# The Arson Murders

David Ferguson

Ironclad Publisher—Douglasville, GA
Paperback ISBN: 979-8-9876678-2-8
eBook ISBN: 979-8-9876678-0-4
Hardcover ISBN 979-8-9876678-1-1
Library of Congress Control Number: 2023901935
Title: *The Arson Murders*
Author: David Ferguson
Digital distribution | 2023
Hardcover | 2023

# Dedication

I'm dedicating this book and my other books to my understanding wife Margaret. She has been very understanding about the time I spend writing and the cost of publishing. I would also like to thank the people that have prof read my stories as I wrote them. I don't think I would have finished the first book without their encouragement.

# Chapter 1

The Atlanta Arson Murders

September 27th 1967

"Amanda. It's Saturday night. I've brought out the next case file. Dad calls it The Atlanta Arson Murders. It starts April 5th 1933 which is about seven months after solving the Wishing Well Murders."

"That last case gave me the shivers, when he was fighting for his life with that trained snake and that evil man Muller was stalking him and his family."

The thought of that man made the hairs on Amanda's arms stand up. "Joseph, I wonder if your dad is going to have another run in with Muller?"

"I don't know, dear. Why don't you join me and we'll find out together."

Amanda took a seat and said, "What do you think our life would have been like if all that Confederate gold hadn't been lost in The Aragon Murders?"

"We would be rich, spoiled and bored. Now let's see how many crimes father solved in this one."

"Before you start, honey, did your folks ever talk about all the fires happening during that year?"

"No. My parents didn't like talking about the past."

"Well, my Mother did, and she remarked that Atlanta hadn't burned that much since the Yankees burned it in 1864."

"I doubt that, Dear. Now, shall I start? It's getting late?"

April 5th 1933
7:00 am Monday

I was on my way to the station when I first noticed a large black cloud of smoke billowing into the morning air. I had just passed the zoo and from this position, I couldn't tell exactly what was on fire. I didn't alter my course until my short-wave-radio crackled to life. "Calling all cars, calling all cars. All cars in the vicinity of Peachtree and Forsyth Streets are to report for crowd control. The McKenzie building at 117 Forsyth Street is on fire. Over."

I waited as car four, six, two, nine and seven, called in that they would be responding. I also called in and said I would be responding as well. If the fire was bad as it sounded, it would be the perfect time to do a robbery. I made a left turn onto Memorial Street and headed towards the largest black cloud of smoke I could see.

As I got into the tall buildings, it became harder to tell which street I should turn on. I got to within eight blocks of Forsyth before I ran into stopped traffic.

Not wanting to abandon my car in the street, I looked around to see if there was another solution. It then hit me why not use the sidewalks? I turned on my siren and placed my blinking red light on the dash indicating I was police.

I slowly drove onto the sidewalk blowing my horn. At first people refused to move until I nudged them with the bumper. As I slowly picked up speed, the public started moving out of the way. I made it another seven blocks when the wind must have decided to change direction.

Instead of it acting as an updraft like a chimney dispersing the noxious black smoke harmlessly into the sky, it created a downdraft that forced the noxious black smoke to swirl ever downwards until it reached street level. I stopped moving forward as the smoke started driving the onlookers away. I looked behind me to see if I could backup when the first wave of people rushed past me. Some were coughing, others rubbing their eyes, and some were brushing away glowing cinders burning them.

I started to get out of my car, when it was enveloped in smoke as well. It happened so fast, I just sat there staring at the burning embers covering my windshield.

**"Well, are you going to just sit there**?" Cochran's serum spoke up.

I snapped out of my trance and ignored him. When I started coughing, I decided to join the crowd heading for cleaner air. I was just about out of my car when the smoke quickly started to dissipate. I looked up and saw the smoke being sucked back up towards the sky. "Cochran! Shut up! I don't have time to argue with you right now."

With everything settled with him, I found myself looking at an empty sidewalk. I continued down the sidewalk until I reached Farmwalt Street. I spotted several firetrucks and police cars at the corner of Forsyth and Peachtree St. It then occurred to me if I drove any closer, I wouldn't be able to leave. People were returning to their cars and would want to turn around. It had been sometime since I had been in this part of town. If my memory served me, this street would take me back to Cooper and then to Whitehall.

Not wanting anyone to clog up this street that was actually an alley, I blocked it with my car. I locked the car and started walking towards the fire. As I reached an opening between two buildings, I got my first glimpse of the 20 story building that was on fire. As I stared at the fire, I thought of Saint Die. It was a small town on the border of France and Germany that had been fought over by both sides. My company had been sent to hold it and the ground around it. As we walked through the burned out buildings, the smells of its destruction had never left me.

"Are you okay mister?" A hobo asked walking up to me.

"I'm fine. I was just, just, thinking about..."

"Of the war in France I bet," he said with that hollow look in his eyes. I tried to give him my change but he turned and walked away.

I walked the rest of the block and saw two firetrucks and two ambulances slowly working their way through the crowd. I guess in my day dreaming, a new crowd of onlookers had replaced the old one. Pushing my way through the dozens of onlookers, I finally reached the police line.

The burning building was the twenty story McKenzie Building. McKenzie Senior, a finical wizard, had built the building in 1892 just after the Cotton State Exposition. It was one of the first 20 story buildings built. When McKenzie Senior died in 1915, his son, Edgar, took over the business. In 1929, the financial market crashed and his building occupancy dropped. The last I remembered hearing was that McKenzie was the only occupant left.

The crowd suddenly let out a gasp and backed up several yards. Flames had erupted out of the sixth floor windows showering dozens of glass shards on the firemen below.

As the onlookers returned, I found myself becoming one of them. The first and fifth floors were venting plumes of black and brown smoke as the ladder trucks sprayed gallons of water into the building.

I spotted several hoses running in the front doors, squirting water out their connections by the gallons. Without thinking, I started walking forward when a policeman shoved me back.

"Where do you think you're going?"

I started to pull out my badge when I spotted Henry Ingram and five other patrolmen. They were struggling to keep another crowd of onlookers in control. I was about to say something to Henry when a gust of hot cinder-filled smoke swept over us.

"Henry!" I coughed. "You'd better push them back another block before someone gets hurt."

"And why don't you follow your own advice, mister."

"Because patrolmen Gregory Tillman," I said looking at his badge. "I'm Detective William Barronson," I said showing him my badge. Then following my own advice, I retreated until I was breathing without coughing.

I spotted a metal police call box and decided to get in touch with a station. Unlocking it with my key I asked for the desk Sergeant. "Sergeant. This is Detective Barronson from the fifth.

We need more men out here at the McKenzie fire to widen the perimeter all around this building."

"I'll check with the Captain, and see if we can get men from another station."

"Why! Are all your men already here?"

"No Detective, We have another fire in the warehouse district as well."

"Okay see what you can do. I'll help out here as well."

Closing up the police box, I started walking back towards the fire when the sixth floor burst into flames again. It was then I spotted the Fire Chief directing his men to hose it down yet again. As I walked up to the chief, I heard more sirens a block or two away indicating help was on the way.

**"Detective. I believe you better listen to this,"** the serum whispered.

"Not! Now!" I yelled hoping that was the end of it.

I could feel the serums rejected emotions swirling around in my body. "Alright! Let me hear it." Suddenly my hearing narrowed while intensifying to the point I could hear the women's screams for help. I stared up into the smoke as my eyes changed as well. Now I could see through the smoke the three women at the tenth floor window as if I was there. I watched in fascination as they screamed and waved to get someone's attention.

They must have seen me somehow looking at them, because they started screaming and waving directly down at me.

"Can you save them!" I shouted to the Chief pointing at the women above us.

"I've got a team already in the building trying to reach them. That last explosion on six I'm afraid has stopped my men from moving up."

A rumbling on the third floor made me look up to see what was happening there. It sounded to me like wooden floor beams collapsing onto the second floor. Seconds later the same sound came from the second floor as well. "Chief, what's happening in there?"

"The floors are collapsing one upon the other with my men still in there." I looked at the Chief and saw tears pouring down his cheeks.

Suddenly his rescue team came stumbling out the front door carrying two of their comrades. "Chief, what are you going to do now, to save those women?"

"I'll get another hose on seven, maybe we can flood the floor below long enough for another ladder team to get to them. If that doesn't work then they'll probably jump to their deaths."

I looked up to see if the women were still at the window. The smoke was so thick pouring out of sixth floor windows, even my enhanced eyes couldn't see through it. I moved around until I got a glimpse of them. There were still three women now with handkerchiefs covering their mouth and noses.

**"I can help you save them,"** Cochran's serum whispered.

I started to say no, when I suddenly doubled over in pain. Cochran, a mad scientist, had injected me with his experimental serum some months ago. I, for some unknown reason, was the only person that had ever lived. At first I fought every time when it wanted to take control, and every time I would lose. Since then, I found it was easier on my health and frankly quite interesting to see what I could do.

"Alright, serum. I expect you to save them."

"Are you alright, Detective. I can have a man help you..."

"I'm fine Chief. It's just my way of talking through a problem."

As the Chief took several steps away from me I could feel the serum supercharging my body until I felt like superman. "Chief! Look at that building next door! Its rooftop is at the same level as the women's tenth floor. What about extending a ladder across to the women and let them crawl across it?" I shouted as more police and fire truck sirens made it impossible to talk.

"That could work but, I'm out of men and officers to do it. Besides, at that height the women would probably freeze or panic once they were on the ladder. And knowing my men, they would all die trying to save them as well."

The serum Detective exploded in verbal abuse until the Chief gave me six men to shut me up.

Rounding them up I said, "I want you two men to get an extension ladder fifteen feet long. I then want you to stand next to the front door of that adjacent building."

"I will then drop a rope to you. Tie the rope around the ladder so we can pull it to the roof. Do you understand?"

"Yes. Sir."

"Now. You four firemen bring enough rope so these two firemen can tie the ladder to it. My plan is to use the ladder as a bridge to get three women out of that building alive. Got it?"

"Got it, Sir."

"Then let's get to it."

I looked up at the three women and signaled I was on the way. We entered the empty building next door and proceeded to the tenth floor using the elevators. Locating the roof top stairs, we broke through the locked door and ran to the street side of the building. I looked down and saw the two firemen holding the ladder just as I had told them to do. Extending the first fifty feet of rope a young firemen tied another one to it and another until it reached the ground.

It didn't take but a minute until I had the ladder on the roof. I had then carried it to the alley side facing the open window. I smiled and waved to the women as the four firemen struggled to extend it.

"Here. Let me help." I put all four of them on one side and me on the other. I saw a look of disbelief as we extended the ladder until it reached the other window.

"Alright you two. Secure the ladder to that pipe and anything else you can find. I don't want to lose the ladder  if it slides loose from their window.

A sudden gust of wind carried the smoke up to us. I looked over the side and saw the seventh floor window blow out as flames shot out of it.

"Please, please help us," the older woman yelled.

"Can you cross the ladder on your hands and knees?"

"I can't, I'll fall," the youngest woman said crying.

"I'll come and get you then," A fireman said removing his equipment.

"I'll handle this," I said taking a deep breath as the serum roared through my veins.

I climbed up on the ladder and started across.

When I left the safety of the building I could feel the heat rising from below.

"Come on serum. Show me what you've got?"

**"Alright. I will."**

Suddenly I found myself at their window. "Good afternoon ladies. Who would like to have a piggy back ride.?"

The young woman that was crying grabbed my neck and wrapped her legs around my waist. Taking a deep breathe, I climbed out the window and raced across the ladder like a mother chimp.

"Get her off of me, I can't breathe."

I raced back to the window and the older women motioned for me take her last. The second middle aged woman wrapped herself around me and I did the same as the first. I was about to head back to get the older woman when I became too dizzy to stand. I could feel the serum beginning to leave my body.

"Where do you think you're going?" I yelled. "There's one woman left."

**"You have no more calories left for me to use. I'm programmed to shut down before I would kill you."**

"If you don't save that woman I might just kill myself."

**"If you hadn't diluted me with transfusions I could have."**

Sweating with exhaustion, I heard the third women scream as I clung to the rooftop wall for support.

I managed to look up and saw her salt and pepper hair burst into flames as I passed out.

$$\underline{\qquad\qquad}\ \lozenge\ \underline{\qquad\qquad}$$

# Chapter 2

April 5th 1933
10:00 pm Monday

"**You could have saved her, Detective, if you hadn't diluted the serum. Why did you do such a cowardly thing?**" Cochran said, floating away.

"**What about me? If you hadn't stopped drinking, I could have saved her as well. It might have taken me a little longer to build up my courage, but I could have done it.**" My alcohol self muttered.

"**William. Don't listen to them. All they want is to control you, remember?**" Margaret said drifting away as well.

"**So! Big man. If you had sacrificed yourself, that woman would still be alive. Now not only are you a drunk, you're a drugged-up coward just like you were in France.**"

"**No! I'm not. You're the one that held me back, not me.**" I screamed grabbing my chest.

"**Come now Detective, I've known you all your life. Remember that day when a dog attacked the neighbor's daughter. You know the one you had a crush on.**"

"**Yes I remember Betty. She got bit and they had to amputate her leg.**"

"**And what did you do Detective? Did you run to her and drive off the dog or did you run away to save yourself?**"

"**I ran.**"

"**And you've been running ever since, haven't you.**"

I felt tears on my cheeks as I found myself on the roof top watching the older woman burst into flames before jumping out the window. As she disappeared, I turned and saw the looks of horror and disgust on the other fireman's faces. They all knew I had let that woman die because I was a coward. I tried to explain to them I didn't let her die because I was a coward.

Then suddenly the firemen grabbed my arms and legs and carried me to rooftop edge.

**"Now you can join her as well, coward."**

"No!" I screamed and screamed and screamed as I saw the pavement rushing towards me.

⬡

# Chapter 3

April 5th 1933
10:30 pm Monday

I woke up screaming and found myself lying in a hospital bed in Grady's burn unit. They were giving me another transfusion of blood while three IVs were replacing the fluids and calories I had burned up.

I tried to move but found my body strapped down to the bed.

"William, you're alright now. Don't struggle so. I'm right here to take care of you." Margaret said with a worried look on her face. "Did you have another one of your dreams."

"Yes, Margaret, I was back on the rooftop arguing with  my selves for not saving the third woman." I said pulling on the straps

"Stop fighting dear. You're still under the effects of Cochran's serum."

"I, I remember the older woman's hair, Margaret, bursting into flames. I watched as her skin melted as her body burned to ashes. I tried, Margaret, to save her, but the serum wouldn't let me." I sobbed.

"What are you saying dear. All three women were saved."

"But, I saw the older woman burst into flames." I took a deep breath and spent several minutes coughing my insides out. I wanted to explain to Margaret she was wrong, but I couldn't stop coughing long enough to tell her.

As my coughing continued, two nurses came to my rescue, one gave me a shot and the other checked my blood pressure and pulse. Whatever, I was given, not only slowed the coughing down, it also calmed me down.

"William, now that your calmer, I'm telling you you didn't see that woman burst into flames. The other fireman got her to cross over the ladder to safety on her own."

"Then how did I get my hands burned?"

10

"The fireman said you passed out and when you came to, you tried to go back across the burning ladder. If it hadn't been for the four firemen pulling you back, you would have burned to death in that building."

"Dear, I see the doctor is coming so behave yourself or you'll have to stay another day."

I could see by the look on Margaret's face she liked what she saw when the doctor entered my room. Doctor Charles Frederick had been assigned by Washington to administer the cleansing transfusion that had been started at Walter Reed. Doctor Charles, as he answered to, was in his late 20's, 6'1", 165 pounds, dark brown hair, blue eyes and a football lineman build.

"Bill, I'm glad to see you're awake. How do you feel?"

"I feel like I've been hit by a truck but other than that I'm fine."

He listened to my heart, took my pulse, and motioned to the nurses to remove the IV's. "Bill, I don't want to scare you or Margaret, but your heart can't take too many more of these transformations.

"I know doctor, I can feel it sucking the life out of me every time it takes over. How many more blood replacements do you think it'll need to get Cochran's serum out of my system?"

"I haven't checked the latest sample, but your last numbers shows a 20% reduction."

"Meaning?"

"I don't believe you'll ever be 100% no matter how many transfusions I give you. The good news is his serum isn't duplicating itself as fast or staying active as long from what your telling me. So my opinion right now is, 89 to 91% clear is the best you can expect."

"Doctor, are you still sending my blood to Washington?"

I could see on his face he was deciding which answer would satisfy me.

"Detective Barronson, I'm not at liberty to tell you because in truth, I don't know myself. All I can tell you is that every pint we take out of you is being picked up by men working for the government. Where it goes from there is not my concern, so I've been told, but I'm sure you can figure out for yourself where it's winding up."

"Thanks for your honesty Doctor, and yes, I assumed it went to a government laboratory. I just hope they can't duplicate it even if it makes super soldiers."

I felt much better after even though I had eaten hospital food. "Margaret is there a paper handy? I'd like to read about the fires.

"I have one right here," Margaret said, showing me the headlines.

## THREE WOMEN SAVED FROM A FIERY DEATH

Three women were saved today from certain death when the McKenzie office building caught fire this morning. The three women were secretaries to the McKenzie family working on the tenth floor. With all exits blocked by fire these courageous women opened a window and screamed for help. It seems their employers had been out of the building at the time the fire started. With fireman unable to reach them from inside the building, it seemed they only had two options. One was to burn to death, or two to jump to their deaths. Either one was going to be a horrible death.

It was at this point our reporter, Jayden Ferguson spotted Detective William Barronson. He was the hero that had saved a child from dozens of man-eating lions just months ago.

With four fireman and himself, he led them to the top of Brant's and Son, ten story adjacent building.

This reporter followed them without fearing for his life to the rooftop as well. I watched as these heroic firemen pushed a ladder across the ten foot alley to the open window. With flames lapping at my heals and cinder filled smoke all around, this reporter was an eye witness to Detective Barronson heroic rescues.

Without any concern for his safety, he personally carried two women on his back across the burning ladder to safety before collapsing from exhaustion. The third woman a Miss Mandy Otis, fifty three stated. "Crawling across the burning ladder was the scariest thing I had ever attempted." Again without concern for himself, Barronson climbed out onto the burning ladder and took her hand. As the flames grew threatening both their lives I heard him say "Take my hand and I'll lead you to safety."

I must admit this reporter felt as if he was speaking to the lord. Without fear of death, they both crossed the burning ladder to safety before our hero collapsed again into a coma. As happy as this story turned out, I'm sad to report 12 other people weren't so lucky. Their names will not be mentioned by this reporter until all the families have been notified.

I started to hand the paper back to Margaret when I remembered the second fire. I opened the newspaper and found the article on page 3.

## WAREHOUSE FIRE DESTROYS THOUSANDS

A fire broke out at a warehouse owned by the McCallum and Sons. The fire was reported by a Mr. Owen. He states he was driving by when he saw smoke pouring out of the building's roof. One firetruck was sent, due to the 20 story McKenzie fire. After a heroic but unsuccessful effort to put the fire out the four firefighters could do nothing but keep the fire from spreading to other warehouses. As of yet we don't know if there was anyone working inside when the fire broke out.

"Margaret, I believe it's time for this hero to get dressed and start investigating the two fires. If they were   set, then Atlanta has an arsonist on its hands."

I headed for the bathroom and felt regret for the twelve other deaths that I didn't know about. I also felt regret for myself as well. People had finally forgotten about the lion story this very paper had played up for more than two weeks. Now with this new fabricated hero story, I'd have to shake another million hands. And if that wasn't enough, I'd have to listen to dozens of different interpretations that would grow the story beyond belief.

Finishing what I had come in there for, I opened the door to find Margaret reading the paper.

"I'll get your clothes, oh great one." Margaret said.

"By the way are you going to part the Red Sea for us this Sunday?" she laughed while bowing.

"No. not Sunday. That's already been done, but maybe Monday, I'll part the Atlantic Ocean just for fun."

"Are you aware there have been a number of small fires reported this year," Margaret said, helping me to dress.

"Five, I believe, one car, two wooden sheds, one wooden garage and a house."

"If all these are set by the same person then yesterday's fires were his graduation present."

Checking out of the hospital, I found I needed someone to drive me home. My car wasn't here and my hands were bandaged and more tender that I had thought.

"Forget something, my hero?" Margaret chuckled.

"Ah.. well...it seems we need transportation home."

"Well, Detective Barronson, it's midnight and by the smell in the air, its going to rain. So what do you have in mind?"

I went to scratch my head and found that wasn't the

smartest thing I had ever done. "Well. I could call the station and get a patrol car to run us home."

Margaret chuckled again while shaking her head. "Come on. I have a taxi waiting."

"Captain, I thought you'd never come out of that place." Hap said opening the door for us.

"Looks like you've been in a fight," he said winking at Margaret. "Who won?"

I didn't answer him knowing full well he knew exactly what had happened to me.

"We're home, William." Margaret said shaking my shoulder.

"Sorry, I must have dosed off. Thanks. Hap, can you pick me up about 8:00 am please?"

"No problem Captain," Hap said pulling away.

I made it to the front porch rocker before I needed to sit down. Margaret sat down in Mildred's rocker and waited for me to say something. She didn't have to wait long as Grace raced out the door and gave me a big hug.

"Grace, please, I can't breathe," I said pushing her away.

"Oh my Bill, your hands. Shouldn't you be in the hospital." she stated gently inspecting them.

"I'm fine Grace, really I am," I said getting up from the rocker.

"You're sure?" Grace said sliding under my left arm and started helping me into the house.

"Grace please. I can walk on my own!" I said pushing Grace away from me.

"William Barronson, that's no way to talk to your sister in law." Mildred said standing at the top of the stairs in her night clothes.

"Mildred, you're a sight for sore eyes. If I was 20 years older."

"If you were 20 years older, I wouldn't give you the time of day.

Now apologize to Grace for being so rude and march yourself up these stairs and go to bed. Land sakes, it's 1:20 am in the morning, and some of us have to get up at 5:00 am."

I walked past Mildred and she gave me a peck on the cheek and whispered, "I'm proud of you Bill, and if you get out of bed before 10:00 am. I'll lock you in your room until then. I'll not have a son in law of mine put in the grave before me."

"Mildred, as uppity as you are, you'll out live us all. Besides, I already had a mother, mother in law, and I'll get up whenever I want." I said waiting for her answer.

When it came it was a smack on the butt. I then knew I was really home once again.

Margaret helped me undress and then told me she would sleep in another room. I started to object but she gave me a kiss, smiled and gently touched my face. "I'll see you in the morning.

I did the three S's before getting into bed. I was about to fall asleep when I heard something outside my window. Not wanting to wake up I ignored the noise several more times before getting up to investigate. The serum inside me told me not to turn on the lights. The hairs on my arms started standing up warning me trouble was about to happen.

I got up and went to my suit coat to get my revolver out of its holster. I fumbled around for it and found the holster wasn't there. I heard a grunt behind me indicating whoever it was was having trouble getting in the window.

Feeling I was about out of time I turned on the lights and found my gun and holster on the floor.

"I wouldn't do that Detective," a familiar voice said cocking his gun.

"Carl Muller. I thought you and Robert Cochran had left the country?"

"We did Detective, and Mein Fuhrer was very pleased to meet him."

"So you went to Germany with that murderer. Then what's the reason for you to come back here. Surely it can't be to kill me?"

I asked hoping that wasn't the reason. "May I sit down? I've had a very long day," I said.

"That you have Detective. I've been watching you for some time, and it amazes me what Cochran's serum has done for you. Extra strength, stamina, reflexes and healing. His serum will make the German soldiers unbeatable on the battle field."

"Okay then, if you know all this, then again, why are you here in my bedroom at... 3:00 am in the morning?"

"Cochran and I need you and your blood. You see you must have Aryan blood in you. Blood that has taken Cochran's serum and embraced all of its qualities."

"Okay I get it now. I'm the only dumb bastard that hasn't died from his injections." I said standing up.

"Then I don't need to worry about you using that gun on me do I?"

"Not at this moment Detective, but when I contact you again after completing my next mission. You'll come with me willingly. And before you say never, Detective remember this. There are other people around you that I can hurt Heir Detective. Like. Mildred as an example. That fat old lady could fall and break her neck while feeding her crows. Grace could be shot and lose her baby, or her husband could turn up missing never to be found.

So you see Detective, there are many ways to make you cooperate. Just ask Bonnie Graves. Oh! You can't! That's because I killed her."

"You damn Huns are all alike. We kicked your ass in WW1 and we'll do it again no matter how many supermen you make.

I'll come when you call, but watch your back because I'll be looking for you as well."

"So be it, Doughboy. I like a good challenge."

Carl backed out the window and dropped to the ground. By the time I got my gun and reached the window he was nowhere to be found.

Now wide awake, I laid on my bed and thought about how I was going to handle this new problem. I thought about going to the FBI, and telling them about this visit I'd had from Muller. After further thought about it, I decided not to tell them anything.

It had been just luck that I wasn't sitting in some military hospital being experimented on, or being dissected to find out why the serum had only worked on me. It was 6:00 am when a pounding on my door woke me up to the birds chirping and the smell of coffee brewing.

"Bill, it's time to get up. I know it's early, but everybody and his brother wants to see you. Besides this taxi driver, Hap, is eating me out of house and home. If you don't come down here soon, I'm sure he'll want me to marry him." Mildred said unlocking the door.

# Chapter 4

April 6th 1933
6:00 am Tuesday

I sat up and started rubbing my temples trying to relieve the pain. "I'll be down in a minute, Mildred. Tell Hap to warm up that so called taxi of his, and tell him I'll need him for the day!"

I headed downstairs hoping I could at least drink a cup of coffee in peace before heading to the station. Finishing my coffee, I felt I could now make it through all the reporters' questions waiting for me outside.

"Bill, not so fast," Mildred said entering the dining room. "I want to see those hands."

I didn't get a chance to object, because Mildred grabbed my wrist and started cutting off the cloth bandages.

"Just as I thought," Mildred said turning my left hand over and over. "I don't know what they smeared all over them, but by the looks of your skin it isn't helping.

Mildred took me by the arm and escorted me to the kitchen sink. In it was a large bowl of brown soapy water. She then took my hands and slowly submerged them into the water.

"Mildred, I don't think this is a... wonderful idea." I hadn't realized how much pain my hands where giving me.

"Mildred, whatever this is in the bowl, you need to bottle it and sell it."

She let me soak for three minutes or so before removing my hands. In that time the angry redness had almost disappeared along with the pain. She gently dried my hand's and inspected them before wrapping them up.

"There, that should hold you until tonight. I'll have you soak them again when you get home."

I left the house and was surrounded by a number of reporters all talking at once. Flashbulbs went off so fast in my face, I couldn't see a damn thing. I tried to answer a couple of questions when a voice asked.

"Tell us, Detective, about your interview last night."

I spun around as if a spring had broken beneath me and found Carl Muller smiling at me. He had a pad and pencil in his hand and a foreign press card in his hat.

"I'm sorry Detective if I startled you. I wouldn't want you to stumble and injure your hands," Muller said pushing his way to the very front of the reporters.

"That's quite okay, mister?"

"Hans Pfeffer, Berlin Press, heir Detective, to be specific."

I noticed the other reporters were all standing around silent watching the two of us, as if it were a prize fight.

"Yes. Heir Pfeffer, I did have an interview with a man that broke into my room last night. Like you, he too was a Hun with no manners."

I watched Carl's face change to anger as I mentioned the word Hun. A low murmur went up from the other reporters at the mention of Hun. It seems the war has been over long enough for this younger generation to think it rude.

Muller stepped closer to me all the while smiling like a cat going to eat a mouse.

"Heir, Detective," he whispered. "Don't forget our agreement. If you think I wasn't serious Detective, here's a memento from our last meeting."

Carl held out his hand and I did the same. "I'll be seeing you Detective," he whispered as he dropped a penny into my hand. As he disappeared behind the reporters I looked down and saw it was an 1864P Indian head penny, the same exact penny I had found on each of the murder victims.

"Detective, Washington Daily Mirror. What does that penny mean? And how do you know that German reporter?"

Suddenly, 100s of questions from dozens of reporters hit me like a wave. I was so overwhelmed I could do nothing but think Muller had done that on purpose. Now more determined than ever to nail Muller, I forced my way to Hap's taxi. "Hap, drive me to the station, before I shoot one of them.

"Okay, Captain." The taxi lurched forward bumping reporters out of the way. Hap did this several times until the reporters got the message. As the reporters moved aside Hap gunned the motor and shot through the opening before it closed.

Pulling into the station Hap said, "Will you look at that, Captain. The place is decked out welcoming you back."

I felt the pain slowing returning in my hands. I wasn't in the mood for a party after my confrontation with Muller.

"Let's get out of here Hap, I don't think I have the strength to handle this right now."

"Where to then, Captain?"

"Just drive around until I tell you to stop. And make sure you use as many alleys and back streets as possible."

I had Hap cover most of the city before telling him to stop. I got out of the car and I said, "Pick me up here at 1:00 pm, and if anybody asks, tell them I went to that store to have a drink."

$$\underline{\quad\quad\quad}\diamondsuit\underline{\quad\quad\quad}$$

# Chapter 5

April 6th 1933
11:00 am Tuesday

I watched as Hap's taxi disappeared into the morning traffic. Feeling I was being followed, I jumped onto the nearest trolley car and changed them without notice every few blocks. By the time I paid my last nickel, the trolley car and I had reached the FBI building at 1620 Fulton Street. It wasn't staffed now but an agent or two did when needed. The main branch for the southeast had moved to Birmingham Alabama in 1930. I had heard Hoover's budget had been cut so deeply to conserve money after the 1929 stock crash.

Entering the ten story building, I found it empty except for a person getting out of an elevator.

"Pardon me sir. Can you tell me what floor an agent might be on?"

"That would be me, Mr.?"

"That's a stroke of luck. My name is Detective William Barronson, of the Atlanta Police Department. I..."

"Oh yes, I should have recognized you from the newspapers, Detective. My name is, Charles Purvise."

"Agent Purvise, I need to speak to you about a matter of importance."

I spent the next hour talking to Agent Purvise. I summarized what had happened to me last year.

"That's quite a story Detective. You say Director Carter is familiar with your case?"

"Yes. So does your boss Hoover. I'm now going to tell you how all this fits together. This morning about 3:00 am  Muller climbed in my bedroom window with a gun in his hand. I was told he was here to take me to Germany to be experimented on." I could see on Agent Purvise face he was having a hard time swallowing my story. "I can see by the look on your face you think I'm nuts. So let's make a call to Washington, and ask to speak to Mr. Hoover."

"NO. I'll do no such thing."

"Alright! Then call Director Carter. Tell him Detective Barronson, wishes to speak with him." I waited in what would have been the dining room as Agent Purvise made his call.

I lit a cigarette and looked out the window overlooking the Roman architecture train station and several sets of tracks. I personally had never given it a thought at how many trains were moving goods and people all over the country. In the five minutes I had seen fifteen trains either heading north or south.

"Detective. I do apologize for having doubting you. Director Carter sends his regards. Now tell me again what this Muller wants from you? But it needs to be short because I was heading out to meet with the Fire Chief. I'm here to investigate it as well."

"Well it's a small world because I was going to do the same."

"Good then. So why don't you ride with me and you can tell me about the fire."

I said "Yes."

As we entered the elevator, I took a good look at the Agent Charles Purvise. He was 5'10", slim build, weighed about 133 pounds, blue eyes, brown hair, dark blue suit and tie. What did make him an FBI agent was his snap-brim hat which every agent had to wear.

As we walked out the door he turned and locked it. I must have given him a strange look because he said. "I'm the only person working here today, and as a matter of fact this whole week. You were lucky to catch anybody here. You see, even I work out of Birmingham."

I got into his brand new 1933 black Ford sedan. This thing was so new it still had that new smell.

"Now, tell me Detective, what exactly can I do for you?"

"As I was telling you earlier. Muller is blackmailing me to go with him to Germany. If I don't, he will make someone in my family pay with their life."

"Did he give you a date and time.?

"No. He told me he had other business here to take care of. But when I'm contacted by him we will leave immediately."

Agent Purvise looked at me with a puzzled look on his face. "I believe Director Carter needs to be in on this as well. How can he get in touch with you?"

I thought about that for several minutes before answering. "Tell Carter, I'm under surveillance, so don't trust the phones. I'll meet him at the zoo bunker Thursday night at 10:00 pm. If he can't make it, then you call my captain and tell him the time."

I didn't say anything else until we got to the McKenzie burned out building. Unlike the Terminal Hotel that had burned last year, the outer walls hadn't collapsed leaving just an iron skeleton. AS we got out of the car I saw several firemen hosing down hot spots of smoldering floor lumber. I spotted the Fire Chief at the same time Agent Purvise did.

"Chief! Come join us please," Purvise said motioning to him.

Chief Mitch Anderson, I later found out, had been the head of Atlanta's Fire Department since 1924. He had started as a fireman in 1909, and had risen steadily in the ranks until he made chief. Chief Anderson was an impressive looking man standing there in his uniform. His height was 6'1", to 6'2" and weighted 250 to 275 pounds of muscle. His broad shoulders and suntanned face oozed authority.

"Chief, had you ever thought of running for mayor or governor?" Purvise asked looking up at him.

"Detective Barronson, who's this that wants to know if I want to run for Governor?"

"Chief, this is FBI Agent Purvise. He's going to investigate along with us as to how the fire started and.."

"As Detective Barronson just said, I'm FBI Agent Purvise, and will be looking into this fire as well."

I could see by the look of the Chief's face he wasn't impressed with this outsider.

"So you're FBI?" Mitch asked looking him up and down. "Are you intending to get your hands dirty wearing that suit and all? "You know Bill, I bet he can't even tie his shoes without his mama's help."

"Mitch don't..." I said stepping between them.

"That's okay Detective. I've been around long enough to know a bluff when I see one. So! Chief Anderson, is it?" Purvise said moving me aside.

"I can see by that doubled up fist that you want to throw the first punch."

I stood in disbelief as the two of them squared off. "Well, redneck take a swing."

"Agent! It wouldn't be gentlemanly of us southerners to not take the first punch from a northerner.

"Very well then." Mitch's right fist shot out so fast neither the Chief or I saw it coming.

"May I help you up Chief? It seems you slipped on something, like your attitude."

Mitch got up, and inflated his chest as far as it would go. "Agent Purvise. "What can I do for you?" he said shaking hands with him.

"I wanted to speak to you about this fire, and all the others that have, shall we say, happened this year." Charles said walking towards the rubble.

"Well, from what I've found out so far, this fire was set with coal oil on the second and third floors. It's a shame detective, because all the loss of life could have been prevented by just putting in sprinkler systems."

I was about to asked a question when sounds of firetruck sirens filled the air. Immediately I look at the sky line and spotted smoke rising into the air.

"I'll drive us, agent. I believe I know what's burning and where. Chief, you want a ride?"

"No! I'll meet you there."

I pulled out into traffic and headed for Washington Street and Mitchell. As we progressed through the traffic I could see the smoke becoming more noticeable as the fire grew.

"Do you think this fire is connected to the last one detective?" Charles asked hanging on for dear life.

"I hope not, because if it is, we have an arsonist on our hands." Turning onto Washington Street I could see flames and brown black smoke up ahead.

"Do you know what building is burning?" Charles asked.

I pulled over to the curb and parked two blocks away. Turning to Charles, I found his face pale and shiny with sweat.

"Are you all right?"

"I'll be in a minute, now that we have landed safely."

I spotted a call box two stores down and headed for it.

"I need to call in and have more men sent here for crowd control."

"What's burning?" Sergeant Sanders asked.

"It's the Fulton Cotton Spinning Company, so send as many as you can because this place is 1500' long."

The Cotton Spinning Company was a long and wide red brick three story building. It was built in the early 1890s by a man named Phillip

Andrews. Its 15,000 spinning machines produced enough cloth to make every uniform the USA armed forces needed in WW1. Since 1929 more than half the employees had been let go. Cotton was being replaced by synthetic materials made from oil.

Agent Purvise and I walked down to the first three firetrucks that had started pumping water into the north end of the building. After several minutes and three more firetrucks, it looked like they were going to be able to save the building. By the time the fire was out one third of the three story, 1500' long building had been damaged, leaving the rest untouched. As several of the trucks left Purvise said, "Evidently the arsonist wasn't smart enough to start more than one fire in a building 1500' long and three stories tall."

"Well. It's possible he was only trying to damage the closed down part. That way, the owner could collect the fire insurance and either stay in business or go out of business. Either way, someone was making a lot of money.

"Let's get back to my office," Charles said. "I need to call this in to headquarters."

"Don't forget to contact Grayson for me."

Making our way back to the FBI building, I left him and started walking back to meet with Hap. I needed to get back to the station as well and advise the Captain of what's going on.

Finding Hap waiting for me, I climbed into his taxi and we headed for the station.

"Captain, have you heard about the latest fire?" Hap asked whipping between two trucks.

"Yes I've just come from there. Luckily the fire department was able to save most of the building. That gives me an idea Hap. How about doing a little detective work for me?"

"Captain, I thought you'd never ask." Hap said smiling at me using his rear view mirror.

"Great! I need you to check around and see if anyone knows who might be bragging about setting these fires."

"No problem, Captain."

"Hap, why do you keep calling me Captain?"

"I guess it's because you look and act like a Captain. I bet you were one in the war."

"No. I was a private, just a home sick private hoping I wouldn't get killed. That reminds me, have you noticed anybody following you today?"

"No, private. No, that's not right Captain. Captain sounds much better than private or Bill for that matter."

I got out of Hap's taxi and found the lobby decorated for the party I had skipped out on. Luckily for me the reporters had gone, along with the Mayor and the rest of his political hangers-on.

"Well it's about time you got here," Grace said pulling down some streamers. I spent three hours decorating this place for you and what do I get! A no show!"

"Grace, I'm sorry. If I had realized you had done all this work I wouldn't have left."

"Okay, I'll think of something to say at the press meeting this afternoon."

"I don't expect there to be one. Didn't you hear about the Fulton Cotton Spinning factory, catching fire today, and the McKenzie building fire?"

"No, I hadn't heard. It seems someone hadn't bothered to informed me." Grace said glaring at me.

I wanted to tell her about the warehouse fire as well but dreaded the reprisals. "Well, Grace, seeing everyone here has kept you in the dark, I'll tell you everything I know about them."

$$\cdots\!\!-\!\!-\!\!-\!\!\diamond\!\!-\!\!-\!\!-\!\!\cdots$$

# Chapter 6

April 6th 1933
1:40 pm Tuesday

To smooth things over with Grace, I told her I'd take her out to lunch as soon as she was done cleaning up. I then left her tearing down pictures of me that had been taken twenty years ago. I knocked on the Captain's door and entered the familiar office that had once been mine.

"Good afternoon, Captain.

"Where the hell were you this morning, Detective? I had everybody and their cousins here waiting for me to give you this medal." Captain Buchanan said, tossing the box to me.

"I'm sorry about that Captain, but I thought meeting with the FBI was more important than this medal."

"FBI? Why? What's going on with the FBI? You know we don't want any federal government agents meddling in our city affairs. Why..."

"Captain, that's why I'm here. Carl Muller paid me a visit last night in my bedroom."

"Muller's back in Atlanta? What the hell did he want with you?"

"Well, for one thing he handed me this," I said handing the coin over to him.

"Isn't this the same coin you found on all the wishing well murders?"

"Yes, and he also admitted killing Bonnie Graves along with all the others that had that coin on them."

"Why would he do that? He must know the whole department will be after him."

"He's a Hun, Captain, and also admitted he was a spy as well. I wouldn't put it past him to have started one or two of the fires to see what weakness we have. Besides, Captain, as you know the Germans think they're superior to us and everybody else in the world. I also believe he wanted to gloat over beating us at our own game."

"So you think he's responsible for all these fires as well then?"

"I don't believe all of them, Captain, or possibly none if we do have a home grown arson. He told me he's here to take me back to Germany.

It seems Robert Cochran is now experimenting on the Germans just like he did here.

I'm assuming he's having the same problem there as he did here. They're all dying except for me."

"How is he going to get you to Germany?"

"By blackmailing me. If I don't go voluntarily, he'll murder someone close to me until I do."

"Then we better get cracking on this, Detective. Get Grace in here and explain everything to her for her afternoon press conference. I'll put out a bulletin to all cars as well."

"I'd rather not, Captain. Do you know how many people would be affected by that? I don't think we'd have enough police to guard them all."

The Captain's phone rang and he spent several minutes talking with the FBI. Hanging up, he informed me Carter Grayson would be dropping by to have a chat about the fires

I went back to talk with Grace before leaving the station. "Grace, my plans had changed and we can't go out for lunch. The Captain wants you to go through the mug books. He thinks our arsonist may have been arrested before and could be out on parole."

"Okay that shouldn't take very long. If I find some candidates, should I bring them to you or the Captain?"

"Probably to the Captain."

"Bill, what are you not telling me?"

"I.. ah, also have one more unpleasant task to do.

Grace after today you'll have to quit the force."

"What! Why?"

"Because, you're pregnant and showing. Department rules, Grace, not mine. So don't fight this, and I'm sure you can come back after you have the baby."

I didn't tell her it would be after they were grown.

I then went downstairs and got in Hap's taxi. "Head for the Fulton Spinning factory fire. "Hap. I have a personal question to ask you."

"Sure, Captain."

"How would you like to join the police force as my driver? I can put you in a much newer car than this one, and it has a police radio in it as well."

"That sounds great Captain, but how can I check around for you? Remember, you asked me to keep my ear to the ground."

"So I did, so I did," I said talking out loud.

"I'll tell you what, Captain. I have a son that has been itching to drive this cab. I'll talk to him and if he agrees, I'll drive for you. But! And I mean a big but. I want a badge and $15.00 a week, plus, plus! Overtime pay for Saturdays and Sundays."

"How much money are we talking about?"

"Let's see, $.15 an hour…for… Saturday and $.22 an hour for… Sundays."

"Or how about this, $17 a week and I'll buy your lunches."

"I can live with that." Hap said.

"I'll have to get the Captain's okay before you can start."

I had hoped he'd take the deal because I was going broke paying him by the mile. As we pulled up to the still smoking building, I spotted Chief Anderson's car parked in the empty lot.

"Wait here Hap. I'll be right back" I started to get out and stopped. "Hap, come with me, I think you need to be in on this one as well."

"Yes, Captain, I was hoping you'd let me tag along."

We headed for the building's North entrance where a patrolman stood guard.

"Is the Fire Chief inside, Leo?"

"Yes Detective. He told me to let you in whenever you got here."

Opening the temporary plywood door a lingering cloud of smoke exited as we walked in. Covering my mouth with my handkerchief we proceeded towards the burned out section. Opening the last door we found the Chief inspecting the damage. Water from the fire hoses filtered down from the second and third floors in small steady streams.

"Chief, isn't it a little early to be inspecting." I said sidestepping a growing puddle. I removed my handkerchief as the air was clear of smoke from all the broken windows.

"Glad you could make it back Detective, and you too Hap as well," the Chief said ignoring the falling water.

"Was it set?"

"I'd say, yes, Detective. I haven't found the exact spot where the fire first started, but as you can see it's quite a large burned out area.

I looked around the burned out room. It measured 50' wide 100' long and 20' high. Bales of wet and partially burned cotton were stacked against outer wall ready to be spun into warn. I started to count the damaged spinning machines lined up in 20 rows 70' long. They would have been turning the cotton bales into yards of cloth in a matter of minutes when the fire started.

"Have you looked at the other floors?" I said dancing from spot to spot as water puddles formed around us.

"I believe we better get out of here. I don't like the look of that floor above us." The Chief said pointing out the sagging wooden beams creaking. We headed for the door when a loud crack fill the air. A second later wood and bales of water-logged cotton started falling from the above floor. The Chief and Hap were ahead of me by 5' as the first bales hit the floor behind me. The amount of water exploding out of them hit me like a wave. Not only was I knocked off my feet, I was soaked to the skin as well. A second section of the floor above gave way to the left of me. This time I covered my face as the second wave pushed me into the wall. I started coughing because I had gotten a mouth full of water just as the wave pushed me into the wall.

"Help me Hap." I managed to choke out as more bales hit the floor around me. I stumbled forward when suddenly two sets of hands grabbed me and dragged me into the next room. As I lay there gasping for air, the sounds of beams  cracking said I needed to get out of here as well.

I suddenly heard a different sound coming from behind me. It sounded like bricks cracking from some tremendous weight pushing down on them. I turned around and saw the wall slowly bowing and bricks cracking from floor to ceiling. I looked up and saw this room had steel beams instead of wooden ones.

That could only mean the two upper floors of wet cotton were unable to break through to relieve the tremendous pressure on the walls.

"Come on Captain, we need to get out of here before this whole damn place comes down on our heads."

I stumbled to my feet and started for the door. As I stumbled along coughing, it became apparent I wasn't going to make it. **"Don't worry Bill. I'll get you out of here."** Cochran's serum said.

Suddenly I could see Hap and the Chief 30' ahead and waiting for me at the open door. **"Let's get moving old man or they can bury you in a shoebox."**

I took off and made it to the door as the brick walls started separating. "Come on you two, the building is collapsing."

I ran out into the sunshine and kept running until I felt I was safe. "There you go Bill. Safe and sound once again. You can thank me later." Cochran's serum drained away and with it my strength.

The Chief and Hap came running up to me and said. "Are you alright?"

I believe so. I'm just a bit tired, wet, and hungry."

Suddenly the ground shuttered under us. We all turned and watched as sections of wall started collapsing. The first floor walls bowed and then suddenly crumbled. Seconds later the second floor wall split and fell apart. This continued until the entire three floors had collapsed taking two other sections along with it. As the dust settled, 250' of the 1500' building was now rubble.

Lucky for us there wasn't anyone else in the factory. Dozens of employees had wanted to get in to collect their belongings. And for once the police had denied everyone including the plant manager.

Hap and I sat down on the lawn and smoked a cigarette while I regain my strength. Suddenly I heard the sound of an ambulance stopping behind us.

"Is anyone injured?" the doctor asked looking at me.

"Doctor. No one was hurt except for me."

"I can see by your clothes you must have been hosed down for some reason."

The Doctor started with me first seeing I was the only one wet. He started with blood pressure, then temperature, then listening to my heart. He moved on to eyes, looked in my throat and last of all my ears.

"Well Doctor what do you think? Will I live?"

"You seem fine, but I still would like for you to spend a day in the hospital."

"I've had all the hospital stays I intend to do for this year. So. No! And I have a gun to back that up."

"As you see fit ah…. Detective William Barronson! I thought I recognized you from the papers. You're the officer that save the three women? I'm very glad to meet you Detective, but didn't you burn your hands?" he said reaching for my bandaged right hand.

I pulled away and shook my head no. "I just need something to eat and drink. Hap let's head out."

"Not yet you two. I need to check you out as well."

"I'm fine, Doctor." Hap said.

"Me too, doctor," the Chief said. "I've got to see to my men and equipment as well."

The doctor was about to leave when he remembered my dirty bandages. "Well at least let me change them for you Detective." I was going to say no again, then I realized if we were to get out of here I needed to let him check them.  As he cut the bandaged away he found my right hand completely healed. Puzzled. He started on the left hand and found it was healed as well.

"You must have some amazing healing power."

"It's my mother-in-law's secret salve." I chuckled.

"I need to meet this woman! Why if it's as good as what I see here, we could make millions."

"Doctor. My hands were not burned that bad. If I had touched a hot stove, the burns would have been the same."

I could see the look of disappointment on his face as the thought of riches slipped away.

"Alright, you three, I'm not going to make you go to the hospital, but if you begin to feel sick I suggest you get to one quickly."

I watched the ambulance drive away before getting to my feet. It took several tries, but I finally made it.

Hap, on the other hand, was on his feet and talking to one of the firemen. They must have known each other because they acted like brothers talking about girls. I looked around for the Chief and spotted him supervising his firemen.

"Hap. Who's the fireman you were talking to?"

"That Steve Bradwell. His father and I went to school together and... Will you look at that." Hap said pointing at the factory.

I turned and looked at the smoldering ruins as if it was the first time. One third of the brick building had collapsed. If I hadn't had the serum in me, I believe I would have died this day.

"Well, I see you two are up and moving now. Detective, how are you feeling?" The Chief asked.

"I'm okay now. If it hadn't been for Hap and you, Chief, I'd be buried under a bale of wet cotton."

"That's okay Detective, I thank you two for your help as well. By the way, what do you think a wet bail of cotton weighs?"

"Dry, 600 to 1000 pounds. Wet, probably 1200 to 3000 pounds each depending on the size of the bale."

"I think then Chief Anderson, I'll call it a day. I need a hot shower and some clean dry clothes. When you get your findings on how the fire started, please give me a ring. Hap. Are you ready to go?"

"I'm with you Captain, on that one."

"Detective? Why does he call you Captain?" the Fire Chief asked.

"It's a long story Chief. I'll tell you another time when I have a day or two."

Once we were back in the car, I closed my eyes and tuned out the world. As the taxi swayed back and forth I thought about Cochran's serum wanting to have a talk. I had done that very same thing many times with my alcoholic self over the years. So I figured it wouldn't hurt just this once to see what it wanted.

"What do you want to talk about, serum?"

**"I want you to stop diluting me with blood transfusions.   Don't you like the powers I can give you?"**

"No, I don't, because every time you appear, I feel my human side becoming more dependent on you."

**"That isn't true. I was developed to enhance your capabilities, not destroy you."**

"That may be, but your programming has a side effect."

**"And what is that?"**

"Madness."

**"Madness! That's nonsense. I'm programmed to.. to. Well. You'll never be able to get rid of me no matter how many blood transfusions you have!"**

"I know that, but you'll be just a reminder then."

**"That's what you think. I'm programmed to survive no matter what you personally want to do."**

"Captain, are you alright?" Hap said.

"Yes. I think... I must have fallen asleep and was dreaming."

"Well, we're just about there."

"And where's that, Hap. I don't remember telling you any specific address."

"Captain, I can assure you, you told me to head home so you could shower and change clothes."

"Okay. Hap, if you say so."

I sat back and closed my eyes and felt the world slipping away again. This time it was pleasant so I thought I'd stay there a while. Then someone I hadn't seen in a long time joined me.

"Bill, you have to wake up now. I know you want to be with us but it's not your time." The beautiful faces of my wife and son melted in front of my eyes and became horned red eyed monsters.

"If you don't leave now, this is where you'll wind up."

I opened my eyes suddenly and found myself in Hap's taxi breathing heavily.

"Are you okay, Captain? You're beginning to scare me."

"What did I say or do this time?"

"Captain, for a second there, I thought you had passed away. You lost all color in your face and hands. I was about to stop when you gasped and opened your eyes."

"I'm okay now Hap, I just have a headache is all."

**"Are you sure about that?"** Cochran's serum whispered.

## Chapter 7

April 6th 1933
5:20 pm Tuesday

Returning home, I found Margaret sitting on the porch with Mildred and felt my heart skip a beat. In the months since getting married, Margaret's face looked ten years younger. Even with the loss of their money to Genovese, the two of them had grown closer.

"My word, William, what have you been into now?" Margaret asked jumping up and started checking me over. "You smell of smoke, ash and your cloths are damp." Margaret started removing my tie and then went for the suit coat. "I just don't understand you sometimes, William. Most men leave in the morning and come home looking the same way. You leave in the morning and I never know how you'll look when you get back. Just look at you, William, another ruined suit and it's only Tuesday."

"Margaret stop!" I shouted at the two of them. "I'm fine, and I'm tired, and I want a shower. So please stop." I started rubbing my temples as the headache returned.

"I'm sorry, dear. Let me help you upstairs," they both said taking an arm to steady me.

In the past months since being injected and bitten by the cobra, I found anger was one of its many side effects along with the physical strain. I hadn't told Margaret or the doctors about that. If I had, I'd probably still be in the hospital being experimented on.

I spent an hour getting clean enough to put on fresh clothes. It has always amazed me when I was young how dirt could accumulate in or on your body parts. After taking a bath or shower, my mother could find at least a dozen places still needing to be washed. On this occasion it was the same, ears inside and out, back of the neck, between the toes, up my nose, bellybutton. Finally after passing Margaret's inspection, we headed downstairs to have dinner. Grace and Lenard were already seated, Henry was also, now being the only boarder.

With everyone seated including Mildred, I asked Mildred to say grace. If Mildred hadn't been at the table, somehow we would have skipped that part. I carved the pork loin and Margaret passed the plates around for each person to take whatever else they wanted to eat. When I sat down to fill my plate I noticed Grace's plate piled to the sky.

"Grace, are you sure you have enough to eat."

"I probably can come back for seconds if you don't eat it all," she said grabbing three slices of bread.

"You can have my extra portion," Margaret said pushing her plate away.

"Margaret, would you like something different?" Mildred asked, looking concerned.

"No, that's okay, Mom. I'll just have a piece of dry bread, maybe that'll settle my stomach."

I looked at Margaret's face and saw how pale she was. Reaching out, I touched her arm and found it cold and clammy. I looked at Mildred and shook my head slightly indicating she was sicker than what she had said.

"I think I left something on the stove." Mildred said, getting up to call the doctor. I got up as well and whispered in Margaret's ear to come upstairs and lie down.

Lenard and Henry could see something was going on and started to get up.

"No." I motioned. Sit down and eat your dinner before it gets cold. Besides someone needs to help Grace with seconds."

I looked over at Grace to see she was busily eating everything on her plate. "Lenard, I hope you keep your job because you'll need the money for groceries."

As I walked Margaret out of the dining room, Grace piped up. "Is Margaret not feeling well again Bill?" she said shaking her head. "My sister is always not feeling well. You'd think she was a princess or something always wanting attention. Pass me her plate please. I hate to see food go to waste"

"Grace, how far along are you now?" I said.

"Seven months maybe eight. Why?"

"I just wondered Grace, because I was thinking of buying stock in commodities, corn, pork, greens."

"Very funny Bill, very funny. By the way, are you going to eat what's on your plate?"

"No go ahead, you can have it as well, you're eating for... ten isn't it?"

"No." Grace said sarcastically, "twenty today."

As I walked Margaret to the stairs, I could see Lenard and Henry pick up their pace on eating. At the rate Grace was going she'd eat their plates as well.

# Chapter 8

April 6th 1933
7:10 pm Tuesday

**M**ildred and I kept changing out cold compresses on Margaret's head until the doctor showed up. He checked her over for about ten minutes and then came to us.

"Your daughter has a cold of some kind. I don't believe it's anything to worry about now, because her temperature is 100. If her temperature increases, then get her to a hospital."

"Are you sure it's not the Spanish flu?" I asked.

"Not from what I see now. I'd be more inclined to say polio, or scarlet fever, measles but flu would be my last choice. There is one other possibility? Is the lady pregnant?"

"No." I said turning a bit red.

"That's a point in her favor. So for right now an aspirin every four to six hours, liquids at least eight ounces every hour. I'll be back in the morning to see how she's doing."

I sat down on the corner of our bed with a damp towel in my hand. I removed the warm one and placed my cooling fresh one on her forehead. "I'm sorry to be a burden on you William. I just don't know what's come over me lately."

"Don't you worry about that Margaret. The Doctor says you'll be up and around in a day or two." I was about to replace the washcloth when Hap poked his head in from the open door.

"Captain, don't forget you have a meeting with the FBI Director at ten."

"Mildred, I have to go out for a few minutes to see someone. Can you handle this alone?"

Mildred nodded yes. I gave Margaret a kiss on her hot forehead and whispered, "I love you."

"Where are you going, William, at such a late our?"

"I'm just running to the store to get some medicine the Doctor prescribed."

Mildred stepped in and gently removed Margaret's hand from mine. "It's 9:10 pm. You better get moving.

I headed out the door and went to Henry's room and knocked on his door. "Henry, are you in there?"

"Yes, come in."

I found Henry sitting at a card table playing solitaire in his night clothes. "Henry, I need you to do me a favor. Keep an eye out for any strangers that might show up. Tell them the house is under quarantine and no one is admitted in or out."

"Is Margaret that sick?"

"No. I just don't want strangers in our house at this hour."

"Yes sir." Henry said, looking for his pants.

I then headed downstairs to find Hap nibbling on leftovers from tonight's dinner. "Hap, if your still hungry bring whatever you're eating along."

As we reached the door I asked Hap, "Doesn't your wife mind you being out this time of night?"

"No, Captain. All she's interested in is how much money I'll bring home."

"Doesn't she worry something might happen to you?"

"Not in a long, long, time, Captain. She thinks I have another woman that I spend money on. I've told her things are slow now, especially me driving this old taxi."

"Detective, I've been meaning to stop by and congratulate you on getting married," Larry, my next door neighbor, said walking towards me.

"Stop right there. Margaret's ill and the Doctor said it could be contagious."

Larry is a lawyer by profession who has been a pain in my ass. "What can I do for you, Larry? Has someone stolen your evening paper again?"

"No. It's more serious than that, Bill. I just wanted to let you know I'm moving out of my lovely home."

"Why's that?"

"Well, with this new stock market crash, I no longer have many clients. I also lost just about all my savings as well."

"Sorry to hear that, Larry. But can we talk about that another time. I have a meeting to go to."

"Okay. Then I'll get right to the point. I, ah, thought you being married now you might be interested in buying my place?"

I wanted to turn the screws to him just like he had done to Betty and Travis' landscaping business.

"I'll talk to Margaret and see what she says. What price do you want for your house?"

At the word price I could see the old Larry light up in his eyes. "Well as you know my place is very well kept. I was thinking, ah, $8,000?"

"$8,000! You got to be kidding. No one would have that kind of money to lend these days."

"Well, I can come down a bit, Bill. I could finance it for a monthly payment of say $45."

"For how long?"

I watched the wheels turning as he calculated his profit, 27 years and 3 months, with a down payment of $1,000.

"I'll have to let you know Larry, but I still think I can do better elsewhere."

"Well, just think on it and I'll get back with you Friday."

About that time Hap blew his taxi horn. "Okay Larry I'll do that." I jumped into his taxi and we headed for the zoo and the bunker I had hoped never to see again.

"Why do you want to go there this late?" Hap asked.

"We're going to meet FBI Director Carter Grayson."

I had been impressed with Grayson's honesty and cooperation on the Wishing Well murders. Reaching the zoo's parking lot, Hap and I headed for the bunker which was behind a two story building. The top floor was the offices where I met Cochran. On the first floor were the snake exhibits which held his King Cobra. The bunker was an old storage room where his laboratory was. It was also the place I had been injected with his experimental serum. As we reached the steps leading below ground, I found myself reluctant to go any further.

**"Come on, Bill. Don't you want to see where we were born?"**

I could feel my heart racing as I struggled to take the first step.

"Captain, why don't I go down and see if the door's locked."

"Good idea Hap, and please stop calling me Captain."

"Okay...Boss." Hap went down into the darkness as I struggled with myself to do the same. "Its locked Boss, but I'm sure I can pick it if you wish."

I didn't have a chance to reply as the outside and interior lights came on.

"Hap. I going to wait here for Grayson and whoever is with him." I lit another cigarette and looked around to see if anyone was walking towards us.

"Boss. I'm going to look the place over just to make sure no one is in here."

I finished my cigarette and decided I needed to be a policeman again. I took a deep breath and slowly walked down the ten steps to the open door. As I entered the hallway I could feel Cochran's serum awakening in me. I took a few more steps, remembering I had checked each room as I came to them. With heart pounding now, I turned the corner and found the operating room just the same. I looked around, expecting to see Cochran pop up out of nowhere.

"Is this where all the girls were operated on?" Hap asked.

"Yes, and so was I Hap, on that very table, but it's just a room now full of bad memories."

**"Bill, why are you so afraid of our birthing table. Just think if I hadn't felt we couldn't work together, you'd be dead by now."**

"What time is it Hap?" I said wiping sweat from my forehead.

"10:15 pm by my watch. What time were they to be here?"

"10:00 pm but they might have been delayed."

We waited until 11:00 pm before I decided they weren't coming.

"Well. Hap, I guess we might as well call it a night. I'll have to call and find out tomorrow what happened."

Hap locked the door and we headed back to the taxi. As I got in I found a letter addressed to me. Opening it I read the following.

Detective Barronson I'm disappointed with you. We made an agreement that you would accompany me to Germany. In exchange, I wouldn't harm any of you friends. You broke our agreement by going to the FBI. Therefore, Detective, you will find your next door neighbors no longer living. I hope you don't break our agreement again as I do enjoy my work.

Major Carl Muller Peiper
Heil Hitler.

"Hap, you better get me home as fast as you can, and I want you to arm yourself as well."

"Boss, what did the letter say that has frightened you so?"

"There's a madman by the name of Carl Muller on the loose and he's threatening to kill people I know."

# Chapter 9

April 7th 1933<br>12:10 am Wednesday

Hap pulled up in front of home and I jumped out and headed for Larry's house with my flashlight in hand. As I reached the porch I stopped and pulled out my gun. The last thing I didn't want to happen was for one of us to get shot by mistake.

"Captain. What the hell is going on?"

"Hap. I need for you to take my key and get into the house and call for Henry, Grace or Mildred. Make sure you identify yourself so that Henry or Grace don't shoot you as a prowler. Then tell Henry to call the station and have them send two patrol cars and two ambulances along with the coroner."

I waited until I was sure Hap was a safe distance away before walking up to the front door. There were no lights on but my flashlight showed me the front door was partially open. Taking a deep breath, I slowly pushed the door open and entered the dark hallway saying. "Police! Larry! It's me, Detective Barronson from next door." When I got no answer I turned on the lights. Larry's and Mildred's houses were built by the same builder. That made the layouts of both houses the same. I called out again and still didn't get an answer. With my gun still drawn, I stepped into the dark parlor to take a quick look around with my flashlight.

As I panned around the room I found nothing out of place. Deciding this could take all night, I found the switch and turned on the lights. To my surprise I found Larry sitting on the sofa with his back to me. Walking around the sofa, I found Larry leaning back with his throat cut. He must have bled out within seconds from the amount of blood all around him.

Turning on more lights as I went, I found Larry's cat hiding behind a basket of clean clothes. When it saw me she  immediately came to me and started purring. I then checked the kitchen, dining room, library and bathroom. Not wanting to go upstairs alone, I was glad when Henry called my name.

"Over here by the back stairs, Henry."

When he appeared he was a sight for sore eyes even if he was in his pajamas.

"Henry, you could have put on some clothes before coming over here."

Henry stopped and for a moment looked bewildered. "Bill I came as soon as Hap said you needed help. So here I am."

"Henry, I've found Larry dead in the parlor. I've checked all the rooms down here and found them empty. That means his wife Beth is upstairs or is visiting her mother. Either way we need to check the upstairs for the murderer."

Just like Mildred's house, the bedrooms were divided on both sides of the house with the bathroom in the middle.

"Henry you take the bedroom on the right and I'll take the left."

We moved to the darkened stairs and turned on the lights. With every step we took, I expected Muller to jump out and start shooting. Reaching the landing, I went to the first bedroom and opened the door. I saw a darker shadow on the floor and quickly turned on the lights. There on the floor was Mrs. Ann Langford, lying face down in a pool of blood. I touched her neck just to make sure she was dead and saw that her throat was cut as well. I continued to check the other bedrooms and found them empty. That left the bathroom and Henry's bedrooms. I started to open the bathroom door when I saw a trickle of blood run out from under it. I tried the door and found it locked.

My first thought was that Henry had run into Muller.

"Henry!" I screamed. When I didn't get an answer, I started hitting the door with my shoulder.

**"I'll do that for you,"** Cochran's serum stated as it took control before I could stop it. I hit the door so hard with my shoulder the door frame shattered along with the door. As I stood there gasping for air I started to throw pieces of door and door frame into the tub to uncover the body under it.

"Bill! What's going on in there?"

I turned and for a moment didn't believe my eyes.

"Henry?" I turned back to the body and finished clearing the debris away.

"Is that Larry's wife?" Henry said backing away from the expanding flow of blood.

"No, Henry. I believe this is his mother-in-law. Mrs. Langford is in that room with her throat cut as well."

Holstering my gun, I went downstairs to meet the police cars pulling up in front. I started to open the door when I saw my hands were covered in blood. I ran to a bedroom and looked in the mirror. My suit coat and pants had smears of blood on them as well as my shoes. It wasn't a minute before I heard the Coroner's Peter Ingram's angry voice.

I made sure the patrolmen could see my badge as I walked out of the back bedroom.

"What do we... have... Oh my God, Bill?" Pete said staring at me.

"Put your hands in the air!" Two policemen said pulling their guns.

"I'm, Detective William Barronson," I said pointing at my badge. "And policeman Henry Ingram is in his pajamas upstairs. I put my hands down as they put their guns away.

"Have you or Henry been injured?" Pete, the coroner asked.

"No. All this blood is from the two victims upstairs.

I could see the relief on Pete's face that his brother was okay as well.

"Okay, show me the bodies." Pete said, looking at his watch.

"What seems to be the matter Pete?'

"I'd wish just once, someone would get murdered in the daytime. That way, at least, I'd get a full night's sleep.

Anyway, Detective, which one do we start with?"

"In the parlor, Pete, is the husband Larry Langford. His throat has been cut. The other two bodies are upstairs. Ann his wife in the bedroom and I believe his mother-in-law in the other bathroom. Both of them had their throats cut."

Pete and his crew started taking photographs and examining the bodies while trying not to step in the blood.

"Pete, if you don't need me and Henry, we'll go home and change our clothes. That way we won't look so out of place."

"Sure go ahead Detective. It'll be a least three hours before I'm done here. And while you're at it, let Grace know I'm thinking about her and the baby."

"Henry, let's go home and change. I must say you look quite hansom in your blue and white striped pajamas."

"I can say the same thing to you, Bill. That blood stained suit does wonders for you blood shot eyes."

"Point taken, Henry."

As Hap and I went out the front door, we got the strangest looks from the crowd as dozens of reporters' flash bulbs lit up the night sky. By the time we reached the front steps dozens of questions were being thrown at us.

"Detective. How many people have been murdered?"

"Is it true you and the homeowner had words?"

"Did you and his wife have an affair?"

"Why is this man in his pajamas carrying a gun?

"Why didn't you listen, Detective. Now tell us why it's your fault they're dead."

I recognized Muller's voice, and started looking for his face. I believe I spotted him several time but when I tried to move some jack ass took a flashbulb picture of me.

The reporters must have figured out I was looking for someone behind them. The thought of them getting a bigger story was like sharks smelling blood in the water. The frenzy got so bad, I was afraid people would start fighting with each other.

Henry and I pushed our way through the reporters and onlookers that were arguing with each other. A woman screamed somewhere in the crowed. It was so high pitched everyone stopped and looked for the woman.

"If you idiots are done fighting! Why don't you people get off my lawn and go home! Don't you think there's been enough deaths tonight, without adding anymore?" Grace yelled from the porch. "And you reporters! Your worse than the rest! Fighting with each other over a story that'll be used tomorrow night to wrap up the garbage!"

"Grace, calm down before you have the baby right here." Lenard said putting his arms around her.

"You heard the lady! I'll give you a count of five before Henry and I start shooting!" Hap joined Henry and myself as we pointed our revolvers at the crowd. "1!..2!.." There wasn't a three, because the onlookers had moved.

The reporters took some pictures before backing across the street as well. I took a deep breath, and let it out very slowly. In all the excitement my other serum self was fighting to get out. "Well you two, it looks like we've defused the situation."

"You did what!" Grace yelled forcing her husband to let her go. "If it hadn't been for me, there would be dead body's all over my lawn!" Grace said breaking down in tears.

"I think we better get inside before Grace starts round two."

"Captain, was she like this when she was a kid?"

"I didn't know her then, but I'm sure that temper was home grown."

We quickly opened the screen door and were met by Mildred in her night clothes holding an 1870's Parker Brothers heavy gauge shotgun. "Mildred, you can put away that monster you're carrying."

"I can still see them waiting across the street. If they think they can break into my house…"

"They're not going to break in here. Besides we all need to have a talk. Larry and his wife and mother-in law have been murdered probably by robbers. I'll talk to the Captain tomorrow and have more police presence until we find them."

After a few minutes of questions I said. "I need to get a few hours' sleep, and I'm sure everybody else does too. Margaret and I headed upstairs. Mildred gave Hap a pillow and a blanked so he could sleep in the parlor.

"William, what is going on?"

"Nothing, Dear."

I got into bed but found I couldn't sleep. I had been so careful to cover my tracks before going to the FBI. I started thinking who might be working with Muller. My first thought was Happy, after all the only thing I knew about him was that he was a taxi driver. Then it occurred to me the Captain or an FBI Agent or may be Mildred. I was so frustrated I felt like my head would explode.

I looked at my clock and then out the window at Larry's house. The house was dark which meant the coroner and police had left.

I got up and looked out the window and saw one car parked out front.

As I stared at the ceiling, I wondered why Muller had chosen Larry and his wife instead of someone closer to me.

I thought about how I would threaten someone if I were him. It then occurred to me the first victim in retaliation would be a neighbor. That way I would get the message he meant what he said. "Damn him."

"What did you say Dear?"

"Nothing, Honey. Just go back to sleep."

My clock said 2:45 am as I made up my mind that I had no intention of going to Germany. Which meant I need to arrest him or kill him.

## Chapter 10

April 7th 1933
3:15 am Wednesday

"It's 3:15 dear. You need to get some sleep" Margaret said turning on the light. "Here take one of these."

"What are they, sleeping pills?"

"Yes, the doctor gave me these in the hospital."

I took one and lay there thinking about Muller.

"It's time to get up dear," Margaret said shaking me.

"What! what time is it anyway," I mumbled turning over.

"It's 9:25, William. You told me you wanted to be up by 6:00 am."

"I lied, Dear," pulling the covers over my head.

"William, you need to get up! Hap, has been waiting down stairs now for three hours."

"Oh. alright," I said stumbling to my feet. "That pill you gave me really knocked me out. What's the name of that pill?"

"Let me look. The bottle says Pentathlon. Take one by mouth at bed time."

"Dear, I believe the doctors are finally right about something. A pill that actually works."

I started to dress when I heard shouting coming from outside. I opened the bedroom window as high as it would go and looked out. Not seeing what all the commotion was about, I leaned out as far as I could without falling. Mildred, Grace, Henry, Hap with our neighbors were pointing to the West and yelling, "The end of the world is upon us."

Being in a higher advantage point, I looked to the West and saw the skyline was brown from horizon to horizon. At first glance it did look as if the sky was of fire. I started to push myself back into my bedroom, when a light rain of sand started falling. I stuck my head out the window again, and stared in amazement as the landscape was being swallowed up by that wall of brown sand. Fascinated as I had never seen a sand storm before, I watched as the brown shifting cloud moved closer engulfing everything in its path. Suddenly, I felt something stinging my face. I started to brush at the bugs unknowing I was actually being stung by wind carrying grains of sand.

"Mildred! All of you get inside and close all your doors and windows, there's a sand storm coming!"

I slammed my window shut and locked it as the storm increased. "Margaret! Start stuffing anything you can find under all the doors. I'll check the other room's windows, and found all of them open. By the time I got all of them closed and sheets under the doors the storm was almost  upon us.

"Mildred! Have everybody close every window and door. And stuff towels under every one of them!"

Margaret and I raced down the stairs carrying clothes we could use to block the fireplace chimney.

"Bill, have you two lost your minds?" Grace said as we stuffed the clothes to stop the sand from coming in.

I ran towards the front door as the storm hit. In an instant, I couldn't see a thing through the glass door.

As the house shook from the hurricane winds, sand started coming in from under the door-sill. With everything stuffed up the chimney I looked for something thin to stuff between the door and the sill. "Margaret. Give me your dress, Hap, get a carving knife from the kitchen." I quickly took off my suit-coat as Margaret handed me her dress. I hadn't thought about what she might be wearing under the dress. Lucky for me she had on a slip which she covered with my coat.

Hap came back bringing me a knife. By then there was several inches of sand blowing across the floor.   Blinking several times to get my eyes to water, I managed to see enough to start stuffing the dress under the door.

When I was done stuffing her dress under the door, the sand could no longer blow in.  As I headed for the kitchen, I spotted Grace and Lenard sitting on the couch holding each other. I then heard sobbing and saw that Mildred wasn't with us. "Mildred! Are you hurt?" Hap said rushing to her side.

"No. I'm not hurt, but my crows probably are, Bill."

"Your crows?" Then I remembered Charlie and the other crows she had adopted along with Larry's cat.

"Bill I didn't tell you, but Charlie never came back after being with me for only one day. I don't know what I did to drive him away."

"Mildred, it's fine. He's just a bird."

"I know, but you had him trained to it on my shoulder and eat out of my hand. Now if the others are killed by this storm." Mildred broke down sobbing again until she saw the fine sand accumulating on everything. "Oh. I better get moving. Y'all need some breakfast, do you?"

I was going to tell her not to bother but if I did she'd start thinking about her crows again. As we left the kitchen I thought of telling Mildred, Charlie hadn't flown away, I had shot the miserable bastard's tail feathers off at the zoo. Bonnie Graves, the trainer of Charlie and other birds, gave Charlie a home with the zoo's wild bird collection.

As the day progressed, we listened to the radio when it wasn't full of static. "Hey everybody!" Hap said "This dust storm, so the paper calls it, started in the mid-west.

"You mean the wind has blown constantly for three days without stopping? Lenard said, shaking his head.

"Not only that. This dust storm will continue on until it reaches the Atlantic Ocean. And you won't believe this. The dust storm could go all the way to Europe."

"Hap. Does the article say how this happened?" Margaret asked.

"Let's see...ah yes. I have to go to page six." Hap turned the pages and then folded it. "Okay, I've found it. It says here the states of Texas, Oklahoma, New Mexico, Colorado, Nebraska and Kansas are in a two year drought. Without rain, the once fertile farmlands have turned into desert. Without vegetation, the easterly blowing winds will pick up the soil and carry it away."

"Then what is the government doing about it Hap?"

"It doesn't say, but it does say we can expect more dust storms."

# Chapter 11

April 7th 1933
2:18 pm Wednesday

Looking out the window for the tenth time, I could see no change. Dust was still settling on everything and the air was still brown. If you looked up at the sun, all you could see is a dim yellow brown ball no brighter than a full moon.

"When do you think this will be over?" Mildred asked, wiping dust off my chair. "I don't know how people out west can stand all this dirt. Look I just wiped that table down just a minute ago, and it's already dirty."

"I don't know Mildred, but I'd say a day or two by the looks of it." I motioned to Margaret and Grace to console Mildred. "Mildred, why don't you let your daughters help you wipe things down. Hap. Let's see if the taxi will crank."

"You're not going out in this with Margaret sick. Are you?"

"I have to, Mildred. This is perfect weather for the crooks to have free reign. I can bet you there's been ten robberies, six or eight shootings, and God knows how many accidents."

Hap and I went outside and didn't get as far as the front porch steps before giving up. "Well that wasn't too smart was it, Boss?"

"I'll call in to the station and tell them we are unable to make it in." I picked up the receiver and found the line dead. Either the lines were down or there were no operators to make our calls.

"William, why don't you take a nap? I'm sure you and Hap could both use one."

"Margaret, I believe you've made the perfect solution to today's problem." I was already sitting in Mildred's rocking chair and before I knew it, I must have fallen asleep.

"I got it running, Captain!" Hap yelled from the front door.

"Hap. Be quiet. You'll wake William up."

50

"It's okay, dear. I was already awake."

"Captain, I don't know how long before the air filter becomes clogged again, so we better get moving"

I kissed Margaret on the cheek and headed out the door. To my surprise, the wind had dropped to a light breeze. "It looks like the storm is about over, Hap." As I got into Hap's taxi, the sky was already beginning to clear. That meant what dust was still in the air was falling to the ground like rain.

As Hap drove along, I was pleased to see he was taking his time. The visibility was improving, but there were many vehicles of all types abandoned on the road. Some had hit other vehicles, some had hit trees, some driven off the road and more were just abandoned. It took more than two hours to get to the station because of blocked streets. When I walked inside, I found the sergeant drinking a cup of coffee and listening to the police radio.

"Looks pretty quiet?"

"You can say that again. I've only booked two robberies and one accident so far today."

"Is the Captain in?"

"Yes, and he'll be a lot happier to see you made it in."

I got to his office without finding anybody else at their desks. Knocking, I entered and found the Captain on the phone. When he saw me I could see he was relieved.

"I made it in, Captain."

"Did you have much trouble getting here?"

"Yes and no. Hap's taxi engine stalled out a couple of times due to a clogged air filter, but other than that, the main problem were abandoned vehicles."

"Do you have any idea yet about the fires?"

"Not much, the Chief thinks both of them were set. As far as the warehouse fire goes, the Chief hasn't been able to get there yet. I didn't get a chance either to see if the other fires we've had this year are related to these fires."

"I see your hands have healed. Didn't you burn them at the McKenzie fire?"

"Yes, but the burns weren't as bad as they looked. That, Captain, leads me to my first question. I would like to put Hap on temporary duty as my driver and partner."

"I don't think that is possible, but I can assign you someone that's already on the police force?"

"Captain, I would like to have Hap as my driver as he knows the town. He also has many connections being a taxi driver that I and the department could use."

"That reminds me I just got a report that said there were three people murdered on your street. Did you know them?"

"Yes, they were my next door neighbors."

"Was it a simple break-in gone bad."

"No, Captain, it was a message sent to me by a man called Carl Muller."

"Who is Carl Muller, and what is his relationship to you?"

I took the next hour to explain what had happened before he was hired as Captain. "So you see, Captain, that was when I went to the FBI building and set up a meeting with Director Carter."

"Did the two of you meet? I should have been informed about it as well."

"Captain, remember the call you got yesterday that said to meet at ten?"

"Yes, that was to inform me that Director Carter would meet me at the zoo bunker at 10:00 pm."

"Well! Did he show up and what did you discuss before I call him up!"

"Captain. He didn't show, and when I went back to Hap's taxi, Muller had left me this note."

I handed it to the Captain and waited while he read it.

"So, Captain, I have someone close to me who is informing Muller about every move I make."

"And you think it could be Hap?" the Captain said bringing out a bottle. "Have one? And while we're on the subject, how are the transfusion working out?"

"Yes, I'll have one and I believe we have about cleaned me out of Cochran's serum that I was injected with," I said taking the glass.

"Alright. Put Hap on the payroll as your driver. Now, what else do you need."

"I need for you to call FBI headquarters in Washington and ask for Director Carter Grayson. I have a feeling he didn't show because Muller murdered him. If he is alive, tell him we need to meet as soon as possible. Don't mention Muller, I want to do that myself."

"Okay, Bill, but I need to be a part of this investigation as well. Do I need to assign the fires to another detective?"

"No. I need to stay on this case so Muller thinks I'm not trying to capture him as well."

"Is there anyone else you think might be working with Muller?"

"Right now I'm not 100% sure who I can trust. I spent the day with Agent Charles Purvise who just happened to be in town. Director Grayson that not did show for our meeting, Happy who's been with me every day, or you Captain, who I know little about."

"Me! You think it's me?" the Captain said, standing up.

"I'm sure it's not you, but I can't cross you off my list until I know if Grayson was on the other end of that call."

The Captain sat back down and said, "I can understand that, Bill, but in the meantime, I'll have two men stationed at your house, and have a patrol car cruise the neighborhood."

I started to leave when I stopped and told the Captain that Grace had resigned because of her condition.

"Good work Detective, I've just the man to take her place."

"Who would that be?"

"The Chief's son, Albert Cooker."

I didn't reply to that. Instead I headed for my desk to see what mug shots she had marked for me to look at.

From what I had been told this Albert Cooker had never had a job in his twenty three years of life. The Captain would be lucky if he knew how to read and write, let alone do a news conference.

I found on my desk had three mug books on it with paper marking the pages I need to look at. I review each one and found none of them fit the profile I was looking for.

# Chapter 12

April 7th 1933
5:31 pm Wednesday

I was about to leave when I got a call, "Hello."

I spent the next several minutes talking to Agent Purvise. He explained he hadn't got hold of the Director in time for him to explain he was on another case. Purvise was to handle the case with my help until he could wrap up the case he was on. I took his number and told him I would be in touch once this dust storm subsided enough to get around.

Now more confused than before, I went back to the Captain's office and confronted him with the news.

"Bill, I can assure you I talked to Grayson yesterday. I don't know what game this Agent Purvise is trying to play. My suggestion to you is take the chance and call this Grayson yourself. That way you'll find out which one of us is lying."

I went to my desk and asked for a long distance operator.

"Operator six two for long distance, who would you like to talk to?"

"I'd like to speak to the FBI in Washington DC. The man's name is Carter Grayson."

"I can try that sir but the storm is causing a lot of static. I can't guarantee you would be able to hear the person on the other end.

"Please try anyway operator. I'll wait at this number for your call back."

Hanging up the phone, I lit a cigarette and waited for the operator. I played over in my mind what I was going to ask Grayson. Accusing an agent of Hoover's being dirty was the last thing I wanted to do. Things where already strained between us and if I pushed in the wrong way I could find myself in somebody's laboratory as a guinea pig.

I lit another cigarette when the phone rang, "Hello, yes this is Detective Barronson."

"I have your party on the line sir. Are you paying or are you calling collect?"

"I'll pay."

"Very good sir." the operator said plugging me in.

"Grayson, is that you?"

I held the receiver away from my ear as the static was so loud. "Det—vie Bar—on—son—can—due—."

"I'm sorry sir, I have lost the connection. Please try later today as all our long distance calling is officially out of service. And sir, you won't be charged for the three dollar connection."

I hung up the phone and headed downstairs to see Hap and tell him the good news. I found him sitting with the Sergeant. They were drinking coffee and telling whopper stories about their weekends in Paris during World War One.

"Hey, Boss, I think I'm going to like working here." Hap said. "I could even do this job if you ever get short."

"I'll try and remember that, but for right now you're my driver. Do you think you can get us home?"

"Without a doubt, Boss, but seeing I'm officially a policeman now I'd better start calling you Detective."

"No. I think Boss is okay for now, Hap. Your job is only temporary. So until it becomes permanent let's leave it alone."

Hap and I headed out the front door and found the dust still settling. When we got to the taxi we found it to be covered in sand. "Hap, where did you get the tarp?"

"Oh, I found it lying around."

"Hap! Where did you get the tarp?" I could see Hap's face turn red as I asked again.

"Boss. I...I found it lying on the ground next to the Captain's new car."

I walked over to the only car that had almost no sand on it and smiled. "Hap did you really find the tarp on the ground?"

"Well almost. It was hanging half off the car and I only needed a small piece to cover the radiator, and."

"I think we better get out of here before the Captain decides to head home for the evening.

As I got in the back seat, I looked at the globed street lights. The sand accumulating on their tops reminded me of snow in the winter. "Hap I hope this stuff will be gone by tomorrow, we have a lot of work to do."

# Chapter 13

April 8th 1933
6:18 am Thursday

I got out of bed to use the bathroom when I heard the sounds of birds. Opening the window, I stuck my hand out and found no sand accumulating on it. I got ready for work and found myself in great spirits. With the dust storm gone I couldn't wait to eat breakfast that didn't taste like sand. "Good morning Mildred. It's going to be a fine day."

I then saw the look on her face and rushed upstairs to Margaret's room. Opening the door slowly I braced myself for not remembering she had been ill. "Good morning," I said finding her sitting up in bed.

"Well, my long lost husband returns. If I hadn't heard from you today I figured I was going to be a widow."

"No such chance." I sat down on the edge of the bed and lightly stroked her hair before giving her a kiss. "How is my darling wife feeling today?"

"I'm feeling much better. In fact, I'm going to get up and join you for breakfast."

"Okay, I'll tell Mildred you're coming down. Do you want the usual. One egg poached, limp lightly buttered toast and water?"

"I think not husband. Tell Mildred to shoot the works today, after all I'm eating for two now."

"Two? What are you saying? Just yesterday you were at deaths door. Now you say you're pregnant?"

"I know dear. You and Mildred are worried. I was myself. You see the doctor told me last year that I probably couldn't have children after the trouble I had. It took me some time to accept the fact that I was barren."

"You never told me about that Margaret. If that's the case, how do you know you're with child now?"

"Well you see, I've been sick every morning for a week now. If you haven't noticed my mood has changed and today I want to eat everything in sight. So Dear, would you be so kind as to get me some ice cream and pickles while you're out today."

"I thought that was an old wives tale?"

"Not today it isn't."

I must have had a strange look on my face as I got in the backseat of Hap's taxi.

"Okay. What's happened to you since I dropped you off last night?"

"Nothing much. I'm going to be a dad again."

"Again?"

"I'm a widower, Hap, and don't ask. Is this your son riding with you?"

"Yes, Captain. This is my son, Ox. We call him that because he's built like one."

"Morning Boss, and thanks for giving my Pa a job. I always wanted to drive his taxi."

"I can see that." I said bouncing around in the back seat.

"I taught him how to drive," Hap said hanging on for dear life.

Reaching the station in almost one piece, I got out of the taxi and found my crushed hat on the floor. Picking it up I just managed to get the door closed before Ox tore out of the parking lot.

"Hap. I believe you'll need to buy a new taxi next week. At the speed Ox's driving he'll tear that one up by then."

"No, Captain, he'll settle down before then, I hope."

"Do you want to put a bet on it?" I said.

"Sure! Two to one on five dollars that he doesn't have a wreck in two days."

"You've got a bet."

As we walked into the station I heard cars crashing and a car horn wailing steadily.

"I believe you owe me five dollars Hap."

"I don't know what you mean, Captain."

"Didn't you hear the horn blowing?"

"No. I didn't hear a thing," Hap said shaking his head in defeat.

I didn't press the matter further as I knew he wanted to have a chat with Ox before paying off on the bet.

I headed upstairs to my desk, while Hap went downstairs to fill out his paper work.

Picking up the receiver I put in my call to Washington.

With the sand storm moving on I got a return call from the operator within minutes.

"Hello."

"I wish to speak to Director Carter Grayson, this is Detective William Barronson in Atlanta."

"Grayson Carter here Bill, what can I do for you?"

"I've been contacted by Carl Muller the other night when he crawled into my bedroom window."

"What does he want from you? And was Robert Cochran with him?"

"I don't believe so, but from what he's after, I'd say Cochran is in Germany somewhere."

"Did you tell him your blood has been cleansed by transfusions?"

"No. Muller has made me an offer that I'm going to have to accept."

"What is the offer?"

"He has threatened to hurt or kill someone in my family along with my friends unless I go with him to Germany."

There was a long silence before Grayson asked, "How do we know he'll follow through on his threat?"

"He already has. My neighbor Larry, his wife Ester and her mother had their throats cut."

"How do you know it was him?"

"Because I found a note he left in my taxi. It said the following,

Detective Barronson I'm disappointed with you. We made an agreement that you would accompany me to Germany. In exchange, I wouldn't harm any of you friends. You broke our agreement by going to the FBI. Therefore, Detective, you will find your next door neighbors no longer living. I hope you don't break our agreement again as I do enjoy my work.

Major Carl Muller Peiper
Heil Hitler.

"I'd like to Bill, but I'm tied up on another case in Chicago. I told Captain Buchanan that the other day that I couldn't meet you at the bunker."

"I never got the message. It seems I can no longer trust Captain Buchanan as well."

"I'll call Birmingham, and tell them to send two men to help you."

"What are their names?"

"I believe they'll send Charles Purvise, and Miles Colton, both have been with the bureau since 1927.

"When do you think you can get down here. I'm not worried about me, Director, but he's up to something that could endanger the county later."

"I'll let you know in a day or two, but in the meantime, whatever you can find out will be greatly appreciated."

I hung up the receiver and decided I needed a cigarette to calm my nerves. As I pondered my problem with Muller, I was happy to write off Grayson and Purvise from my list. The Captain on the other hand had risen to the top of my list. That left Hap for me to verify one way or the other. Scratching my head in frustration, I decided to send Hap out in the field. If he is as good as he says he is, then I should get a lead on who the arsonist is.

I wanted to call the FBI number listed for Birmingham but decided I needed to wait until Grayson talked to them first.

"Well Captain. It looks like I'm in the police force now."

"Remember Hap. This is only temporary. we'll have to show the department that your worth making you a full time employee."

"Captain, with the two of us, this Muller will be in jail within a week."

"Hap, your forgetting Muller isn't our primary job. I been assigned to arrest this arsonist. So I need you to get with Ox and check your sources to see if they have anything on this guy?"

"Okay Captain. But what about me being your driver?"

"Being a driver won't keep you employed."

# Chapter 14

April 8th 1933
10:11 am Thursday

I looked at my watch and decided it was time to talk to Birmingham. It being 9:11 am their time someone should be working by now. I picked up my phone and asked the operator for an out side line. When I heard the double click I knew someone was listening.

"Operator. I need to call the FBI Headquarters in Birmingham Alabama."

"And do you wish to speak to?"

"Agent Charles Purvise. Tell him it is Detective Barronson calling."

"Very good Detective Barronson. Who do I charge the call to?"

I thought about that and decided if I could get a reaction from the person listening in. "Bill it to the Atlanta Police Department number under Captain Wade Buchanan." I heard a click telling me the Captain had hung up.

"Go ahead please."

"Agent Purvise?"

"No this is Agent Miles Colton, Detective. Agent Purvise in on assignment in Portland Oregon since the first of the month. May I ask why you want to speak to him?"

"Are you sure. Because I spend most of the day Tuesday with him in the Atlanta office."

"Detective. I'll have to check with Washington on that and get back to you. Do you remember me Detective? Grayson and I worked on the Wishing Well Murders with you."

"Yes, now that you mention it we did. How's the wife and kids?"

"Doing well, and how are you doing with the transfusions. From what I hear, every lab in the country has at least one bottle of your blood."

"I'm coming along fairly well. What I called about is I talked to Director Grayson and hour or so ago.

He was to called there and assign Agent Charles Purvise and you to work on the Muller case with me."

"As I said, Bill, he's not in Atlanta. The last I heard he was in Portland Oregon. Describe him to me."

I explained to Miles I had spent the day reviewing the McKenzie fire and the Fulton Cotton fire. I then described the man to him in detail.

"That's not him Bill. I will drop what I'm doing and head your way. We can't have people pretending to be agents. It's nine thirty here, I should be at your office by one."

"That sounds great, and if you can spare two more men, I think you're going to need them."

I went back upstairs to the Captain's office to inform him of my conversation with Agent Colton. If he was the one listening in I expected him to ask about the long distance charges.

"Well I'm glad you're getting that settled Bill. I was beginning to worry that things could get out of hand."

"Not to worry Captain. Agent Colton will handle it from here." Now all I have to do is find the impostor that calls himself Purvise and hold him until Colton gets here."

"Did you have any luck with the mug shot books?"

"No. I could check on a couple of them that seem to fill the bill, but right now no one does."

"Then what do you have in mind now. We just can't sit here and wait for another fire."

"I'm going to see John McCallum Junior. I want to see what angle he could put on them after all he and Vito were tight when Marco was here."

"Then you better get to it Detective. You're burning daylight and you can't afford to if you want to keep your job. And one more thing before you go Detective. I've charged that call to Birmingham to you. So don't get to  upset when you find your pay a little short."

"That's okay Captain, I'll make it up in overtime." I said closing his door.

# Chapter 15

April 8<sup>th</sup> 1933
11:28 am Thursday

I signed out another car and headed to the Flat Iron Building. I wanted to speak with John Junior about the arsonist burning down his warehouse. It had taken Grace some digging around until she found out who actually own it.

I pulled into the parking lot, and found it almost empty. I sat there for several minutes gauging the time between trains. I was wearing my last suit and didn't want it covered in smoke and coal cinders. I lit a cigarette, and after smoking it, I decided I had enough time to make it to the front door. I opened the car door and listened for a trains whistle. Nothing. There wasn't even any smoke rising from the train station as I slowly walked to the buildings entrance. Opening the door, I found the information desk was unmanned and the lobby empty. From the look of the dirty dust covered desk it hadn't been manned in over a year. I spotted a large hand painted sign on a wooden tr-pod stand next to the elevators that said:

Due to the Market Crash of 1931
Please do the following

1. Check the list below for which floor.
2. Push button for elevator doors to open.
3. Push button to close doors.
4. Move lever up and watch the floor number light up.
5. Move lever to center to stop at floor that is lit up
6. Doors will open automatically

John McCallum. CEO& President Office s on Floor 6

I followed the instructions and stopped the elevator on floor two just to appease my curiosity. When the door opened I found no lights on except the exits. I did this at every floor and found the same thing until I reached the sixth. As the door opened, I saw John sitting behind his father's desk using the window sunlight as electricity.

"Detective Barronson. It's been a long time since we met. How's my sister doing?" he asked looking over his horn rimmed glasses.

"Very well, as a matter of fact John, I just found out Margaret's going to have a baby."

"Baby! Well I hope it's yours and not Marcos. It would be a shame if he's born with black hair and olive skin now wouldn't it."

The cruel look on his face made me want to wipe that look off his face. "That would have to be a miracle too, wouldn't it, John?"

"What do you mean by that?"

"Not much considering your father and Caroline, his mistress, could be your parents. No! that's not right either. Well... never mind, I'm sure you remember your mother's name no matter what it is." I said lighting a cigarette.

I watched the self-satisfied smirk melt from his face,  and be replaced by the one I knew better. "John I didn't come here to banter with you. I wanted to know, and I'm sure you know, there have been three bad fires just this week.  The Fire Chief Mitch Anderson has surmised that one of the fires which happen to be your warehouse was set by an arsonist."

"Are you implying I paid somebody to burn down my own warehouse? I lost $50,000 worth of merchandise that had already been sold."

"If that's the case you wouldn't mind telling me who the insurance company is?"

"That is none of your business, demoted Captain."

I could see on John's face he was trying desperately to talk his way out of it. "John. I'm not here to try and pin anything on you. All I'm after is this guy's motives for setting these fires."

"I'm a busy man, Detective, since my father and great, great grandfather were murdered last year. As a matter of fact Detective, how's the investigation going now that you're back on the street?"

"I'm sure you know better than I about who murdered them."

"If you're looking for someone that knows, why don't you talk to your wife. Everything would have been just fine if she hadn't broken the engagement with Genoveses son, Marco."

"And if she hadn't, you'd still be an errand boy for your Father and the Major. So stop blaming Margaret for not wanting to spend the rest of her life being knocked around by that bastard Marco. Now I have one more question."

"No! There will be no more questions, Detective." John said pointing at the elevator.

"Alright, John, will you inform your secretary to show me to the elevator, so the operator can take down to the lobby? Oh! by the way, John, that girl at the information desk needs to do some housecleaning. The lobby is very dusty after that last dust storm."

John jumped to his feet clinching his fist. I figured I had pushed him as far as I could without getting into a fist fight. "Okay. John, I'm going." I got up from my chair and headed for the elevator ignoring his four letter words. As I got into the elevator, I said, "Nice talk President, secretary, elevator operator and janitor. That last one I mentioned needs a little more training though, and y'all have a nice day now, you hear?" as the doors closed. I heard a thump. John must have thrown something heavy at the doors. I thought about what he could have used, and the only thing I could think of was a shoe.

As the elevator descended, I could hear John yelling profanity until I reached the lobby. I started for the door when I started laughing. The arrogant SOB had insulted my wife and if I didn't laugh about it, John would have a bloody nose by now.

I made it to my car without getting covered in black coal smoke from a passing train. As I waited to turn into traffic a cloud of black smoke covered me and my car.

I always hated breathing in that smoke as 1000's of trains passing through Atlanta daily. Now with this last stock market crash, thanks to Roosevelt, I'd be lucky to see 300 trains a day.

That was bad for business but good for my lungs not having to inhale their smoke. I did like the new President, because he did repeal prohibition making my life much easier. The problem with that was the Mafia instead of pushing booze has started pushing drugs to make their revenue.

I was heading towards the station when I decided to make a detour. I wanted to see if Agent Purvise was in the building. I parked in front of the FBI building instead of in their private lot. If I need help in arresting this so- called agent, I wanted as much public exposure as possible. As I walked up the four steps leading to the front door I double-check my revolver. I expected the doors to be locked but found one side to be unlocked. Walking in, I found the lobby deserted and unusually cold for this time of day. I started towards the elevators and with every step I took  echoed off the high marble walls and floor. I hadn't noticed the first time I was here that this place was large enough to park 50 cars in here without them ever touching.

Upon reaching the elevators, I pushed the call button and  waited for a door to open before pressing the button again and then again. Stepping back I looked at the floor indicator arrows and found none of them moving. I spotted the stairs and started climbing until I reached the first floor. As I stood there looking around, I felt a strange silence. As I walked down the row of dust cobwebbed desks a chill ran up my spine. This place was a mausoleum now for the FBI.

"FIRE, FIRE, FIRE." I yelled breaking the silence. When I got no reply I climbed to the next floor and repeated my call. By the time I got to the tenth floor screaming, fire, fire, fire I found myself alone and hoarse. As I walked around I remembered this floor had been occupied by Purvise and his partner. Finding no one here I looked at my watch and found the time to be 3:45 pm. I decided this had been a wild goose chase and started down the stairs. I reached the lobby and headed for the front doors and found them locked.

"What the hell is this?" I said banging on the thick glass.

"You idiot! While I was climbing all these stairs shouting fire, Agent Purvise had slipped passed me and locked me in. As I looked out the door it became clear I could be in here for days. As I lit a cigarette it became clear I was going to have to break out. I removed my gun from its holster and fired three shots at the brass lock. I was going to shoot a fourth, but the echoes bouncing off the granite walls had made my ears bleed.

**"You shoot another bullet, I'll stop repairing the damage you're doing to your ears."** Cochran's serum stated.

"That's alright. I didn't ask you to repair them in the first place."

"Alright, then, fire away and see what happens?"

I started to pull the trigger just for spite. It then occurred to me I was being manipulated by Cochran's serum to do just that. I had been told by the doctors that had studied me in Washington, "The more you let the serum take control the stronger it will get."

I returned my gun to its holster and pushed on the door. At first it didn't open, so I kept pushing with no results until I lost my temper. "Damn you door! Open!" I gave it a good kick and heard the door swing open.

Once I was outside I could see a crowd building across the street. As I headed for my car, I realized they were pointing at me as three police cars pull up. The first one out of the car was Henry, reaching for his revolver.

"Henry! It's me Detective Barronson."

"Detective Barronson! What the hell were you shooting at?" the police officers asked putting their revolvers away.

I told Henry to follow me up to the doors. "Henry I got locked in buy an FBI Agent that's pretending to be an agent."

# Chapter 16

April 8th 1933
4:14 pm Thursday

I headed back to the station when a call came over the radio. "Detective Barronson, over."

"Detective. I've been calling you for over two hours, over."

"Sorry, Sarge, over."

"There's a Miles Colton here that says he was to meet you at 1:00 pm, over."

"Tell Agent Colton I'm on the way in and will explain everything once we meet, over"

I found Hap in the lobby waiting for me.

"Boss, where have you been? I must have had the Sergeant call you a dozen times."

"It's a long story, and I've got Agent Colton waiting for me in the Captain's office."

"While I'm up there, how about you fill the tank and have the fluids checked. I expect we'll be doing a lot of driving tomorrow."

I started up the stairs when I remembered I had sent Hap out to see what he could dredge up on our arsonists. Rubbing my aching head, I made it to the third floor.

"Well, look who's finally showed up for work."

"Alright, you two. I'm not in the mood for any ribbing right now."

"Well I'm sorry to hear you don't feel good. Should I get you some aspirin, or would a drink be more to your liking."

I pushed past Detective Lee as if he wasn't there. When I got to the Captain's door, I shot them both a bird before knocking.

"Come in."

I opened the door and found the Captain and Colton having a drink. Both were smoking a cigar and by the off color of Colton's face, he was having trouble smoking it.

"Well, now that everybody is here on time we can have our meeting."

"I apologize for being so late, Agent Colton. It was good of you to wait so long."

I took a chair next to the window and waited for the Captain to say something.

"While we were waiting, Agent Colton explained to me about Muller and Cochran. So, can you explain to me what super powers you now possess?"

"At the moment, Captain, no. Now before you get angry, Captain, I need to tell Agent Colton that I spent the last three hours in your FBI building looking for Agent Purvise."

"Are you telling me the building was open?"

"Yes, and I walked right in and went to the elevators. We had met in the lobby and spent most of the day at the first two fires with Fire Chief Mitch Anderson. I forgot to tell you, Captain. As we met, his partner was taking the fake agents downstairs to lock them up.

"Now wait a minute. Are you saying the fake agents locked up the other fake agents?" The Captain asked, shaking his head.

"That's correct Captain. At the time I thought Agent Purvise and his partner were real agents."

"That I am Detective. Agent Colton, I presume. I'm Agent Walter Purvise. Charles is my older brother."

"Then why didn't you tell me you weren't Charles Purvise?"

"You didn't ask. So I let you think what you thought was the truth. Besides I didn't know you from Adam."

I looked at him and smiled. "Upon reviewing my thoughts, I didn't ask your first name. Well then, I need to read you in on my background."

"No need Detective. I've read your files and spoke with Director Grayson at length about your problem with Muller."

We finished our meeting and I headed out to meet Hap. Captain Buchanan asked Agent Colton and Purvise to stay.

"Well, How did it go, Captain?"

"I'm beat. Let's go to Kim's place and have something to eat. Then you can tell me what you've found out."

Hap pulled into the lot and found my personal parking spot no longer there. As we walked into the diner we found things had changed there as well.

No longer was the diner staffed as it had been just a month earlier. Now you sat yourself and waited for a waitress to bring you a menu.

Behind the counter was a cook instead of two. Looking around, I could see the place wasn't very clean. There were finger prints on the windows and dried spills on the floor.

After five minutes I went to the counter and asked the cook if a waitress was going to wait on us.

"She hasn't come in yet. If you want something you'll have to sit at the counter."

"Is Kim working today?" I asked heading for the office.

"She's not in, and hey, you can't go back there."

I flashed my badge and continued into Kim's office. I found a man sitting in her chair going through her papers.

"And who might you be?" I asked, showing him my badge.

"If it's any of your concern, I'm an auditor with the Central and South Bank of Georgia."

"Isn't her loan with your bank? You people didn't? Did you? You called in her loan didn't you?"

"I didn't Mr.?"

"Detective William Barronson."

"As I just said, the bank called in the loan not me. I'm here to see how much this place can be sold for."

"Wouldn't it be wiser to have the place open and making money to pay off the loan. I'm no banker but I'd say one hundred percent return is much better than an eighty percent loss."

I didn't get anywhere with him so I went back to Hap and told him we'd try another place. As I got in the car, the police radio was calling for me to call the station.

"This is Detective Barronson, Sergeant. Over."

"Detective, the Captain wants you back in his office. Over."

"Tell the Captain I'm on my way and should be there in ten. Out."

I didn't have to tell Hap to step on it as the siren and light were already on.

Weaving in and out of traffic at a breakneck speed, I could see Hap was having the time of his life.

"Can you slow down a bit," I said bouncing from side to side in the back seat.

"Captain, this new car of ours could do a hundred I bet. It sure out performs my old taxi. Why, I don't think it ever went over forty five with the wind behind me."

With tires squealing in protest, Hap pulled into the station parking lot and stopped on a dime. I looked out the front window and saw a number of patrolmen talking and pointing at us.

"Come on Captain. The Captain is waiting," Hap said opening the back door for me.

I stumbled out of the back seat using Hap to help steady me. "Hap, you just gave me my first and I hope last white knuckle flight I'll ever have."

"Captain, come on now. It couldn't have been that bad. Why in my younger days I drag raced at Lakewood Raceway in the winter. I have two trophies and a picture to prove it."

Hap and I walked towards the policemen without further conversation. As we walked past the patrolmen, one of them said, "Hey Detective, where did you get the fighter pilot?"

"Maybe he found him in France still looking for Germans to shoot down." another patrolman laughed while opening the door for me.

Before the door closed I said, "Maybe he could be assigned to drive each one of you around for a day or two."

I didn't wait for a reply, but the laughter stopped suddenly.

I knocked and we walked into the Captain's office and found Agent Colton and a new man talking about college football.

"You made good time, Detective."

"Who's the new Agent?"

"Detective William Barronson, I want you to meet Agent Samuel Emey. He will be working with us as well." Agent Emey was even younger than Colton. The only difference in their appearance was Colton had on glasses and Emey didn't.

"This is Hap. He's just been hired today to be my assistant."

"The Captain and I have both been talking with the Director about your neighbors' deaths and the threat to your family. Upon his recommendation Mr. Hoover will be sending an additional twenty agents."

"Well, that's a relief. Now I have some ideas as how to arrest Muller.."

"Bill. The FBI is not only here to protect you and your family. Agent Colton will be taking over the investigation as well." The Captain said.

"Sir, Captain. This man is after me. Why am I being taken off the case?"

"Because Hoover thinks there could be something else going on beside taking you back to Germany. You yourself even said he has something else he has to do. And before you fly off the handle, this is a federal matter now."

I was going to argue the point but could see Hap and I were outvoted. "Then I'm assuming you want me on the arson case."

"Exactly, Bill. Now if you gentlemen don't mind. I've got work to do as well."

Hap followed me as I left the building as fast as I could. "Captain, slow down. We need to talk."

I got in the passenger seat and lit a cigarette to calm my nerves. "Hap! I'm not going to stop my investigation on Muller. That man has threatened our family and I'll be damned if I'm going to stand by and let him kill another."

"I agree, Captain. Which case do you want to work on first?"

"That reminds me. What did you find out on the street anything about our arsonists?"

"Not so far, but I need to check some other sources I know."

$$\text{———————}\bigcirc\text{———————}$$

# Chapter 17

April 8th 1933
7:04 pm Thursday

We hadn't left the station more than ten minutes before I heard the sounds of fire truck sirens echoing off the buildings.

"Detective Barronson, calling Sergeant Sanders. Over"

"Sanders here. over"

"I hear the fire truck sirens. Where is the fire? Over"

"1624 Atlanta Avenue SE. over"

"Thanks. over"

"Hap. There's a fire next door to Mildred's."

I grabbed the open window door and hung on for dear life as Hap accelerated to seventy miles an hour. As we weaved in between streetcars, trucks, cars and pedestrians, I could see Hap was really having a good time. Hap accelerated as he passed the last car before reaching Atlanta Ave. "Hap! Slow down or you'll flip the car!" I hadn't got the words out of my mouth when Hap made his turn without slowing down. With tires screaming and me hanging on for dear life, the car weaved from side to side as Hap fought for control.

"Tree, Hap!" I closed my eyes and waited for the sudden stop. When it didn't happen I opened one eye and found Hap smiling at me.

"We're here Captain."

As I slowly got up from the car floor, I looked out the window. Flames had just broken through the roof of Larry's house, creating a huge cloud of black smoke. The fire trucks couldn't have beaten us here by thirty seconds, because they were just hooking up their hoses.

I found Mildred, Grace and Margaret standing on the porch watching the firemen work. As the first hoses shot water into the second floor windows, it was apparent the house would be a total loss. As the sun set, the fire increased in intensity as the fire hoses were turned on adjacent homes to keep them from catching fire. It was at this point I thought I saw someone moving from shadow to shadow as the fire light grew brighter.  I poked Hap and motioned for him to follow me into the house.

"I think our arsonist is hiding in Larry's backyard and watching his handy work."

Hap and I slipped out the back door and worked our way to the back fence. Larry hadn't put up a fence between his house and Mildreds so his cat could do his business in our yard.

Mildred had planted azaleas, and other tall plants to block their view of each other. Once we reached the back fence, I started crawling my way through the bushes into Larry's back yard. I had Hap wait on Mildred's side just in case the arsonist broke through the bushes trying to escape me.

With scratches on my face and bugs in my hair, I cleared the bushes as the rest of the roof caved in. The firelight was so bright now most of the shadows had disappeared. Not wanting to alert my arsonist, I laid down on the wet grass and slowly moved forward.

I must have covered 15' when I heard movement in the bushes in front of me. Creeping closer, I could just make out his outline in the dimming fire light. I took a deep breath to fortify myself and burst into action.

"Don't move! Police," I shouted, grabbing him from behind as he started struggling.

Suddenly he screamed. "Hey! Let go of me you masher!" she said as I felt her breasts.

I was so shocked at him being a her, I let her go. My face suddenly stung from a slap that turned my head to the left as far as it would go.

"I'm sorry miss. I..."

Another slap in the opposite direction drove my head far to the right. There was another slap coming when I reacted and grabbed her wrist.

"I believe we're even, miss. Now tell me what you're doing hiding in these bushes?"

"Let me go, you brute! You're hurting my arm!" she said wiggling to break free.

I could feel the serum beginning to take control as she fought like a tiger to break free. "Hap! come help me! I have a tiger by the tail over here!"

I suddenly felt the serum take full control. I grabbed her by the waist and picked her up off the ground as if she was a feather. With her kicking and screaming, I headed for the street as two policemen came running towards me.

"Here!" I said tossing her to the two policemen. "Put her in your car and keep her there until she calms down. I want her name, address and what she was doing hiding here!"

The cops took one look at my face and didn't say a word. They just grabbed her by both arms and headed for their car. I watched them struggling to keep hold of her as they tried to get her in their car. Once handcuffed I could see she was a teenager and a hobo by the looks of her clothes.

As the rage slowly ebbed away, I headed for the house when Hap came plowing through the bushes.

"What do you need, Captain?" he said gasping for air.

"How about a drink and a meal. I'm starved."

# Chapter 18



April 8<sup>th</sup> 1933
9:00 pm Thursday

Hap and I returned to the house and found everyone on the porch watching the firemen as they hosed down the last of the flames. The second firetruck was already packing up  and would be heading back to the station.

"Mildred, Hap and I haven't eaten all day. Do you have anything to make sandwiches with?"

"Sandwiches? I can do better than that, Bill. Give me thirty minutes and I'll have a five course meal on the table," she said rushing into the house.

"What was all that about with that girl?" Margaret asked.

"I don't know yet, Margaret. At first I thought it was the arsonist watching his handy work from the bushes. I didn't expect to find a kid hiding there."

My serum hadn't fully left me yet, giving me its night vision as a bonus. I could see the girl crying and arguing with the policemen in the front seat. One of them was saying if you don't answer my question you're going to  jail. Her reply wasn't very polite, because he slapped her across the face. He called her a tramp that wasn't fit to be on the street.

My night vision faded away leaving me just a human again. I started to go into the house holding Margaret's hand when an idea crossed my mind.

"Margaret, come with me, I need your help with the girl I captured."

We walked over to the police car just as the engine turned over. I held up my hand not to leave as officer Long rolled down his window.

"What do you need, Detective?"

"I'd like to take that wildcat off your hands, if you don't mind."

"I don't mind at all, Detective," he said getting out of his car and opening the back door. She's all yours."

"Margaret, would you take this young lady upstairs and give her a bath and some clean clothes if we have any her size."

"I don't want a bath or your clothes, you pervert," she said looking for a way to run away.

"Okay, then miss. You won't be able to sit at our dinner table and eat as much as you like. You see, Mildred has asked me if you would like some dinner with only one stipulation."

"And what would that be?" She said, wiping her nose on her sleeve.

"Take a bath so we all can eat together. The way you smell now, even a dog would refuse to eat next to you."

I could still see the distrust on her face and wondered how many times she had to fight off unwanted advances.

"What's your name?" Margaret asked taking her dirty hand gently. "Besides, cleanliness and Godliness go side by side."

"My name is Nancy Gamble, and I still don't trust you people. Especially you cops" she said wiping tears from her dirty face.

Margaret led Nancy into the house and up the stairs to our room. I went into the kitchen and informed Mildred we had one more guest for dinner. As promised, Mildred had a dinner worth is weight in gold. Fried Chicken, rice, pinto beans, turnip greens, cornbread, gravy, fried potatoes, ham, black eyed peas, snapping beans, and I was sure there was something for dessert as well.

We were all seated at the table when Margaret and Grace brought Nancy down the stairs in a dress. It was a little large on her mainly due to her being so thin. I'd give her a week with Mildred's cooking, the dress would fit just fine.

"Now young lady what is your name again?" I asked.

"I already told you. It's Nancy Gamble."

I thought about turning her over my knee and giving her the spanking she deserved. Margaret must have seen my intentions. "William. Remember she's just a child that's been on her own."

Taking a deep breath to calm my anger, I took a good look at her now that the dirt had been removed.

Nancy I guess you'd say was a dirty blond. Her hair was short and had been cut with either a knife or scissors to make her look like a boy.

Her complexion was dark, due to being out in the sun and her eyes were pale green. She still had on boy's shoes because we didn't have any other shoes that would fit her little feet. As she sat down at the table she was shorter than anyone else. I'd say 5' 2" tall and weighed maybe 85 pounds. When Mildred saw her. she headed towards her as if in a trance. "Oh my word child. You're so pretty." Mildred said leading her to an open chair next to her. Without asking her. Mildred started putting food of every description on her plate. "Now child, you eat slowly because if you eat too fast, your body will reject it, and we both know what kind of mess that would make."

Now, the rest of you pigs make sure you don't eat it all."

At that remark Nancy gave a little chuckle and started eating. We all finished eating and sat talking while Nancy and Mildred talked to each other. By the third plate, Nancy said, "Thank you for the wonderful meal, Mildred. Now I'll be on my way."

"I don't think a lady should be out on the streets at this time of night. I'll fix you a place for you to sleep tonight, and in the morning after breakfast you and I will see what we can do."

Mildred lead Nancy to her room to get her ready for bed.

I was about to head upstairs myself when Margaret and Grace stopped me. "Just a minute, you three. There's a table full of dishes, not including the kitchen, that need to be washed and dried. Us ladies think it's about time you men learned how."

"Margaret, I have to get up early and Hap hasn't seen his wife all day?"

"And poor Lenard? Well, poor Lenard doesn't have an excuse. So here is the deal." Grace said winking at me.

"Hap, help clear the table, Lenard fill the sink and start washing the dishes. Bill, ah, you ah, dry all the plates and we women will do the rest, okay?"

I could have gotten out of doing anything but if I wanted any sleep, I'd better do what the bosses wanted. While Lenard was getting himself set up to wash, I helped Hap to clear the table and put away the leftovers.

As Lenard washed his first dish I found the time to be 12:20 am. I sent Hap on his way home after dropping the third plate in a row. By the time I dried my last cup, it was all I could do to take a shower and slip into bed. As the cool sheet settled on my naked body, I turned out the light and blew Margaret a kiss. Margaret must be down stairs with Grace and Mildred fussing over the new girl. I yawned once before falling fast asleep until Muller appeared.

"Remember, Heir Barronson, we have a boat to catch. Mein Fuhrer and Heir Cochran are waiting to drain your blood."

Then some loud annoying clanging woke me up.

# Chapter 19

April 9<sup>th</sup> 1933
6:45 am Friday

I stumbled out of bed still half asleep and stubbed my toe on that same damn wood chair again. Still not fully awake, I tried to sit down on the bed. But with my usual grace I missed the bed and hit the floor with a thud. "Damn it!" I yelled, holding my foot and rocking as tears filled my eyes.

"Not again, William," Margaret said pulling the covers over her head. "Why." she yawned, "Why don't you throw that damn chair out the window or give it away?"

"I like that damn chair, Margaret."

"Then move it! I need my sleep, and why are you so clumsy in the morning anyway?" she hissed putting the pillow over her face.

Now awake and mad at her and myself, I got up from the floor and sat down in the offending chair. "Why do you hate me so much, chair?"

"Because it knows you'll walk into it twice a month! Now go away and let me sleep!"

Ignoring my throbbing big toe, I got up and pulled the covers off of her and threw them on the floor. Feeling vindicated, I ambled towards the bathroom when I stubbed my toe on that same damn chair. With tears flowing down my cheeks I limped on into the bathroom to shave. As I stood in front of the mirror I said. "I'm the man of this room, and if I want a chair against that wall, then I better have one there" I mumbled to the mirror, lathering my face. I sharpened my straight razor when the sound of window glass breaking told me Margaret had heard every word I said. Not wanting to see what she had done, I finished shaving. After showering and doing everything else I could think of, I walked out into the bedroom. I found Margaret in bed with the covers I had thrown on the floor sleeping soundly. I felt a breeze on my naked body and saw the curtains moving. I walked over to the window and found broken glass on the floor. Carefully stepping around the glass, I looked out the window and saw my chair broken into three pieces.

As I stared at my chair, not believing mild mannered Margaret could do something like that, I heard a woman scream. I looked up and saw two older woman pointing at me.

"He's naked, Martha!"

"Yes he is, sister."

"I just can't believe it, Martha. In this day and time to see a naked man standing at his window, and look he waved!"

I moved away from the window embarrassed at what I had done to the spinster twins. They probably hadn't seen a naked man since 1870. "Well I hope you learned you're lesson." I said dressing in front of the mirror. "Never argue with a woman who's having a baby."

I went down stairs and found Mildred at the front door being dressed down about a man naked at one of her windows.

"I can assure you, ladies, I have no one living here that would do such a deed." Mildred said looking over her shoulder at me.

"Mildred! I'm tell you there is a man naked. He was standing in front of a broken window staring at us as if we were naked."

Mildred whispered, "Was he good looking."

"Well ah... he was rather." both sisters said, grinning at each other.

"Ladies, I do apologize for being naked. It seems I sleep walk sometimes, since the war, and find myself waking up to embarrassing circumstances."

"Oh! I see Mr.?"

"Detective Barronson, ladies."

"Well, Detective, I believe you need to see a doctor about that."

"I have to get back to cooking breakfast. So if you'll excuse us." Mildred said closing the door. "I never could stand those two spinster sisters always walking the neighborhood looking for something to gossip about at church. And, that brings me to you, William. What were you doing staring out the window naked as a jay bird? And! Who's going to pay for a new window?"

"Mildred. I'll take care of the window. And as for me being naked at the window...well I'll get back to you on that."

Mildred looked at me and blushed. "I bet you will you, old dog, you."

"Mildred. Shame on you for thinking thoughts like that. And at your age."

"What about my age. I'm up before you are and in bed after you're asleep, young man."

"I meant no disrespect, Mildred. Not to change the subject but how is Nancy doing? I saw you two having a lot to talk about last night."

"I think she'll be fine once she gets some meat on her bones. From what she told me last night, she's been on her own for over six months."

"Six months! What about her parents.?"

"Both died from a high fever is all she knew. It seems they didn't believe in doctors according to their church teachings."

"Did she tell you what state or city she lived in?"

"I believe she told me Chicago or close to it. I don't know. All I do know is that poor girl has been floating around the country trying to just stay alive. Now, leave me alone or you'll never get your breakfast."

I went into the kitchen and poured a cup of coffee. As I looked out the window, I saw Hap pull up. When Hap didn't appear at the door, I went out onto the porch and spotted him talking to one of the firemen. Whatever was being said it must have started a heated argument.

I started to head towards Hap just in case a fight broke out. I made it to the steps when I noticed there were only two firemen left watching the smoldering ruins of Larry's house. The fire truck must have left leaving two men with pitchforks and a hose to handle the hot spots. "Hap! Breakfast!"

Mildred's breakfast was just hitting the table when Hap came in and took a seat. The ladies of the house must have slept in because the four of us, Lenard, Hap, Henry and I devoured everything Mildred brought out.

I watched Hap finished off the last pieces of bacon and coffee and seemed to be looking for more. Mildred was standing by the kitchen door, getting madder by the minute.

"Mildred, that sure was a wonderful breakfast."

When I didn't get a reply, I looked at Hap. He was using his fingers to scrape the sausage gravy bowl clean.

"Hap. I believe it's time to go. Henry, do you need a ride into the station?"

I scrambled the two of them into the car and got behind the wheel. I smiled at Mildred standing on the porch and said. "We won't be home for dinner, Mildred. Would you let Margaret know?'

"I hope not, because you four ate everything in the house."

I waved good bye and headed for the intersection of Boulevard and Atlanta Ave. I looked at Hap still chewing on something. "You know Hap, you're making Mildred very angry with you overeating."

"Why's that, Captain? Isn't food put on the table meant to be eaten?"

"Yes it is, but not everything. Some of that food we ate was for the girls."

"I'm sorry about that, Captain. It's such a treat for me to have breakfast like that again."

"Doesn't your wife cook for you?"

"No. My wife's been dead some ten years now. She died of the Spanish flu when I got home from France."

"Then who's the woman on the phone yelling at you?"

"My landlady, and before you say anything, she doesn't cook. And my son is married, and living with her parents.

I'll make sure I don't come around until your meals are done." Hap said sadly.

"If you don't keep stopping by for your meals, Hap, I'll fire you myself. Just make sure you leave some food for the others is all I'm asking. And I'm sure Mildred would agree."

As we pulled into the lot, I spotted the FBI cars parked beside each other. Each car was black. Each had four doors. Each license plate was the same except for the last number.

# Chapter 20

April 9<sup>th</sup> 1933
8:59 am Friday

I let Hap park the car while Henry and I got out. I headed for the front door while Henry went in the break room. A large drop of rain hit the sidewalk in front of me leaving a muddy splat mark in the sand.

"Detective Barronson, I'm glad you got in so early. Let's go over to the FBI building. My men are waiting to have a meeting with you over security for you family."

"I'll need a minute to let the Captain know where I'm going so he can send Hap to join us."

As we road along Agent Colton seemed to be in deep thought. I didn't want to interrupt, so I looked out the window. Storm clouds were building, and the city was hoping it would be a heavy rain. Since the dust storm the other day, everything was covered in a fine coat of sand. In some places like alleys, the sand had accumulated to six inches deep. As we pulled up in front of the FBI building rain started in earnest. Within two minutes you could see brown streams heading down to the storm drains. A sudden break in the rain let us dash up the steps and reach the entrance door without getting soaked. I opened the door and marveled at how quickly the door had been replaced.

Once inside, I found the lobby neat and clean. If I hadn't been here yesterday, you would never have known the place had been closed. We headed for the elevators that now had two guards flanking them. They also had the information desk and telephones manned as well.

Colton and myself entered one elevator. The other two agents took a separate one. I lit a cigarette as the elevator rose towards the tenth floor without an operator.

A bell dinged and the doors opened "This is the tenth floor Detective." Agent Colton said seeing my reluctance to move. "I assure you Detective we're on the tenth floor. So please follow me."

I followed Colton down the long hall to a lit office. As I entered the office I found Agent Purvise waiting for us.

"Detective, nice to see you again." he said holding out his hand.

# Chapter 21

April 9th 1933
9:15 am Friday

**"A**re you feeling a little lost, Detective?" Colton said smiling at me.

"Just a little, so why don't you explain it to me." I said sitting down.

"It's quite simple. Purvise has been assigned to protect you ever since you left Washington. We had an idea Muller or someone like him would try to abduct you."

"You see, Detective, it was just my bad luck you finding me leaving this building. I didn't want to blow my cover so I pretended I was sent here about the fires."

"If that's the case, then why did you let my neighbors be murdered and their house burned down?" I could see the agents were beginning to squirm as he looked for an answer.

"Well?" I said staring at them.

"I'll answer that." Colton said. "It seems agent Purvise fell down on his job. He states he didn't know Muller had  threatened your families lives in order to get you to Germany."

I looked at the three of them wondering if I should trust them or not. Deciding I didn't have a choice I said, "Then how do you propose to catch this Muller? And don't tell me to wait till he tries to murder someone in my family!"

Not wanting to lose my advantage in this discussion I started to talk.

"Look at the black smoke outside the windows!" Purvise said. As I turned around to see what all the commotion was about, I heard the familiar sounds of fire engines sirens wailing. We all walked to the windows, and spotted the  billowing smoke rising from the Union Station Terminal.

From my advantage point, I could see people running in every direction as explosion after explosion wracked the  building. Even a passing train's box cars had caught fire from the flying debris as the burning train moved on. I felt our building shudder as the once beautiful Pennsylvania Station designed roof collapsed in on its self.

As I kept watching, the first of four fire trucks arrived. From this height of four stories the people looked like ants running around. Within minutes, the fire fighters had figured out they might as well let it burn itself out.

We returned to our seats, amazed at how quickly the building had destroyed itself.

"From what we have just witnessed, Detective. I believe you need our help on these fires as well," Agent Colton said lighting a cigarette. "Do you have any clues as to who's doing this?"

"Not as of yet. Things are happening so fast, the Fire Chief hasn't been able to spend much time investigating."

Colton went to the phone and made a call. When he was done, he stated five investigators and a profiler were heading in our direction.

I felt, for the first time in a week, that things were going in the right direction. I was sure the Fire Chief, the Chief of Police, and the Governor, will all want to lead the investigations. In my opinion it didn't matter who was in charge, as long as we found who's doing this.

"Gentlemen, I believe we all need to get going on our prospective jobs. Agent Colton, you and I should keep abreast of what going on," I said.

I excused myself from the meeting, as what they were talking about didn't concern me. Pressing the button that said lobby, I felt uneasy as it headed down without an operator to stop it before plowing into the concrete floor.

As the doors opened, I quickly walked out into the lobby as the door started closing. "I don't like or trust you, you robot driven monster."

It felt good to know I had mastered the workings of the elevator by myself. I opened the door and found the pavement dry as a bone. If you hadn't seen it raining yourself, you'd never in a million years guess it had rained at all. As I headed in the direction of my car I didn't expect to find Hap waiting. To my surprise, I found Hap asleep in the back seat with a smile on his face. I was about to wake him up when I remembered the breakfast he had eaten.

As I looked around, I noticed the streets filled with all sorts of moving vehicles. None of them were moving because of the fire. I decided to let Hap sleep and decided to take a walk. It would give me time to figure out who and why was he setting fires.

In all the excitement in the past two days, Muller had absorbed all my thoughts. That left the arsonist alone to become as famous as Machine Gun Kelly. As I walked along stopping to look in windows, I noticed the same two people.

At first I thought Agent Purvise had assigned tow agent to keep an eye on me. I walked a few more blocks and spotted another man tailing me. One was behind me, the second man was across the street and the third was in a car. I walked another block and stopped just to be sure.

I took out my cigarettes and lit one. The man behind me did the same and gave himself away. He was smoking his cigarette the European way. The driver must have seen I knew who he was because he pulled away from the curb. I pretended I hadn't reacted as he quickly change smoking the American way. I continued on down the sidewalk, tipping my hat to ladies, and smiling at babies in carriages. I spotted a familiar alleyway just to my left. I had been a beat cop back then and used the shortcut to catch a number of pick pocket thieves.

I went into a drug store, said, "Sir. Can I buy a roll of pennies from you?"

"I'll have to go to the safe?"

"Okay." I said discretely showing him my badge.

I walked out of the drug store and gave a penny to a street kid.

"Thanks mister. Can I have another?"

"Tell your friends over there playing baseball in the alley, I'm giving away money."

Thirty seconds later I had 40 kids standing around me begging for a penny. I handed out a few so I could see where the two were and spotted the car as well.

"Alright, kids, it's time to play 52 pickup."

I took what change I had in my pocket, added it to the pennies and tossed them into the air.

As the kids and adults scrambled to pick up the money, I took off running down the 200' long alleyway. In my younger days, it had been easy task. Now, after years of no physical activity, I wasn't sure I'd make it to the end. As I reached the alleyway's end in utter exhaustion, I heard their echoing footsteps.

**"If you let me take over. I'll get us out of your mess."**

"If I let you take over I might never regain control."

With burning lungs, I ran across the street and entered Ham's Meat Market & Deli. I went to a back table and collapsed into a chair. I could see everyone in the place was looking at me as if I was going to rob the place.

"Don't worry, folks. I'm trying to hide from an ex-girlfriend's husband. And no, I didn't know she was married."

I motioned to the girl behind the counter to bring me a water and coffee. I downed the water and said, "May I have another please."

"I'll bring you a pitcher."

It didn't take long before the first German walked passed. Then the second appeared, and called to the first man to come back. As they stood there in front of the windows, a woman joined them. She must have been in charge, because she started giving them the what for while shaking her finger at them.

I thought about confronting them but decided the odds were in their favor and I'd be kidnapped. Instead, I sat there and concentrated on remembering them. The two men were of average height 5' 8", young say 24 to 28, slim built 125 pounds and had the look of being military trained. The woman was 5' 5", brown hair, and wore a brown suit and hat with a white blouse. Her makeup was heavy, and reminded me of the Paris women. It also occurred to me what she was wearing wasn't American either, probably Parisian as well.

When she was done talking, the two men went in different directions, I assumed, to look for me. I watched as she lit a cigarette and walked to the deli door. Once inside she looked around and didn't find an empty table.

"Miss. You can sit with me if you don't mind. I'll even buy you a coffee."

"That is very kind of you. Waitress, bring me a cup of what you call coffee. I'll be sitting with this gentleman."

As she marched to my table, people stepped or moved out of her way.

I stood up and pulled out her chair so she could sit down. "Thank you. You must have been brought up in Europe. These Americans have no manners when it comes to a woman of class."

"You'll have to excuse us Americans. We've done away with all that tradition that Europe has fought over for the last 500 years."

As the waitress brought her the coffee, a cloud of perfume surrounded me. It was so thick and heavy I started  coughing.

"Are…you okay... Mister?" The waitress asked, looking down on me.

"Yes. I am."

"I am Gertrude Becker. And your name?"

"Detective William Barronson of the Atlanta Police Department."
I saw one eyebrow raise slightly as my name sunk in.

"My. Such a long name? Does that mean you are polizei?"

"Police, yes, I'm a policeman. What country are you from, Gertrude Becker?"

"Switzerland. I'm.. ah sorry, my English is not good."

"That's no problem. We get a lot of foreign speaking people here, especially Northerners.

"Northerners? I do not know that country. Is it in America?"

"We've often wonder that ourselves. Well, nice meeting you." I said tipping my hat and heading for the door. I made a right turn and stepped into the next shop. I wanted to see what Becker would do next. I didn't have long to wait before she appeared and walked to the curb. The same black sedan that had been following me pulled up and stopped. I didn't catch the whole conversation as she conversed with the driver in broken English before getting into the car.

Once they disappeared, I retraced my steps back to the FBI building and found Hap wide awake waiting for me.

"I was about to send the cops out to find you. Did something happen to keep you up there for so long?"

"No problem, Hap. When I found you sleeping, I decided to take a walk to clear my head."

I didn't mention being followed by three me and a woman because I didn't want to alarm him. I thought about telling Agent Purvise about these new players in town. "Hang on a minute, Hap. I just remembered I left my lighter up in Purvise office."

As I walked up the steps I spotted the black sedan turning the corner. With no time to spare, I raced back to my car and ducked inside.

"Captain, what's going on?"

"Has the black sedan stopped?"

Hap looked around, "No, it must have kept going."

"Okay. Then let's head home. I need to clear a couple of things up with the ladies of the house."

Hap pulled up in front of Mildred's boarding house. "Hap, head back to the station and gas up the car and then return here."

"Captain. I already did that."

"Well... Then go get something to eat and we'll talk about this later."

# Chapter 22

April 9th 1933
4:45 pm Friday

I walked up the steps to the front porch and stopped to look at what was left of Larry's house. It had burned to the ground, leaving just a large pile of burnt lumber and a few skeletons of burned out furniture.

There was still one fireman turning smoldering piles of what was now charcoal with a pitchfork. He must have been bored, because he spent most of his time looking across the street at the Johnson twins. They were sitting on the porch, probably talking about boys and pointing at something. I turned to see what they were pointing at, and spotted a dark colored parked car with two men in it. It was two houses down from Mildreds and was an unmarked Atlanta police car.

I opened the front door and found another policeman drinking coffee. The other officer I assumed was watching the back door and eating whatever Mildred had fixed for him.

"Detective Barronson, Mike and I have been assigned to protect everyone in this house."

"Thanks, Dave, but I believe you boys can go. There's more important work for you to be doing than guarding us."

"Very good Detective, I'll advise the Captain that you released us."

Once they had gone, I asked for everyone to meet down in the dining room. While this was happening, I took Mildred aside and asked her about Nancy and what were her intentions.

"Bill, I'm not totally sure yet about that. One minute she wants to leave and the next she wants to stay."

"Then let me ask you this. Is she going to live here until she makes up her mind?"

"I would like her to stay. She can work for her room and board Bill"

About that time, Nancy walked in, smiling. She must have been listening to our conversation.

"Bill. I can clean and cook, and do whatever Mildred wants if you'll show me how, Mildred?" Nancy said pleading.

"Please, please let me stay, I don't have anywhere else to go." Nancy said tearing up for Mildred.

I wanted to say no but the look on Mildred's face told me it was a lost cause. So with that question answered, we headed into the dining room and took a seat. I counted noses as I looked around the table. Grace, Margaret, Mildred, Nancy and me were present. Lenard, Hap and Henry were all working.

"I have asked all you here because I have a proposal to make. I want all of you to leave Atlanta until Carl Muller is found and captured."

"No!" Grace said, popping up out of her chair. "This Muller guy doesn't scare me. So no. I'm not leaving."

"I can't leave either." Mildred said. "Besides, how will we live?"

"Alright now. Let me explain. I'm going to the FBI and have them put y'all up in a safe house. The reason for Muller killing Larry and his family the other night is he wants me to accompany him to Germany because of the serum Cochran injected into me. I don't want to go into details right now. but if I refuse, he's threatening to kill one of you until I do."

The room got quiet for several seconds before Grace popped up again. "I don't care if he wants to burn the house down with me in it. I'm not leaving!"

"Grace, we have talked about your stubbornness many times." Mildred said nodding her head.

"Yes mother. But."

"No buts Grace! You're still not too old for me to spank even in your present condition."

At the thought of that, Grace's eyes became as large as saucers. I myself would pay good money to see that.

"Margaret! What about you, are you going to give me any trouble?"

"No mother. If my husband wants me to leave him to face danger alone... I'll, I'll understand." she said breaking
out in tears.

I covered my face and started rubbing my forehead just above my eyes. "Alright! Everybody! Forget what I just said!

No one leaves this house unless we all leave together!" I didn't know how I was going to protect all of them but I'd figure something out. I got up and went to the porch and waved for the two FBI agents to come inside. "I'm going to make a phone call to my Captain, and I want you to hear what I say."

I went to the parlor and picked up the receiver. "What number please."

"Connect me to HL-5764, please." I hear it ring three times before the phone was picked up. "Sergeant Clark."

"Sergeant, this is Detective Barronson. I need to speak with the Captain."

"Captain Buchanan."

"Captain, this is Detective Barronson. I've sent your men  back to the station. I think it's a waste of manpower to have them here just to protect my family. If you would, Captain, have a car come by the house every hour after it gets dark."

"I appreciate the men Bill. With all these fires going on I need every man I can get. The Mayor is fit to be tied and wants him dead or in jail. I'll inform the desk to schedule a car for once an hour after dark."

I hung up the phone and returned to the dining room. "Well that's taken of, a car will come by every hour all night." I could see their mood improving so I continued on while the iron was hot. "Alright. Now that we have settled your two questions, I believe it time to set some ground rules."

About that time the two agents came into the room and introduced themselves. "I'm Agent Jayson Long and this is Agent Mike Jones. We will be here to protect you day and night, along with several others."

"Have a seat agents. I was about to go over the ground rules.

1. As of today none of you are to leave without one of the agents accompanying you. If more than one of you want to go out, then all of you will have to go together this includes Nancy, Margaret, Grace and Mildred.  This will include Lenard, Henry, Hap and myself when were home."

"Now Bill, I think your overdoing it a bit." Mildred said. "I have many things I need to do like groceries, and..."

"Mildred. I don't care. One agent will go with you either by yourself or in a group but not alone. If this can't be adhered to, then you leave no choice but to send you all to Cleveland."

"Why Cleveland? Why not Hollywood or Chicago?" Grace asked.

"Cleveland, Grace, because there's nothing to do in Cleveland."

I could see on Grace's face she wanted to argue the point until she got her way. I turned to the agents and motioned for them to follow me. I was tired and the only way I could end the argument was to leave the room.

"Bill! I'm not finished with you yet!"

I walked out onto the porch with the two agents. "I wanted you two to see what I have to put up with."

"We totally understand, Detective."

"Then, if one of them gets out without one of you, there will be hell to pay."

Grace opened the screen door and Mike stepped in front of her. "Mrs. Please go back inside. You're making yourself an easy target for anyone with a rifle."

"But I wanted.."

"No buts Mrs. The meeting's over and you need to return inside. Or would you like to be locked in your room all day?"

Grace's face was beat red, but she returned inside sputtering to herself.

"Is that how you want us to handle them?"

"Yes. They can be mad at me all they want, but they'll thank me when this is over."

Margaret and I headed up the stairs when I remembered Hap should be returning shortly. "Margaret, Henry is the only one using that room?"

"Yes Bill, Hap can stay in Henry's room for tonight."

"Mildred. Until this is over with, I'd like Hap to stay here as well."

"William. The man eats enough food to feed three men.

I need five dollars a week from him to cover his food bill." Mildred demanded.

'Mildred. Now be reasonable. I..."

"Five dollars a week! Or he can't stay! You'd think I was running a free boarding house! Not only do I have my family to feed, I now have Nancy, Henry, Hap and two agents to feed on a $15.00 a week budget." Mildred said walking into the kitchen to make coffee and snacks for the agents.

"Captain. I'm back. Is there somewhere you want to go?"

"No. And the reason I sent you away is that as of now you'll be living here until Muller is caught."

"Great! I'll go get my things."

"Take Agent Mike with you. And by the way, you'll be sleeping in Henry's room."

"Henry's room?"

"He has two beds, unless you want to sleep on the floor?"

"No problem, Captain, I think."

I quickly got ready for bed and slipped under the clean cool sheets. It had been a day or three since I had gotten more than four hours sleep and I was determined to get eight tonight. When the clock struck 2:00 am, I found myself smoking a cigarette as Margaret sawed red wood trees down with her snoring.

## Chapter 23

April 10<sup>th</sup> 1933
2:00 am Saturday

I got dressed and headed down stairs to check with the agents. As I reached the bottom of the stairs, I heard a man and a woman talking. Not wanting to disturb them, I slipped up to the doorway into the parlor.

"So far everything is going as planned. Mildred has accepted me completely as a hobo. The others seem to follow her lead without questioning anything I say." Nancy said.

"That's what I had hoped for. So from now just play your part and I'll be contacting you when I'm done."

Not wanting to be caught snooping, I slipped into the bathroom. I waited until I was sure he was gone and Nancy had returned to her room. I tip-toed into the parlor and found Agent Elder asleep in a chair snoring. As I looked around the room, I spotted a cup of coffee sitting next to him. **"There's something wrong, isn't there? Let me out and I'll find out for you."**

"Get back in your cage, serum." I mumbled under my breath. I looked at the snoring agent and decided I had nothing to lose by waking him up. Making as much noise as I could, I walked over to Jayson and said, "Wake! Up!" When he didn't respond, I touched his shoulder, again no response. I tried once more to wake him and still didn't get a response. With my internal alarm bell ring I started looking for Agent Mike, not caring how much noise I made.

I started with the kitchen, then to the dining room, then to the front porch. By the time I found the porch empty Cochran's serum had kicked in without me knowing it.

**"I'll find him for you."**

I took a deep breath and could smell every living thing around me. Sniffing occasionally to follow Mike's scent trail, I found him in his car talking to his headquarters by radio.

"Detective. What are you doing out here?"

"Have you been talking to Nancy just a few minutes ago?"

"No sir. I've been outside checking the grounds. Why do you ask?"

"Nothing agent. I must have been dreaming is all."

"I did find Agent Jayson asleep in the parlor. I believe he's been drugged."

"Drugged? We better get in there and check to see if everyone is alright."

"Everyone's okay, Bill. If they weren't, I would know it."

"What are you saying Detective?" Mike said getting out of his car.

"I meant, Mike, I already checked before finding Jayson asleep. Does he take anything to help him sleep?"

We started back towards the house when I saw Hap, step out onto the porch. He lit a cigarette and sat down smoking and drinking coffee.

"What are you doing up so early." I said noticing the coffee.

"Couldn't sleep, the beds too soft and it's too quiet here."

"Where did you get that coffee?"

"From the agent inside. He was making a fresh pot. I told him I didn't mind cold coffee, so I poured me a cup of his leftovers."

"How do you feel?" I said, looking carefully at him.

"Fine. Why?"

"I found the agent asleep in the parlor with cold coffee cup sitting next to him. I thought it might be drugged?"

"Drugged? No, he was catching some shut eye. You don't think they stay awake all night do you? Why do you think he was drugged anyway?" Hap said putting down the cup and looking at me for an answer. "I don't have an answer for that, Hap. All I can tell you is I found him asleep in the chair and I couldn't awake him."

Just before regaining control, I tasted a different man's scent. "Damn it!" I said.

"Hap. I either dreamed hearing a conversation between Nancy and a man or its real."

"Have you asked her who she was talking to?"

"Not yet. And for now, Hap don't tell anybody. Now let's help Mildred by making breakfast."

## Chapter 24

April 10<sup>th</sup> 1933
4:50 am Saturday

"**O**h my God! What have you done to my kitchen?" Mildred yelled looking at the two of us covered in flour.

I had her apron on and Hap had on her spare. Mine was white with little pink flowers around the edges. Hap's was white trimmed in black with kittens on it.

"It's almost ready Mildred, so why don't you take a seat and I'll bring you a cup of coffee."

"I appreciate the thought Bill... Ah, the oven door is smoking. I believe your biscuits are done."

I watched Mildred's eyes as she graded each food item we had made so far. Bacon C+, Biscuits F, Toast F, Grits D Gravy DD. Coffee unknown. And Eggs not cooked yet.

I was about to say it wasn't as bad as it looked when Mildred broke out in a laugh. "You two take off my aprons and go upstairs and clean yourselves up while I... I do something with this... this ah? breakfast."

I was not about to argue with the chief and neither was Hap. As we climbed the stairs, I heard a cuss word echo through the house. I looked at Hap and he looked at me.

"I don't think she likes my biscuits, Hap?"

"Why's that? They looked okay to me?"

"I think they were a bit on the heavy side."

"Heavy side?"

"Didn't you hear that plate drop and break just a second ago. That was the plate I stacked the biscuits on before we were run out of the kitchen."

"Okay. So how much did each weigh?"

"I wanted big ones so I'd say they were half a pound or more each."

"You two come down here!" Mildred said shaking her big wooden spoon at us. "Don't! Ever step into my kitchen again and try to cook or bake, or fry, or even get a glass of water! Do you two understand?" Mildred stormed back into the kitchen.

"What are you two laughing at!" I said to the two FBI agents as they headed for the porch.

# Chapter 25

April 10th 1933
7:21 am Saturday

ap and I headed for what was left of the Union Station Terminal. I hoped Fire Chief Anderson and some of the FBI investigators would be on the scene. As the sun grew higher in the sky, I could see thin wisps of black smoke rising into the sky. Trying several streets we hoped weren't blocked with onlookers, We still found ourselves several block away. Discussed, I radioed in, "Sergeant, can you tell me how many people are at the fire."

"From what the radio newscaster said there are more than 125,000 people watching the firefighters looking for survivors."

"Well Captain, what do you want to do now?"

"Hap.." A fire truck flew past us with sirens wailing. "Follow that truck, Hap."

As we raced down the street, I could see the packed crowd parting several blocks ahead. They reminded me of Moses parting the Red Sea as we passed through them. I looked out the back window and saw them flow back together as if they were water.

Seconds later we came to a sudden stop. I got out of the car and saw the police barricade being opened. I could see  the terminal was 85% destroyed by the fire. The walls facing the street had collapsed blocking the street with bricks. What was left of the roof had become a giant smoke stack, pumping out smoke from a new fire. Luckily, the railroad tracks and passenger loading dock walls had withstood the collapse. There was some rubble spread  across the three rail lines, but workers were already clearing them. Atlanta's livelihood depended on trains transporting everything North, South, East and West.

As we went through the blockade I said "Let's park over there, Hap. It's out of the way and we can walk the rest of the way to the Terminal."

As we crossed the first set of tracks, I could see a train waiting to go South as they cleared the tracks. Crossing the second set, the train

I had seen catching fire  was being unloaded and reloaded into other boxcars.

As we crossed the last set of tracks, a number of employees were picking up clothes, shoes, luggage,  briefcases and assorted papers of all sizes and

descriptions. Hap and I walked up the three steps to the terminal platform and spotted Fire Chief Anderson talking to four FBI people. One was Director Grayson who must have flown in late last night. Agent Colton and Samuel Emey, an arson investigator, were two and three. The fourth man I didn't recognize, until he turned around, was Director of the FBI J Edgar Hoover.

"Detective William Barronson, I've heard good things about you. How would you like a job with the FBI?" he said shaking my hand.

By the looks on the other agents' faces, I no longer was a friend but a competitor. "I'll have to think on that, sir. Can I give you my answer in a week?"

I could see his disappointment and knew I had a tightrope to walk if I wanted to come out of this in one piece.

"Chief, have you any idea how the fire was started?"

"I've got a pretty good idea. So why don't you all follow me." Chief Anderson walked through what had been the entryway leading into the enormous terminal. "As you can see, when the explosion blew out the street windows, it also weakened the brick walls as well. It didn't take a second for the weaken street wall to collapse outward. That in turn weakened the roof causing it to collapse in as you see it here. Now I'll show you where the explosion took place."

We worked our way around the rubble until we reach a large crater in the floor. It measured 15' across, and 12' deep.

"This is where the explosion took place. What you see is what remains of the boiler heating room system." The chief said continuing. "I believe the gas line was cut in order for the room to fill with natural gas. If you look down and to the right, you can see where a doorway and hall once were."

Agent Samuel Emey then said. "Upon my examination, Mr. Hoover, I found traces of dynamite and wiring leading up the stairs to a battery and a time clock."

"Why wasn't the outside door locked?" Hoover asked, looking at me as if I was the Mayor.

"Someone must have had a key. Or worked here," I said.

"Chief, what about Fulton Cotton fire, are they related?"

"I'll answer that, Chief. From my preliminary inspection I found coal oil was the accelerator. It was poured on a number of bales of cotton. Then it was set ablaze with a timer as well." Agent Samuel said.

"As for the McKenzie fire, I found the same thing. It was also set using a timer." The Chief said, backing away from the expanding crater.

"Then it means we have two arsonists." Colton said.

"No! We have one arsonist and one saboteur pretending to be an arsonist." I said, looking at Hoover.

After I used the word saboteur, no one said a word until we returned to the FBI building. I stood by the window watching the different crews work to make the Terminal operational once more.

"Detective Barronson, will you elaborate on your statement?" Hoover asked.

I explained once again about Muller, and the threats he had made and carried out. I also told them about yesterday's run in with what I suspect were German agents.

"So, Mr. Hoover, I believe we do have a saboteur and or

arsonists that likes to watch their handy work. This last fire is too sophisticated for our local people to have committed."

"If what you say is true, then Germany is committing an act of war?" Hoover said, reaching for the phone.

"I'd hold off on that, Director. If I were you, I'd gather more information from other countries on Germany's    intentions. I can't believe a country would want to go to war in this world's economic state."

We spent several more hours talking about who should be doing what. It was finally decided I, being local, would work on catching the arsonist. The FBI would take over the case on Muller and the German agents.

# Chapter 26

April 10th 1933
1:32 pm Saturday

I left the FBI while they discussed among themselves what their next move would be. As the elevator descended to the lobby, an idea came into my head. I found Hap asleep in the car and banged on the door.

"Emergency! Emergency! All cars respond! It's past Hap's lunch time so hang on to your food." I said getting in the front seat as Hap grabbed the mike. "Hap, don't call in, I'm pulling your leg."

"What! What happened," he said rubbing sleep out of his eyes. When he realized it was a joke, he picked up the mike and said. "Calling all cars, Detective Barronson is buying lunch for anyone that has a seat at Rick's place." Hap said smiling at me in retribution.

"Very funny, Hap. Now I'll have to take half of the cost out of your pay. Let's head for the newspaper. I want to check something out."

"All cars, all cars, free lunch has been canceled, repeat canceled."

Heading across town while ignoring calls to return to the station, we parked in front of the Atlanta Times building. Upon entering the building, I felt the cool air-conditioning and thanked Mr. Carrier, the man that had invented it.

We went to the Information desk "May I help you, gentlemen?" Alice asked.

"We would like to see the City Editor, please." I showed her my badge.

"Just a minute, please."

I watched as Alice plugged in her connection line and wondered how she could remember which one was which.

"I'm sorry Detective. He's not in his office." Alice said.

"Can you see if you can find him, please."

"I'll try. This is a big place and he could be anywhere in the building."

I counted as Alice plugged into one connection after another asking if he was there.

By the 29th connection Alice must have found him. With relief on her face she said, "He'll be right down, Detective. Have a seat. Would you two care for some sweet tea or coffee?"

"I'll take a glass of ice tea." Hap said smiling all the while. "I'll take the same, Alice."

Hap and I waited and waited until we ran out of cigarettes. "Alice, call him again and tell him he's got five minutes to get his butt down here before I shut this place down."

Four minutes and fifty five seconds later the elevator door opened and a balding middle-aged man walked out.

"I'm so sorry, Detective. I forgot about the time." He said, holding out his hand. "I see Alice has made you comfortable. Now what can I do for the police?"

"For one, you can tell me your name."

"Oh! Sorry, I'm Lincoln McBride, City Editor."

"Mr. McBride, I wish to look at all the photos and news reels taken from the last four fires."

"Ah.. well.. ah.. that could be very time consuming Detective. You see there's hundreds of feet of film and the same for photos. I don't... ah."

"Mr. McBride, I don't care if it's thousands of feet, and thousands of photos. I intend to look at every foot of them. Or. I can shut this paper down for impeding my investigation into who is responsible for them."

"Okay, okay, I get your point, but I want exclusives on whatever you find."

"That's seems fair. I'll even throw in the exclusive when we arrest him or them."

I let Lincoln return to running his paper so he could get the evening edition out. "Alice, I believe you know all the departments and who runs them?"

"Yes, I do."

"Then I want you to escort us upstairs to the film department."

"Detective. I can't abandon my desk."

"Can you get someone to fill-in. I'll square it with your boss."

Hap walked next to Alice talking as if he was in high school, trying to get a date for the prom. Not wanting to interfere with his pitch, I dropped back and looked at the drab green walls. As we walked into the room, the first reel was being installed. Once he was done, another man came in and introduced himself as Peter Long.

"Are you the camera man that took these films?"

"Yes. Along with my associate."

"Alice. Thank you for your help."

"Thank you for the break, Detective." as she started to leave, she gave Hap a smile and a wink.

"I cleared my throat, "Are you ready to work now Hap?"

"Oh…ah, sorry Captain. Yes I'm ready now." Hap said with a very red face.

As the first reel came on the screen I asked the following question.

"Peter. I'm interested in knowing if you remember any person or persons trying to get his face on camera?"

"Not that I can remember, but if they did, it'll be on one of these reels."

"Did you camera any of the onlookers?"

"Yes. I did that at each fire."

"How many hours of film do you have?"

"Twenty minutes depending on the action."

"Did you go back the next day?"

"Oh yes. You see we sell what we call news shorts to wire services and theaters all over the country."

I looked at my watch and found it to be after seven.

"Why don't we call it a night gentleman, and start fresh in the morning."

I was about to tell Peter to stop the film when I spotted a man trying to cover his face.

"Peter, where did you take this?" I asked as the reel finished.

"Let's see. I think it's at the Fulton Cotton fire, but let's look at the canister. It will have the name, date, and time." Peter picked up the canister and brought it to me.

# Chapter 27

Fulton Cotton Spinning Company Fire
First of three reels

April 6th 1933
11:40 pm Tuesday

"**D**o you have a way to look at this frame by frame?"

"Yes. We'll have to go downstairs for that."

Taking the elevator to the third floor, we entered the movie and photo processing department. I was amazed at all the different equipment it took to produce a two minute film. I gave Peter the canister and watched as he threaded the film onto a hand cranked viewer. "So this is how, Detective, each frame is viewed."

I watch as he turned the handle and the first frame appeared on the screen. It took twenty minutes before the frame came up that I was looking for.

From what I could make out the person was male, about 5' 10", slim build. He was wearing a work shirt with a name badge above his left pocket. "Go forward one frame. Now go back two. What are you looking at?" Hap asked.

"I'm trying to read the name badge. See if he turns just enough that I can get a clear look at it."

"Let me see, Boss," Hap taking my place. I can't read it either, but I'd say he works at a gas station."

"Pete. Can you make a blow up picture of this frame?"

"Sure, I can make you one. 8x10" or 10x12" or a big as you want."

"I think 10x12" would be great. So, when will it be ready?"

"Monday, if I don't spend all day looking at more films."

"I think we can get along without you for a while. How about the photos. I'd like to take a look at them as well maybe, I'll get lucky."

Hap and I lugged two large boxes of photos to the car and secured them in the trunk. I didn't want to put them on the back seat because of Hap's driving. The last thing I wanted to see was them blowing out the rear seat windows while doing 60 in a 30 speed zone.

"Well Boss, what do you think? Is this the guy?"

"I can't be certain but if we spot him in any of these photos or in any other news reels we might have our man."

A sudden gust on hot wind shook the car as sand started settling inside the car.

"Another sand storm Boss" he remarked, rolling up his windows."

"I got the back windows."

As we crept along, the swirling sand was so thick you couldn't see a thing beyond five feet.

"Hap, I have a feeling we'll be spending the night in the car." It wasn't a minute later the engine started coughing as the air filter clogged with dirt and sand.

"We'll make it, Boss. Don't you worry about that."

"I'll bet a dollar we don't."

"I'll take that bet, Boss. By the way we're one house away from Mildreds." Hap said as the motor died. "Well. I guess we'll have to make a run for it."

I covered my nose and mouth with my handkerchief and opened the door. A gust of sandy wind blew my hat away as I started for the porch. As we staggered along, I kept my eyes closed as much as possible. Once I reached the porch steps I opened my eyes just enough to see the screen door. With my last burst of energy, I stumbled to the front and  pounded on it.

**"Let me help you."** Cochran's serum said.

I was about to give in when a hand opened the screen door and pulled me inside.

"Where is Hap?" Mildred asked, walking me to the sink.

"I'm not sure. We must have gotten separated." I said flushing my eyes with water.

"I'll find him."

"Mildred! You can't go out there. It's too dangerous!"

I washed my eyes several more times before heading towards the front door.

"William! You're not going out there in your condition."

"I have to. Hap's out there."

I started to pull my arm away when the front door opened. Mildred with a large fish bowl on her head was leading Hap    towards the kitchen sink.

"My God, Mildred. What do you have on your head?" Hap said opening his eyes.

"How did you think of using a glass bowl, Mildred?" Hap asked.

"Don't you need to wash your eyes out?" I asked.

"No. I kept them covered with my handkerchief. Mildred. Can I try your helmet on? I want to walk around outside."

"No.

Hap, this bowl was my mother's and..."

Hap went to put it over his head when he lost his grip.

"Oh! Damn!" Hap yelled as the bowl shattered when it hit the floor.

# Chapter 28

April 10$^{th}$ 1933
6:12 pm Saturday

"Hap, I think you made a bad mistake with Mildred. If you ever want to eat her cooking again, I'd apologize again for breaking her mother's bowl."

"Mildred, I didn't drop it on purpose. Please tell me what I can do to set this right?"

"You can leave me alone while I'm making your supper."

I felt sorry for Hap as he climbed the stairs with his head bowed. As he reached the top step, he heard Mildred say "And make sure you wash your face and behind your ears. Or they'll be no supper for you, young man." Mildred said tapping her foot on the wood floor. "Men, they're all the same. No matter how old they get, they always need mothering. Now as for you, Bill!"

"I'm going upstairs right now, mother." I said heading for the stairs.

After dinner, Hap, Lenard and I went into the parlor while Margaret and Grace cleaned up. "Nancy, why aren't you helping with the dishes?"

"Mildred said I didn't have to. So I came in here to listen to the radio."

"That was nice of Mildred. So, Nancy, tell me about growing up in Maine?"

"I didn't grow up in Maine." she snapped. "I grew up in Ohio. In a small town just outside of Dayton, Detective."

"Please call me Bill. So you grew up on a farm outside of Dayton?"

"No! Not a farm. My father worked in the steel mills and my mother was a seamstress."

"Did you grow up in a house with a white picket fence?"

"No! We lived in a two room boarding house."

"Did you have any brothers or sisters?"

"Yes, but they died when I was ten."

"What did they die of?"

"Flu, I guess. Why are you asking me all these questions?"

"I'm just wondering is all. Being a detective it's natural for me to find out what kind of people are living under our roof." I could see Nancy was getting very agitated, but I needed to find out who she really was.

"Did you work as a seamstress as well."

"No. I helped out in the diner down stairs. You see my father drank, a lot. When he died, we both worked two jobs to keep a roof over our heads. Then my mother died a year later, and I had to make enough money to live on." I felt  Nancy broke out crying when Mildred entered the room. I felt bad for pushing her so hard. So to smooth things over I got up and took her hand. "I'm sorry, Nancy. It's just my nature. I don't mean anything by it"

I patted her hand and found it to be soft and smooth as a baby's butt. If she had worked in a diner and then been living on the street, her hands would be dry and rough. Taking my seat again, I looked at my wife and said,

"Margaret, I think it's time to go to bed. Hap, I'll see you in the morning about six. Hopefully, this stuff will be gone by then."

Upon entering our room, Margaret asked, "What was all that about? You scared that poor girl to death."

"No dear I didn't. That girl is putting on an act. She said she worked in a diner and been living on the street. That girl's hands have never seen a day of work in their life."

"What do you mean by that, William?"

"Her hands are smoother and softer than yours."

"It's because of her age, William."

I didn't press the matter, because no matter what I'd say, the women of the house wouldn't believe me. I was about to get into bed, when I heard a knock on the door.

"Bill. It's me, Grace. I need to talk to you a minute."

I opened the door and Grace quickly entered the room. She took a seat and covered herself up as best as she could.

"Bill. There's something not right about Nancy. I can't explain it, but I don't believe a word of what she told you tonight. And yes, I was listening in."

"Grace! What are you doing in my bedroom in your nightgown. You should be ashamed of yourself."

"Margaret stop! Grace feels the same about Nancy as I do. She was just telling me..."

"I don't care what she was telling you. She needs to get back to her own bedroom and husband."

Margaret went to the door and opened it. "Leave, sister."

Grace stormed towards the door and stepped on Margaret's foot as she left the room.

Margaret yelped! "I'll get you for that!" she said, chasing Grace down the hall.

I heard a door slam shut and figured Grace had outrun her sister. "Margaret..!"

"I don't want to talk about it, William!" she said storming into the room and getting into bed. "Now come to bed or you can sleep on the couch. And what's the matter with you, letting her into our bedroom in her night clothes."

"Margaret, she's married and seven months pregnant."

"So? I don't go into her bedroom naked with her husband there," she said burrowing her face into her pillow.

I shook my head in surrender and didn't say another word before turning out the light.

I laid there for another hour reviewing in my mind what Nancy had said. I decided in the morning I would find out if she really was from Ohio or not. So rolling over, I closed my eyes and heard the alarm ring a second later.

# Chapter 29

April 11th 1933
6:02 am Sunday

I met Hap downstairs, devouring every plate of food Mildred set in front of him.

"Morning, Boss. You're just in time for breakfast," he said clearing another plate of flap jacks.

"I don't have time, Hap. I need to get to the office pronto. So eat up."

My eyes grew wide in disbelief as Hap finished off five flap jacks in thirty seconds.

"Okay, Captain. I'm ready to go," he mumbled through a mouth full of flap jacks.

I watched Hap pick up a cup of coffee to drink it but his mouth was so full it dribbled down his chin instead.

Hap jumped into the front seat and started the car. I looked around and saw a half inch of dust covering most of the ground. It then occurred to me the car was free of sand and dust.

"When did you clean the car?"

"I think it was four o'clock when I started. Why?"

I got in the car and told Hap to drive to Western Union on Powers Ferry Road.

"Why are we going there Boss? There's one a lot closer on Piedmont."

As we drove along, I watched as people started cleaning off their cars, sidewalks, and porches. It was Sunday and a good many people went to church no matter what. Hap parked in front of the small one story building and found two people working. I went inside and wrote out this telegram and had it sent.

Daytona Police Department

Please advise me if you have or can check on a Nancy Gamble age twelve to fifteen. Stop She states she lived in a small town outside of Dayton. Stop Father and mother both dead six to twelve months ago. Stop  Father was a steel worker Stop.  Mother seamstress. Stop

Detective William Barronson
Atlanta Police Department

"That will be thirty five cents." I gave the clerk the money and said, "Send the reply to the station." We then proceeded back to the station, and unloaded the boxes of photos and took them down to the break room. Not only was it cooler, it also had enough tables to lay them out.

"I'll start with this box, Hap. Why don't you take the smaller box and use those tables? In three hours, we had gone through most of the photos without success.

"Let's call it a day, Hap." I said throwing a hand full of them back into the box.

I rubbed my dry eyes, hoping they would water enough so I could see again. "Let's store them in the evidence room for now."

"Hap. I have some personal business I've been meaning  to take care of. So let's take a ride."

Hap and I headed west on Bankhead Hwy until we reached our destination. "Hap. Slow down and pull into Whitney's Nursery. As I got out of the car' I spotted Travis arranging vegetables on his stand to sell.

"Good morning Travis. How's your wife Betty?" I said walking up to him. "I see your back selling vegetables again. How is that working out for you?"

"We're doing alright Detective." Betty said walking out of the storage building.

"Betty. It's good to see you again. I thought you two would be in church today seeing it's Sunday?"

"What are you doing out here Detective?" Betty said joining her husband. "If it's another one of your hare-brained ideas, you can just get back into your car and drive away."

"Yes, I came to talk to you about another idea I have in mind and..."

"And before you say another word, Detective, if it has anything to do with Larry Langford!"

"Larry Langford and his family were murdered, Betty. I found them dead two nights ago."

"Oh, dear God. I'm so sorry to hear that Bill. He wasn't a very nice man, but I wouldn't be a good Christian if I didn't forgive him." Betty said.

"Please excuse my manners Mr.?"

"Happy, ma'am, but you can call me Hap," he said taking his hat off. "It's easier than using my Christian name."

"Would you two like something to drink?"

We went to their modest two story farmhouse that hadn't seen paint in a number of years. I started to take a seat when Betty rushed past me and started brushing the sand off.

"Don't worry about that Betty, the damn stuff is everywhere."

Betty's living room looked just like any other farmer's. It was wooden planked floors, walls and ceilings. Betty had furnished the place with the bare necessities now twenty years old or older. They were the typical hard working backbone of America since this country's beginning.

Betty brought us a glass of tea. I noticed it didn't have any ice in it and after taking a sip it didn't have any sugar either. Setting the glass down I could see on Betty's face she was embarrassed.

"Would you care for a glass of water instead. Our well water is cold and pure."

"No thank you Betty. We're fine." I said eyeing Hap not to say yes. "Now let me get to the point. I know you had a bad experience with Larry, and that you didn't want to have a Chinese boss."

"Chinese boss? What are you talking about?" Travis asked sitting straight up.

I could see Betty hadn't told her husband about the deal with Wang. So not to have any bad feelings I said, "Travis. A few months ago I got this wild notion. A man named Wang would replace Larry in the landscaping business. But with the collapse of the stock market, landscaping isn't a good business to get into."

"So what are you proposing now?" Travis asked.

I could see the hope in his eyes and the doubt in hers.

"How much land do you own on this farm?"

"The bank has taken all but three acres."

"Okay. I had hoped you had more, for this new plan of mine. How about you two jump in my car and visit two friends of mine."

# Chapter 30

April 11th 1933
11:20 am Sunday

I could see in their eyes it would be the ride of a life time. Especially since it was just a Sunday afternoon ride.

I told Hap the directions and sat back to think about how I was going to get everyone on board.

"Bill. Can you turn on the siren? I always wanted to ride in a new police car with the siren going." Travis said with hope in his eyes.

"Hap. Turn on the siren and let's show them how fast these new cars can go."

As we raced down the road doing sixty five Travis head was looking out every window in glee. Betty on the other hand was looking at the floor and praying we wouldn't die.

"Turn coming up, Boss. I'll have to slow done."

It didn't take five minutes before reaching Ester Bradford's and Ruth Taylor's farm. In the time since being out here, the place hadn't changed much. The porch had been shored up enough to get to the front door without killing yourself. Most of the tall grasses and sapling pine trees had been cut down. What had changed a lot was the backyard. It now was a vegetable garden fifty feet by thirty feet and was ready to be planted.

"Good afternoon Mrs. Taylor. Are you responsible for this garden?"

"Yes sir, me and my kids take good care of it."

"Ruth Taylor, this is Betty and Travis Whitley. Let's go inside so they can meet Ester Bradford."

"Entering the house, I found it greatly changed. No longer were there pictures of her husband hunting or drinking with his buddies. Now it looked like a well-cared for interior with pictures, chairs and the dining room table and chairs appropriated from the Aragon Hotel.

I introduced everyone, and we all took a seat at the dining room table.

Ester brought out a picture of ice tea and Ruth brought out several plates of finger food. I could see the look of astonishment on the Whitney's faces. Not only did they have ice in their ice tea, they had sugar in it as well.

"This is a nice visit, Bill. But what do you have in mind now that we have all met?"

"Well Ester. I was hoping you would ask. I see you have done some work on the place. What I don't see is any changes outside. Why didn't you hire some men to help you run the place?"

"I tried, but nobody wants to work for two women."

"Well. I hadn't thought of that. Two women living  together is questionable." I said rethinking how I was going to get them all together. "Okay then. Here's what I want to propose. Ruth, Ester, you have what one hundred and fifty acres of unplanted farmland. Travis, you have three acres of land that the bank hasn't taken. Correct?"

"Correct."

"Well, here's my thinking. If you three pooled your resources and worked this land together, you could all profit from the profit you would make. Now before you give me a thousand reason why it wouldn't work, let me say this. We've had two dust storms from out west. That means no crops being grown out there. Which means food shortages, which means higher prices for what you produce and sell."

"That's not a bad idea, but where are we going to get money for seed, gas, pesticides, machinery?" Travis said.

"Are you going to give us money Bill, Ester, Ruth?"

"No," we all replied.

"Then who?"

"Chang Fu Wang."

"A Chinese. You can't be serious Bill!"

"Why not. Chinese save all their money, and besides, I'm sure he could provide enough help to get this place going. And once going, Travis, you can buy your land back for pennies. My wife is a McCallum and would know how to start a corporation. I also want all of us to meet at Wang's Cleaners in town. No! Better yet we'll all meet here in two hours."

Hap and I raced back into the city and pulled up in front of Wang's Cleaners. Walking in, I found his wife working in the back. I bowed to her and asked where her husband was.

"He at Lee Chang. They play Mahjong Sunday. Sunday slow business only I work. He play."

Hap and I walked around the corner and knocked on the door of Lee Chang's door.

Lee came to the door to tell us he was closed. When he saw the two of us, Lee opened the door and invited us in.

"Detective Barronson, and your driver Happy. What may I do for you today," he said eyeing Hap's old cloths. "I have just the clothes for you Happy. It will make you the most dashing man in the city." he said taking Hap's left arm and leading him to the already made suits.

"Hang on Lee. We didn't come for clothes, not yet anyway. I want to talk to you and Wang."

"May I ask what it is about? If I might be so bold."

"I prefer to talk to you both, please."

We were led to the back office behind a curtain. The smell of incense was stronger back here as we entered a smoke-filled room. There were three tables occupied by two people each playing a game called Mahjong. A very young, and very beautiful woman was pouring tea. Once she saw us all the players turned to look at us. I bowed slightly and that act seemed to break the ice.

"Detective." Wang said. "What you doing here? Did someone rob me? Take wife please?"

"No. Everything is fine. Even your wife."

"That too bad, I must pray to Buddha more."

"I want to talk to you about a business opportunity."

I immediately got everyone's attention in the room.

I spent the next hour explaining my plan before they understood my intentions. "Well Mr. Wang, What do you think  of my business proposal?"

"I, for one, must admit it sounds too good to be true. But Detective, you have been a friend to me and my family. So yes we will help."

Chan and Lee got in the back seat and we headed to the station. "I need to pick up another car so Hap can drive you to the farm while I followed behind."

# Chapter 31

April 11<sup>th</sup> 1933
3:10 pm Sunday

I pulled up to the farm I found Hap was already inside with Wang. "Well, I see everyone is here. Hap, did you introduce everyone?" I could see both sides were uncomfortable with each other. The women and kids were at the table. The Chinese were standing by the door smoking.

"All right, you four. If we're going to work together, then we all need to sit at the table." I spent another hour before I got my idea excepted by everyone. "Okay now this is the contract I'll have my wife type up. Chan and Lee will provide the capital and man power to repair the farm equipment and buildings. Ester and Ruth will provide the land, meals and education. Betty and Travis will work the land with help to plant and harvest. Margaret, my wife will draw up a corporation contract making all of you board members, and equal partners."

"What you mean education?" Chan asked.

"The ladies well teach your workers English."

"No Want."

"Chan we need to communicate with each other so the work gets done." I could see he wasn't about to change his mind. "Chan. Then you provide men that can interpret. You know, speak both English and Chinese."

I looked at my watch and found it was time to stop.

"Captain I'll take Chan and Lee back to their home.

"Good idea. I'll take Betty and Travis back to theirs."

I turned on the headlights and headed for the paved road. As we bounced along on the dirt road, Travis spoke up.

"I'm still uncomfortable with the Chinese, Bill."

"Why is that?" I said looking at him in the rear view mirror.

"I don't know. Maybe it's their slanted eyes. Or their lack of showing any facial expressions. That's it! You don't know what they're thinking."

"And they're not Christian!" Betty said.

"So. They're not Christian. I'm sure they think the same thing about you. They're not Buddhist. But you have one thing in common. The United States dollar."

I dropped them off and headed for home to tell Margaret what I had volunteered her for. Upon reaching Mildred's, I found every parking spot filled except for Larry's driveway. Not wanting to keep looking, I pulled into Larry's driveway and got out of my car.

"Well, old friend, what are you doing out so late?" I said stroking the late Larry's cat.

I don't know what name Larry had given you, but I think I'll call you Larry." For some reason Larry's cat had attached itself to me as if we had been buddies for years.

"Detective Barronson, I didn't know you're a cat person. I would have killed the cat as well?"

"Detective, don't try to alert the FBI watching your house. I would hate to have to kill them along with your cat." Muller said smiling at me from in the shadows.

I could see Muller was daring me to do just that. In the short time I had known him, Muller had told me he had thrown down the same gauntlet to a French officer over his wife and killed him.

"No." I said. "I'll stick to our agreement."

"Then you better make sure the FBI men don't get in my way, Detective. I wouldn't want anything bad to happen to your friends out in the country. Not after all the work you have done to get them to work together."

I was about to tell him I had had enough of his threats. As my anger grew Larry no longer wanted to stay in my arms.

"Go." I hissed as the cat took off for Mildred's.

I took several deep breaths and found I could no longer taste or smell Muller. I tried several more times to pick up his scent without success. I became even angrier at myself as I headed towards the house. Just as few months ago I could have followed his smell for hours. Now after diluting the serum, I was almost like every other human. I walked up onto the porch sweating even though the temperature was fifty degrees. I sat down in a rocker and waited until I could regain control of myself.

"William, what are you doing out here?" Margaret asked, feeling my forehead.

"Come on, husband. You'll catch your death out here."

Margaret took me into the parlor and sat me in front of the fire in the fireplace. As the heat warmed me, Margaret rubbed my cold hands to get the circulation moving. As I sat there staring at the flames, I looked for the other me that Cochran had made. "Margaret! I can't find or feel him anymore." I said, sitting up.

"Are you sure dear? You've said that before, you know."

"Yes I know, but I can't feel it any longer. I'll have to go to the hospital and have my blood checked, just to make sure."

I gave Margaret a kiss and started rubbing my temples. I had wished for this day many times, and now that it was here, I felt regret for doing it.

"Margaret, I'm sure and don't tell a soul!"

"Well, the master of the house is home, I see. Is the inhuman eating machine here also?" Mildred asked, looking around for Hap.

"He had an errand to run for me, but he'll be here shortly. So you better get the food ready, because the longer he has to wait the more he eats," the three of us said at the same time.

Mildred left the room and started banging pots and pans in the kitchen to get ready for him.

"I feel sorry for her sometimes, William. It seems she does nothing but cook and clean for us."

"Where's that Nancy? Isn't she supposed to be helping Mildred?"

"I didn't want to say anything bad about her but every time Mildred asks her to help out, she has an excuse."

"I'll take care of that!" I said heading for her room.

"William, don't! If Mildred wants to let her lay around, then it's not your place to say anything."

"All right, I'll let it go this time. Oh, that reminds me I need to talk to you about contracts. Can you draw one up?"

"I've never had, but I've reviewed every one John or the Major has ever drawn up."

"Margaret, if I put together a rough draft, could you have it ready by tomorrow? Okay, then here is the meat of the document."

"This seems pretty straight forward. I can give you a rough draft tonight to look over."

"Captain, there's another fire. This ones at the Flat Iron Building."

"The Flat Iron Building! My brother lives there, William!"

I grabbed my hat and headed for the door.

"I want to come?" Margaret said grabbing her coat.

# Chapter 32



Not wanting to argue, the three of us got into my police car and headed for the city. As we sped along, I could see the glow in the night sky.

"Is that glow coming from my brother's building?"

"Yes. But from what I've seen, it's not a very large fire."

As Hap turned onto Peachtree Street, we followed a fire truck to the burning building.

"Hap. You hang on to Margaret, and I'll go and see if her brother is okay."

Giving her a quick peck on the cheek, I crossed the police line and started looking for Fire Chief Anderson. I stopped and stared up at the third floor. Smoke was pouring out the windows meaning the fire hadn't reached that floor.

"Hey you! Get out of my way!" A fireman said pulling a hose.

"What did you say?"

"I said get out of the way! Damn you! Or I'll have the police get you out of the way!"

"George. It's me, Detective Barronson!" George was one of the firemen that had help me at the McKenzie fire. I grabbed his hose and helped to unravel it as it filled with water. Seeing he was struggling to hold it, I went to help when another fireman got there first. I heard the building crowd gasp as flames shot out of the third floor windows. For a second, it looked as if the building would be a total loss. Three waiting ladder trucks with hoses started pouring gallons of water into the building. Four other firemen turned their hoses on the second floor fires. Within three minutes, the flames had disappeared on one and two. Two minutes later floor three's fires were out.

"Alright, you three. Start with the first floor and work your way to the top. If you come across any hot spots, let me know by coming to a window. The same goes if you find bodies. Injured people bring to a window and we'll use a ladder truck to get them down." Fire Chief Anderson said.

"Hey, you! Get back behind the police line before you get somebody killed," another fireman said.

"He's okay, Mike." Mitch said walking up to me.

"Looks like we won this one, Bill." Chief Anderson said looking at the smoking windows. "What are you doing down here on a Sunday night."

"My wife's brother lives there Chief. Have you seen him?"

"No, and so far we have only found one body. It was a patrolman I believe his name was Henry."

"Henry Ingram!"

"That I can't say. You'll have to go to the coroners for a positive ID."

I walked away from Chief without saying a word. If Henry Ingram, my oldest friend, was dead, Muller was the man that had murdered him.

"Did you find him?" Margaret asked before seeing my face.

"William what's the matter?"

"I think Henry Ingram was murdered here tonight."

"Henry? Our Henry? Who told you that, and what about John McCallum. Is he dead too?"

"No. John isn't dead, Margaret he's just missing. He might not have been in the building or he was trapped when the fire started. So why don't I take you home as it will be hours before they check every floor."

I helped Margaret unwillingly into the back seat. I had to threaten her with handcuffs before she resigned her stance on staying. By the time Hap stopped in front of  the house, Margaret had fallen asleep. I looked at my watch and found the time to be 4:30 am.

"Well Hap, it looks like another sleepless night."

I woke Margaret up and the three of us quietly entered the house. Mildred greeted us and whispered, "Did she find her brother?"

I shook my head no, and continued on to our room to put her in bed. Tiptoeing out of the room, I went back downstairs and found a pot of hot coffee and biscuits.

"Hap. I see you've already started eating, and by the look on Mildreds face, you must have devoured a number of them."

I poured a cup of coffee and heard a smack and Hap yelp.

"You've had enough, you pig!

Those two are for Bill." Mildred said pointing her finger at him.

"Sorry Mildred," he mumbled through a mouth full of food. "I was so hungry, I just couldn't help myself."

"You need to see a doctor Hap, I think you might have a tape worm?"

"Tape worm, what's that?" Hap asked picking every last crumb off his plate.

"It's a worm that lives in your intestines making you want to eat all the time. If I remember right, my uncle died from one in 1882 when his stomach exploded and a five foot worm fell out." Mildred glanced at me and winked.

Hap set the empty plate down and backed away from the table. "A worm! Inside me! I think I'm going to be sick."

Hap headed for the bathroom and we both tried not to laugh. "Well maybe that'll slow down his eating. I've never seen a man eat so much and still stay skinny." Mildred handed me the plate with the last two biscuits on it.

"I'll pass Mildred if you don't mind. I have some bad news to tell you. Henry was found dead at the Flat Iron Building fire."

"Henry! Are you sure?"

"I'm not one hundred percent sure, but a body was found and was taken to the coroners. I intend to go there when it opens to make sure it is him."

A wave of fatigue swept over me as I settled on the couch. I was about to drift off when the two FBI agents came in and woke me up.

"Detective Barronson, I've had a communication from the Director. He wishes to see you in the morning at his office."

"Did he say why?"

"No, just that he wants to see you."

"Thanks, for letting me know. Now let me have some sleep before I shoot one of you."

# Chapter 33

April 12th 1933
7:43 am Monday

I opened my eyes and found the place strangely quiet. Getting to my feet, I stumbled to the bathroom before doing anything else. Now with that out of the way, I went to the kitchen and found it empty. Alarm bells started ringing in my head. This was the first time ever that Mildred hadn't made breakfast. I went to her bedroom door and knocked softly. When I didn't get an answer I knocked harder and called her name.

"Mildred. Are you all right?" I waited for thirty seconds before trying the doorknob. It was locked. "Mildred! I'm coming in!" I shouted and then kicked the door as hard as I could.

"Are you looking for Mildred, Detective?" Nancy asked walking up behind me.

"I believe she said she was going to the store or something like that." Nancy said touching my ear and stroking it.

"I'd stop that, Nancy, if I were you," Margaret said grabbing her hand.

"I'm sorry. I didn't mean anything by it. Honest."

Nancy pulled her hand away and gave me a wink before walking away.

Margaret's head snapped around and gave me a look as if it was my fault. "What are you two doing here at Mildred's door?"

Red face with embarrassment I started to tell her I couldn't get Mildred to answer the door. I then heard a click and the door opened slowly.

"Yes, Bill. What can I do for you?" Mildred said, through blood shot eyes.

"Mildred. What's the matter? I've never seen you looking like this."

Her long bedroom hair had savagely been chopped off in different lengths. She had a blood clot forming on her lower lip indicating someone had hit her. Her nightgown once white was spattered with blood as well as being torn.

"Mildred opened the door and I could see the room had been ransacked. I was about to step in when Mildred collapsed into my arms. I picked her up and placed her on the blood stained bed.

"Margaret, get some wet washcloths and clean her up. Nancy! Nancy!!! Go call for an ambulance, now!"

I looked for Hap, but he must still be asleep upstairs. I stepped away and let Margaret do what she could until the ambulance arrived. I slowly started examining the room for clues as to what had happened here. Whoever had done this was looking for something Mildred had. All the dresser drawers were open and empty. Mildred's and Nancy's clothes were thrown around the room. A chair had been cut open and the insides pulled out. I opened her closet door and found everything on the floor as well. I was about to turn around and check the bathroom when I spotted a safe.

Several of Nancy's dresses had been thrown on it. Whether it had been intentional, I couldn't tell. Moving them aside, I tried the handle and found the safe was locked. Evidently, this must have been what they were after. Knowing Mildred, she wouldn't give them the combination, so they tortured her hoping to get it. I then went to the bathroom and found the medicine cabinet open and empty. Whatever had been in there was now broken on the floor. I carefully pushed the door closed and found a message taped to it.

Detective, you're trying my patience
with your futile attempts to find me.
Tell the FBI to back off Detective or
next time it could be your wife that's
been assaulted.

Carl Muller

I pulled down the message and stuffed it in my pocket. I didn't want anyone here to see it except the FBI and me. I could hear the ambulance siren coming closer. I picked up the phone. "Sergeant. I want to report a break in."

---⟨◇⟩---

# Chapter 34

April 12th 1933
8:43 am Monday

I hung up the phone and found Grace, Lenard and Hap waiting to talk to me. Who I didn't see were the two FBI agents that were supposed to be protecting us.

"Don't anybody ask and don't anybody move until I tell you to. Hap, get your gun and come with me." I had a very bad feeling as we stepped out onto the front porch and looked around. "Hap. check out the FBI's car to see if one of them is there. I'll head around back and take a look for them there."

I waited as Hap headed for their car. Once I was sure he was okay I headed for the back door. I opened the door and found my missing agents. Both were lying in the grass face down. I slowly walked towards them making sure I wouldn't join them. As I knelt down, I saw both of them were shot in the back. I rolled one of them over and saw the look of astonishment of his face. I spotted two coffee cups and  several cigarette butts around them. They must have been talking about their wives to let their guard down this way.  I continued looking around and spotted two sets of foot prints under Mildred's bedroom window.

"Captain. I didn't find either of them in the car. They must be in the house somewhere asleep." Hap said walking out the back door.

"That's okay Hap, I found them dead over there." I backed out slowly using my footprints as a guide. Once clear, I headed for the sidewalk to meet the ambulance as it pulled up.

"Follow me." Lenard said leading them into the house.

I met Hap on the porch and waited until Mildred was loaded into the ambulance. "I'm going to ride with them." Margaret said.

"What about me?" Grace said heading for the ambulance as well.

"Lenard. Why don't you drive them to the hospital. That way the doctor won't be bombarded with questions. Hap and I have other business to attend to before we can join you."

"Okay Hap. Now that they're gone, let's have a good look around before the coroner and police show up."

I started with Mildred's room while Hap checked the kitchen. I went to her window and found it had been jimmied. Leaning out the open window, I got a better view of the footprints. The man's shoe prints looked to be tens. The other set was small, probably sevens, which indicated a young boy or a woman belonged to them.

I backed up and found both sets of footprints in the room. The smaller ones must have been rifling the drawers and closet. The larger set went straight to the bed where I found spots of blood on the sheets. A sudden flash of insight hit me.

I ran out of the room, knocking Hap and the incoming coroner out of my way.

"Captain! What's going on?"

"I need to call the hospital! Mildred's life is at stake!"

"Operator. Connect me with Grady Hospital immediately this is Detective Barronson.

"Hello. This is Grady Hospital. May I help you?"

"This is Detective William Barronson, I need to talk to the Doctor who's treating Mildred Adams."

"I'm sorry Detective Barronson, she is in the emergency room at this moment. I can have him call you when he can?"

"Listen Nurse. Is Doctor Charles Friederick in the building?"

"Just a moment I'll check... Yes he is. Would you like to speak to him?"

"No. I thought I'd just call him because I have a hang nail. Yes please, it's a matter of life and death."

"Doctor Charles, Detective. Do you need another transfusion?"

"No, and yes, but a Mildred Adams is in your emergency room and she might have been injected with the same serum I was."

The doctor didn't answer me because he had hung up. I hung up the phone and saw the look on Hap's face. "I could be wrong, Hap."

"But if you're not, and she dies, Captain, I want this Muller to hang by his neck until he is dead."

"If she dies Hap, we'll hang him together from the tree outback."

I wanted to go to the hospital but I needed to go to the coroners and find out if the body was Henry Ingram. Then I remembered the coroner was in the backyard. "Hap. Why don't you go to the hospital and see how Mildred is doing," I could see Hap was worried about

Mildred. It seems in the short time Hap had known Mildred he had become smitten.

I was about to find the coroner when Nancy appeared out of her room.

"What's all the noise about, Bill?" she said yawning.

"Is Mildred making breakfast because I'm hungry." she yawned again heading for the kitchen.

"Have you been asleep all this time?"

"Yes. Why do you ask? And where is Mildred? I'm hungry."

"Mildred's in the hospital, Nancy. It seems someone broke into her room last night and beat her half to death."

"Oh that's just terrible, Bill. Did the FBI agents catch them?"

The hair on the back of my neck stood up at Nancy's lack of concern for Mildred's injuries. I watched as she played with her hair while walking back and forth provocatively.

"I see the lack of concern tells me you already knew Mildred had been attacked."

"I don't know what you're talking about, Bill. I was in my room all night asleep and why would I hurt a kind old lady like Mildred. I can get anything out of her I want by just asking. You see she thinks I want to be her daughter," she said giving me a know it all smile. "Anyway I couldn't get into her safe in the closet. If I had I wouldn't be here now talking to an old man like you."

I wasn't sure what happened next but when I came to, Nancy was sitting on the floor nursing a red slapped face.

"I'm leaving!" she shouted, getting to her feet.

"You certainly are, because I'm putting you under arrest for burglary and assault."

"You can't do that to Mildred, she won't stand for it!"

She screamed breaking into tears as I handcuffed her.

I dragged her to the porch and called for a policeman to come here.

"Yes Detective."

"Here. Take this kid to the station and book her for assault and burglary. Have them put her in a separate cell and make sure she gets some police breakfast."

"Nancy, you're going to love breakfast. Powdered eggs, stale dry toast, and warm water."

As he dragged her kicking and screaming to his car. I noticed a bruise on her face and hands. I felt sorry for the patrolman as he and his partner struggled to get her into the car. As they pulled away I waved goodbye. I couldn't hear what she was screaming, but I'm sure it wasn't polite.

I took a deep breath to calm my nerves, and headed for the backyard to see what the coroner had come up with. I found Pete still examining one of the bodies. The other was on a stretcher heading for the ambulance.

"Pete. Was the body they brought in last night your brother Henry?"

"No. It was Henry Gordon. He was a grandson of Mayor Gordon of Marietta."

"How did he die?"

"I haven't started his autopsy yet, but he had several bullet wounds in his back. He pulled one out and found it to be a 7.65x 22mm  or a .30 caliber in our standard of measurements."

It took a minute to remember that size bullet was used in a 1900 model German Luger. "What do you think about the two agents murdered? Could it be the same gun as well?"

"I'll have to let you know later, but my first guess would be yes."

"I've finished taking pictures, Detective. Are there any others you want taken?"

We walked around the crime scene, first outside and then inside. When we were done he had taken eight more pictures.

Now that they were done, I locked up the house and rode with the coroner to his place of business.

As I followed the coroner into the building, I found the two dead agents already on their respective tables.

"Pete. Would you do me a favor and remove the bullets first from each man?" In thirty minutes I had three Luger. 30 caliber bullets. "Pete, I'm headed for the FBI Building if anyone calls looking for me."

I hailed a taxi and headed for the FBI building. When the taxi pulled up, I found the place was abuzz with agents and reporters. I got out of the car and was immediately inundated with reporters.

"Detective. Is it true your landlady was accosted in her own home?"

"Why were there FBI agents guarding you home?

"Did you shoot the agents thinking they were burglars?"

"Why, what about this, have you ever, did you know." The reporters yelled until I couldn't think straight.

I was about to explode in anger, when four agents pushed through the mob and escorted me into the building.

"I'll take you to Director Hoover's office. He's been waiting to talk to you."

# Chapter 35

April 12th 1933
11:36 am Monday

I entered Hoover's office and found a dozen men answering phones, filing reports and going in and out of his office. I started to take a seat when an agent motioned for me to follow him into Hoover's private office. I took a seat and waited while Hoover was on a phone talking to someone in Washington. I looked around the office and found it to be quite different than the one I had. The desk was half again the size of mine, and had three phones of different colors on it. At the moment, he was talking on the red one, while the other two were ringing. His desk was already covered knee-deep with reports, and a teletype machine was working overtime in the corner.

Not ever seeing a real teletype machine, I got up and watched as it typed out message after message.

"Detective, please return to your seat." Hoover said hanging up the phone.

"Sorry sir, I just wanted to see how that machine works."

"That's okay, but if you read one forget what it said. Now tell me about the attack on your household last night."

At first I was surprised he already knew about his agents and that the house was attacked. He even knew about the Flat Iron Building fire and the death of an officer.

"Well now, Detective Barronson, it seems you're a target for more than just your blood. As for these fires, my men have discovered they also have a connection with Muller."

"Is that why the Governor and the Police Chief are sitting outside as well?"

"In part yes, but the main reason for them being here is that you'll no longer work for the Atlanta Police Department."

"Well, before you ask for my badge and gun, I'd like to know where this bodyguard named Purvise is. It seems every time something happens to me, he's nowhere to be found. Sir!"

The door opened. "Director Grayson, tell me about agent Purvise. Is he assigned to protect this man?"

"Yes sir he is. I assigned him myself. Why?"

"I should say there is. I want to see him immediately. Now where was I…ah… oh yes. I remember now."

As Hoover fumbled around with his thoughts. I figured I was either being fired or was going to become a lab rat again at some Army laboratory.

"I can see by the look on your face, Detective, what I'm about to tell you will come as a surprise." Hoover said motioning to an aide.

The aide carrying a folder handed it to Hoover and left the room. Hoover opened the folder took out his gold pen and signed it. "There. This makes it official, agent Barronson." He handed the file over to me to read.

The United States of America under the FBI and the Department of Defense, William Barronson, is offering you this temporary position of Special Agent in the FBI and a Major in the Army and Navy. You will be in charge of all investigations in the state of Georgia deemed important to you and the FBI. Upon your signature this position will be reviewed once a year by the Director of South East Operations. "Well, William Barronson, what do you think about the position?"

"Director. I'm not sure if I can do the job. You see less than a year ago..."

"I'm aware of your history William. I'm also aware of the plot by Major Gabriel McCallum and his son to secede Georgia from the United States. So, sign the damn thing, so I can get back to work in Washington."

After signing, I was then told the newspapers would be informed I had been suspended from the police department. The reason given would be lack of progress in catching the arsonist burning down Atlanta.

A photographer took my picture handing the Chief my badge. It was then sent to every paper to be put on the front page that I was suspended.

Feeling I might have made a mistake, I headed for the door when Director Grayson came up to me.

"Don't look so dejected Bill. You'll be of great value to us now that you're an agent. Now, come with me."

I walked with Grayson to the elevator and entered it. Grayson pushed a button that said basement. The door closed automatically and the elevator started down.

"I guess this is progress Sir. No need to have an elevator operator anymore."

"Yes, things are changing, but it'll be sometime before all the new improvements come into being."

The door opened and I found myself in the basement which was a storage area. There were wire interlocking cages on both sides of the hallway. Each separate cage was labeled with what was stored inside. We stopped at the last interlocking cage. The sign read small arms and ammunition.

Grayson unlocked the door and went to a locked cabinet. He unlocked it and opened the double doors. "See anything you like agent?" he said, stepping back smiling.

The cabinet was filled with different handguns all on display. Forty fives, thirty eights, magnums, wheel guns, automatics, long barreled, short barreled and more.

"I'll stick with the same type of gun I carried with the police force," I said examining one I particularly liked.

Grayson handed me a box of bullets and said, "Now this isn't the old west and you're not Bill Hickok, understand?"

"I understand sir. By the way, Director what am I being paid?"

"Oh! Sorry I forgot. $5.00 a day and $2.00 a day for expenses. And I remind you, all expenses need receipts. Now is there anything else?"

# Chapter 36

April 12<sup>th</sup> 1933
2:13 pm Monday

I spent the next hour with different departments like payroll, expense report forms, transportation when it arrived. By the time I was done, my head was so full of information I thought it would bust. I left the building and jumped on a streetcar heading for the hospital.

"William, Doctor Charles Friederick wants to speak to you about Mildred." Margaret said looking at me strangely.

"What's happened, William? And don't tell me nothing. I know better than that."

I took Margaret aside and whispered, "I've been suspended  from the police department for lack of progress on the arson cases."

"Oh no! It can't be. What about the FBI, can't they intercede on your behalf?"

"No. It's final. The Captain and the Chief were both present. Let me see the doctor, and we'll talk later."

I went to the nurses' station at the end of the hall and asked for Doctor Friederick. I took a seat and lit a cigarette while waiting for him.

"Detective Barronson, nice to see you again. I thought I'd seen the last of you with your last transfusion."

"Doctor, have you checked Mildred's blood for the serum?"

"Yes, and it's negative. I did find heroin in her system which should be wearing off just about now. As for the cuts and bruises, I think she would heal faster at home. Now, while you're here, let's see what your blood looks like."

"I'm fine, doctor. I'm in a hurry and."

"Nurse, take Detective Barronson into that room and draw five tubes of blood for me please."

"But. Doc. I."

"Come along with me Detective, this won't take but a minute. And if you're a good boy I'll give you a lollipop," she said, dragging me by the arm.

I did get a lollipop from the nurse, and was sucking on it when I returned to Mildred's room. I could see she was feeling much better. "What did you do to deserve that lollipop?"

"I gave blood just in case you needed a refill. After all, it's high test or used to be."

"Well, anyway I don't see why I didn't get one. Now where are my clothes? I have dinner to prepare and a bedroom to clean."

Hap took the girls home and then headed for Kim's closed diner. Once they had left the hospital, I waved down a taxi.

"Where to, Captain?" Ox said smiling at me.

Ox was Hap's son, who had taken over his taxi when Hap went to work with me. "How are things going, Ox?"

"Not too bad. I'm making enough money to keep the old girl on the road. Now, where to?"

I gave him the address of Kim's diner and we headed in that direction. As I rode along, I thought over what I had  gotten myself into. I understood me being suspended from the force would ease Mullers suspicions. As for the FBI, I would have to separate myself completely from them as well.

Ox pulled into the diner's parking lot and parked in front of the door. "What are you going to do here, Captain?"

"Ox. I'm not a Captain anymore. So please call me Bill."

"Okay. Bill, but.."

"Enough! Ox. Just give me a minute, will you?"  A tilted for sale sign in the dirty window made me feel sad. I had eaten in Kim's place every Thursday for years. I took a deep breath and closed my eyes. The smell of her fried chicken made my mouth water in anticipation.

"Captain. I just heard you've been suspended from the police force. Is that true?" Hap asked, parking next to us.

"Yes. I'm afraid it is, Hap."

"If that's the case, I'll quit two. What a bunch of damn idiots they must be. You're the only man that can solve these fires."

"Enough, Hap. It's done. So keep your job if you can and maybe the Captain will let you drive for him. That way you can keep me informed as to what is going on."

I got back into the taxi and told Ox to drive me to Ray's Pool Hall. I think it was time to have another chat with the Atlanta Mob.

Ox pulled up in front of the place and parked. I got out and looked in the window at the same three men playing pool.

"Gentlemen. Nice to see you three again." I said walking in the front door. "Bartender, seeing it's legal once again, give them a drink on me."

"What the hell do you want, cop. We haven't broken any of your laws. We even tip big every time we order food."

"That's good to hear, but I want to have a word with the boss. If he's available?"

I ordered one of their iced coffees from the bartender. He looked surprised that I would order it seeing prohibition had been repealed. When he sat it in front of me I asked, "Didn't we talk about you opening up a coffee shop?"

"Yes we did. Now I remember you. You're Detective, Ah! Barronson right?"

"That's right. I'm the guy that was after Johnny Knox."

"And you broke the place up looking for him. So did you catch him?"

"Yes."

"Detective Barronson, or should I call you Mr. Barronson seeing you're on suspension."

"Mister will do for now, Mr.?"

"Well' seeing we've done business before, I don't see how it could hurt for you to know my name. Pastor Alton Lyman."

"Pastor! I never would have thought of that in a million years. Which one?"

"Let's keep that a secret for now, until we know each other even better. Now what do you want to see me about?"

"As you well know, I'm on suspension because of not catching the arsonist. Seeing we worked together on the Wishing Well Murders, I was hoping we could do it again on the arsonist."

Pastor Alton ordered a drink. As he waited, I could see his wheels turning. I knew asking him for more help was going to cost me something I didn't want to accept.

"Exactly, what kind of help are you looking for Mr. Barronson? I want you to understand, the more help I give you, the more it's going to cost?"

"I understand that Pastor. I'm hoping I'm able to justify the cost to myself."

"Well then, let's see how much you're willing to spend. Shall we?"

I asked for a shot of whiskey before starting the negotiations. "Okay, here's what I need from you and remember this arsonist is costing you business as well."

"Agreed."

"I need your people and their connections to be on the lookout for this man or men. Also if they hear anything on the street about a man name Muller, I would like to be advised."

The Pastor drank his drink and lit a cigarette as he thought over my proposition. "Just to clarify. You just want me to either give you his name or where he might strike next. Not eliminate him, correct? What about this man Muller?"

"Correct on the arsonists. As for Muller I'll take care of him myself once you find him."

"Then here's what it's going to cost you. Tell your boss to leave my betting parlors, pinball and gambling parlors alone. I'll let you raid one of my houses on occasion just to be fair. After all, you have a squeaky clean image to maintain."

I took a deep breath and lit a cigarette also. I knew the cost was going to be high, but damn.

"Now you realize I've been suspended from the force, and don't have any control over that even if I wasn't suspended."

"I realize that William, but you have connections and can let me know in advance on a raid. Correct?"

I didn't answer him, because I knew I'd be under his thumb for the rest of my life.

"I can see by the look on your face we need to bargain some more, William. Well, how about this Detective. Let me know whenever an outsider, or shall we say competitor, comes to town.

As for the rest, we'll save that for the next time you need my help."

"I agree to those terms. You can contact me through the  taxi driver. His name is Ox."

I hated to put Ox on the spot, but I had no other alternative at this point in time.

I was about to leave, when an idea popped into my head. Pastor, I have something else I'd like to talk to you about. Are you familiar with Kim's Diner?

"Yes. She had the best fried chicken in town. I tried to go into business with her, but she wouldn't accept any of my offers. She's a spunky woman, and I do like her"

"Then you know the bank foreclosed on her loan. I went by there today and saw a for sale sign in the window. I don't want to know but a smart Realtor could buy it for nothing."

"Then rent it back to her for a small profit for now."

"I'll have to think on that and let you know at a later date. Now, if there's no other business we need to discuss?"

I thanked him for his time and headed for the door.

"Hey mister you forgot to pay for your drinks" the bartender said.

"Oh. That's right, I wouldn't want to break the law now would I."

The bill was forty five cents, so I gave him fifty cents and left the nickel as his tip. The look on his face wasn't happy as he picked up the nickel and dropped it into the register.

"Now this is for your coffee shop, Ray." I slipped him a dollar and headed for the door before I got touched for more. Once outside, I was feeling pretty good about what I had accomplished today. As I got into the taxi, I remembered Nancy was sitting in jail. My original plan was to question her about last night.

"Ox, we better head for the station. I need to have a talk with the Captain."

"Okay, Bill. Should I wait for you there?"

"Yes. It shouldn't take but a minute or two. Then take me home."

## Chapter 37

April 12<sup>th</sup> 1933<br>
4:23 pm Monday

I sat back in the uncomfortable seat, and thought more about Nancy and her answers. She had mentioned she knew about the safe and couldn't open it.

That statement alone made me suspicious that Nancy wasn't who she said she was. "Ox. I've changed my mind. I need to go by the Western Union office on Powers Ferry Road.

I got out of the taxi and entered the small office. I found the same man behind the counter. "Have you received a reply yet?"

"Ah Detective Barronson. Yes, I just received the telegram. I quickly opened it, and read the following.

To Detective William Barronson. Stop
Atlanta Police Department stop

Have check on your Nancy Gamble Stop
Found only one recorded death of Gambles in last year. Stop. They lived in Old North Dayton Town. Stop.  No information on any children living or dead that we can find. Stop. If you require more information. Stop
I'll be at your disposal. stop
Detective Roy Farsight. stop
Dayton Police Department. stop

I folded the telegram and put it in my pocket. Detective Farsight had confirmed the Gamble family had lived and died  there last year. But he had no proof that a Nancy Gamble was their daughter. So this left me with one choice. Is she who she says she is or is she an impostor?

I left the building and got into the taxi. "Ox, lets head for home."

Suddenly my door opened and Muller stood there with a Luger pointed it at me. "Move over, Detective." I slid across the seat and he slipped in beside me. Pointing his Luger at the back of Ox's head he said," Am I going to have any trouble with you my friend?"

Ox, shook his head no, and looked in the rear view mirror at me. "Do as he says, and you'll be okay. Isn't that correct, Heir Muller?"

"If he minds, Mr. Barronson. Now as we head back to your home, William, I expect you Ox to drive slowly. Will that be a problem for you?"

"No sir! No problem. Shall I head that way now?"

"If you please. Now William, you had a blood test today. Tell me, what did it say?"

"I don't know. I didn't wait around to get the results."

"Detective. I like that better than calling you William. Are you sure about your answer." he said cocking the Luger."

"Heir Muller. I just told you I haven't been back to the hospital to find out the results. If you want, we can do that now."

"It's not necessary. I already know the results. You see, I wanted to see if you were lying to an old friend."

"Okay. Heir Muller, then what did you find out."

"According to your deceased doctor, your blood is 89% clear of Doctor Cochran's serum injected into you."

"Then there's no reason for me to go with you to Germany, is there?" I said keeping a careful eye on the Luger.

"Not quite, Heir Detective. I'm no Doctor, like Doctor  Cochran calls himself. So, your blood could still be of some value, along with your organs. You see, I would get to do the dissecting on you, once he's done with you."

"Then you better shoot me now, because there's no way I'm going to Germany with you, you Hun bastard."

"Now, now, don't forget about your family. I paid Mildred a visit last night. Should I visit Margaret tonight? Or how

about the pregnant Grace. She could lose the child if I tried hard enough. Or maybe your old friend Henry, would he be a better choice?"

"If you do. I'll hunt you down and do the same thing to you, Heir Peiper, no matter what country you're in. You see there's one thing you've forgotten about."

"My government has all my blood from the transfusions. I'm sure I could get a pint or two injected back into me. Then I could hunt you down, just like Cochran's cobra could."

The taxi stopped in front of Mildred's as I looked into his eyes. For the first time since meeting him, I saw fear behind in his eyes.

"Then it looks like it's a stalemate for now, Heir Detective, but just to be sure we understand each other."

Muller opened the door and slid out, all the while pointing his Luger at me. Smiling all the while, he put two slugs into Ox's head and one into my right shoulder.

"Now if you please, Detective. Get out of the taxi, we're going for a little plane ride."

I opened my side of the taxi's door and got to my feet.

"This way Detective, or I'll shoot whoever is in the house."

I looked at the porch, and saw two men with their guns pointed at Hap and Henry. When Hap saw his son slumped over the steering wheel, Hap exploded and decked his assailant.

"Ox, Ox! No, not my son, you bastard!" Hap started to point his gun when Mullers shot hit him knocking him off his feet.

"Henry! Drop the gun! Or you'll join Hap and his son." Muller yelled.

"Henry! Drop the gun, and see if you can do anything for Hap. There's nothing you can do for me now."

Henry dropped his gun and backed up towards the porch wall with his hands in the air. I walked slowly around the taxi holding a handkerchief over my bleeding shoulder. As I reached Muller I saw Hap trying to sit up as Margaret  and Henry ran to help him.

Muller gave me a wicked smile and aimed for Margaret.

"You're a good shot, Muller, but if you pull that trigger I'll ram it down your throat." I said walking up to him.

With my good hand I grabbed his gun arm and started squeezing as hard as I could. The look of surprise on Muller's face told me he knew the serum was taking effect.

"I was just making a point, Detective. Now shall we go?"

I let go of his arm and he pointed the Luger at Henry and Hap. "Back up slowly towards the sedan three cars down."

I could see both of them wanted to try for their guns even though one of them would die trying. Don't!" I yelled as Muller placed the barrel next to my head.

"Get in, and remember, I'm a very good shot."

I opened the door and slid in next to Gertrude as Muller slid in next to me. In the front seat were the two men that had been following me.

"I believe you've met, Detective."

"Not those two in the front seat."

"Otto is our driver. Rudolph is your guardian, and you already know Gertrude, and of course, me." he chuckled poking my gunshot shoulder. "Gertrude, see what you can do for his wound until we get to the plane."

"Heir Muller, I don't understand you sometimes. There was no need for you to shoot Larry's family or for that matter Ox. He was just the taxi driver."

"My plan was to kidnap you without anyone knowing. Now that you forced our hand, we'll have to race to the airport before the FBI." Gertrude said removing my suit coat.

"Frau Gertrude, just take care of his wound and let me worry about the FBI and the police. Otto, start driving and head for the airport."

I was surprised Gertrude was so efficient in handling my wound with what little we had to work with.

"There. I think that should hold you until I get to my first aid kit."

"Were you a nurse in the war?"

"Yes. I was a nurse and a surgical assistant on the Western front."

"Then why didn't you become a doctor after everything you learned, when the war was over?"

"Because, when you Americans showed up I had been a nurse since 1914 and a doctor since 1917. In that time, I saw thousands of men, women and children die from lack of medical supplies. Unlike you Americans who had the best of everything, we only had the very basics."

With that said, I leaned back in the seat and kept my mouth shut. I pretended to be asleep and listened as Muller told them what his plan was to get out of the country.

"Heir Muller, we're at the airport."

"Make a turn here, and drive up to the gate. I'll hand the guard this pass." Muller said.

I pretended to be asleep when the car stopped at the gate. I thought about trying to signal the guard until the steel barrel Luger pressed deeply into my ribs.

"Don't try to warn him, Detective. The man has a wife and family, and it would be a shame to make them fatherless."

The bored guard looked at the pass and opened the gate. As the car accelerated Rudolph, headed towards a hanger on the north side of the airport. As we neared the hanger, I sat up and checked the surroundings. The terminal building was lit up as if it were daytime. There were three twin engine DC-1s parked close to the terminal. One was loading passengers and two were discharging theirs.

As we pulled up to the hanger, two men started opening the hanger doors and revealed another DC-1. Unlike the airlines, this plane had no markings of any kind.

"All right, Detective. It's time to take a ride. And I warn you don't try anything that'll get you killed. Cochran and the Fuhrer would be most displeased if their prize guinea pig came home in a box," Muller said using the gun to show me the way.

I was helped up the boarding ramp by the two men accompanying Muller and Gertrude. Unlike Gertrude's gentle  hands, these two roughed me up every chance they got. I tried to walk down the aisle but was pushed instead and put in the nearest seat.

"Thanks dummkoph's, you two just tore open my wound again."

One of them turned and slapped me across the face. He was about to do it again, when Muller grabbed his wrist and broke it. The man screamed and backed away in fright. Muller said something in German and they left the plane.

"I apologize, Detective, for their roughness. These new recruits are so fanatical, they forget sometimes where they are. Would you care for a drink before we take off?"

"I wouldn't mind one or two and by the way, where are we flying to?"

Ignoring me he said something to Gertrude in German and took a seat across from me.

"What do you think of my plane?"

I hadn't had a chance to scope the place out so I might as well. The cabin was a DC-1 with a couple of modifications. Instead of twenty four seats on both sides this one only had six. They were arranged two to a table with two tables on either side. The other two seats were  sofa chairs, I assumed for reading. Behind the tables was a small bar, a galley kitchen, two bunk beds and toilet at the tail. It even had curtains on the windows. Up front was the pilot and copilot cabin. It was closed off from the rest of the plane by a steel door.

"Very nice Carl. Did you design it or did your boss?"

"Gertrude, put two drinks on the table and then check his wound. It seems these Americans can't take a little pain."

Gertrude did as she was told and checked my bleeding wound. "Heir Muller, the bullet needs to come out, or he won't make it to New York."

"Well, if you're that worried about him, why don't you take the bullet out, doctor? I saw you butchers when I was injured, hacking off their legs and arms instead of trying to save them." Muller bellowed. "And what was your excuse? You didn't have time to do surgery because there were so many wounded. Wounded! Half the wounded died of shock or infections."

"They died, Heir Muller, from lack of medicines, that's why! And if I was that bad a doctor, why don't you take the bullet out, it if you dare."

Gertrude slapped him across the face with an ashtray. It must have been heavy, because he didn't get up.

"Detective, I'm going to attempt to remove the bullet in your shoulder. I don't have the right instruments, but I'm willing to try if you are."

# Chapter 38

April 13th 1933
2:18 am Monday

I awoke to the familiar smell of food cooking. At first I thought I was back home in bed until I heard the sounds of engines. A sudden bright flash of lightning followed by a clap of thunder told me I was indeed in an airplane.

"What's going on? Are we going to crash?" I yelled as the plane bounced and shook from the rough weather.

"Take it easy, Detective. We're in a pretty bad thunderstorm but the pilots say everything with the plane is running normal."

"What about the bullet? Did you get it out?"

"Yes. I have it right here," she said showing me the bullet.

"Don't worry, I'm fine too, Detective, except for this lump on my forehead which Gertrude gave me." Muller said poking my wound until I winched.

I sat up on the bed and wished I hadn't. Between the plane bouncing in the rough air and my hangover, I struggled to not to visit the toilet right now. Without anything but whiskey to dull the pain, I had consumed most of their supply. I laid back down while Gertrude and Muller hung on for dear life. About the time I decided to get rid of some alcohol, the plane shuddered and lost power. I could hear alarm buzzers going off in the pilot's cabin when the door opened. The co-pilot stuck his head out and shouted "Right engine is on fire. We may have to make an emergency landing."

This was my first time flying but my insides were telling me the plane was losing altitude. I looked around the cabin to see what I could use to soften the crash. There were two bed mattress, two pillows and blankets to cover our heads with. The pilot's door opened again and he yelled "We're going down. Do the best you can to protect yourselves."

Suddenly the plane starting losing altitude and I started tearing the beds apart. Luckily the bed frames where bolted down. I stuffed the mattress between the legs facing the front of the plane.

I piled the two pillows behind it to cover our faces. That's when I saw Gertrude and Muller hanging on to the table. I stumbled towards them when the plane tipped twenty degrees to starboard. At first I didn't think I would get to them before crashing but suddenly the plane leveled off. Reaching Gertrude, I grabbed her around the chest and dragged her to my bed and pushed her under it. I climbed in behind her and gave her a pillow to cover her face.

Muller must have come out of his trance because he stumbled back to us and tried to pull me out.

"Make your own, damn you!" I yelled, kicking him where it hurt most.

"Get out or I'll shoot you!" Muller fumbled for his gun when the plane hit the ground belly first. I hung on to Gertrude as the plane bounced several times before stopping. The sudden silence seemed unearthly until I heard Muller's voice. It was just my luck he hadn't broken his damn neck in the crash.

I laid there holding Gertrude, unable to see anything until a lightning bolt flashed.

"Gertrude, we need to get out of this plane. "Nein, nein" she whimpered covering her face with her hands.

I tried to get her to move but she refused to budge.

"I'm going to find the exit door, so don't panic."

I felt around and found the legs of the bed. Slowly unwinding myself from Gertrude, I felt my way towards the pilot's cabin until I touched their door. I then moved to the right and felt around for the door handle. I didn't find it because it was on the left side of the plane. Reversing my steps I found the handle and tried to lift it without success. I tried several times using both hands but my right arm was too weak to make any difference.

"Move out of the way, Detective. I've got two good arms and hands," Muller said squeezing past me.

A sudden flash of lightning lit up his face. I could see he must have hit his head on something because blood was streaming down both cheeks.

I heard Carl grunt, and then a thump, as the door open a few inches before stopping. "It's stuck in the mud, damn it," Muller said.

"The nose of the plane must be buried in the dirt. We'll have to try the back exit if we want to get out alive."

As we moved towards the back of the plane, a feeling of dread crept over me. As I neared the middle of the plane, a  flame appeared where the cook top used to be. Its light brightened as it started feeding on its surroundings. Now I could see the interior and the exit door 10' away.

Gertrude screamed at the sight of the flames and raced past me in blinding fright. I tried to stop her, but she plowed through me like an offensive lineman. I started to go back after her when Muller grabbed my arm.

"Forget her. You'll both die in here if you don't."

Muller pulled the exit door leaver and swung the door all the way open with ease. Muller jumped out onto the grassy ground and motioned for me to jump. I could hear Frau Gertrude crying and pounding on the forward door that wouldn't open. "I'm going back to get Gertrude. You can either help or run."  I wasn't six inches from the door when a bullet passed close to me. "I said jump or I'll shoot you where you stand."

"Be my guest. I'm sure the Fuhrer will understand."

I started towards Gertrude but the fire had spread and the heat was more than I could stand. "Alright, Heir Muller, I'm coming out." I jumped to the ground and found Muller nowhere in sight. I ran around the plane to get to the forward door. Lightning still flashed in the distance as the storm moved on. I stumbled on some rocks and scraped my knee as I reached Gertrude's outstretched hand. "Is that you, Detective?"

"Yes. Let go of my hand so I can get this door open."

Another flash of lighting showed me the door was hung up on some rocks and dirt. I started digging with my hands as fast as I could as the light behind her got brighter.

"Oh, please hurry. The fire is spreading and it's getting hard to breathe."

"Give me a minute more and I'll try the door."

I grabbed the door and gave it a pull. It moved about four more inches before it hung up on the pile of dirt it had created.

"How bad is the fire?"

"It's getting pretty bad, William. Maybe I can squeeze out the opening."

**"Let me try"** the serum said taking control

I grabbed the door and pulled it opened another 2,' before I couldn't do any more. My shoulder was bleeding and the pain was so intense, even the serum couldn't stop it from sapping my strength.

Gertrude was about half way out and seemed to be hung up on something. "My suit is hung up on the door handle."

"Then I suggest you take it off before the fire gets to you." A small explosion inside the cabin blew smoke out of the door. It seemed like an eternity until I saw Gertrude slide out the door in her slip. I grabbed her and started running. We didn't get very far because a barbwire fence was blocking our way.

"I think we're far enough away to be safe now, Gertrude."

"What about Carl and the pilots?"

"Carl got out first and ran away. The pilots, I can only assume died on impact." I could just make out Gertrude was shivering as the serum disappeared. I put my good arm around her and we held each other as the plane consumed itself.

As we clung to each other, I noticed the sky becoming lighter. "The sun will be up soon, and then we'll go looking for help. In the meantime, we might as well sit down, because we can't get any wetter than we already are."

# Chapter 39

April 13th 1933
5:08 am Tuesday

I must have closed my eyes because suddenly I felt someone shaking my shoulder. "Are you two from that airo-plane over there that crashed in my field?"

I opened my eyes and saw a man that had to be a hundred by the looks of his skin. He was average height and very thin. His cap was faded red along with his blue shirt, buttoned up to his neck. His blue jean overalls were also faded but his work boots were new.

"Yes, sir. We were on that plane. Might I ask if we could get this woman to your house? She needs some medical attention and could use a drink of water?" I hadn't noticed before but he was carrying a double barreled shotgun.

"You and her got a name?"

"I'm William Barronson, and this is my cousin Gertrude Becker."

"My name is Samuel Hodgekins, and this here woman behind me is Emma, and my youngest son Mark." Sam said, spitting tobacco juice out of his toothless mouth.

"Emma, give this here woman a drink of water and see what you can do to get her dressed. It ain't fittin' for a woman to run around here in her night clothes."

Emma helped Gertrude to get up and wrapped a blanket around her. "I'll take her to the house and fix her up while you decide what to do with him."

By the time Emmy got her to the pickup truck dozens of pickups and the local police were showing up.

"Land sake Samuel, what did I tell you about shootin' at them hawks. Now I got to explain to the law about how you shot down an airplane."

I got to my feet and said, "Sheriff, Sam didn't shoot us down. That storm last night did it."

"And who might you be? And what you doin' with a bullet wound in your shoulder?"

I took out my badge and showed it to him. "I was transporting a man called Carl Muller back to Atlanta to stand trial for murder."

"After the crash, Muller got lose and shot me while escaping. I couldn't go after him because my cousin needed help getting out of the burning plane."

I'll call the sheriff's office in Marion and have them send a car out here to confirm who you say you are."

"I thought you're the sheriff."

"No. Just the constable in these here parts."

I was led to his pickup truck and handcuffed to a ladder in the back. We headed to Sam's farm house to pick up Gertrude. As I rode along the sun came out from behind some clouds and showed me the wonders of nature. The plane had landed in a wide valley somewhere in the tree covered Smokey Mountains. As we pulled up to Sam's farm, I noticed he had two dozen cows in a field and three horses in another. The house and barn and chicken house were all close together.

The handcuffs were removed and I was escorted into his house. "I'm not going to put the cuffs back on if you promise not to cause any trouble."

"I promise, no trouble. I am an officer of the law."

"Then, don't make me regret it.'"

"Sam, you have a beautiful farm here. My dad would've been proud to know you."

"Did he have a farm in your neck of the woods?"

"Yes, not as nice as yours. I grew up on it until the city bought it for expansion."

"That seems to be the way of the world now. More houses and more concrete. Pretty soon there won't be any land left to farm." Sam said rolling his own cigarette.

"Alright, you two. Come to the table. I have some food for y'all to eat and you, mister, go outside and wash up before coming to my table." Emma said.

"Emma, can you help me take off my suit coat?"

"Land sake, mister. That shoulder of yours is a mess. You men don't seem to learn about shootin' each other, do ya." she said, washing the wound clean of mud.

"Ouch! That hurts!"

"It's gonna hurt more if it festers. I've never seen such a poor job of fixin' a wound. Is the bullet still in there?"

"No. Gertrude took it out just before we crashed. What do you mean by that last remark, ma'am?"

Emma put her hands on her hips and looked at me just like my mother did when I did something wrong.

"You men are always either gettin' cut, fallen, bitten, fightin' or shot. If it wasn't for us women mendin' your wounds, I'd have more time for myself."

Emma spent another thirty minutes working on my shoulder before she was satisfied I was going to live. I, on the other hand, wasn't sure. "Alright now. You're fit to sit at my table now."

I thanked her and started for the breakfast table when I heard a car pull up.

"Well. I see you're still alive, Agent Barronson, ma'am," the Sheriff said tipping his hat to Gertrude and Sam's wife. "I see by your wound you had a run in with this Carl Muller."

"How did you know about that?"

"Your boss in Washington told me about this Muller and the lady over there. He says for me to tell you to get back to Atlanta and leave Muller to us. He has agents on the way here to help."

"What about Miss Becker?"

"She's to return to Atlanta with you, where my agents will then arrest her."

I looked at Gertrude to see if I was going to have a problem, but from the look in her eyes, she wasn't going to be any problem. In fact, I'd bet ten to one she would have no problem in telling Washington everything she knew about Muller. As we were about to leave, I thanked Samuel and Emma for all their help and promised I'd let them know about the removal of the wrecked plane. Sam said "You leave that plane right where it is. That plane will make me more money as an attraction than planting."

"He's right, you know, Agent Barronson. People will come from miles around just to see it." the Sheriff said. "Now let's get you two to that flat piece of land about a mile down the road. Your Boss is having a plane land there to pick you three up."

# Chapter 40

April 14th 1933
2:18 pm Wednesday

We landed at the Atlanta airport and taxied up to Eastern Air Transport Building to deplane. While in flight, Gertrude and I spoke about Muller and her relationship to him.

"Gertrude, you know that you're in serious trouble with the US Government?"

"Yes, I realize that. I'm hoping to get a better deal by telling them everything I know. Thank you for saving my life, by the way. It seems my comrade was too busy running away to help me."

"I'd like to ask what made you join this Nazi party? It seems a very cruel and uncaring party towards its followers."

"Their idea to rebuild a Germany for Germans made us feel good inside. You see, your form of government was corrupted by money and communism was for the Russians. So when the Nazi party said they were for Germany, we all joined."

"So how long have you been a member?"

"Three years, I joined right after college."

The plane stopped and we walked down the boarding ramp together. At the bottom of the stairs were two policeman and two agents. Gertrude went with the agents and the police took me to Grady Hospital once again. When I awoke from the shot I was given, I found Margaret was asleep in a bed next to me. Grace was pacing back and forth, mumbling to herself.

"Grace, what are you saying?"

"Bill, You're awake! Margaret, he's awake! Look he's awake!"

"Grace, let her sleep. She's probably been up all night."

"Oh damn, I forgot they gave her a sleeping pill to calm her down. I can tell you she was so upset, I thought she'd have the baby right here. I know it's not time yet, but you never know, Bill, about these things and..."

"Nurse! Nurse! I need help. This woman is talking my ear off. Can you please put her to sleep as well?" I asked, as the nurse walked into the room.

"Detective, only the doctors can do that. What I can do is to take Grace back to the waiting room, where the rest of them are."

"No! please, no! I'll promise not to say another word, well maybe four of five. Besides, I'm pregnant and due anytime now myself and you wouldn't..."

"Out!" the nurse said, pointing at the door. "The waiting room is just down the hall.

"No! I won't go!"

"Grace! Go sit down before you have your baby right here. We'll talk later after I take another nap."

With Grace out of the picture, Director Grayson entered the room. He turned off the lights closed the blinds and put a do not disturb sign on the door. He then went to Margaret's bed and checked her chart.

"Director. What are you doing here?"

"I wanted to see for myself how bad your wound was."

"With the drugs I'm on, I could go ten rounds in a boxing ring."

Grayson moved a chair next to me and sat down. "I think we and, I mean you, have had enough of this German."

"I can agree on that but what about his threat? You know he killed Hap's son yesterday."

"I know. So here's the plan. I want you to follow it now that Gertrude has talked."

"What has she told you?"

"From what she has told us, Carl Muller is here not only for you. She mentioned his secondary plan was to set up a Nazi recruiting cell in this area. It seems that's how he met Robert Cochran along with Bonnie Graves while working at the zoo. She didn't know anyone else he had recruited  because she states she's only been in the states for three days."

"Do you think you can trust her?"

"I believe we have turned her to be a double agent for us. For this cooperation, Gertrude would be given asylum to live in the USA.

# Chapter 41

April 15th 1933
10:30 am Thursday

I was discharged from the hospital with the doctor's orders to stay at home for two weeks before trying to use that arm. I was in a wheelchair being pushed by Margaret as we exited the elevator. Every other time, I had always exited out the backdoor to avoid the press.

This time, I was going out the front door to the waiting herd of reporters. As I neared the glass double doors, flash bulbs went off by the dozens, blinding me. Anger arose in me because this was all Grayson's idea and I was too stupid to say no. As we neared the doors, the reporters started yelling and pounding on the glass to get my attention. I now knew how the Christians must have felt being led into the arena to fight the lions.

"Detective Barronson, tell us how you feel. Who shot you? Why did he shoot the taxi driver? Is there a women involved? Why didn't you shoot back?"

"Enough!!! I intend to give you a statement"

As I looked at the crowd of reporters, I spotted Gertrude and the two men who had driven us to the airport. I also spotted the five FBI agents mixed in with the reporters that were keeping an eye on her as well.

Clearing my throat I stood up using Margaret as a crutch for better effect.

"Gentlemen of the press. I'm here today to ask for your help in catching the man that killed Hap's son and shot me for not following his orders. His name is Carl Muller. He is one of two men wanted for the Wishing Well Murders. I had tracked him and his partner Robert Cochran, the Atlanta Zoo's Curator, who has since fled the country. In a bunker on the zoo's grounds, he and Muller were creating a serum made from cobra and human brain cells. Between them they are responsible for murdering the following people: Caroline Hadley and her daughter Linda; Bonnie Graves, a zoo employee; Lish Jones, a grounds keeper; Doug Miller, a reporter; Larry Langford and his wife, my neighbors; my Doctor Charles Friederick, and now Hap's son, Ox, my taxi driver.

"As far as we know, Robert Cochran has fled the country and is hiding in Germany. Carl Muller is here in the Atlanta area to take me back to Germany. The reason is that I was injected with the serum, and to my knowledge, I'm the only person who hasn't died. This makes me Cochran's Frankenstein monster, and he wants his lab rat back to experiment on.

A $10,000 reward is offered for the where abouts of Muller and his capture. My last known contact with him was in Virginia, near the Tennessee border."

The reporters exploded with more questions so fast I couldn't make out what they were asking. Captain Wade, my city boss, stepped in and started answering questions. I kept my eye on Gertrude with the feather in her hat and pointed to the FBI the two men she was working with. I think she figured out I had seen her and her two friends. To make her look good, I shouted and pointed. "Stop that woman in the blue hat, she's one of them."

One thing you can count on in this country of ours is that reporters smelling a story will react like a pack of wolves.

Instantly the reporters surrounded the woman, taking pictures, asking questions and pulling at her clothes to get attention. If it hadn't been for the police and the FBI surrounding them, I don't think she would have made it.

Margaret wheeled me back into the hospital lobby and we headed for the back exit. As we reached the elevators, Grayson joined us. Not wanting the elevator operator in on our conversation, we talked about the weather and how my arm was doing.

Once the elevator doors closed and headed for the first floor, we started to talk.

"That was a fine speech you made out there, Bill. By this afternoon's papers, Muller will be the most wanted man in America. By the way who's going to cough up the $10,000 reward money?"

"I thought being an agent. Uncle Sam might loan it to me."

"Loan it? At what interest rate should your uncle charge you?"

"Whatever he wants, because I don't intend to pay it back."

"Before we part company, why did you expose Gertrude to the press?"

"I wanted to make sure the two agents with her believed she hadn't talked to me."

"That makes good sense. You two did spend some time together. Well, I'm sure we'll be seeing each other again. Margaret, take care of him and make him rest."

"Sir. That's like telling a bird not to fly."

When Grayson walked away, I got out of the wheel chair and walked towards the exit. Reaching the exit door Margaret and I found several orderlies smoking outside. They must not have been on break, because when I opened the door they all dropped their cigarettes and went back inside.

"William this is probably a dumb question. Who are you working for?"

"As of now, I'm back on the Atlanta police force."

I spotted Grayson getting into his car and he and his driver pulled out of the parking lot.

"Will you look at that," Margaret said. "At least he could have offered us a ride. I'll go back inside and I'll call for a taxi."

"No need Margaret. I think that's Hap pulling in with my car. Where is Grace? She's going to need a ride home as well."

"Grace went home because she said she didn't feel well."

"Sorry to be late, Captain. I had to make arrangements for my son."

"That's okay. Let's head home so I can change suits. This one has a hole in it which I hoped Wang or his brother can repair."

## Chapter 42

April 15th 1933
11:43 am Thursday

Hap pulled up in front of the house and everyone ran out to see me. They had already heard my plea for help and the response was overwhelming.

I walked into the house and stopped dead in my tracks. Nancy stood at the foot of the stairs wearing an outfit that made her look eighteen.

"Well, who let you out of jail?"

"I did." Mildred spoke up glaring at me.

"Now why would you do that. Nancy and Muller tried to murder you, Mildred. She even admitted wanting to rob you for the money in your safe."

"I know all about the safe. I caught her the second day she was here trying to open it. As for the break in, I know it wasn't her. They weren't after me, they were after her. It seems her father and mother were killed because her father testified against the local mob."

I looked at Mildred trying to decide if this was another of Nancy's lies or was Mildred still wanting to protect her as if she was her own. I looked at Nancy standing there looking like an innocent angel and decided not to push this any farther. Mildred's mind was made up about Nancy and she wouldn't change her mind until she was caught red handed.

"Alright Mildred, I'll forgive the past indiscretions, but I better not find her loafing on the bed while everyone else is pulling their weight."

I walked past Nancy without saying a word and went up to our room to change my suit. Struggling to get my suit coat off with one hand was quite a task. In the movies, a gunshot like mine didn't slow them down a bit. In real life it hurt like hell even to move it, let alone pull a gun and shoot.

"Here, let me help you with that coat. Now, drop your pants while I get one of your three remaining suits out."

"Any one will do except the blue one. It's the last one your father bought for me and I can't afford another $800 to replace it."

"There now," Margaret said, straightening my tie.

"Except for the sling holding your right arm, no one would ever know you were shot."

I sat down on the bed and said, "I want you to keep this a secret just between us." I reached into my inside pocket of my old suit and brought out the two Western Union telegrams. I handed them to Margaret and waited for her to read them.

"Margaret. I need you to keep an eye on Nancy. I believe she's helping Muller to break into Mildred's room. I found two sets of foot prints outside Mildred's window. One set a male and the other set a woman. This story about her parents being murdered for testifying against the mob doesn't hold water! Every cop within fifty miles would have known about it and her."

"William. I think you're trying to make a case against Nancy that isn't justified. You're assuming everything you see, no matter what, has to be hers. Did you find a shoe that fit the print?  I'll admit this girl isn't as pure as she pretends, but a murderer? No! No. I won't help you hang her until you show me proof, not suppositions."

I took the telegrams back from Margaret and jammed them in my pocket. I wanted to argue this more because I knew I was right about her. Hell, it's my job for Christ sake. I've broken cases with less evidence than this, I said to myself.

"Okay Margaret. Maybe I've been a little hard on her but!"

"No buts. Now go to work. I have a headache and would like to lie down."

I closed the door behind me and headed down the stairs. As I reached the dining room, I heard Mildred and Nancy giggling and talking in the kitchen. I started to listen in but if I got caught, I'd alienate everybody. So pretending I didn't hear them talking I yelled, "I'll see you tonight Mildred for supper. Do I need to pick anything up?" I didn't get an answer so I slammed the door and decided Hap and I would eat out tonight and show them I could be stubborn as well.

"Mildred, what do you think that was all about?" Nancy said with a smile look on her face.

# Chapter 43

April 15th 1933
2:23 pm Thursday

I got in the police car and said, "Hap, head for the station. We have some work to do." In all the excitement I had forgotten about the arsonist and the photos.

"Hap, why don't you take some time off."

"I don't need or want any time off, Captain. All I want is to find Muller and make him pay as the good book says. An eye for an eye and a tooth for a tooth."

"I completely understand, Hap. I would do the same thing, but don't let it eat away at your insides as I did."

"Captain, just make sure you keep me informed about his whereabouts. I have a few army buddies that would be willing to make him disappear for good."

As Hap pulled into the parking lot, I was amazed at all the police moving about, directing traffic.

"Did you see the line of people waiting to get into the building? What do you think they want?" Hap asked, parking.

"I believe each one of them knows where Muller is and thinks they'll get the reward."

Not wanting to start a riot now that everybody knows who I am, I told Hap to head to the FBI Building instead. If I was right, Gertrude was now firmly back in Mullers good graces.

"Calling Car 54."

"Go ahead, over"

"The Captain and the Chief want to see you in the Captain's office as soon as possible, over"

"I'm about to meet with Director Grayson at the FBI building, over.

"I'll pass the word along Bill, but I'm sure they won't be happy about it. out"

Hap parked on a side street and I motioned for him to come with me. If we were to get Muller, I wanted neither Hap or me to go after him alone. As we walked into the building, two agents met us. I could see each was packing a weapon.

"We want to see Director Grayson."

"He's busy. You can leave a message at the desk. If he wants to see you, he'll call down. Otherwise, I'll escort you out of the building."

"Agents. I'm Detective Barronson, the man Muller is after. I need to speak to Grayson about our case."

"Detective Barronson, I thought you'd be home recuperating from the gunshot wound." Agent Colton said.

"Can you tell these two agents it's okay for me to pass?"

Colton nodded to the agents and we walked towards the elevators, discussing Mullers possible capture. "With all the media coverage on him, we estimate he'll be caught or killed within 24 hours. I wouldn't worry about him anymore." Colton said, as we stepped into the elevator.

When the elevator doors opened, Director Grayson was standing in front of us.

"Well, I didn't know you were coming Detective, Hap.

I was just about to head down stairs to discuss Muller."

"I'm sorry, Director. I should have called you."

"No problem. Let's go to my office instead."

Hap and I took a seat as Grayson ordered to have coffee brought in. "Now, Bill what is on your mind." Grayson said as we accepted the coffee.

I took a deep breath before wondering if I was doing the right thing. "I'm here because... I believe I've put you and the FBI in a compromising position." I said lighting a cigarette to calm my nerves.

"Alright." Grayson said knowing what was coming next.

"Are you talking about the speech you made today?"

"Yes, when Hap and I got to the station, there were hundreds of people lined up I'm sure with information as to the where abouts of Muller."

"I see. Then what exactly do you think I can do?"

"I want you to put out a statement to the press that there's no $10,000 reward. I'll also talk to the news media and give them a statement that I wasn't in my right mind due to the gunshot wound."

"Well that is already in the works Bill. It seems Mr. Hoover wasn't too pleased with your first statement either. Hoover did put a reward out for information on the capture or whereabouts of Carl Muller though."

"And what would the amount be?"

"$500 and if I were you, I'd give Mr. Hoover a call to explain yourself. As for your police department, I'd do the same thing if you still have a job."

I used a phone in another empty office to call Mr. Hoover. It was bad enough with all of them in Grayson's office as I apologized. I sure didn't want them to see me grovel even more than I did with them.

It took some fancy explaining to Mr. Hoover, but when I hung up, things were back to normal between us. I called the Chief of Police office, but found he was in the Captain's office waiting for me. I was about to hang up when a call came in for me. "Hello?"

"Bill, this is your Captain calling. Where the hell are you?"

"I was just leaving Director Grayson's office."

"What were you doing there? Having tea, while we are being overrun with people?"

"No, Captain, I was on the phone with Mr. Hoover." There was dead silence for a few seconds before he came back on the line. "The Chief wants to talk to you."

"Detective Barronson, you have left us in quite a mess here with your statement to the press."

"I know that, Sir. I was about to call and have the reward canceled with my apology."

"That's good to hear Bill, because I have already done that for you. Now I think it would be best for you to take a few days off to let things cool down. Besides, I hear you were wounded in the shoulder."

"Yes Chief, several times."

Hap and I left the FBI building and for the first time in days, I felt things were getting under control. As we drove back towards home, a spring shower started washing the Midwest dust off our streets. As the rain blew in the car window, it reminded me how Margaret had always loved the smell. I could always find her on the front porch rocking every time it rained.

"Well Hap, if the FBI gets their man tomorrow, all we'll have left to do is catch the arsonist that likes to set fires." I started rubbing my forehead to relax the pain behind my eyes when Hap called out.

"Captain. Wake up. We're almost home."

I opened my eyes and looked around trying to get my bearings. "Where are we?" I said, trying to clear my head.

"I said we're almost home, and are we going to call it a night?"

"I believe so, Hap. Why?" I said rubbing my forehead.

"I need to gas her up if we're going any distance?"

"No. You can gas up in the morning. All I want to do is to take two aspirins for this damn headache." Hap parked in Larry's driveway and we rolled up the windows. The rain was still coming down as we walked towards the house. As each rain droplet hit my hat, the pain it was causing started to diminished. By the time I reached Mildred's yard, the pain was gone.

"William, come on now. You're getting all wet," Margaret said, holding an umbrella over her head.

"You don't need that umbrella," I said throwing it away.

As the rain increased, I put my arms around Margret's growing waist and started dancing."

"William! I don't understand you sometimes." she said smiling at me. "I haven't danced in the rain since I was ten."

"I don't know if you two have lost your marbles. Dancing in the rain, you'll catch the death of cold." Mildred said from the open screen door.

"Should we go in, Margaret?"

"No, not yet. Let's keep dancing."

"Didn't you two hear me! Dinner is almost ready, and I don't allow soaking wet children to ruin my furniture," Mildred said, stepping out onto the porch.

"We'll be in shortly, Mother." I said as we continued to dance is the rain.

I saw Mildred shaking her head in wonder as she opened the screen door. On my next turn, Mildred was smiling at us. I believe if she had a beau, Mildred would be out here dancing as well.

"Mildred. Why don't you come out here and join us?"

"I'll do no such thing. Why, if the neighbors saw me dancing in the rain, I'd be sent to Milledgeville."

"How about a dance with me." Hap said offering his arm.

"Don't be such an old fool, Hap. We're both too old for that kind of nonsense." Mildred said getting a good look at Hap. "You're as wet as those two dancing in the rain, and as I just said, no dinner until you're dry, old man. Margaret opened the screen door and pointed at Hap to go to his room. "Alright you two. I think the neighbors have gotten an eye full, so if you're not at the table in ten minutes, it's no supper for you."

Margaret and I both heard the wooden front door slam shut. "Well, I guess we better go in and change now that we have had our shower." I changed out of my wet clothes and into a bathrobe. Margaret did the same except she had a towel wrapped around her wet hair. "Do you think we'll make it to the table before the ten minutes are up?"

"We'll make it on time even if I have to carry you. So let's go." When we entered the dining room, everyone smiled and blushed at the same time except Grace.

"Did you two have a nice time dancing in the rain?" Grace said, looking at her husband as if he should do something romantic like that.

"Mildred, we made it with a minute to spare." I waited for a reply, but didn't get one until she walked into the room.

"Well, aren't you two a pair." she said looking at both of us. "Are we having a pajama party?" she said, setting the food on the table away from Hap.

"Mildred, you said we had to be at the dinner table in ten minutes or no supper. You didn't state what type of clothes, and we did make it here before the time was up."

I looked around the table and saw everybody with their heads bowed. I, on the other hand, looked Mildred straight in the eyes, waiting for her reply.

"Well, seeing this is the first time you two disobeyed me, I'll let it slide. Now go put some clothes on while I make sure there will be enough food left." she said, glaring at Hap.

"Yes ma'am."

It didn't take but five minutes for the two of us to get dressed. As we sat down and looked around the table I felt I had a family again. Hap was eating and talking, Henry was doing the same. Grace and Lenard weren't talking, which meant she was mad at him again. Nancy sat quietly nibbling while watching and listening as each person spoke. Her eyes darted to that person speaking and stayed there until they were done. I could see her mind as a Dictaphone machine recording everything everyone said.

"Nancy! What have you been up to?" I shouted, deliberately breaking her concentration.

"Oh!" she said dropping her fork in surprise. "I.. ah didn't do much, sir." she said, turning bright red.

"Nancy helped me a lot today, Bill. We went to the market and did..." Nancy cut in and quickly said. "We looked at... ah.. clothes and stuff.. and then went to lunch. It was so much fun wasn't it, Mildred. I hadn't done anything like that in forever."

"Bill, stop the third degree. I don't want any more of your interfering. I'm quite old enough to handle any problems I think need addressing with Nancy."

I nodded my head yes and glanced over at Nancy. She still had that little girl look on her face except for the slight wicked smile. When Nancy saw me watching, she gave me a quick wink and a bigger smile that said got you again.

Not wanting to cause anymore discomfort at the table, I excused myself and went into the parlor. Shortly after  taking a seat where I could look out the window, Margaret joined me.

"William. I don't understand why you get so upset with Nancy. She's just a kid."

"I don't know, Margaret. There's something about her I just don't like." As I looked out the window at the rain, a thought crossed my mind. I got up and went back into the dining room. "Hap. I need to talk to you now."

"Can't it wait till I'm done eating."

"Alright. But make it quick. I'll be on the porch." I looked at Nancy and could see the worried look on her face.

I gave her a slight smile and a wink, just to make sure she knew I had figured her out.

I headed for the porch to wait for Hap when Margaret said, "I'll come and sit with you."

"No, dear! I have police business to talk over with Hap." I could see she was putting two and two together when Nancy walked by without speaking.

"Okay, Captain. What's so important?"

I pointed to the far end of the porch and headed in that direction. "Hap. I think I know who the arsonists is." I whispered, looking around to see if anyone was listening.

Hap gave me an unbelievable look. "Who might that be?"

"Nancy."

"Nancy?"

"Quiet, damn you. I don't want her to know I know she's been setting the fires."

"How did you come up with that dumb idea?"

"When did these fires start? I said, waiting for his answer. "Come on Hap, when she got to town, right?"  Hap still didn't answer, but I could see the wheels turning.

"How are we going to prove she's the one?" Hap asked, still not sure he believed me.

"It shouldn't be that hard now that I know who to go after."

"Captain, I think you're on the wrong track on this. I don't see how she could have gotten around town without Mildred knowing."

"That may be, but I'm positive she's up to no good." I thought about Bonnie Graves and how I had been duped into thinking she had nothing to do with Muller or Cochran at the zoo. "Hap, Muller killed Bonnie Graves because of our dating relationship. If Nancy is aligned with Muller, I don't want a repeat performance from Nancy."

"I see your point now, Captain." Hap said, seeing Nancy peeking out the window at him.

# Chapter 44

April 16th 1933
6:26 am Friday

The alarm clock went off and for once, I didn't want to throw it out the window. I got out of bed and immediately Margaret wrapped herself up in the covers. I showered and shaved and did what nature had required. "Alright, you handsome devil." I said looking in the mirror. "It's time for you to get dressed." I gave myself a wink and went back into the bedroom. I started to get dressed when I noticed Margaret was sleeping in the middle of the bed, snoring like a drunken sailor.

I smiled, and shook my head in disbelief. If this was going to be the norm, then I needed to see if they make larger beds than a double. I looked at the size of the room and figured it would hold a double double or a triple double if they made such an animal. I then wondered how Lenard slept on his double bed. Grace was farther along than Margaret, and if she was as restless as her sister, then I felt sorry for him as well.

I finished dressing and was about to leave when I spotted a folder on the dresser. I opened it, and found Margaret's hand written notes about the co-op I had asked her to draw up.

As I skimmed it, It looked professional from a non-lawyer's point of view. I made a mental note to discuss this with her later today.

I went downstairs and found Hap busily eating for two along with Grace, Lenard and Henry. I grabbed a cup of coffee and told Hap I'd be outside. At this time of the morning, the air was cool and the humidity was low. I sat down in a rocker, and looked out at the neighborhood. Several lawns hadn't been cut and a number of neighbors were missing. It then occurred to me there were several empty parking spaces along the street as well. Puzzled, I walked back into the dining room and asked Grace. "Have several of our neighbors moved out?"

"Yes, the Jones, the Adams, the Bowens and I believe the Masons will be leaving tomorrow. Why?"

"Is this because of what happened to Larry's family?"

"No. It's because the bank has foreclosed on them. It seems most of the fathers have to go West to look for work'"

"West! What's out west but desert?"

"I don't know, Bill. All I know is it has to do with water."

I refilled my coffee cup and went back outside to mull over what Grace had told me. I hated to hear about our neighbors' foreclosures, but it might be a good opportunity for me to buy one. Before Larry's death he had wanted me to buy his house. I had talked to Margaret about building a new house on Larry's property. But with foreclosures popping up on our street, I might be able to buy one of them. I was about to get another cup of coffee when I heard the faint sounds of sirens wailing in the direction of downtown. I ran out into the street and could just make out black smoke in the distance. I ran back into the house and yelled. "Hap! We have to go. It sounds like we have another fire."

We raced to the car and Hap started the engine when the short wave radio blared into life. "I need cars 26, 18 and 44 to do crowd control at Pryor and Forsyth Streets. Has anyone seen or heard from Car 54?"

"Car 54 to dispatch. What's the emergency, over"

"The Winecoff Hotel is ablaze, Bill. There's been a number of casualties already and a number of people trapped on the upper floors, over"

"We'll head that way, out." As we headed in that direction, I noticed Hap was very quiet. "Hap. Have you made arrangements for your son?"

"Yes, it didn't take but a couple of hours. Why do you want to know?"

"I just wondered. You seem quiet today and I thought it might have something to do with his burial. Are you going to have a service? I'm sure Mildred would be more than happy to help you with it?"

"No service, Bill. I'm actually a very private man. That's why I joke around so much. It's my defense against a world that scares me to death.

So no, no service or wake please. I just want me and my son is all." I could see the sadness in Hap's stature as we pressed on towards the fire and the deaths it had incurred. As we got close I could see it resembled the McKenzie fire in many ways. The first two floors weren't on fire. The third and fourth were fully involved and pouring smoke and flames out of every window. I spotted three people hanging out the fifth floor window waving for someone to help them. Unlike the McKenzie building, this hotel sat on the point of a triangle where the two streets met. This section of town had been developed in the 1890's with 4 and 6 story buildings. The Winecoff Hotel had been constructed in 1905 and was 12 stories tall with a parking lot behind it. That parking lot meant there was no way for to reach them from another building.

"Can you save them?" Hap asked, pulling into an alley to park."

**"No, I can't help either. I've spent too much energy on healing you and your shoulder."**

"No, Hap, I'm just a normal man today. Besides, there's no building close enough to reach them."

We raced down the street, pushing our way through the onlookers, until we reached the police line. "Come through Detectives. I was told you were on your way here."

We got to within a 100' of the fire trucks, before being stopped. In the time it took for us to get there, the trapped women had moved to the 7th floor window.

I wanted to look away, knowing they would either jump or burn to death on the 12th floor rooftop. Things looked hopeless as more and more smoke poured out their window as the flames grew in strength on the fifth. "Please God, help them." Hap said, with tears building in his eyes.

Evidently, he must have heard Hap's plea, because suddenly the top three floors collapsed onto the second floor. Smoke and burning cinders blew out the windows scattering them on the firemen below. It happened so quickly it must have created a vacuum that sucked most of the flames out.

Fire Chief Anderson immediately directed five ground firemen to direct their water into the second floor windows. With the heat and smoke reduced, an unnoticed ladder truck backed up close to the building. It raised its ladder to the sixth floor and started pouring water directly into the window below the trapped people.

"Try to come down the back stairs one at a time and walk slowly towards this window!" I heard a fireman yell.

A minute later the first woman appeared soaking wet at the adjacent window. Another ladder truck had also extended its latter just a foot below her window. "Look Hap, the Fire Chief is running up the ladder as if he were a kid."

I wondered why he didn't send his men up there? "Isn't the Chief a little old to be doing that?" Hap said, looking at me strangely.

"I guess not, Hap, look!" We watched as Mitch reached the 6th floor just under the 7th floor window. Without hesitation Mitch grabbed the woman around her waist and threw her over his shoulder. She must have fainted because his next trick was to slide down the ladder. Mitch did this four more times in less than 20 minutes. As he reached the ground with the last person, the crowd people started applauding. Reporters broke through the police and started snapping pictures.

"Captain, I guess you have some competition now." Hap said, looking at me.

With the fire now mostly out and the people saved, the onlookers started melting away along with the reporters.

"Hap, go ahead and bring the car up now that there's a place to park. In another hour the last onlookers will be gone along with most of the fire trucks." I wanted to speak to Mitch about his superhuman exploits. I started walking over hoses being deflated and through puddles of water until I spotted him. He was talking to the FBI arson investigators and two men that had to be insurance agents.

"Mitch, I know it's early, but do you think this fire is linked with the others?"

"It's possible Detective, but we'll know more when we can get inside." Mitch said, looking at me strangely.

# Chapter 45

April 16<sup>th</sup> 1933
11:46 am Friday

I could see by the look on Mitch's face, he needed to rest. "Gentlemen, it's lunch time and from what I can see, Mitch could use some downtime as well."

About that time Hap walked up. "Hap is there a diner close by?"

"Yes...ah...Bill. Two blocks down on your left. It's a bar but he also serves food."

"Let me go to my car first. I need to put on some dry clothes." Mitch said, walking away.

"Hap. Wait for Mitch while I take them to?"

"Patrick's Bar and Grill."

I found the place with no trouble. Hap, being a taxi driver, knew more about Atlanta than I ever would. I opened the door and walked in behind them. To my surprise, the place was bigger than it look. "Gentlemen, welcome," the bartender said from behind the bar.

"We would like a table for seven please." At the mention of seven customers, his eyes like up with delight. "Right this way. He led us through a door and into a back room.

"This is where I put large parties. That way I don't lose the regular customers that only have an hour for lunch." He sat us at a table away from the entrance. "I'm sure you need privacy to discuss your business. I can put up a false wall if you need more?"

"No, this should be fine, and there will be two more joining us."

"Very good Sir. I'll keep an eye out for them. Shall I send a waitress back?"

"Just coffee for now will do."

Once he was gone the agents said, "I believe this place use to be a speakeasy among other things."

We ordered and discussed each fire and their relation to each other. "Well, gentlemen, it seems we all agree that someone or ones are setting these fires. We all seem to agree he or they are pyromaniacs.

"If this is the case, then he or they won't stop until they are caught or killed in one of their own fires." the agents said.

"I've never heard that word before. Isn't he just a fire bug?" I asked, writing that name down to look up later.

"No. We consider a fire bug likes to set small fires and likes to watch them burn. Usually it's kids fascinated by it until they get burned.  A pyromaniac sets fires because he has something mentally wrong inside him that demands it. Sort of like an alcoholic, or a smoker that has that other self-nagging him until it gets what it wants."

"If that's the case, then we need to alert the public so they can be on the lookout."

"That's probably your best bet for now, Detective. It's going to take a lot of eyes looking for them before you can catch him." The FBI arson agent said.

"What about the Fire Insurance gentlemen?"

"As of today there have been two belonging to the same company. This fire, I'm happy to say, was not insured. So who ever owns this property will have to pay the full cost."

"What about you, Mitch? Do you have any thought on who the arsonists might be.

"In my time as Chief, I haven't ever seen this many fires set alike. It's possible someone has come here from another city like Chicago, where, pardon my pun, it got too hot for him."

"We'll check on that once we get back to Washington, Bill."

"You sound as if your leaving us?"

"I'm afraid so, Detective. We leave in the morning."

"Leaving? No one told me that! Let's go Hap, I have an FBI Director to chew on."

Hap drove straight to the FBI building as I thought about what I'd say to Grayson. "You know, Hap, it seems like every time we have a plan of action, it gets changed without telling us." Instead of parking on the street, Hap headed for the private parking lot under the building. Showing my credentials to the guard, Hap park next to the elevators.

I was about to press the elevator call button when the doors opened.

"I hear you're looking for me, Detective?" Grayson said.

"Yes, Sir, I am. I want to know why you're pulling both arson investigators off the job?"

"Why don't we go to my office and discuss this in private. I have some wonderful new coffee from Java..."

"I don't care if it came from Mars, and I'm not going anywhere until I get an answer."

"Do you need any assistance Director?" Two guards asked walking up behind us.

"I don't believe so, Mike, but why don't you stay close just in case. Now, Detective, I suggest we go to my office where you can calm down and discuss this." Grayson said in a stern voice.

I looked into Grayson's eyes and saw this was the last request he was going to offer me. Taking a deep breath to relax, I nodded okay. I took out a cigarette and offered one to both Grayson and Hap.

Hap took one gladly but Grayson refused. When the elevator door opened, we followed Grayson to his office.

"Now, Bill. Before you go off half-cocked, I want you to know that Director Hoover has need of these men in other cities. Now would you two like a cup of this excellent coffee?"

Again seeing it would be a wise choice to do so, I accepted his explanation and coffee. When the coffee was brought in, I took a sip and felt as if I had gone to heaven.

"I see you like the coffee, Bill. How about you, Hap?"

"It's amazing! Where can I buy some?"

"It's not sold in the USA just yet. If you'd like, I'll have a pound sent to you."

"That would be great, sir. How much would it cost?" Hap said, pouring another one.

"Well, take it as a gift. The cost to buy a pound and ship it to you runs about five dollars a pound. How many would you like?"

"None, thank you. I'll stick to 40 cents a pound.

"Director, can we get back to my problem?" I said pouring another cup as well.

"Now that everybody is relaxed, tell me what is bothering you, Bill"

"It seems every time we put a plan of action together, it get changed without us knowing it."

"In that note, Bill, I don't get informed of what you're doing or have done until it's already done. Like your $10,000 reward. Do you know how much trouble that caused me."

"So Detective, it seems we both agree we have a communication problem. So you tell me and I'll tell you before either one of us puts it into action."

"Yes, sir. I'll make sure we talk at least once a day."

"Excellent then, once a day," Grayson said, standing up.

"Bill do you realize I haven't pulled your agent status, and for you, Hap, I believe you need to be one as well."

"An FBI agent? Me! Really!"

"It's not permanent, Hap, but I can see the two of you work very well together, and by God, he needs a partner to keep him in line."

"An agent? Will I get paid?"

"Would $3.00 a day work for you?"

"Yes Director! That would be excellent."

"Good. I'll call payroll and get you signed up. Now agents, I have other matters to attend to."

# Chapter 46

April 16th 1933
1:56 pm Friday

We left the building and headed for the police station after Hap filled out his paperwork. "Hap, I need to check in with the Captain seeing it has been two days since doing so." As we pulled into the parking lot, we found people still in line wanting to tell us where Muller was hiding.

Not wanting to attract attention, we headed for the back entrance.

This entrance led directly to the locker room, break room and holding cells. Taking the back steps up, it occurred to me we had all the photographs downstairs that we had gone through from the newspaper.

"Hap, pull up to the back door. I'll get some help to load up the boxes and we'll take them back to the newspaper."

"When I'm done with the Captain, I'll meet you downstairs."

I went up the back stairs so as not to get waylaid by the public or the policemen interviewing them. I reached the third floor and opened the door. I expected the detectives to give me hell, for offering such a large reward. To my surprise I found the room empty. Feeling they would return any second I rushed over to the Captain's door and knocked. "Come in!" the Captain growled.

I opened the door and found the Captain unshaven and drinking J&B scotch. "Well, look what the cat has dragged in. My long lost Detective that has caused me all this trouble."

"Captain I'm sorry about that. I was sure the place would be empty now that the reward has been canceled."

"Oh! You mean the winos, hobos, and hundreds of out of work families from three states! Is that what you're talking about, ex Detective!"

"Captain, didn't the Chief tell you he would straighten this out with you?"

"I believe the Chief has been tied up with the Mayor, and Governor after he talked to you."

"Give me five minutes and I'll end this, Captain." I left his office and walked down the front stairs until I reached the lobby. When they saw me everybody pushed past the police to reach the stairs. "Good people of Atlanta!" I screamed as loud as I could. "Carl Muller has been found dead in the Virginia woods. He died in the plane crash along with the pilot and co-pilot. So please leave the building as the reward has been canceled."

To my surprise there wasn't an uproar. People just turned around and slowly exited the building. "Sorry, guys, for all the trouble I've caused." I went back upstairs and entered the Captains office without knocking. "Well, Captain, it's done. I'll clean out my locker.."

The Captain's phone rang several times before he answered it. Whoever was talking on the other end didn't let the Captain say a word. After five minutes the Captain hung up and glared at me. "I should kick you off the force, Barronson! I should run you out of town on a rail! But…! I.. can't! So you and that hack taxi driver get out of my sight!"

I left his office and found a number of detectives had already returned to their desks. I started to say I was sorry, but they all turned their backs to me. Not wanting to push the issue, I went down the back stairs and walked outside to meet Hap. "Captain, what happened in there. You're white as a sheet." When I didn't reply, Hap asked again. "This has something to do with your speech this morning? Is that why all the people are leaving?"

"Yes, and so are we." By the time we pulled out of the lot, there were less that ten people waiting in line. "They must be the stubborn ones." Hap said, pulling out into traffic. "I guess so, Hap, but for now let's concentrate on getting to the newspaper."

"Detective Barronson. What can I help you with today?" The Chief editor asked.

"I want to see more of the films on the fires. I'm hoping to spot the arsonist watching his creation."

"Well you're in luck, I have a man that can run them for you. Just follow me to the projection room."

We followed Lincoln McBride up to the fourth floor and entered the small projection room. "Take a seat and I'll have the projectionist run them for you."

"Thanks for being so understanding." Hap and I watched every reel they had in slow motion. We both spotted several candidates that had been filmed two or more times watching  the fires. As the last reel ended, "You can shut it down now there's no need to see another one."

We headed for the door when the editor in Chief came out of his office and handed us a newspaper.

"I want to thank you Detective for giving me my byline."

I opened the paper and couldn't believe the front page with my picture on it. I started reading the byline.

ARSONIST STRIKES AGAIN
POLICE HAVE NO CLUES

Detective William Barronson now reinstated in the police force has been looking for the arsonist without success. After an exhausting day of researching through our film and photograph files no leads have surfaced. In order to help the police in catching him. This newspaper will offer a reward of $100 to anyone that can give us any information leading to his arrest.

"Well what do you think Detective?"

"I think you've just run him to ground."

"Why's that? He'll probably want to get his picture on the front page now that he's famous."

I scratched my head and looked at the Chief, "Well, I hope you're right."

We headed back to our car, "Let's have a talk with the preacher Hap. Maybe he might have a lead or two for us."

"Captain, do you really think the Atlanta Mob is actually going to find our arsonist?"

"Well Hap, we just had strike two. I hope strike three isn't around the corner."

"Captain, don't get too discouraged. We have a lot of people besides them looking for him."

"You're probably right, but damn. I can't believe no one knows anything about him. Hell, he must have a family or a girl somewhere that knows what he's been up to!"

I looked at my watch and found it to be after three.

"Let's stop for a quick lunch Hap."

"I thought you'd never ask. I know a little place you might enjoy. I believe you know the woman."

Hap pulled in front of what used to be a tailor shop.

As I got out of the car, I noticed the unlit neon sign was still above the door. "Hap. What are we doing at this empty store? I'm tired, and in no mood for a joke."

173

"Captain, look at the signs in the windows."

I started to open the car door when I looked at the first hand written sign.

NOW OPEN
Kim's Home Cooking

It was printed in bold red letters on a white background. I followed Hap through the front door, and found Kim and a cook working. The place was about one hundred feet long by thirty feet wide. It had a long counter with a flat grill, and all the other necessary equipment behind it, on the left side were six four top tables with four chairs each.

"Bill! I'm so glad to see you, and Hap it's good to see you again to." Kim said giving us a hug. "I'm so sorry for your loss Hap, and what happen to you, Bill?

"Got beat-up, shot, plane crash, and surgery. You know just a normal day being a cop."

Kim laughed, "Are you two here for something to eat?"

When we said yes, her eyes lit up. Kim led us to a table which reminded me if her old place. Once we had sat down I looked around and found we were the only people in the place.

"Kim, how long have you been open?"

"Ah.. a week, but I'm sure it'll pick up."

She gave us a menu and I spotted my favorite meal, fried chicken.

When we were done eating, Kim refused to take our money. Not wanting to argue I gave her a big hug and slipped a fiver in her pocket.

"Don't you worry Kim. I'll have this place full of customers by tomorrow."

"Captain. What are you going to do to get customers into her place?"

"I think the boys at the different stations would come if I offered to pay for the first 50 breakfasts."

"That's a great idea, Captain. I'll let the Sergeants know it will be for tomorrow morning breakfast."

Hap started the car and got on the radio as he pulled into traffic. By the time we were a mile down the road six police stations and eight fire stations had been given the news. "Hap when we get to our destination you better let Kim know what going to happen tomorrow."

# Chapter 47

April 16th 1933
5:56 pm Friday

We walked into Ray's Pool Hall and for the first time  were greeted as friends. "Afternoon, Detective." Jerry said looking at my right arm in a sling. "Did you have an argument with your wife?" Everyone in the placed laughed including me.

Jerry Smith was a big man that must have worked on his daddy's farm. He stood six feet tall, two hundred and ninety five pounds and muscles bigger that my head. We had butted heads a couple times in the past but respected each other as army veterans.

"No Jerry. I was shot by a German that killed this man's son."

The laughter stopped and Jerry lumbered up to Hap and gave him a hug. He turned to give me one, but I backed up pointing at my arm.

"You his friend, little man?"

"Yes we are. My nick name is Happy but most people use Hap."

"So Hap. You lost your son to that Muller German guy that's in the paper?"

"Yes, and if you find him.." Hap couldn't finish wiping tear away.

"We find him, what would you like us to do with him?"

"Don't kill him. Bring him to us. We have a tree he needs to meet."

"Is the Pastor around? I need to speak to him."

"No. But I can send Earl to go get him." Raymond said from behind the bar.

Raymond Brown was also an average size man, five eight, one hundred and thirty pounds, balding and always chewing on a tooth pick. Raymond had to be a lieutenant because none of them ever gave him any lip.

"Raymond. I have to ask you a stupid question."

"Okay, but first, you want to try one of my coffees?" he asked munching on the toothpick.

"Sure. By the way, did you ever do anything with your idea of a coffee house?"

"No. Maybe when I retire, I'll do that rather than opening an Italian restaurant. So what do you want to ask him?"

"Why are you using non Italian last names?"

"Well, it seems the Pastor wants to fit in better down here with you locals. We Italians are getting a bad rap in the newspapers, so this way we fit in better with you English."

I looked at Ray and almost laughed. He looked at me and just shook his head and shrugged his shoulders. If I went to New York City and told them I was an Italian, I'd be laughed out of the city.

"Detective. It's good to see you again." Pastor Alton Lyman said. "I see by the look of your shoulder, you had a run-in with someone." the pastor said, shaking my good hand. "Now what can I do for you today?"

"I'm sure you have already heard about the Winecoff Hotel fire this morning."

"Yes, that was quite a shock for the Winecoff family seeing they didn't have fire insurance."

"Yes it is. How did you know about them not having fire insurance?"

"Just a lucky guess," his men chuckled.

"I need to see if your people on the streets have any information as to who is setting these fires."

"I don't have much, but what I've been told, the man starting the fires isn't going to stop. Evidently, he has a grudge against the city."

"A grudge? Hell, that could be half the people in the city."

"Don't get too discouraged yet, Detective. Information on him should be forthcoming in a day or two. By the way, this man Carl Muller seems to be a bigger fish to catch than the arsonist. I also have some information on him as well."

I could see the pastor was wanting to barter for this information as well. "Okay, what is your asking price?"

I saw a crooked smile appear on his face. That smile changed his appearance from a nice middle aged pastor to a cruel heartless old man that would sell his mother for a dollar.

"Well Detective, here is my offer, and I believe it's a good offer. Before you say no, I want you to think very long and hard because I won't offer it again."

"Okay... but if it's against my morals, I don't care if it's a $1,000,000, the answer will be no."

"Understood. So here is my offer.

1. I will provide protection for your friends and family. I know the FBI and your own police said they can do it, but look at what's happened so far.

2. This protection will be provided to you for the rest of my life. That means no robberies, thefts, muggings,

injuries or anything else well ever happen to your family.

3. I want men and any future men I deem a threat to my business, will be handled by you the police.

4. I want in on this co-op deal you're putting together as well as any other venture that might arise.

5. To sweeten the pot I can get some of your black mail money back from Vito.

Now, before you give me an answer, I want you to think on this and let me know by tomorrow."

I was about to tell him where he could put this proposal when something inside told me to wait. "I'll think about your proposal, Pastor, but some of what your asking is going to be hard for me to swallow."

"Well then, Hap, what do you think of my proposal? Wouldn't it be prudent of the Detective to be assured his family would be safe. Just think in a short time you and Mildred could be married and rich. Wouldn't it also be nice not to worry about what happened to your son, would happen to Mildred?"

Hap looked at me wondering if he should say something or not. Hap had only been an officer for a very short time, but I could see in his eyes he thought the proposal was more than fair.

I had seen how something this simple could entangle you into a life of crime before you knew what happened. My father had always said "If it looks too good to be true don't do it."

"As I said Pastor. I'll talk about with the other members and I'll let you know tomorrow."

I don't think we got thirty feet outside the pool hall when Hap started in on me.

"Captain! Just think no more worries about us losing our loved ones." Hap said with eyes the size of saucers.

"Besides getting some of their money back from this Vito guy. Come to think about it, what money and who is this Vito guy anyway?"

"That's a long story Hap. I'll go into that at a later date. Now I think it's time to head home, I need to talk to Margaret."

As Hap drove, I kept thinking about the Pastor and how he was slowly working his way at making me a member of his mob. I had hoped not to involve him in the co-op but as things got worse with the banks, money was becoming very hard to borrow.

Pulling up to the house, I got out of the car and told Hap to gas her up and have her washed before coming back. Between the smoke and ash from this morning's fire the car could use a good cleaning inside and out.

I walked up the steps and opened the front door and heard the tap, tap, tap of a typewriter. Not wanting to scare Margaret in her condition I called out. "Margaret!"

"I'm in the small library working at Mildred's desk." I hadn't been in this room before, so when I walked in it was quite a surprise. The room itself wasn't large, eight by nine feet with a small couch, a reading lamp and potted plants on the North wall. Mildred's desk, chair and two paintings of her father and mother were hung on the East wall. On the West wall where book shelves loaded with hundreds of books. The South wall was the doorway and on each side of the opening were more bookshelves. There were a few books on them but mostly had pictures frames of Mildred and her parents as children.

"Margaret, I see you're working on the co-op papers?"

"Yes, why?" she said turning around from the ancient typewriter.

"Where did you find that old machine.?" I said looking at the manufacture medal plate. "It says here, Imperial model 5 1878.

"Mildred remembered she had stored it in the basement. She said it was her fathers but she didn't like to type on it."

"Let's sit. I have something to discuss with you first before talking to the others."

I was about to start when Grace and Mildred came into the room. Mildred had a tray with four cups, a pot of tea and some cookies. Grace set a small round table in front of us. Mildred set the tray down and started pouring tea.

"How did you know I wanted to speak to Margaret!"

I looked at Grace who was now as big as a house and saw her blush, indicating she had been listening outside the door. Mildred, looking over her shoulder, said "Might as well come sit too, Nancy. That way you'll know what we're about to find out."

Nancy stepped out from behind the hall wall and took a seat on the floor next to Mildred.

"What about the agents, Mildred?"

"Don't worry about them. They're in the dining room having an early dinner."

# Chapter 48

April 16<sup>th</sup> 1933<br>6:56 pm Friday

"**I** wanted to do this one at a time, but seeing we're all here, I might as well tell you now. I have been talking to a pastor who I won't name. This pastor, has connections with the Atlanta Mob. He has offered us protection for as long as we need it. He also has offered to help me in catching the arsonist and Muller as well."

"This pastor." Mildred said. "You stated he has connections with the Atlanta Mob?"

"Yes. Mildred."

"His name wouldn't be Alton Lyman? Would it."

"Yes Mildred, but how do you know him,"

"I met him once a long time ago." Mildred said looking down at the floor.

I immediately knew were she had met him. It was at the Aragon Hotel where she had work as a hostess. "Isn't he one of your father's partners' son? I remembered you talking about him."

"Yes, I believe I did mention him to you."

"Well, anyway Pastor Alton also wants to help fund the co-op Margaret has been writing up. He also states he can get some of your money back from Vito Genovese." I looked at their faces as they thought it over. "Well that's his offer Mildred, Grace, Margaret and Nancy."

"You mean I'm included too?"

"Yes even you Nancy." Mildred said stroking her hair

I could see Grace wanted to accept the offer, because she didn't want to give up her share in the first place. Margaret also liked the offer as well, because of her not marring Vito's son. That left Mildred and I could see in her eyes she wasn't going to agree. "Mildred, I wish to speak to you alone." I said motioning for the others to leave. Once everybody had left the room I shut the solid oak door. "Let's move closer to the window to make it harder for them to overhear. "Mildred I can see you have doubts. Is it the pastor or the money?"

"It's both Bill. When we all had money my family changed from being one to being greedy and hateful. I don't want to see that happen again if I can help it. As for the pastor, I had hoped our paths would never cross again."

"Can I ask why, or is it none of my business?" I picked up Mildred's tea cup and refilled it. "Here, drink this."

I waited as Mildred took sever sips before handing the cup back to me. "Bill.. When things got bad after my parents died, and the Major was trying to destroy me as well. I met Alton Lyman at one of the dinner parties at the Aragon Hotel. He took a shine towards me and I let him be my guardian for... When I told him I was pregnant he made me have an abortion and then dumped me."

"Mildred, I'll tell the pastor we decline his offer."

Mildred took a deep sigh and let it out slowly. "No Bill, tell him we all agree, but make sure you don't mention me. He's long forgotten about me and I'd like to keep it that way. I also want you to swear to me you'll put that bastard in the electric chair for killing my baby."

I walked back to the door and snatched it open. They all must have been listening because as the door opened Margaret, Grace and Nancy fell on the floor. "Have you lost something down there?" I said helping them up. Once they were all seated, "Has anyone to offer before voting?"

Mildred got up and said, "I can see it's beneficial to be protected as long as he lives. It would be nice to get some of our money back as well. As for you William, it could help your carrier to catch the arsonist. As for this co-op project you're trying to put together. I'm sure he's just like my father. Once the co-op starts to grow, he'll be there to take it away from us. So I vote yes."

"Yes!" Grace screamed struggling to her feet. "That Pastor mobster is as bad or worse than Marco and his father were to all of us."

"Grace. I've said my piece." Mildred got up and headed for the kitchen.

"Well! Mildred! I vote, No! No! No!"

"Okay. Grace. Please sit down before you have the baby right here."

"Margaret, how do you vote?" I asked.

"I can agree with my sister on all the bad things that could happen if voting yes, but then again there's a lot of positives."

"Like what! Getting some of your money back to buy back into your bankrupt corporation. It's just like you Margaret. You're only concerned about yourself." With tears pouring down her face Grace raced out of the room.

"Well, I'm not sure just what happened but I hadn't voted one way or the other." Margaret said leaving the room as well.

That left Nancy and myself in the library. Taking a deep breath I said, "Nancy. What do you think about the pastor's proposal?"

"I think you should take it. So my vote is yes."

I was surprised at how quickly she had made up her mind.

"Are you sure?"

"Yes, and I'll tell you why. This pastor isn't as smart as he thinks. If I understood you right, he said his protection will be provided to you for the rest of his life. Not your lives, but his life, and how long does he expect to live? So I vote yes and hope he dies next year. Isn't he an old man, Bill?"

"I believe he's in his sixties, and for once, Nancy, I couldn't agree with you more."

"Yes father, something like a fall, or a car accident, or even a gun shot." Nancy said smiling at me.

"Ah! What did you call me?"

"Father. Bill. I've decided you're more my father than the one that abused me and my mother."

"Now wait just a minute. Nancy. I'm not your father. We don't even look alike!"

"Don't be afraid dad, I won't tell anyone what you tried to do to me unless you force me to. You see, Mildred can't live forever either, and I intend to be her loving adopted daughter that'll inherit everything. So daddy, don't cross me, or Margaret might find out." Nancy got up kissed me on the cheek, and left the room.

I wanted to smoke a cigarette and drink the biggest drink I could find, but my hands where shaking so badly I couldn't get the pack out of my coat pocket. Remembering the brandy decanter in the parlor, I raced to it and poured several drinks before I regained control of my wits.

"What are you doing?" Mildred asked staring at me with a glass in my hand.

"I needed one to steady my nerves, Mildred. You see the vote as of now is two yes, one no, and two undecided."

"Who's undecided?"

"Margaret and myself."

"Then, Nancy voted yes. Well I'll have to make her something special just for her dinner tonight."

I wanted to tell Mildred about Nancy, but all I could hear in my mind was her calling me daddy.

"Well what's going on you two. You both look like you've seen a ghost." Margaret said looking at my empty glass.

"Don't look at me like that, Margaret. I just found him here drinking my brandy."

"William! What do you think you're doing with that brandy decanter?" Margaret said tapping her foot in anger.

I put the decanter down along with the empty glass and walked out onto the porch.

"Alright, William. Are you going to tell me what made you take a drink?" Margaret said sitting down in a rocker.

"It's just been a very bad day dear. I thought everyone would be pleased with my solution for financing the co-op."

"Well maybe this will help. I've decided to vote yes if you do? Does that help?"

"Yes, it does solve that problem. But what about Grace?"

"I'll have a talk with her and I'm sure shell agree by tomorrow."

I sat on the front porch with Margaret and rocked slowly back and forth, thinking about what Nancy had said. It was clear now she was a master at deception, and if I didn't do something to discredit her soon, Mildred would adopt her.

"Are you going to talk to the others involved in the co-op?"

"That I'm not sure of. There are six of them and I believe the Chinese will vote yes. The two women on the farm should vote yes. That leaves Betty and Travis who have already been burned once by Larry. So they are the key as to whether it's a go or no go."

I sat thinking and thinking what to do about Nancy, and then it came to me. I needed to lay a trap for her and her man that likes to set fires.

# Chapter 49

April 17th 1933
6:17 am Saturday

Not wanting to wake up the wife, I quickly got dress and headed downstairs. The familiar smell of breakfast reminded me I promised Kim I would fill her place up with customers. With a cup of coffee and the first cigarette of the day I got on the phone I rang up the Desk Sergeant.

"Sergeant Mike Sanders."

"Mike, this is Detective Barronson. I want you to let the men know that I'm buying breakfast for the first 50 men that eat at Kim's Home Cooking grand opening."

"Kim's Diner, Hap call yesterday and told me you were doing that to help Kim get her new place running."

"Oh yes I forgot he was going to handle that. By the way did he say how much each man could spend?"

"Let see, I wrote it down. Ah, 50 cents with tip."

"That much?"

"Yep, and it's too late to back out now, because the place was pack when she opened. I must say after the mess you made with the men this will go a long way to redeem yourself Detective."

"That's good to here, and tell them again that I apologize for losing my temper."

"Operator, connect me to the newspaper please. When their operator picked up I asked for the City Editor.

"Hello."

"Mr. McBride, this is Detective Barronson.

"Detective, is there something I can help you with?"

"Yes, I want to place a half page add how would I go about placing it?"

"Well an add that size is going to cost $5. how many days do you want it to run?"

"For that price it'll have to be just one day. Can you work up the ad for Kim's Home Cooking grand opening for me?"

"Kim's place, I remember it closed. Yes it did, the bank foreclosed on her."

"I'll have a nice add drawn up by my staff, and just for you and her I'll charge $5 for five days for everything."

I hung up the phone and made myself two bacon biscuit sandwich for a quick breakfast and headed for the door.

Remembering I hadn't given Mildred a peck on the cheek, I went back into the kitchen and found her teaching Nancy how to cook. I stood at the door a second and watched how easily Nancy could manipulate Mildred.

"Mildred." Immediately Nancy backed away and looked down at the floor waiting to be scolded. Ignoring her I said, "Mildred, Hap and I probably will not be home for dinner."

It then crossed my mind I also needed a copy of our proposal. If that wasn't enough I also had forgotten I needed to take my suits to the cleaners. Returning to our room I found Margaret up and writing madly at the table.

"I'll be done in a minute dear. It's in pencil but at least you'll have something to show them."

By the time I had gathered up my dirty suits, Margaret had finished and was putting it in an envelope for safe keeping.

"Here's one copy at least. You know I wish someone would invent a copier of some kind."

"If they did just think of how many typists would be out of work. Besides who could afford one that would be the size of a dining table and where would you put it."

With the envelope in my suit coat pocket, a large stack of dirty suits, two bacon biscuits and a mug of coffee, I headed for the door. Lucky for me Hap had pulled up in front of the house. Seeing me struggling not to fall down the stairs Hap got out and took my two biscuits and coffee. With my hands free I opened the door and drop them on the back seat.

"Wouldn't it be easier to bring one or two to Wang's Cleaners instead of six?" Hap said devouring one of my biscuits.

"Probably. Hey! That's my breakfast."

"Captain, haven't you always said, possession is nine tens of the law," he said finishing off the other biscuit.

I stood there in disbelief as Hap drank my coffee as well. "Captain, that sure was tasty. Thanks for bring it."

"Don't think nothing of it Hap. I'm always happy to help a friend. So if you don't mind waiting I'll go get myself another breakfast."

"Oh was that your breakfast? I though you brought that for me?"

I could feel my face turning red with anger. I stared back towards the house when Hap said, "Captain, what should I do with the breakfast Mildred packed for you? Eat it to?"

"Hap if you touch that food I'll, I'll, drive every day for a week."

"That's a very tempting offer," Hap said opening the passenger door to show me brown bag and thermos of coffee.

I picked up the food and got into the front seat. Hap got in the driver's seat and started the car. "Where to me Lord." he said smiling.

"Oh, shut up and drive to Wang's. Besides I need to keep you busy enough to earn all this money your making."

"Money? I haven't seen a dime yet. So when do we get paid anyway?"

"Today or Monday. Whenever we get back to the station."

Hap mumbled "About damn time."

Working our way through the Saturday traffic I noticed it was a lot lighter than normal. It seemed with the depression deepening more people were walking or taking public transportation than driving. Hap pulled up in front of Wang's Dry Cleaners and found the place already open for business. We walked into his store and I dreaded what his answer would be.

"Good morning, Wang. How is your lovely wife this fine day?" I said putting all my suits on the counter and bowing slightly.

Wang didn't say anything until after inspecting every suit. "You pretty rough on clothes. What you expect me to do with this worn out suits?" he said pushing them back at me.

"Wang, what's the matter? Did you have another fight with your wife?"

"No. Wife gone. She leave me for neighbor. Now I have all work here to do by self."

"But wasn't that what you wanted a month ago. Now you can get another wife from China, a younger one. One you can train to be traditional wife."

"I no want wife never. I have three women on way. They will be working here until pay off cost to bring them here.

"How long would that be?"

"Ten, twenty year or until I want new ones. Much better than one wife, I think."

"Now, isn't there anything you can do for my suits?"

"Let see again please."

Wang looked them over and kept shaking his head no. He did it so many times I was surprised his head didn't fall off.

"I try, but material wore out, might come apart. You best see Chang for new suits, save you money."

"Okay, if you say so, you're the expert on this. Now Wang I have here a paper for us all to sign when it is made official. Will you look it over and tell me if you and Chan would sign it."

Wang opened the paper and put on his glasses before handing it back to me. "Who this pastor offering all this help? He a gangster?"

"Okay, I sign."

"Just like that you'll sign?"

"In China we have same. It part of doing business. This money he wants. How much time do I have?"

"Not sure yet. I'll let you know if everybody agrees to sign."

I left Wang and went around the corner to Chang's Tailor shop. He too was already open and was waiting for a pigeon to enter his store.

"Good morning, Lee. I see you're already open." I said bowing slightly. "This is a friend his nickname is Happy. I need some new suits."

With the word suits, Lee's eyes lit up with dollar signs. From out of nowhere three men appeared and started measuring and showing us fabric ties, shirts, socks, and shoes. Within one hour, Hap and I had purchased five suits, shirts, ties, socks, and shoes.

When the whirlwind stopped Hap and I were in our car looking at each other's stunned face.

"Did I just buy five suits?" Hap asked. "I...ah didn't intend to buy any. What I'm wearing is still okay even if they're out of date."

"Me too. I only wanted two suits, but he said yes to the proposal and where else can you get all that for $100?"

"The second hand store for twenty dollars on Fifth St."

$$\sim\!\!\diamond\!\!\sim$$

# Chapter 50

April 17th 1933
10:37 am Saturday

We stopped at Kim's to picked up a coffee because Hap had drunk most of mine. "Will you look at that, Captain? A waiting line out the door. It seems your idea had caught on better that expected."

"I think we better pass on the coffee. Let's head for Ester and Ruth's farm to get their signatures." As we pulled up to the farm house it was looking much better than the last time I was here. The weeds had been mowed down by several goats tied up around the place. The porch had been worked on but needed a carpenter. It didn't take five minutes to get both women to agree to sign.

"Okay Hap. Let's head to Betty and Travis Whitney farm. If I can get them to sign also will be in business."

We pulled into their place and found them working on their vegetable and plant stand. "Morning y'all, how are things with you two?"

"Not well, William, the bank has come after us again."

"Well I have a new proposal, and if you sign it's going to benefit you and everyone else by years end." I brought out the proposal and let them read it.

"We trust you on this William, because you're part of this co-op. So where do we both sign?"

We headed back into town and stopped at the Ray's pool hall. As we walked in I saw the pastor talking to a stranger.

"Well if it isn't Detective Barronson. I see your carrying a signed copy for me to sign as well."

I handed him the papers and watched as he signed them.

"Just a minute Pastor. This is only a pencil copy, I'll have a typed copy signed by all and notaries to make it official."

"We don't need a notary Detective. Because this co-op is you and your friend's business. I'm just the silent partner that expects a 30% return. As for the legal end that's up to you." he folded the papers and put them in his coat pocket.

"I hate to ask this so soon Pastor. But when do you think you'll have an answer on the money from Vito?"

"It's already done Detective. Now that everyone has signed, Mildred, Grace and Margaret will get $50,000 apiece. The other $150,000 is my processing fee. Do you have a problem with that?"

I wanted to drag him out of that chair and show him what I thought of his processing fee. But as I looked around there were to many men with guns. "Who's you friend sitting with his back to me."

"No one you would be interested in Detective. So if you don't mind, I have other things to take care of.

As Hap and I opened the front door, a young man pushed past us as if we weren't there. "Excuse me!" Hap said turning around.

"Excuse me for what cop?" he said daring Hap to challenge him.

"Hap. Let it go. There's to many of them, and I'm sure we would lose this fight." I grabbed Hap's arm and dragged him into the street.

"He couldn't whip me no matter how many of them help him."

"I'm sure you could, but for now, let's make sure we remember every detail of what he looks like."

It took some doing but I managed to get Hap into the car. As we headed back home to tell the family the good and  the bad news. Hap asked, "Just how much money did this Vito guy take from them?"

"I'm not sure Hap, but I'd say a conservative guess would be to $2,000,000 in gold coin."

I grabbed the back of the front seat as the car's tires screamed in protest as we came to a halt.

"2,000,000 in gold! Are you kidding Captain. If I had that kind of money I'd be living in Paris or Rome, not Atlanta, running a boarding house."

With horns blowing and gestures being made. I got Hap to continue on to home. I found Margaret in the library beating on the old typewriter. "How many copies have you typed dear?"

"Damn this machine. Margaret said pushing herself away from the desk. As I walked closer I found a rusty key had jammed halfway towards the paper. "OH. William, I didn't hear you come in." she said pinning some loose hair back into place.

"Well, I got everyone to signed except Grace and Lenard  to get the ball rolling."

"I hope Grace doesn't find out that. You know what kind of temper she has."

"I was hoping you would help me with that. My Captain wants Grace to come back to work after the baby is born. Do you think it might make her change her mind?"

"Well I'm sure she'll be happy about the job. I think we will need something else to sweeten the deal?"

"I do have one more card up my sleeve. Veto is going to return to each of you $50,000."

I could see the disappointed in Margaret's face. I could also see in her face something was better than nothing.

"That might do it, but I need a different typewriter than that one."

"How many more copies do you need to make. 9 or 10 just to make sure we have an extra copy."

"Wow, that many. How many have you completed?"

"None." she said pointing at the overflowing trash can.

"Margaret, I have an idea. Why don't we go to your old office and type them there?"

"That's an excellent idea. I'm sure John won't mind us doing that."

Heading out the door I noticed for the first time Margaret was showing almost as much as Grace was. Opening the front door of the car, I helped her in and sat in the back. "Hap. drive us to the Flat Iron Building when I remembered it too had been torched. As we neared the building I could see construction workers working on the outside three floors that had burned. I was sure the bottom floors below ground were damaged as well from water.

Parking in the side lot, we entered the unlocked side door. As we reached the elevator the smell of smoke and burnt wood was almost overpowering.

I pushed the button for the elevator and seconds later the doors open. To my surprise an operator was at the controls. "What floor please?"

"Let's start with the fourth floor." As the doors opened we found only a few workman repairing walls.

"Which floor is John Junior on. I'm his sister and would like to see him."

"He's on six Miss."

When the doors opened I found the place had changed dramatically since my last visit.

Now there was a secretary sitting ten feet from the elevator. There was a temporary wood wall behind her She had a desk, chair, a lamp on the desk and a Sears picture on the wall. To one side was two chairs and a coffee table  with three magazines on it.

"May I help you?" she said looking as if she smelled something bad.

The woman was in her thirties, dressed in a gray suit with her brown hair pulled back in a tight bun. She wore black rimmed glasses bright red nail polish, and red lipstick.

"Yes I'd like to see my brother please. I'm..."

"I know who you are. Margaret Barronson and no you can't see John. He's much too busy to see a half-sister that betrayed him. Now if you don't mind or if you do, the elevator is behind you."

"Now just a minute!" I said.

"William don't, please. This was a mistake. Let's just leave so I never have to see this place again. Miss or Mrs. whatever your name is, give John this from me."

Margaret leaned over the desk and slapped the woman across the face. "That's for your rudeness and this is for Junior!" Margaret swept everything off her desk onto the floor and then headed for the elevator.

"Well! I can see why his family never thought much of you."

As the elevator door closed, the rude woman was on her knees picking up her things.

"Stop on five, please." Margaret said.

"It would be a pleasure, Miss. I've been wanting someone to do that for a long time."

The elevator door opened, and Margaret walked to the nearest desk that had a typewriter on it. I knew immediately what she wanted to do. "Margaret, I'll carry that and why don't Hap and you, look in the drawers for ribbons, paper and whatever else you need. I believe you're owed that much for all the years you put up with him."

As we got back on the elevator with everything we could carry an idea started forming in my mind.

When I closed the car trunk, my idea had crystallized. "Margaret, if I had some way to get your desk down here and to home."

"That's all right William. I think we did all right for the spear of the moment."

"Is there anything else I can do for you Miss."

"It's Mrs. But no thank you. You've done enough. I wouldn't want you to lose your job on account of me." she said handing him $2.

"Margaret, don't spend another minute worrying about what John thinks. You're going to have a family and a co-op to take care of. Maybe someday you'll be able to buy him out."

"Son what's your name?"

"Claude, Claude Henson."

"Claude, how would you like to make $5."

We drove back home and at every stoplight I chuckled.

"What are you laughing about?" Margaret asked.

"Oh. Nothing dear." By the fourth stoplight I could see both of them were getting irradiated with me. "Alright, I'll tell you. I paid the elevator operator to turn off the power when he leaves."

"When does his shift ends?"

"11:00 pm. I also asked if he could block the exit door as well.

# Chapter 51

April 17<sup>th</sup> 1933
11:37 pm Saturday

We got all our loot unloaded and I left Margaret typing away at 100 words a minute. It had occurred to me it was time to see Doug and Clair Hutchinson's at their pawn shop for a proper desk and chair.

"Clair it's me, Bill. How are you today?" I said entering the store.

"Well I'll be. Detective Barronson I thought you'd forgotten all about us." she said giving me a big hug.

"How's that man of yours?"

"Why don't you just ask me?"

I backed away from Clair and saw Doug standing with crutches behind the counter.

"Now you look like the old Doug I used to know before your hair turned so gray."

Clare whispered, "Don't say too much about his looks please."

I nodded okay and went to the counter. "I see you're working on walking."

"Yes and I can even talk now that my broken jaw has been repaired."

I didn't acknowledge his struggle to support himself to shake my hand.

When I touched his hand, I almost pulled away. It was cold and clammy but at least he could still use it.

"What are you here for?"

"I need a desk and a chair for Margaret to do her typing on. She's going to be my co-op secretary." I thought about that one more time before asking. "Clair, you're the book keeper here, if I remember right?"

"No, that's Doug. He kept the books. You should know that."

"Oh yes, that's right." I said knowing full well he was.

"I need someone to handle all the paperwork for this  co-op. You know like paying and receiving."

"I thought you said Margaret was your person for that."

"No. She's going to have a baby soon and I need her for other work. You see I not only work for the police department, I also work for the FBI as well."

"I think that job is just what Doug needs right now. His spirits have been low since his recovery isn't going the way he wants."

"Doug, I need to ask you a question."

"What could that be that you need a cripple for."

"I don't need a cripple. I need a man that can squeeze a penny out of a nickel. You might not be 100% physically, but your book keeping is. So how about handling the books for the co-op?"

"I'll also need Clair to help also as it's not a penny out of a nickel, it's two pennies," Doug said laughing slightly.

"Now it won't be much money to start with, but it will build as the business grows, and I still need that desk and chair."

As I started to leave, Clair gave me another Hug.

"Thanks, Bill. He needed that." she whispered.

"Clair make sure every penny is accounted for because we have a partner that will be auditing the books as well."

"Where to now Captain?"

"Let's go to the City Property Records building on Prior Street. I have a feeling I know what and why the fires were set."

As usual all the parking spots were full in and around all the government buildings. Not wanting to wait for a spot. I got out and told Hap to keep looking. Walking into the building, I saw the time on the clock read 12:25 pm. Lunch, as always for government employees, was 12:00 to 1:00 for the entire building. That really meant their lunch, which should have been an hour, was actually two. I looked around and found one of the guards and showed him my badge. He started to give me some excuse about why he couldn't let me upstairs, when I showed him my other badge.

Now having his full cooperation, I went to the fourth floor where the deed records office was located.

I found the door unlocked and entered the empty office. "Hello! Is anyone here?" I didn't get an answer so I went around the counter and opened the door to the records room. It was twelve feet wide and eleven feet deep with 12 rolls of shelves. All the shelves were filled with large leather bound books labeled A-Ae B-C so on. I opened one and started looking at it to see if I could find the one O wanted to look at. It didn't take me long to figure out I could be in here for the rest of my life, and not find what I was looking for.

So deciding to wait, I returned to the outer office and took a seat. I lit a cigarette and watched the clock as the hands slowly crept towards 2:05 pm. The first person that walked in the door was a young man thinner than a sapling and just about as tall.

"Well. It's nice to see someone works in this place." I said looking at the clock that said 2:35 pm.

I showed him my FBI badge and watched him shrink an inch in fright.

"I didn't mean to be so late sir. I'm new here, and I was told everybody took two hours for lunch. Am I being arrested? Because if I am, can I call my mother first?"

I so wanted to play along, but I didn't have the time and hell, he'd probably faint if I did say yes.

"No. Not this time, but remember, lunch is one hour not two. Now Mr.?"

"Malcolm sir. Brad Malcolm."

"Brad. I need your help in locating these properties. Can you do that for me."

"Yes sir. I can. What's the first one."

I started with the address for the McKenzie building. The kid looked like a scared rabbit, but he sure knew where and which book to look in. I gave him the second and then the third and fourth address. When I had what I was looking for I said. "Thank you Malcolm for your cooperation and I'm advising you not to tell anyone else about this."

"Yes Sir. Mister FBI agent. I won't tell anyone."

"I hope not Malcolm, because if you do, I'll have to tell your mother why you are in jail."

As I walked out of his office, it took every bit of willpower not to laugh. I met Hap at the front door as he was walking in. "Ah. There you are, Captain. I parked right outside. It seems everybody goes home early around here as well as coming in late."

I looked at the clock and the time was 4:15 pm. The sign on the door with the hours said nine to five.

"Where to now?"

"Let's head back to the station, or better yet let's go to the zoo."

"The zoo! What for?"

"I thought I'd visit my old friends the lions to see if they remember me."

"The lions, I thought you'd never want to see them again after fighting 20 of them off you to save that child. It give me chills every time I think about it. 20 man eating lions the paper said. How did you do that anyway?"

"Just one at a time, Hap. Just one at a time." I started to laugh hard for several seconds. Each time I thought I had stopped, I'd see Hap's face in the rear view mirror and start laughing again.

"I hope you're enjoying this. I don't see what's so damn funny myself. Twenty lions only six bullets and ten dead lions."

I started laughing again until my sides ached so bad, I said, "Hap! Please stop talking my sides are killing me."

When we reached the zoo I had Hap park as close to the office buildin' as we could. I wanted to have another look in the bunker just to make sure Muller wasn't hiding there.

# Chapter 52

April 17th 1933
5:05 pm Saturday

I purposely led Hap towards the lions exhibit so he could see how inflated the story had become. As we walked along talking about the fires, I stopped and leaned on the top rail metal fence.

"Well. What do you think we should do next to catch this arsonist?"

"Well. We could... Damn!" Hap yelled at the top of his lungs as the lions started bellowing for dinner. "Why you." He stopped and stared at the lions in disbelief.

"There are only six lions here. What happened to the rest?"

"Hap, that's all there ever were. I just wanted to show you how absurd that story has become. 20 lions Hap I could I or anyone survive 20 lions."

"Okay. So someone embellished the truth a few times. It still doesn't change the fact that you saved that little kid."

"Alright. Let's drop it Hap, I don't want to ever hear anything else about it. Now let's get a drink and go to a quite spot Mathew Jones had shown me."

"Mathew Jones wasn't he the colored man that died at Grady?"

"Yes. Cochran had injected him as well with his serum. I found him alive by the wishing well. Grady Hospital put him in an iron lung to help him breath until the doctors could figure out what happened to him."

"Then how did he die?"

"Sometime during the night Muller unplugged his machine."

Walking down the overgrown path, I found the spot that led to Mathews private sanctuary. Pushing through the azalea bushes until they opened to a clear area with a table and two chairs. In the months since his death, nature was reclaiming what Mathew had so tenderly kept up.

"Is this the place you were talking about?" Hap said scratching his face and arms.

"Yes. But it looked a lot different when Mathew was alive."

"Let's go sit by the lake instead of here. The weeds are as tall as I am." Hap said.

I followed Hap to the lake and we took a seat under some pines. I purposely took a seat on the picnic table facing away from the wishing well. Even then I could feel its presences bring back the unwanted memories of so many deaths.

"Okay. Captain. What do you want to show me? It looks like the zoo has closed for the day."

I brought out the folded piece of paper I had written on. I laid it on the picnic table so Hap could read it. "Hap. I had this idea to check who owned the buildings that had burned so far. Here's what I found."

McKenzie Building owner McKenzie family
Fulton Cotton Spinning Factory owner McCallum family
Warehouse owner McCallum family
Railroad Terminal Georgia Southern
Flat Iron Building owner McCallum family
Winecoff Hotel owner Winecoff family

So far all the buildings that have burned are owned by McCallum except for the two hotels."

"Why would they burn down their own properties?"

"Because. John McCallum Junior, Winecoff and Mc Kenzie are broke. When I visited him a few days ago at his office he didn't have one employee or electricity. Now he has the money to repair the office building, hire a secretary and turn on the lights."

"Well Captain, he must have gotten money from the insurance company to repair the building. I'm sure he has to repair the other buildings as well. If I was an insurance company I just wouldn't hand over thousands of dollars with no strings attached."

"Hum, I see your point Hap, but there's another way they might be trying to use the destruction. With the buildings burned out, it would cancel all long and short term leases.

Then they could condemn them and rebuild a more modern building or buildings."

If I was them I pad the books so that I could claim bankruptcies, canceling my debts and by it back from the bank at pennies on the dollar with the money I skimmed off." I could see I had lost Hap awhile back "Hap I can see you don't understand."

"No…I think I understand alright, I just can't believe they would do something like that."

"It's simple Hap. You buy a junker car for $5. You fix it up for $10 and insure it for $50. Then you wreck it collect the $50 and then by the car back for $7 and sell it for $70."

"Okay I see, then they must have hired someone to burn them down, right?"

"Correct. If They hired someone, they'll have to get rid of him, at some point. Otherwise he'll black mail them to death."

"Well, Captain,  I believe it's time to pay John McCallum a visit and see if we can stir the pot a bit. When do you want to do that?"

"Tomorrow, I'll call in for an appointment with his rude secretary. I'll use the name Wilson from the Department of Internal Revenue."

"I see." Hap said smiling. "You want him to sweat."

"Exactly, and better yet. I'll use the FBI phone number in Washington just in case he calls to verify."

Checking the time, I told Hap we needed to head back home as the zoo was close. Following the walking trail back towards the parking lot I remember the night Bonnie Graves and I had our first date. I had been called back to the zoo because they had found another body. She hadn't stayed in the car as I had asked her. Instead she came to the crime scene walking down this very trail. Once she had seen the body I believe she might have had a change of heart. It's one thing to say people must die for your beliefs, it's another to see one. I sighed in regret because Bonnie was quite a woman, and I might have married her if she hadn't been murdered by Muller.

"Captain," Hap whispered, "Isn't that Muller up there about a hundred yards ahead of us?"

I strained my tired eyes to see who Hap was talking about. For some reason Muller's name cause me to have a headache. "I don't think so Hap."

"It's got to be him. See he's heading into that building up ahead."

"Then we better check it out, if you're sure it's him."

Running to the door we found it unlocked. Opening it slightly I remembered this was the building Frazier worked in to cut up meat for the animals. Slipping into the dimly lit building I remembered the layout. Meat lockers were on the left, hay straight ahead. Bags of bird seeds, nuts, and coolers for fruits on the right. "Is that the man your talking about?" I whispered as the figure walked under a ceiling light. The light didn't illuminate him very much as he walked into the shadows. "I think it could be him, Hap."

"What do you think he's doing in here?" Hap whispered.

I put my finger to my lips to indicate this place echoes like a cave. We slowly crept along the same aisle listening for his movement. Once he had turned the corner we had lost sight of him. Upon reaching the end of the isle I peeked around the corner and saw a meat cooler door open. "Hap, he must have gone into that cooler for something?"

"May be he's got weapons or money stashed in there somewhere."

"That's a thought, so let's wait here and see what he comes out with." It didn't take long before he came out the door carrying several pieces of meat. Setting it down on the cutting table, Muller then went into another cooler. This time he had a basket of fruits and vegetables.

Placing them on the same table he picked up a long carving knife and sliced himself off a very large steak.

We watched as he gathered his booty and started toward the backdoor.

"Dinner for one Herr Muller. We thought you might ask us to join you," I said pointing my revolver at him.

"Why if it isn't our guinea pig and his rabbit companion." he said setting the food down.

"Captain. Let's take him to our tree and string the Hun up." Hap said as the anger grew on his face.

"Not quite yet Hap. I think we need to find out what his real mission is."

"Come, come, now Detective, you know I came back for you and your blood, remember."

"Yes. I remember you threatening me and my family if I didn't cooperate you'd murder them." I said walking towards that smug face.

I wanted to pull the trigger so bad my hand started shaking. Hap looked at me and he too was having the same problem.

"You're not going to shoot, Detective, because you know I'm after much larger fish than you. Now don't get me wrong, you're needed for the fatherland but once the war comes we'll need them more."

"Gentlemen if I were you two I'd put your weapons down."

I heard several clicks behind me as a cold revolver barrel touch the back of my head.

I uncocked my gun and held it up for them to take.

"Very wise Detective. Now turn around so I can see your faces."

We turned around and looked into the face of Gertrude Becker and her two henchmen.

"Gertrude. I thought the FBI was holding you?" I said not wanting to give her double agent secret away.

"They were Detective, until the German Ambassador spoke to your President. It seems in what you call hands across the water is why I was released."

I looked at Gertrude's hate filled face and wondered if she really was working on our side.

"Well, seeing you've got the upper hand now, Gertrude. What do you have in mind for us this time around?"

"That's very prudent of you Detective Barronson, or should I say Agent Barronson."

"Captain. I thought we had an agreement that the people responsible for killing my son were going to hang!"

Hap started moving towards Muller with his hands clinched in a fist.

I grabbed Hap's shoulder and hit him as hard as I could squarely on the jaw. Hap went down like a felled tree and didn't get up.

"Thank you Detective. I didn't want to shoot him, but I would have even though he has a good reason."

"Now, if you please Detective, my men are going to tie the two of you up."

When they were done tying us up on the floor, I knew it would take some time to get loose if ever. "Your men are quite the experts at tying people up Frau Becker. Is this common practice in Germany?" I wanted to keep her preoccupied with me instead of on the surroundings. Muller had left his carving knife on the butchers table and I wanted it after they left.

"Auf Wiedersehen Detective Barronson, I hope we don't meet again unless it's in Germany." Gertrude said turning the lights off.

We laid there in pitch darkness and I started sweating, thinking of Cochran's king cobra stalked me in the dark. I started rolling in the direction of the butcher's table. On the third roll I hit one of the table legs and thanked God I hadn't missed it. As I struggled to get to my feet the smells of zoo animals filled my senses.

**"Would you like me to help you?"** the serum asked in a sultry voice.

"No, I can do this without your help."

As I struggled to get to my feet, I could feel the serum waiting for an opening. It didn't have long to wait because the table I was using as a brace slid backwards. I tried to  keep my balance but failed and hit my head on the concrete floor. I laid there as my head throbbed to the point I thought I was going to throw up.

**"My, my, William, you do punish yourself for no good reason."** I had given the serum the opening and it took control. As I opened my eyes I could see everything around me. Hap was lying three feet to my right still unconscious. The table had slid a foot away behind me and the coolers were five feet from me. I started to roll towards the coolers and I tried to stop it.

**"Back off!"** the serum screamed making my headache again.

**"I said I'd get you out of this mess you made."**

"Okay. Just be quick about it."

It was still a strange feeling my body doing things without me in control. My body rolled up to the cooler wall and within seconds the serum had me sitting up and then standing.

**"See. I can be useful. Now I'll walk you over to the table and cut the ropes."**

Before I could say a word, I was standing next to the table and cutting the ropes with the knife. I felt the ropes part and slowly move my numb arms around to get the circulation going.

**"There you go William. Now go turn on the lights and I'll let you retake control of your body."**

"You're going to voluntary let me take back control?"

**"Flip the light switch and see."**

I flip the switch and blinded myself. It took several seconds until I could see again without squinting my eyes.

I turned my hands over and over until I realized I was in control again.  "Serum, I feel for the first time we have an understanding."

**"I believe we do to."**

# Chapter 53



April 17<sup>th</sup> 1933
11:25 pm Saturday

"Come on Hap, wake up," I said untying his hands. "I didn't hit you that hard."

I could see movement and then Hap opened his eyes.

"You hit me damn it. What the hell...ah, what happened to you?" he said looking at the lump above my right eye.

"Me? I got tied up for a while doing other things. That's why I let you sleep."

I could see Hap looking around and putting two and two together. "Why didn't you wake me, and before I forget, thanks for saving my life."

"Hap. Helped me to the car." It seems in all the excitement I had forgotten about my right arm that used to have stitches. Favoring it, we entered the darken house and turned on the hall light. I made it to the kitchen before needing to sit down. My entire body ached from the beating I had given it. "Hap. Help me get my suit coat jacket off."

"Captain. I think you need to go to the hospital. Your shoulder looks pretty bad."

"Here, let me look at that." Nancy said walking into the kitchen in her night clothes.

"What do you know about wounds?" I said glaring at her.

"I know a lot about them. I've stitched up a cut or two in my day Bill. You see my dad was always injuring himself on the farm and ah."

"Farm? I though your father worked in the steel mills?"

"Well.. We had a farm until he lost it gambling?"

I was about to argue the point but when she opened my shirt and took it off, the pain changed my mind."

"Oh that's not bad." Nancy said touching the wound gently. She asked Hap to give her a wet and dry towel. "I think with some pressure on these missing stitches It'll stop the bleeding."

**"Give me a few minutes and I'll have you fixed up proper."**

I looked at Hap and he looked at me with the same expression.

For a kid of fifteen, she seems to know a lot for her age. Ten minutes later my shoulder had stopped bleeding and a new bandage was covering it.

Five minutes later my bruises and scratches were cleaned and dressed as well. "Now, Would you two like a drink to relieve the pain?"

"Now just a minute Nancy! Who the hell are you, and where did you learn all this nursing?"

Nancy didn't answer me as she left the kitchen. A minute later she returned carrying Mildred's tray of brandy and set it on the table. I watched in disbelief as she filled three glasses and handed one to Hap and me. "Down the hatch, boys." Nancy emptied her glass and set it back on the tray. "Anyone for another?"

"Now just a damn minute. What's going on here?"

"Well I guess I can tell you now that Muller is on his way back to Germany. You see, I'm not fifteen, I'm twenty three. I'm also a special agent for the FBI. And my job was to keep watch on the house. I know what you're going to say but I've played this part before. You see, I was brought up in Vaudeville playing the little girl with my parents. I had to give it up when I reached eighteen because I wasn't able to hide this figure anymore." She said pointing at her chest

"Then why the bad girl routine? And telling me I was your father. Do you know how badly that scared me?"

"She scared you? Are you telling me you haven't been with other women besides your first wife and me?" Margaret said entering the kitchen.

"I...ah...I. Wait just a minute! You knew she was a plant didn't you!"

"Not at first. But I figured it out when Mildred started defending her."

I look at Hap, "Did you know about this?"

"No Captain. I swear I didn't know."

"Okay. So you're an FBI agent and you knew Muller was heading back to Germany without me."

"Yes."

"Then why did you leave us tied up?"

"You'll have to talk to the Director on that. I wasn't there. I was here in the house under guard by your orders. If I was there. I can assure you I wouldn't have left you to get free on your own."

Chapter 54

April 18th 1933
9:09 am Sunday

I awoke with a headache right between my eyes. I covered my face with the pillow thinking the bright sunlight was causing the problem. Laying there I cleared my mind and thought about relaxing in a bathtub of warm water. The pain started relaxing and in a few minutes it was gone.

**"I took care of that for you."**

I threw the pillow and found Larry lying at the foot of the bed purring. His large green eyes stared back at me as if I was going to ask her a question. When I didn't, she got up and started rubbing on me for attention. I scratched his head for a minute and then got up.

I still wanted to take a long hot shower to relax my aching body but couldn't. My shoulder had seeped a little blood during the night which meant it hadn't closed all the way yet. So after taking a sponge bath, I got dressed and headed down stairs. I found Mildred as usual in the kitchen fixing me something to eat.

"How do you always know when I'll be down for breakfast?"

She smiled at me while holding out a plate full of food.

"That's my little secret Bill, but you can call it mother's intuition. Now go sit down, and don't tell me you're too busy to eat something! Well! hurry up, you're in my way and I have to keep working on dinner before church."

I ate enough to satisfy Mildred. As I sipped on a cup of coffee I wondered where Margaret and Hap were. It wasn't like Hap to pass up food of any kind even when it wasn't cooked for him. I checked the parlor and found it empty and decided the only place left would be the library. I approached the door when I heard the click, click, click of the typewriter. I entered the room and found the two of them there. Margaret was typing and Hap was reading the finished copies of the co-op agreement.

"Well Captain, you're looking a lot better this morning than you did last night."

"Yes. I must admit sleep does wonderful things for your constitution. Margaret are you typing up the proposals?"

"Yes dear. This is the last set."

"Last set. How long have you been up?"

"Not long. I couldn't sleep because the baby wanted to play ball with my kidneys. I'll be done here in a minute. So you can deliver them today if you wish."

I decided to get another cup of coffee and waited for Hap on the porch. The day was sunny and the humidity and temperature were pleasant. Dogwood trees were in full bloom along with all the spring flowers. I had just sat down in a rocker when I heard the telephone ring.

"I'll get it Mildred. It's probably for me anyway."

I went to the parlor and picked up the heavy receiver with my left hand. As I put it to my ear it occurred to me this phone could be quite a weapon if used right. "Hello. This is Detective Barronson."

"Just a minute please. Long distance calling," the operator said. Go ahead please. I have your party on the line."

"Bill this crackle crackle, FBI Director--- Grayson."

The connection was a bad one. It was full of static it was causing me not to hear every word.

"Director, where are you calling from?" I shouted knowing it didn't make any difference.

"I'm in --- Tennessee. The plane--- down all killed--- Muller------."

"I'm sorry sir." The line went dead. "Shall I try and reconnect you?" The operator asked.

"Do you know where he was calling from, operator?"

"Blakeville Tenn. Sir. Shall I try to reconnect?"

"No. I'll wait for him to call back."

I hung up the phone and went to the radio cabinet.

Opening the doors, I turned it on and played with the dial until I found a news station.

"This is WSKN in Knoxville, Tennessee. As we reported earlier this morning a Ford Trimotor passenger plane has crashed just ten miles outside Knoxville.

An eyewitness to the crash has told us the plane was being chased by two by-wing Grumman FF Army fighters.

"Mr. Peter's how did you know they were army planes?"

"I'm not at liberty to say, all I can tell you they are out newest fighter."

"Well folks it looks as if the government is involved in this crash. I wonder if the army shot down the plane? Ah, folks we have to break for this important message from our sponsor." I turned the volume down and got another cup of coffee. The last thing I wanted to her was an ad for something I'd never buy. When I returned to the radio I slowly turned up the volume.

"We're not allowed yet to the crash site but I can still see a large black cloud rising from the area where the plane went down." a pause. "Folks I have just been informed that a man by the name of Anderson has witnessed the downing of the Ford Ti-Motor passenger plane. How did that make you feel Mr. Anderson to know you'd find dead bodies when you got to the crash site?"

"Well. You see the fighter planes weren't shooting at the passenger plane. They were shooting at a strange flying object that looked like a saucer."

"Thank you Mr. Anderson for that eye witness report."

"But what about the. Hey!"

"Get him out of here he's probably drunk on moon shine. Sorry folks. Well. I now see the police chief heading in this direction. Chief can you tell our listeners did anyone survive this horrific plane crash?"

"At this time we have found six bodies. We believe two were the pilot and copilot. One was a woman and the other three men. As for identifying them we'll leave that up to the FBI."

"Which airline did the plane belong to?"

"Eastern by the markings."

I turned off the radio and found Mildred, Hap and Margaret standing at the door.

"Does that plane crash have anything to do with us?" Margaret asked.

"I don't know for sure, but I'd say yes."

The phone rang again and this time the connection was much better.

"Detective Barronson. This is Director Grayson. I wanted to advise you that Carl Muller, Gertrude Becker, are officially dead."

"Then you did have it shot down?"

"No. They were following them until they landed for refueling. We Had agents stationed at every airport within the planes fuel range."

"If that's the case then why did it crash?"

"The pilots said the plane suddenly exploded in midair. We believe Muller and his spy ring had outlive their usefulness."

"If you knew they were leaving the country, why didn't you arrest them last night?" I asked wondering what the hell was wrong with Colton and Purvise.

"They were under instructions not to is all I can tell you now."

"Okay, then how did you know what plane they were on."

"The pilot had sent an SOS to the tower and left his radio key open so we could track them as well. In the meantime I'll leave Nancy there until she gets reassigned to a secretarial position or terminated if that's alright with you."

"Terminated? Why?"

"This was a temporary job that need a girl. It's Hoovers policy that no women will ever become full time field agents."

I hung up the phone and found everybody standing in the doorway. "Why are the FBI agents leaving?" Grace asked with arms folded over her belly. "Aren't they here to protect us? And what about the four creepy looking men that just showed up that smell like garlic."

"Grace! Stop taking. I can't get a word in edgewise."

"Now just a minute Bill, just because you're a detective doesn't mean..."

"Go head Bill, I'll keep Grace quite." Mildred said struggling to keep her hand over Graces mouth.

"Thanks Mildred. Now. I was on the phone with Director Grayson. He was telling me about another plane crash in Tennessee. It seems Muller and his spy ring all died when the plane blew up in midair. That's why the agents are leaving. The other four men were sent here by the Atlanta Mob to help with the protection. They also will be living once I inform them. Does that answer all your questions, Grace?"

"Let go of me mother!" Grace gave Mildred an evil look before tuning on me. "How do we know they're the ones on the plane?"

"You'll just have to trust me on that Grace, and before I forget the Captain told me that he'll give you your job back once the baby is born."

"Really! You're not kidding are you?"

"You can call him if you wish."

"Hap. bring the car around."

"Do you think that is wise Captain in your condition?"

"I think so Hap. I'm in no condition to climb a mountain, but I'm sure I can handle your driving. Just stay under 80 miles per hour please."

"William. It's Sunday. Can't we spend one day a week together?"

"Margaret." I saw the disappointment in her eyes, and decided things could wait till Monday.

"Breakfast is ready. So you better sit down and get what you want before Hap gets to it."

We all ate breakfast and I offered Hap to drive everyone to church that wanted to go. Mildred, Hap, Grace and Lenard excepted. I was surprised that Hap wanted to join them in church but I figured he had an alternative motive, Mildred.

# Chapter 55

April 18th 1933
1:09 pm Sunday

Once they were gone Margaret and I went onto the front porch and sat in the rocking chairs. There was a gentle warm breeze that relaxed every muscle in my body.

"Detective Barronson. May I have a word with you?"

I opened my eyes and found Nancy standing in front of me head bowed. If I hadn't known she was 23 I would have taken her to be 15. "Nancy! I'm so sorry. In all the confusion I forgot about the message Grayson wanted me to give you."

"I'm fired. Right?"

"Oh. William. How could you be so cruel as to not tell here."

"Now wait a minute. Grayson said that you would be transferred into a secretarial position. He didn't say where, but I assumed he wanted you to stay here until he gets in touch with you." I was about to say something else when Nancy said, "I'm fired. If I was going to be transferred he would have already said so. I'll go pack my things and leave before they get back from church.

"William! Can't you do something? Call Grayson and remind him what he can do with that FBI job and Badge."

"Margaret. Please give me a minute. Grayson said she might be let go. So I was thinking why couldn't you be a private eye detective working under my name."

Nancy, Margaret and I went to Margaret's office and work out the basics to set her up in business. "Dear. Let's stop for now. I need to lie down for a while."

"That's sounds like a good place to stop. You and Nancy can work out the rest tomorrow." Nancy helped Margaret up the stairs while I went looking for Hap who had just returned from church. "I see you're still eating Hap." Mildred gave me a pleading look to please get him out of her hair. I winked at Mildred and said to Hap. "Let's take a drive while Mildred makes enough dinner to feed all of us."

"Do we have too?"

"Yes. Now put your shoes back on and let's get going before the sun goes down."

Hap and I headed first to Ray's Pool Hall. We entered the place and found only the bartender.  When he saw us he seemed happy to see us. "Good afternoon Raymond. I see you're working on your coffee's. Is that why you have several cups already poured. Or are you expecting company?"

"Afternoon Detective. You're just in time to try several new coffee respites."

"Okay. Hap pick one and I pick up another." Hap drank his quickly." Taste like Hazel Nut?"

"That's correct."

I picked up my cup and found it to be almost empty. I took a sip and immediately spit it back into the cup.

"I see that one is a no," Raymond said drawing a line through it. What about yours?"

"I liked mine. Can I have another?"

"Ray. Is the Pastor available?"

"Yes. He's upstairs working on next week's sermon."

"Hap. Stay here and sample Raymond's coffee. Be honest about them, the man is thinking of opening a coffee house."

I climbed the stairs slowly. Not only were they steep there wasn't a hand rail for me to hang onto. Reaching the top floor, I found it to be offices. There were three regular windows open, one on each side, front, right and left. Two desks faced the stairs on opposite walls leaving a hallway to a third desk. The pastor was sitting behind the third desk. A secretary or bookkeeper not working today must set in the other two. Today I found two men were sitting in the chairs looking board as hell.

"Good morning Pastor. I said climbing up the last few steps.

"Hold it right there mister."

"It's alright you two. This is Detective Barronson, he has joined our little group. Come, come, up Detective and take a seat, I see you have another folder for us to look at."

"Yes." I said ignoring the two guards while handing him the folder.

"My, my, someone must have a legal secretary working for them." he said opening the folder.

I watched as his eyes moved across the pages devouring each word until he finished it. I could tell by the satisfied look there wasn't going to be any problems.

"Very professional work Detective. Is this the copy that's going to the governments to make our co-op legal?"

"Yes. It hasn't a notary stamp or all the signatures yet, but I thought you'd like to see the final documents."

"Seeing your here, shall we sign Detective?"

"I haven't got the other signatures yet..."

"You can bring me one if you wish later. Right now the only one I'm interested in is your signature."

I thought that was a bit strange but if he's happy with only mine, then I'm happy to.

"So Detective. Now all I have to do is give you the money I promised you to seal the deal."  The pastor got up from his chair and went to a large safe I hadn't noticed. He spun the dials several times until a click let him, opened the heavy door. He seemed to be looking for something that should be in there and wasn't. I was about to back out of the deal when he said, "Ah. Here it is." The pastor brought out a thick leather brief case and set it on the floor. He then closed the safe and returned to his desk and handed the case to me. "Now we are partners Detective."

I opened the case and saw packs and packs of $100 bills.

"I can assure Detective that there is $150,000 in that case. If you wish to count it then by all means be my guest. He handed me another sealed envelope and said,

"That envelope is the $25,000 start up money I promised you."

I was so stunned by this much money in my possession, I couldn't get a word to come out of my mouth.

"I see by the look on your face this is more money than yell ever see in a lifetime."

Suddenly the shock of all that money disappeared as the two guards grabbed one of my arms and squeezed. "Let me remind you Detective, this money is for the co-op. So be very careful who will handle your finances, because if you fail to make good.

A number of you will be visiting the East River in New York."

"I understand and have put things already in action. I would also like you to pull your men from my place."

"I thought that was part of our agreement."

"It was but it seems Muller and his agents died in a plane crash today."

"That's a shame, I was looking forward to meeting him."

We left Ray's Pool Hall and headed for Doug's Pawn Shop without stopping for anything in between. I had shown Hap the money and he was as nervous as I was with it in the car.

"Captain, are you going to give them all the money?"

"No. I only want Doug and Clair to know about the $25,000 start up money. We entered the store and found the two of them eating dinner. I noticed at once Doug's spirits were much improved. I handed Doug his copy of the co-op agreement. "They signed their copy and mine as well. You'll get another copy once everybody has signed to keep as well.

"That means we're in business." Doug said smiling at the brief case.

"Yes we are Doug, but before you celebrate. I need to inform you of his verbal demands seeing you'll be handling the money and ledgers. The backer who is not on the document has his own bookkeeper who will inspect your books once a month. He tells me this man can find any little mistakes and if he finds one you, Clair and me will disappear from the face of the earth. So I want both your assurances that every penny spent will be accounted for. If you can't do this Doug. Then don't take this money." I opened the brief case and set the stack of $25,000 on the counter.

I watched as Doug's eyes lit up as he stared at the money. With trembling hands he reached for it when Clair stopped him. "No dear. Leave the money alone. I love you Doug, but I know in my heart that temptation will be too great. So Bill please put it back in the briefcase and get the hell out of here." she said tearing up her copy.

Chapter 56

April 18$^{th}$ 1933
2:15 pm Sunday

Hap and I headed for the door when an idea crossed my mind. "Clair I have another idea. Doug and you can still handle the books just not the money. This way we'll have a double check on everything we buy or sell. What do you think?"

"I think it is a great idea Bill. What do you think dear?"

"I think it would work fine. I' m ashamed that the money is too overpowering. I would have found a way to alter the books in order to have more than we should. It was the same thing with the Confederate Coin. I just had to have it and look where it got me. I'll promise you this in front of y'all that the ledgers will balance with there's every month."

"Okay then, here's you typed copy. Now go to work and sell something even if you have to discount it Doug." We all laughed.

Next we went to Wang and Chan and set up things with him as well. He gave me $5,000 also to start the business. I assured him he would have a formal receipt. I did sign the one he had which seemed to satisfy him. Both Hap and myself were surprised, when Wang gave us our new clothes we had bought for free.

Now feeling everyone knew I had all this money I told Hap to head for the house. I wanted Mildred to put it in her safe. I had thought about a bank, but the run on them had closed most of them down. The ones that were still open I didn't trust either. Once I deposited that much money the bank could close its doors and abscond with the money.

As we pulled up to the house I found Margaret and Grace rocking on the front porch talking. Parking in Larry's drive way we walked across the lawn with his Larry my cat following us.

"Well don't you look like a business man carrying that brief case," Grace said struggling to get up.

"How far along are you now Grace?"

"Eight months and I can't wait for it to be over," she said rubbing her bully. "Now what secrets do you have in that case?"

"He probably has a $1,000,000 in there or maybe two," Margaret said as the two of them laughed.

We headed into the house and I found Mildred reading a book to Nancy. "Mildred, I need to put something in your safe."

"Okay, is it money to start the co-op business?"

"Yes and no."

Now the whole house was interested in the briefcase I was carrying. As we entered Mildreds bedroom, I waited for her to open the safe before sitting the briefcase on the bed.

"Now all of you and especially you Grace need to sit down." I opened the case and took out the first stack of money and handed it to Mildred. I then handed her two more stacks.

"This can't be the money for the co-op Bill. There's got to be $50,000 here."

"That's correct," and started handing here six more stacks.

"William, what have you gotten yourself into?" Margaret said wide-eyed with concern.

"Bill. I'll not have stolen money in my house," Mildred said starting to hand it back to me.

"Mildred. It's not stolen. There is $150,000 there that belongs to the three of you. Our partner was able to get that much money back from what the Genovese family blackmailed from you. This $30,000 is the start up money for the co-op."

Mildred took the money, locked the safe, and spun the dial several times.

"Bill. I think this money needs to go to a bank."

"I thought of that, but what bank can we trust not to close its doors once they have the money."

"I have a suggestion?" Nancy said stepping forward. "I would open a small business close by, with a large safe."

"Where would we find an empty building with a safe?

Nancy thought a minute. "Why not buy an empty bank. I believe there's one two miles away.

That way we'd run the place and use Henry and some off duty policeman as guards."

"Your idea has some merit Nancy. Let's go check that bank out."

Hap, Nancy and I got in my car and we followed her directions. Hap pulled up and parked at the corner of Boulevard and Woodland. We got out and Nancy pointed at an empty store front. "I thought this would be a good place for me to open my detective agency."

"How does opening your detective agency and looking for an empty bank have anything in common?" Hap said.

"Easy." We followed her around the corner and walked a short distance to a brown brick two story building. It must have been built in the last five years because it was the ugliest building I had ever seen. Whoever had built it had spent as little money on it as possible. From the front entrance all you were looking at was a simple glass door with two windows flanking it. If it hadn't been for the sign, you would have taken it as a warehouse.

"It sure is plain," I said peaking in the dirty windows.

"That it is but wait till you see the inside." Nancy unlocked the door and we walked into a dark cobweb dungeon.

From what I could make out there were three teller windows. One small desk a chair and dust in everything. "So where is the vault, Nancy."

"Back behind the counter. Hap go get our flashlights out of the car. I don't know about you but I can't see a damn thing."

Five minutes later Hap handed me a flashlight. I turned it on and looked around the room finding it was as ugly as it was in the dark. "Come on you two, I'll show you the safe. We walked behind the teller windows and opened a wooden door. As we entered the hallway it reminded me of the bunker hallway. A shiver ran up my spine at the thought of being operated on again.

**"Don't worry about that, Bill. This place is only a bank."**

We walked passed the bathrooms and then opened another door. To my utter surprise there in front of me was an open round vault door. As I stepped inside the walls had four shelves lining them.

"Is this what I think it was, Nancy?"

"I'm not sure but I believe a lot of money was kept here and it wasn't by the government."

We left the bank and went back to the car. I stopped and looked in the window that Nancy had said it could be her detective agency. "It looks a little small Nancy, and out of the way. Wouldn't be better to have an office downtown, say on the tenth floor."

"Probably, but you see the backdoor opens out onto an alley and so does the bank. That way I can keep an eye on the place as well."

We headed back home and dropped off Nancy. We then headed for Kim's place. "I believe I know what your plan is Captain. You want to get Kim to move back to her old location. Right."

Hap pulled up in front of Kim's new location and we found it nearly empty. As we walk in, I spotted Kim and the cook sitting at a table looking very dejected. "Hap! Bill! I'm so glad you stopped by. Can I fix you something?"

"Yes. But first I want to talk to you about moving."

"Moving? I can't afford to move. As you can see there's not much business after all the other shops close at five."

That's what I wanted to talk to you about. Your old location is up for sale. How would you like to reopen it?"

# Chapter 57

April 19th 1933
6:15 pm Monday

I hadn't slept well that night because every time I closed my eyes I started thing about what the pastor had said. "If you lose the money for whatever reason, it'll be the East River for you and them."

I looked at the clock and decided I might as well get up. I got dressed and tip toed to the door hoping I wouldn't wake Margaret up. Turning the handle ever so slowly I opened the door just enough to slip out. I was about to close the door when I heard, "Have a good day dear."

"You to dear." I closed the door and sat down on the stairs and put my shoes on. "Captain. Why are you putting your shoes on now." Hap yawned heading for the dining room. "Because I didn't want to wake up Margaret." I yawned as well. "Hap help me up." We both walked down the stairs smelling the coffee brewing.

I sip coffee while Hap attacked three breakfasts before he was ready to go. My first stop was to the Whitney's to give him a typed copy and to tell them to put a list together of what they needed. Hap then drove to the Bradford farm and I repeated what I had told the Whitney's. As we headed back towards town, I got a call from the station.

"Detective. There's been another fire reported in Vine City. I don't think it has anything to do with the others, but I thought you'd like to know."

"Hap. I think it's time to use the siren." We were forty minutes outside Atlanta, so by the time we got there the fire was out. One house had burned to the ground and the ones on either side had been damaged as well.

"I spotted the Fire Captain directing his men and headed in his direction. "Captain. I'm Detective Barronson from Atlanta, due you think this one has anything to do with our fires?"

"No. It seems that young man standing next to his mother was playing with matches."

I looked over my shoulder and saw the boy was five or six.

When he saw me looking at him he hid his face in his mother's dress. "Well then Captain. I'll leave you to finish putting this one out."

As I headed back to my car I saw a policeman talking to the mother. I got into the car and Hap said. "I'm sure they'll have a talk with the parents as well about his kid playing with matches."

I called the station and told them this fire was unrelated to ours. "Detective. A call has come in from a Mildred Adams. She says it's an emergency." Hap headed for the house with lights and siren blaring.

"Do you think the FBI was wrong about Muller being dead?"

As we pulled up in front of the house I found several people on the porch talking. I jumped out while Hap parked in our usual spot. As I started up the steps I heard a woman scream from the upstairs window. I Pulled my gun and rushed into the house looking for Muller's men.

"What are the guns for?" Lenard asked sitting in the parlor with a drink in his hand.

"Then who is screaming?" I said putting my gun away.

"It's Grace, Bill, she's in labor."

"Labor! Why haven't you called for an ambulance. She needs a doctor, nurses, and other hospital things."

"No hospital Bill. There isn't time. Anyway, Mildred knows how to deliver babes and I really don't trust hospitals anyway."

"Here. Have a cigar and a drink. Mildred told me to boil some hot water, but so far they haven't used a drop. Do you think it's to keep us from interfering with the delivery?" Lenard asked poring himself another drink.

"Lenard. I think you'd better slow down on the drinking. By the look of your eyes, you're about to pass out."

"Margaret entered the room and said. "It's a boy Lenard." When Lenard didn't answer. "He's either fainted or asleep."

"Just like a man. He's more interested in a baseball game than in becoming a father."

"Margaret, he's passed out from drinking so much to steady his nerves. I'm sure a baseball game doesn't compare to having a baby."

"Well you better not pass out when we have ours." Margaret said glaring at him.  "Not after all the work I've been through so far, and you're going to be in the room when I have him."

"Now just a minute Margaret. My jobs to pass out cigars and.."

"And get drunk! I'll not have it William. I'll not have it!" she said heading back upstairs in a tiff.

I looked at Hap and he looked at me. "What the hell did I say to make her so mad?"

"I'm not sure Captain, but whatever it was I wouldn't say it again." Suddenly I felt very tired as people rushed up to see the baby. I sat back in the overstuffed parlor chair and closed my eyes.

**"I see you're in trouble again with your wife again."**

"No I'm not, she's just jealous of her sister."

**"That reminds me you also have a brother as well."**

"I don't have a brother. I'm an only child."

**"Not that kind of brother, my kind of brother."**

"Captain. Wake up! You're talking to yourself again." I heard someone saying. I opened my eyes and found Hap shaking me. My heart was racing so fast I thought it would tear itself out of my chest. I grabbed Hap's arms and pushed him away. "Why are you shaking me?"

"Captain! Bill! You were having a bad dream, and talking out load to someone."

I let go of Hap's arm and sat back in my chair thinking about what the venom had said. There's another one of me out there. Another one.., with the insight and enhanced powers I've been struggling to get rid of. I could feel the sweat trickling down between my fingers as I struggled to regain control. "Sorry Folks," I said to a dozen people looking at me. "I had a dream I was delivering the baby instead of Mildred." I got a few chuckles of understanding from the women.

I taking out my handkerchief, and wiped the sweat from my face and rubbed the throbbing pain between my eyes.

"William. What's the matter?" Margaret said in a concerned voice. When she reached me the look on her face scared me again. "Margaret, what's the matter?"

"Your face is so white."

"Oh, for a minute there I thought you were in labor and I was delivering it."

"William your soaking wet, and you smell bad. Let's get you upstairs and into the shower. Then you're going right to bed. I'll have no man of mine running around sick."

I struggled to my feet and felt Margaret's arm slip around my waste and lead me towards the stairs.

"I believe my shoulder is bleeding again?"

"I'll deal with that when we get to it."

She lead me up the stairs as people stepped aside to let us pass. "What was Grace's baby, a boy or girl?"

"A boy. And I hope he's as stubborn as his mother is."

I had a shower which seemed to revive me some. My wounded shoulder hadn't bled when the water hit it. "Your shoulder looks find William and I didn't find any blood on your shirt."

**"Don't worry about your shoulder. It's already repaired."** The serum whispered in my head.

"Let's go see the baby honey?"

"You're not going anywhere but to bed, and tomorrow is your Monday. So for the rest of today consider this your Sunday."

"Margaret. I can't take the day off."

"If God can rest on the seventh day, so can you on the eighth."

I didn't argue any longer with Margaret, because the fact was I wasn't sure myself how much longer I could stand up.

"I thought you took a shower?"

"I did."

"Well you need another one."

"How about a bath instead."

I sat soaking in the hot water as every stiff, bruised or sore muscle began to relax.

Margaret, being concerned about me, was washing my back with a warm washcloth.

"Your wound is looking much better than yesterday. You must have an exceptional body to heal this quickly."

"I do. It seems my mother's side of the family have always been quick healers."

"Well then, I hope our son will inherit some as well."

I just smiled and nodded in agreement. I hadn't told Margaret or anyone in this household about my special abilities. I hadn't ever given it a thought that my blood could be passed on. I started counting back the months to when Margaret had gotten pregnant. My calculations put me infected three months before our son's conception.

"Alright dear. The water has gotten cold, so out you go."

The hot water had done its job very well. I was so sleepy all I wanted to do was crawl into bed and sleep till tomorrow.

# Chapter 58

April 19<sup>th</sup> 1933
4:43 pm Monday

I woke up to the sounds of Grace and her crying baby. Evidently it must have been feeding time, and knowing Grace she didn't want to get up. I rolled over and found Margaret had pulled the covers over her head.

Not quite awake, I got out of bed and stubbed my toe on the  chair once again. Grabbing my foot with my right hand, I made an attempt to sit down on the chair. I sat down alright, by missing the seat and hitting the floor with a loud thump.

"What, who was that?"

I turned and found Margaret sitting straight up in bed still asleep.

"It's okay dear, just lay back down and go back to sleep." For once Margaret did what she was told, she laid back down flat on her back and started snoring. When my  toe stopped throbbing, I got to my feet and glared at the chair as if it had done that on purpose. I grabbed the chair and limped to the window. "I've had enough of you getting in my way, chair. It's either me or you chair, and being the master of this house it's going to be you that's going out the window. I opened the window as much as it would go and forced part of the chair out the window. The rest wouldn't fit no matter what I did. Frustrated, I was about to break the top window pane out when I started to laugh.

"Bill," I whispered to myself. "It's a chair, and it's not alive. Just move it or hide it or better yet remember it's there and walk around the damn thing."

Pulling the chair out, I set it down as quietly as possible so as not to wake Margaret.

"Did you two finally make up?" Margaret mumbled from under the covers.

"Yes dear now go back to sleep."

"I'd like to if you'd stop fighting with the furniture."

I quickly got dressed and put on one of my new suits. I had picked a charcoal gray suit which made me look like an executive.

As I studied myself in the mirror I decided I needed a handkerchief in the top left pocket. I then strutted down the hall with my new matching hat and walked into the dining room. I found Nancy, Lenard, Henry, and Hap already seated. When they saw me strut in I didn't get the reception I expected.

What I did get was cat calling and who's the fancy New York City dude. I didn't say a word, instead I fixed my plate and started to eat when I realized this was dinner.

"Well it's nice to see someone dresses up for dinner." Mildred said looking at me and smiling.

I looked around the table and saw everyone looking at me as if I was naked. "What's the matter?" I said not wanting to admit I didn't know what day it was. When everyone was done I motioned for Hap to follow me. Once on the front porch I could see by the sun it was the same day. "Today is still Monday?"

"Yes it is Captain. For a minute there I wondered if you thought it was Tuesday by the way you looked at the food."

"I must admit I wasn't sure what day it is."

"Bill, I have the desk sergeant on the phone. He needs to speak to you."

We walled back into the parlor and picked up the receiver. "Detective Barronson."

"My, it's been hours since you checked in."

"I'm sorry I should have called in after leaving Vine's."

"There's been another fire this afternoon. The Captain is under the impression you already there. So it would be a good idea to get there as fast as you can."

"Where is it?"

"The old opera house on Marietta Street."

Hap and I raced to our car and headed into the city. As usual there was an accident that slowed us down. "Hap I'll walk the rest of the way." I could see the black cloud billowing above what had once been the business district in 1889. It had never opened as the opera house. Instead it became the state capitol building until the new one was built in 1899.

I was three blocks away from the fire when an explosion sent a large rolling fire ball into the air. It was so powerful a number of upper floor windows shattered. Glass shards fell among the onlookers sending them into a stampede for cover. I got knocked against the wall as a bleeding woman with a head wound raced by me. I started to go after her when I saw a number of people lying in the street with cuts, bruises and broken bones from being run down by the stamping crowd.

"You!" A man shouted. "Come help me with my wife. She has a broken ankle and can't walk."

I ran to the man and helped get his wife to her feet. "I don't think this is going to work mister. Your wife has passed out from the shock."

"I'll carry her then! Can you help me left her into my arms."

**"Why don't you carry her yourself. You know I have the strength."**

Suddenly I picked the woman up in my arms and headed for

a nearby store. "You can't bring that woman in here!" The owner said blocking our way. "Look, this woman has a broken ankle and cuts from broken glass."

"I'm sorry mister, but I have no place for you to put her down, look." As he stepped aside I saw his place was already filled with dozens of people. "Who here is not hurt!" For what seemed an hour but was only seconds three men and a boy stepped forward. "Look this woman his hurt badly. I need you to get these people out.."

Another explosion rocked the building shattering more windows. Women and men screamed as glass hit the pavement exploding into hundreds of deadly spears. "Captain! Over here!"

I turned around with the woman in my arms and saw Hap pulling up with the car. Disregarding the glass Hap jumped out of the car as I ran towards him. We put the unconscious  woman in the back seat. I moved to let her husband get in but found him injured a well.

**"I've got him."**

# Chapter 59

April 19th 1933
10:53 pm Monday

With both of them in the back seat we headed for Grady Hospital. By the time we got there, the place was abuzz with hundreds of injured people. I showed my badge several times to get some help without success. "You!" I said grabbing an orderly who was pushing an empty gurney. "This way." I led him to our car and showed him the two injured people.

We put the husband on his gurney as he was closest to the door. "I trust you to come back with another gurney. That's her husband you have there."

As the wife disappeared into the hospital, I said "Well done Hap."

"Thanks Captain, but I think we need to go home. I have a few cuts that needs some attention."

I looked at Hap and saw several cuts on his face and hands. "Let's go inside hand have a doctor look at you?"

"I don't need a doctor, but you look like you could use one."

**"Don't worry about your cuts. I'll have you mended in no time."**

I looked in the mirror as saw dried blood on my face and hands as well. "We might as well go home and get cleaned up." I said feeling the serum losing control.

"Car 54 to dispatch, over."

"Will be out of touch. Have received minor injuries and need some medical attention, over."

We headed for home and reached our destination just as the sun was setting.

"Well, hear goes Hap." I said getting out of the car.

"What do you mean?"

"You'll see once they get a look at us."

The first person to see us was Mildred, "Have you two been fighting." she said looking the two of us over.

"I'll take me all night to patch you boys up. So get into the kitchen so your wives don't see you.

"Why's that, Mildred?"

"I don't need to deliver another baby, that's why.

I'll get Nancy to help with you Bill, why I clean this old man up."

"Old man. I'll have you know young lady that I saved two people today without a thought to my safety." Hap took off his suit coat and turned around. "See, a piece of glass cut me open when we were getting them into the back seat."

Mildred Help him remove his shirt before examining the wound. "My that's a nasty cut, Hap. I'll have to sow it up." Mildred winked at me as she opened a draw and brought out a large needle. I had seen her use it once before to sow up a turkey for thanksgiving. "Turn around now Hap."

The next thing I heard was Hap hitting the floor as he  passed out.

"Well, I see it isn't superman after all Bill." Mildred Nancy and I picked up Hap and placed him face down on the kitchen table. "I guess I shouldn't have scared him that way." Mildred said wiping blood from off his back.

"He did take quite a beating and that cut on his back looks deep, Mildred."

"I see Nancy has cleaned you up already. My poor man here needs both our attention. So why don't you head for bed while we finish up here."

I didn't argue because the serum had used up most of my energy in repairing me. "Bill, I how is it that your wounds are so superficial compared to Hap's?"

I started to give her a cock and bull answer when her eye's widened in amazement. "You, ah, Bill," Nancy said touching my arm to see if it was real. "You just..."

"I heal fast Nancy. It's been a trait of mind that my mother said came from her side of the family."

"That's amazing, Bill. Has anybody told you.."

"Yes. And they say I'm a freak of nature. So some people are strong, others are geniuses, in math, science, music. I just happen to heal quickly."

"I wonder if your son will have the same trait?"

"I don't know, Nancy." As I climbed the stairs I felt a knot in my stomach. Would some of Cochran's serum transfer to him as well.

$$\text{---------} \otimes \text{---------}$$

# Chapter 60

April 20th 1933
7:43 am Tuesday

"Where to Captain." Hap asked looking as if he had just got up.

"Hap, why don't you take the off. I'll let the Captain know you were injured yesterday."

"No Thanks Captain. I'm, fine...now that I have two band aids on my little cut."

"Okay then let's head to the motor pool to swap out this car for another."

Hap headed towards the station mumbling to himself. "Hap, what seems to be the matter?"

"Mildred! That's what's the matter!"

"Why are you mad at her. Didn't see fuss over you last night while she cleaned and stitched your cut and scratches."

"And what about that joke she played on me with that turkey needle."

"I believe you were embellishing your wound just a little, weren't you?"

Hap didn't answer. So I left it alone as we pulled into the parking lot and parked in front of maintenance. "Hap. I'll go see the Captain and see if we can get a replacement. Maybe they can clean the blood off the seats easily."

As I walked in the back door I heard them talking about the fire. "Detective Barronson did you hear about Mitch Anderson's exploits last night?"

"No, what exploits are you referring two?"

"Well. It seems he ran into the burning building and saved a Hobo from burning to death. Then later when the second building exploded he saved three firemen that had gotten trapped. At the rate he's going hell be a bigger hero in this town that you."

I shrugged my shoulders and said, "I didn't know we were in competition. The only thing he and I have in common id to save lives. As for the rest of it he's more than welcome to be in the limelight."

As I headed up the stairs I heard one of them say. "Well isn't he and ass today, letting the fire department become number one in the city."

I knocked on the Captain's door and entered. "Detective, I see you recovered nicely from yesterday's explosions."

"Yes, I was lucky. Just a few cuts and scratches is all."

"How about you partner?"

"He took a few deep cuts to his back and arms but other than that he's okay."

"I see by this morning's paper Chief Mitch Anderson was quite a hero yesterday. I also see we weren't mentioned. Why's that?"

I explained what had happened when the windows were blown out and people were hurt. I also embellished Hap's rescue of me and the injured woman. "So Captain, I believe Hap should be award a medal for bravery."

"What about you?"

"I don't need any more headlines, Captain. But if you award Hap it would reflect on the whole department. Especially if it get in the afternoon paper."

When I walked back to maintenance I found the car being worked on. I also found Hap asleep in the waiting room. I didn't wake him until the car was ready for us. It seems all they had to do was swap out the seats from a wrecked model. "Hap, it's time to go."

"Okay, Captain. I was just resting my eyes."

"I'll drive Hap. The Captain wants to see you about yesterday."

"Okay, are you going to wait?"

"No I believe you're going to be there awhile. So call me on the radio and I'll swing by and pick you up."

Hap, got out of the car and had a worried look on his face. "Hap, I want you to know that I'm proud to have you as my partner."

"Thanks Captain, I've enjoyed our time together as well."

"I heading for the Flat Iron Building to have a chat with John Junior, and don't get upset you're not being fired."

I worked my way through the traffic and hundreds of pedestrianizes crisscrossing the streets like ants. When I finally reached the parking lot. As I opened the door I heard the whistle of an approaching train. I dash to the front door and entered it as a cloud of swirling smoke tried to follow me. After brushing off smoke soot I found the lobby refurbished. The only difference was there wasn't an information desk with a pretty woman behind it. Disappointed I walked to the elevators and noticed a black information sign with white movable letters was mounted to the wall. It was labeled by floors one through ten with letters stating offices to rent. The only floor occupied was the tenth floor and it belong to the McCallum Corporation.

President offices 1010
Vice President    1008
Law Offices    1003-1005

I pushed the call button for the elevator operator. When the doors opened there wasn't anyone in the elevator including the operator.

Not sure what to do next, I stepped into the elevator and looked around I spotted a roll of numbered buttons 1 2 3 4 5 6 7 8 9 10. I pick the number one. The elevator doors closed and the elevator rose to that floor.

As the doors opened I looked at the unfinished rooms and pushed the number ten button. The elevator started rising faster than any other I'd been in.

**"I don't like this either. Give me control."**

"I will not. And don't you try to take control either."

I said as the number 10 light up and the elevator slammed me to the floor in an emergency stop. I staggered to my feet waiting for the door to open. Not wanting to touch the control buttons, I counted to ten and then pressed the open button. Nothing happened so I punched it several more times before it finally started to open.

**"Hurry, before this thing's doors close on you."**

I didn't hesitate a second when I saw I had enough space to get out. The shock of making it out unscathed had me in a trance. All I could do was stand there and look at the open doors.

"Are you alright?" A man's deep voice said. When I didn't answer he touched my shoulder. The act of doing that broke the spell. "Oh! Yes, I was just admiring this new pilot-less elevator.

"Oh yes it's quite a remarkable machine. I'm thinking of have put one in my building. That way I can eliminate the operators." he said stepping into the elevator.

"Well, I have a feeling you'll change your mind in a minute about eliminating their jobs. Just make sure you  touch the L button first."

I turned and headed down the hall indicating McCallum's office. I couldn't have been 10' from the elevator when I heard a scream and said. "Just wait till it stops."

At the end of the hall was a door with the number 1010.

I opened the door and found the same rude secretary sitting at her desk.

"Can I help you?" she said recognizing me.

"Well if it isn't the smiling, cheerful Miss. Rudeness. I see you've already taken your ugly pill for the day." I said walking up to her desk.

"Mr. McCallum sees no one without an appointment!

Trying not to lose my temper, I smiled and showed her my badge. "Here is my appointment."

She looked at my badge and then touched it. "I can get one just like that at the five and ten." She pointed at the door with her pen and said, "Out!"

Not wanting to hit her, I stepped around her desk and handcuffed her to her chair. I then stuffed my handkerchief in her mouth and headed for the inner door. I knocked twice and opened the door to a room that would have been his fathers. John Junior was sitting at the Majors old desk looking over a number of papers. "I thought that was you out there harassing my secretary. Didn't she explain you need to make an appointment?"

"Well. It's nice to see you again John.. Junior.."

"Don't call me junior. My father's dead. So I'm in charge now and I'm just John!"

"Okay, John. I'll give you that point, and you also have acquired your grandfather's rudeness."

I took a seat in front of his desk lit a cigarette and waited for him to surrender.

I finished my cigarette and lit another while John kept ignoring me. "I can do this all day John. Or I can take you downtown to jail and I don't mean the station. You see I've been given privileges with the FBI. They have a nice cell in their basement with your name on it."

"So it's the FBI. My lawyers will have me out in hours."

"Not if they don't know where you are."

I watched Johns eyes narrow and then saw them surrender.

"Okay. Detective, what do you want?"

"Now, see. Isn't that much easier. If you had cooperated earlier, I would already have been here and gone. So here is what I want to know." I opened my suit coat and brought out a folded piece of paper and laid it on his desk. "It says here, that you own most of these buildings that have burned. The last time we met, you didn't have a nickel to rub between two fingers. Can you explain where all this money has come from?"

"Are you insinuating I had them torched for the insurance money?"

"Well.. Yes."

John flipped a switch on his intercom and said, "Come to my office and bring your files with you on all the building that have burned."

Shortly a well-dressed man that must have been a lawyer and another man shorter and older came in behind him carrying the folders. John introduced them, "Philip Lee Anderson. my lawyer, and Bryan Cobb, my accountant. Bryan. Give the Detective the folders and explain anything he ask you."

I started with the McKenzie building. As I scanned the file I found the building wasn't insured for fire. I see here you had bought the McKenzie building."

"No we were in the process of buying it. Now that it burned are offer will be significantly lower."

"I see the warehouse fire was insured for $250,000."

"Yes, and we did collect that much."

"What was in the warehouse that cost that much?"

"We were storing Andrew Carnegie library books and art pieces while the inside was being remodeled."

I checked out the other fires along with this building's fire and didn't find anything suspicious. "Is there anything else you'd like to see, Detective."

"Yes, but that'll wait." I looked at the three of them and didn't see any telltale signs that said they were lying. "John, do you think you're being targeted?"

"I don't see why. I've managed to satisfy all the creditors."

"What about enemies. Is there anyone that stands out."

"As a matter of fact there is," John said smiling at me.

"Your mother in law, Mildred and her two illegitimate daughters."

"I doubt that. You're to insignificant a person for them to worry about you any longer. I on the other hand find you a very significant person."

"Why would you say that, Detective? Cobb asked.

"Any corporation that has this many fires in such a short time is either in finical trouble or is being forced to sell out." I could see I had hit a nerve with John, as for Cobb his stone face told me the same. "Well gentlemen, I think that's all the questions for now."

"Any time Detective," Cobb said standing up and walking towards me. "Let me walk you to the elevator."

"That's okay, I'll take the stairs. Besides I need to uncuff your secretary." I walked out the door and found she had already been uncuff.

"I believe these belong to you Detective?" he said handing them back to me.

"Thanks, I wondered where I had left them."

He grabbed my arm and tried to drag me towards the elevator. "I can find my own way out." I said sticking my 38 into his rib's.

"Tony, let the Detective go." Cobb said standing in the doorway.

"I don't like a man that treats a woman like that."

"Tony…Let the man leave. I'm sure he didn't mean to hurt your friend."

Tony let go of my arm and slipped his hand inside his suit coat. "Tony," I said. "I apologizes to you for me tying the lady up." That seemed to satisfy him. When I reached the exit door I looked at Cobb. "Tell John I said hello to Vito Genovese the next time he's in town."

It took me some time walking down that many stairs, but it was a lot safer that using the elevator. When I got to the lobby I found Tony waiting for me. "Tony, what did your boss tell you?"

"He said," I could see on his face he was trying to remember what Cobb had told him. "He said for me to make you an offer."

"An offer?" I said reaching for my 38.

"Yes, he says you need to make an appointment next time."

"I's that all?"

"Ah, no. He said to tell you next time I can deal with you if you don't make appointment."

I got back into my car and heard Hap on the radio.

"Captain, I'm ready to go. Over."

"I'll be there in thirty."

When I reached the station, I found Hap talking with the desk Sergeant. "Well, how did it go?"

"Much better than I expected. I'm being given a medal for bravery."

"Is that for saving the three of us last night?"

"I knew it was you, Captain. You.."

"I did nothing of the sort. Besides if it wasn't for you the woman could be dead instead of being in the hospital."

"What did you find out about McCallum?"

"I'll tell you on the way over to last night's fire."

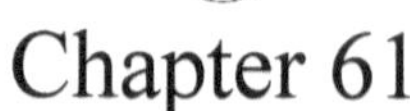

# Chapter 61

April 19th 1933
11:43 am Monday

It took some time to reach the old opera house fire. Even though it had been almost 24 hours since the fire had  started. I counted five firetrucks still hosing down the two block damage. "Hap park here. I see Mitch Anderson talking to a number of reporters."

"Hap and I walked over to the group of reporters interviewing Mitch. When the reporters saw us the immediately ran over to us and started throwing questions at Hap. Feeling a little left out I worked my way out of the crowd and joined Mitch who had the same look on his face as I had. "Can you tell me what started the fire."

"Well, from what I've inspected so far it looks as if it started in the back room, by some hobos no doubt. It then spread to the upper floors and the to the front offices."

"What about the explosions?"

"At first we thought it could be gas leaks, but I don't believe that's the cause."

"Can we have a look at the second building, or is it still too hot?"

"We can take a look, but there's still a lot of hot spots."

"Let's take a walk anyway. It looks like Hap well be tied up the reporters for some time." As we walked along another smaller explosion blew bits of flaming lumber into the air. "I see what you mean by hot spots." As I looked around it occurred to me that three buildings on this block had burned almost to the basements. It then occurred to me that the Aragon Hotel had blown up in the same manner.

"Mitch I also heard you save three of your firemen that were tripped in one of the burning buildings."

"Yes." he said nervously looking away from me.  "I was telling the reporters about it when you two showed up."

"I must admit that you must work out a lot to be that strong, and by your looks you didn't get burned?"

"I got lucky is all."

"It seems you have gotten lucky twice since meeting you, and that reminds me. I've wanted to ask you. Have you ever met a man named Robert Cochran?"

"Cochran? No I haven't. Is he somebody I should know?"

**"He knows who Cochran is. He has some of me in him."**

"Hmm, that seems unlikely Mitch. He was the curator at the zoo."

"At the zoo? I don't ever go to the zoo."

"Then how about a man named Muller. He's German and worked at the zoo."

"No. I already told you I don't ever go to the zoo."

"Well maybe you met them at a bar or restaurant?"

"Is there some reason you're interrogating me about them?"

"No, but it seems you've done some extraordinary feats of strength, that I could only do." I could see Mitch was becoming agitated as I pressed him.

"I don't know what you're trying to insinuate, but I never met those two men and as for the other, it's none of your business."

Mitch walked away from me and started talking to some of his men indicating our talk was at an end. "Captain, I'm sorry about taking so long. Is there something I've missed?"

"Not much. It seems Mich thinks some hobo's started the fire which spread to the other buildings."

"From what I can see, they could have started the fire. But the explosion's no, there had to be something like dynamite stored in them as well."

"You know Hap I believe you could be right about that."

"Why's that?"

"You remember the Aragon Hotel explosion. I was investigating the McCallums plot to rebuild the Confederacy. I found in the hotel basement they were stockpiling weapons stolen from Fort Bragg."

"I see where you're going with this, Captain. They must have been storing weapons in more places than the Aragon. If that's the case then why didn't you know about it?"

"Because they all died in the basement looking for the Majors stolen gold."

"If that's the case we need to have all the buildings inspected in Atlanta for more caches."

"That's a tall order, Hap. I believe we need to inform the FBI about it." We returned to our car and headed for the FBI building. As we entered the building I spotted Agent Miles coming out of the elevator.

"Morning. Agent Miles, do you have a moment?"

"Good morning Detective, and you too Hap. I was just about to head to your station to advise you about the plane crash."

"Excellent. We were on our way here to do the same. How about a coffee at the shop across the street."

The three of us sat at a booth in the back right corner. The place looked a lot like Kim's place. A small counter seating five people, six tables and four booths. I could see the hungry look on Hap's face and decided we might as well have lunch while we talked.

"So. Is Muller and Gertrude actually dead?"

"Yes. All the bodies in the airplane have been accounted for. Our people in Washington are waiting on the bodies to be ship to them for better identification."

"Then how do you know Muller and Gertrude are dead?"

"We only found one woman's body. Lucky for us her body wasn't in the burning wreckage.  She must have been blown out of the plane before it crashed. As for Muller, we found a burned body that matches his description. That's why we're waiting on his autopsy verification before letting the German embassy know of their deaths."

"It's a shame, Gertrude, didn't take Grayson's offer seriously, or maybe Muller suspected she had become a double agent. The paper also states you have to fighter planes shoot them down?"

"We didn't shoot them down, the plane's wing exploded and  the plane dove into the ground. The State Department wanted them alive to make a political statement to Germany. The German ambassador was pushing for them to be extradited to Germany for trial."

"But now that they're dead it doesn't matter. Or does it?" I said looking at Hap to see if he agreed.

Our food came and we ate and talked until we were done. Lighting a cigarette, I asked, "I'm going to bounce a theory off of you before we talk to Grayson. I'm sure you are aware of the fire and explosions."

"Yes, I was going to ask you about that."

"I'm sure you're familiar with the McCallum case. Hap and I think the Major and his other conspirators had more than one cache of weapons."

"That sounds reasonable. Do you know for sure that the explosions were munitions and not gas leaks?"

"Not yet, the fires aren't out yet, but if there is proof then it's possible there could be more stored in other buildings as well."

"I see your point. Let's go back and discuss this with the director Grayson."

Hap and I left the FBI and headed for the station house to inform my Captain about our theory. "Hap. Find a drugstore, I need some aspirin. My head is killing me."

"It'll be a minute, the traffic has stopped for some reason."

"Calling all cars. A man has been seen in the 700 block of Broad Street. He is believed to have set a fire now in Gambles Department Store. The suspect is white male five foot six, brown hair, wearing a Georgia Tech sweater. He was last seen heading east, Over."

"Pull over Hap. So we can get out. If he's still heading East, we should be seeing him shortly."

I forced the headache to back off enough for me to see. I spotted a drug store across the street and headed for it ignoring the horns blowing in protest. Showing my badge I grabbed a pair of sunglasses and the aspirin and left a dollar on the counter. Rushing out the door, I downed four aspirin and put on the glasses. Not wanting to look out of place I bought a paper from the news stand and pretended to be reading it.

I didn't have long to wait before I spotted the man walking slowly towards me. I wasn't one hundred percent sure it was him until he stopped and kept looking around to see if he was being followed. He must have felt something was wrong, because he turned and went into a dress shop.

Taking my time. I slowly walked up to the window and looked in. He was talking to a woman behind the counter and from the smile on her face he was flirting with her.

I was about to walk in, when I stopped and let a woman go in ahead of me. I pretended to be with her and started asking questions as if I were shopping for my wife.

"Do you think miss my wife would like a dress just like the one in the window?" I said smiling.

"How would I know. Now get away from me before I call a cop."

"Miss. Can I ask you the same question? I said walking towards the counter. "You see it's her birthday and.. don't you move mister. You're under arrest."

I grabbed him by the arm while shoving his face onto the glass counter. I reached for my handcuffs when he tried to get loose. "What do you think you're doing?" The sales lady said hitting me with her receipt pad.

I yelled at the sales woman. "I am the police!" It didn't seem to sink in because she kept hitting me in the face as hard as she could. The sales women must have found something harder and heaver to hit me with because suddenly I saw stars. She hit me again and I felt his arm slip from my grasp.

**"Do you want me to do something about her?"**

"Yes!" Suddenly my head cleared as the clerk was winding up for the coup de grace. I reached over the counter with my left hand and grabbed her chest. She was so surprised by that she didn't see my right fist cold-cocked her. I started to turn around, when I heard Hap's voice yelling "police."

"Hey! What do you think you're doing? I haven't done anything wrong!" the man said.

Hap pushed him up against a waiting room couch and pointed his gun at him while handcuffing him.

I went behind the counter and found the sales woman unconscious. I spotted a water cooler and drew a full cup. I then threw it in her face to wake her up. She moaned slightly, so I did it again until she regained consciousness. I don't treat women in this manner unless they become a threat. "Are you alright lady?" I said helping her to her feet.

"Why am I all wet?" she said glaring at me. "Did you do this to me?" she said drying off her face. "You're the guy that hit me!" she said looking in the full length mirror at her bruises. "I want him arrested for assault, officer" she mumbled to a uniformed policeman entering the store. It took her a minute to realize that we all were cops as well. "So you're all really policeman?"

"Yes. And to prove it, you're under arrest for injuring one." I said showing her my bruises. I looked around for the other woman to arrest but found she was nowhere in sight. We drove back to the station with Gavin Whitney next to me in handcuffs. After booking him, I could see he was still cocky so I asked him.

"How do you feel about this cell Gavin?" I looked around and started pointing out the fine points. "Gray walls, no window, spring steel bed, mattress one inch thick, toilet next to bed, one pillow and blanket, and the best for last, cockroaches."

Gavin was a young man in his late teens, brown hair, and brown eyes. He stood 5' 5" and weighed 125, and probably wasn't the man we were looking for.

I sat there letting what I had just said sink in before continuing, "This will be your room for possibly thirty years if you're lucky. Or it could be your room for a year before being electrocuted."

"Now wait a minute. I didn't shoot anybody. I just set a couple of fires. The man told me it would be alright."

"A couple of fires?  You care to tell me which ones? It might just save you from the chair?"

"Well. I guess I can. I set old man's Procter's shed on fire, and the Gambles Department Store."

"What about the big fires like the McKenzie building?'

"No! I didn't do those. I did the shed and Gambles because it was my initiation to join Gama Delta FY fraternity. So does this mean no chair right?"

"Who in the fraternity told you to do this?"

"I went upstairs and told the Captain about Gavin and the fraternity and his initiation. "Captain, I believe it would be more effective if you and some men raid this fraternity. Arrest all of them on arson charges to get their attention."

I returned to Whitney's cell to talk with him about the other fires. I found him in good spirits talking with another man waiting to be processed.

"Well. good afternoon Detective, are you here to let me go?"

I had the guard open his cell so I could sit down on his bunk next to him. "Gavin how old are you?"

"I'm eighteen, why?"

"Gavin. If you were fifteen then you'll be considered a minor, but you're actually eighteen, so you'll be treated as an adult."

"What's the difference?"

"Three to five in a reform school with a psychologist, or   ten to fifteen years in a jail."

My statement didn't seem to bother him either so I pressed on. "Now tell me about the Department Store. Why did you set this one Gavin?"

"I didn't Detective, but I know who did. You see he was showing me the ropes and I.."

I slapped the kid across the face opened handed. "Do you think it's funny to destroy property and burn people to death!"

"No," he said rubbing his bright red cheek.

"Then what the hell is the matter with you!"

Tears formed in the kid's eyes as I raised my hand to hit him again. I dropped my hand grabbed him by his shirt, and jerked him to his feet. I slapped the cuffs on him and led him to my car.

"Hap. Take us to the coroners. This man thinks it's fun to set things on fire."

When we got to the coroners, I jerked him out of the back seat and dragged him down to the autopsy room. Pete was there and had a body on the table covered with a white sheet.

"Bill. What are you doing here so soon after the fire?"

"I've brought this kid responsible for that fire. He seems to think it's funny to burn things down. Pete this is Gavin, he wants to see some of his handy work."

Pete looked at Gavin and pointed for him to stand next to him. "So Gavin, you like to set fires?"

"No Sir, I told you why."

"Well then, you can thank your lucky stars. You see most of the arsonists wind up on my table because they made one mistake. And that one mistake will have you looking like this when they find you."

Pete pulled the cloth off the body, "Now this is what your handy work will do to you and the people trapped in your fires."

The body was a male. His clothes had burned away with all his skin, ears, nose, eyes and hair. His mouth was open indicating he was screaming as the flames devoured him.

I picked up a large empty porcelain pot for Gavin as he started to throw up. What I didn't anticipate was him passing out. After Pete revived him with some ammonia I took him back to jail. Once he was settled I asked, "Well what do you think of your new profession?" Gavin didn't say a word he just sat there looking at the floor and shook uncontrollably.

"I.. I had no idea that people would look like that when burned. Honest."

"Well you're young, and haven't murdered anyone yet, but I need to know who the other person that was training you. If you don't tell me, then you leave me no choice but to charge you with all the fires and the deaths. So what will it be Gavin, life or death?"

"Alright. I'll tell you Detective, it's Mitch Anderson."

"You mean Fire Chief Mitch Anderson?"

"Yes Detective. I swear by God almighty."

I looked at the kid and couldn't decide if he was telling the truth or not.

I had known Mitch for twenty years. He had started out as a rookie in 1900 and was one of the principal people in making the department what it was today. "Then the collage thing was all a lie! Right?" I rushed out of the cell and called the Captain. Lucky for me he was still getting the warrants when I got a hold of him. I returned to Gavin and cell and continued to interrogate him until I felt I had the truth. "Hap, let's return to the newspaper and look up  some of the old headline fires to see if the man responsible was ever caught.

# Chapter 62

April 19<sup>th</sup> 1933
3:33 pm Monday

Hap and I reached the Times and walked up to the information desk. "Good afternoon Miss. I wanted to have a look at the old daily papers going back to 1890." I said showing her my badge.

"I'm sorry Detective, I don't believe we keep them that far back. Why don't you check with the public library, I believe they have what you're looking for."

"Miss. I believe you must be new here. I was here a few months ago and they are kept downstairs in the archives."

"I don't believe that's correct. Let me call upstairs." However she got in touch with must have bent her ear, because her face was bright red when she hung up. "I'm so sorry Detective's. I had forgotten that old man Peter worked downstairs. I haven't been down their myself but he visits with me a lot just to talk to someone. You see.."

"Then it's okay for us to go down stairs?"

"Oh yes. I'll press the button to unlock the door.

When we reached the archive storerooms the old man remembered me and asked, "What do you want to see today, Detective?"

"Let's start with 1890. I'm looking for anything on Chief Mitch Anderson and any fires that were written up."

The first 1890 article was on the establishment of a full time fire department instead of volunteers. The first mention of Mitch Anderson was in 1900, when he became a Captain. As Hap and I thumbed through 1901,02, 05,07, we found every important fire was handled by Mitch and his crew. This seemed to continue until 1912 when he became Chief. After that there wasn't any mention of him until 1922 with the Oxcart Hotel fire. As I read the byline the reporter stated that a man's body believe to be the arson was found dead in the basement.

"Hap. Take another look at your articles about Mitch and see if there's any mention of catching the person who had set them?"

It didn't take but ten minutes to see that all the fires were accidental according to the Chief.

An overloaded fuse box, flammables stored to close to a heater, lit cigars or cigarettes falling into a waste paper basket, but never a purposely set fire until the Oxcart.

"Hap, when we get home tonight remind me to have Nancy check with several other cities."

"Okay but what is she to check on?"

"Well I was wondering why with all the advancements Mitch has brought to the fire department why he doesn't have a full time investigator besides himself."

We left the newspaper and headed for the house when another call came in on a fire. This time it was the fuel depot at the airport. Turning on the siren and red light, we raced across town as the black cloud increased in size and height.

"My God Captain, will you look at the size of that smoke?"

I looked out the front wind screen and couldn't believe my eyes. The black smoke had to be five thousand feet in the air and a mile wide and we were still a mile away.

By the time we got to the fire, the flames were forty feet high above the fuel storage tanks. I got out of the car and immediately felt the heat. It was so intense I thought I was on fire myself. Getting back into the car we backed up as far as we could until blocked by other onlookers.

Getting out of the car we ran back to the down the dirt road and advised people to run for their lives. Upon reaching the paved two lane road we found it blocked with onlookers' cars. Hap and I tried to get them to move their cars so that firetrucks, police and ambulances could reach us. I went to the first car and showed him my badge. "You need to get out of the way."

"I don't have to do anything. This is a public road and you.."

I pulled out my revolver and fired a shot into the air. Hap did the same to get the cars out of the way until the firetruck reached us.

"Thanks whoever you are."

As the trucks passed us you could still feel the heat at this distance. "Captain, do you think well have a police car left to return to?"

A sudden explosion shook the ground as the fire lit up the darkening sky. "I'd say no Hap. So I guess we better start walking back towards town and find someone that has a phone so I can call in for a ride."

It was just my luck that by 1:00 am we spotted a taxi heading toward downtown. We both ran out into the street and blocked the road while waving our arms. For a moment I thought he'd run us down but he did stop.

"I yelled police," and held up my badge in his headlights. Reaching the driver we found he already had two passengers. "Sorry folks. If we scared you but we need a ride back to the station."

"Where is your car Detective?" the driver asked checking my papers closely. "I already have a paying customer so.."

I didn't let him finish because I knew he was about to drive off and my feet hurt. So I opened the rear door and got in while Hap got in the front seat with him.

As we headed for the station, I found out the couple had just gotten married in Nashville and were on their honeymoon. Their plane had just landed for refueling when the fire broke out. I had the taxi driver drop us off at the first call box I saw and paid him for the ride. Thirty minute later we entered the house and found everyone asleep. We were about to head up the stairs when Hap made a proposal.

"How about a midnight snack?"

I hadn't thought about that, but my stomach agreed with him in a second. So creeping into the kitchen as if we were kids. Hap opened the icebox and smiled in delight.

"Jackpot."

I grabbed a couple of plates while Hap brought out two baked chickens, potato salad and a chocolate pie. It didn't take us but fifteen minutes to polish everything off. It then occurred to me we may have eaten tonight's dinner.

"Hap. I think we're in trouble with Mildred now for eating all this food."

"How's that Captain? We just put everything back into the icebox and go to bed. In the morning we acted as if we knew nothing about the missing food."

"So your saying lie to Mildred about what we just did."

"I wouldn't advise that you two." Mildred said standing at the doorway.

"It's all his fault!" Hap said pointing at me.

"Hap. If you were as tall as your lies you'd be 70' tall. So. You two go to bed and I'll come up with something for dinner tonight."

"Maybe one of your beef roast?" Hap said smiling.

"Maybe for us. But for you a hot dog."

# Chapter 63

April 20th 1933
6:28 am Tuesday

Hap and I met with Nancy and I gave her what information we had found at the Times yesterday. "Just to be clear Bill. You want me to return to the newspaper. Recheck your findings on the Chief. You also want me to run down any former fireman either retired, quit, fired and see what they have to say about him."

"Correct."

We headed for the door when I remembered we need to apologizes to Mildred for eating tonight's dinner. "Captain. Do you think I'll be forgiven. I sure hate to miss her dinner tonight."

"I'm sure everything will be alright. Mildred has a loud bark and no bite. But if I were you I'd only eat one helping unless she says you can have two or three or maybe four."

I wanted to head back to the fire but when I saw the sky gray with its smoke, I decided against it. When the squad car pulled up we headed to the station to pick up another car. "Thanks for the ride." we got out and headed for the motor pool door. "Morning Howard."

"Not you two again." he said shaking his head. What did you need now? Wait! I know, another car, right?"

"I hate to say this but yes. Do you have a spare?"

"Where's your car?"

"At the airport on fire."

"As a matter of fact I do have one car available. It's parked out back. "Mike! Bring the car around that's parked out back."

"I appreciate you being so understanding."

"I totally understand Detective's, but I think this car will hold up better than the newer models. Ah here it comes now."

"Captain! A 1928 Ford model A. Isn't she a beauty."

I didn't say a word, but looked at Howard who was trying his best not to laugh.

As we pulled out of the lot we got some strange looks from our fellow policeman. Hap on the other hand was like a kid in a candy store. "Captain, I think we should keep this car." he said changing gears smoother than he ever did with our last car. "They just don't make them like they used to."

"I'm pleased you like her, but this care isn't built for comfort. Maybe I can get the Chief to sell it to you?"

"That would be great! I'm sure Mildred would love a Sunday afternoon drive."

I thought about that and didn't want to bust his bubble, but I don't think.. well on second thought, she might.

We reach the main firehouse which was on Roswell and Peachtree Street. It consisted of a two story brick building built in 1909. It had an attached building that  housed three fire engines, 14 men and a training center. The Chief's office was on the second floor facing Roswell Street.

"Hap I have an idea. I'll go in first and see if he's here. If he isn't, I'll get someone to show me around. That should give you the chance to get to the chief's office without being seen." I opened the door and found a young man behind a desk reading the newspaper.

"Can I help you sir?"

"Yes. I'm looking for Mitch Anderson."

"I'm sorry sir. He's been at the airport old storage fire. I don't expect him back until late today."

"I'm from the Washington Times. I was to get a one on one interview for my paper."

"Well. I don't know what to tell you. Can I take a number where you're staying."

"No. I was to get a story and fly out tonight, but I've got a better idea. Why don't I interview you and get your view of the man instead?"

"Well. I don't know about that sir."

"I can put your picture in the paper along with the article. So why don't you show me the station while I take notes." Lucky for me I always carry a small note pad and pencil. I kept him busy answering questions until I couldn't think of anything else to say.

"Well now that you know everything about the training center and how we handle calls. Let me show you the upper floors."

I looked at my watch and found we had been talking for 45 minutes. "I see by that sign there's no smoking. So I'll step outside and smoke one. Do you have any coffee available. I sure could use a cup." I headed for the door as he climbed the stairs to go to the kitchen. I opened the door and found Hap sitting in the car napping. "Hap! Wake up!"

Hap opened his eyes and yawned. "Captain. It's about time you showed up."

"Did you get his address?"

"Address? Oh you mean the chief home address?" he said wiping sleep out of the coroner of his eyes.

"Hap. Your pressing your luck. Did you get his address or not?"

"As I remember, Captain. His door was lock and it took me some time to unlock it. Then his desk was also lucked and…"

"Did…you…get…his…home…address?"

"Yes. 1134 Northside Drive, phone number NS3214. His wife's name is Beverly. He has two children Mark 34 and Cathleen 30, they both live at home."

"Now how do you know that?"

"He has a picture on his desk of the three of them."

"That's very good work Hap. But way all the drama in telling me?"

"I just wanted to prove to you I can get results as well."

"You're talking about Nancy, aren't you?"

"I could have done the research just as well as she can."

"That's very true Hap. But I need a seasoned partner that I can trust to watch my back when things don't go well. So cheer up old man. If you keep up that type of attitude you'll never be promoted to full detective. Now let's head to 1134 Northside Drive. I want to see what kind of house a Fire Chief lives in on a $7,245 salary."

# Chapter 64

April 20th 1933
11:28 am Tuesday


s Hap pulled up to the mailbox I couldn't believe the size of his home. If I put Mildred's Victorian house next to this one it would have taken four of them just to be seen from the road. "Hap. Let's see if anyone is home."

Hap drove us up the circular dive and stopped in front of the main entrance. As we walk up the six steps I couldn't get over its size. "Captain. What do you think this monster must have cost to build?"

"I don't know, but I'm sure it's more than he makes in ten years." I knocked on the front door several times before someone opened the door. "May I help you?" A maid said looking at us as if we were beggars.

"I'd like to speak with Mrs. Anderson please."

"Mrs. Anderson is not at home."

"When do you think she'll return?"

"I'm not sure. You see she's in Jamaica for an extended vacation."

"What about Mark or Cathleen?" Hap said trying to look past her.

"They are not at home either. I believe they went with their mother to Jamaica as well. Now if you're done asking questions. You can go around back and the cook will give you something to eat." she said closing the door.

I looked at Hap.

"I know what you're thinking, Captain, but now isn't the right time."

We got back into our police car and headed for the oil fire to see if I could locate Mitch. After seeing his house, I began to believe the kid in jail. As we neared the still burning fire we ran into hundreds of onlookers, dozens of news photographers, cops, ambulances, firetrucks and every type of car you could imagine.

Hap spotted an empty driveway to turn around in "We might as well leave, Captain. Will never get through this crowd."

A woman with a baby in her arms came out and said we could park here for twenty five cents.

I checked my pocket and found I only had a fifty cent piece. "I'll give you this if I can park here all day."

Before leaving the car behind, I wrote down the address just in case the car wasn't there when we returned. I thanked the woman again for letting us park here before Hap and I started walking down the sidewalk. It didn't take a minute before being swallowed up in a mass of people. At first I asked them to step aside but found being polite didn't work. "Hap. Show your badge and don't answer any questions as you move past them."

After what seemed a lifetime of togetherness we reached the police line barricades. "Boy are we glad to see you" I said showing the policeman my badge and ID.

"Hey! Were the press. How come they can get in and not the news media?"

As we walked away I heard the policeman say. "Because you people are so stupid you'd wind up in the hospital with third degree burns."

We zigzag between ambulances, firetrucks, personal cars, leaking fire hoses and a food truck. "You boys look like you could use a coffee?"

"You read my mind," I said taking the offered coffee.

"By the looks of you two, you're not volunteer fireman."

"No. we're police detectives. Have you seen the Fire Chief?"

"Not lately, but I believe you could find him somewhere over there."

"Thanks. How much do I owe you?"

"Nothing. This is a red cross disaster truck." He said pointing at the red cross on the truck.

We headed in the direction of the largest bulling black smoke. As we passed a fireman we got the strangest looks.

"Hap, I believe they think we're nuts." We hadn't walked another yard when a lieutenant in fire gear stopped us.

"You two can't be here." He stated not an inch from my nose.

"Yes I can." I show him my badge.

"I don't care if you're the mayor. Get yourselves back to the food wagon before you get yourselves killed."

I was about to argue the point when a loud explosion changed my mind.

"If you see the Chief. Tell him Detective Barronson would like to talk to him."

"If I see him, I'll tell him. But don't count on it. Now go!" A smaller explosion vibrated under our feet as another large black cloud rose into the sky. We headed back to the food truck and accepted a coffee as it started to rain. You boys want to come inside out of the drizzle."

"Thanks. But here comes the chief now." As he marched towards us Hap said. "The Chief cuts quite a figure in his red fireman's getup. That ax he's carrying makes me think of a Viking heading into battle."

"That ax is quite a weapon, Hap. So be on your guard if he decides to use it."

"Detective Barronson, and your side kick Hap. Why are you here? The fire won't be out for another day at least."

"I have a few questions I need to ask you about some past fires."

"Look. Detective. I've got an out of control fire to fight, and I don't have the time to answer your questions right now."

The Chief looked at the burning gas tanks as one suddenly went out probably from lack of fuel.

This left two more tanks still shooting flames twenty feet into the air and smoke a thousand feet above them.

"Alright Chief, but I want to see you at the station as soon as the fires are out."

"You know where to find me, Detective."

As he walked off I could see the difference in his stride. Her no longer walked like a leader.

Now came the hard part of getting back to our car and out of the traffic jam built up behind that.

# Chapter 65

April 20th 1933
8:42 pm Tuesday

Hap parked the car in our usual spot. We both felt as if we had gone through a ringer as we walked towards the house. It had taken hours to get back to the car and several more to get to an open road.

As we reached the porch steps, I barely had enough strength to climb them.

**"What's the matter. You miss me and my strength?"**

"No. But it would have been nice to get a little boost of energy." I decided to sit a minute before going inside.

"Are you talking to me? Or is it your other self again?"

"I'm just talking to myself, Hap. In the shape I'm in I didn't want to face a cross examination just yet." I started rocking slowly and thinking how glad I was that the day was over. I closed my eyes and took a deep breath of cool fresh air that didn't smell of fuel oil. The next thing I remember is Henry waking me up.

"Bill, wake up! And you too Hap. You'll catch you're death of cold out here in this night air."

I opened my dry bloodshot eyes and saw the ugly face of Henry shaking my shoulder. When I came to enough to think straight I said, "Henry. Do you know you're shaking my wounded shoulder?"

"Oh. I'm sorry Bill, I didn't realize it was that shoulder."

I rubbed my eyes to get them to focus while yawning.

"What time is it anyway, Henry?"

"3:00 am."

I woke up Hap while Henry headed on to work. We both felt as if every muscle in my body was abused by yesterday's hike.

"Captain. I wonder why no one woke us up? It's not like Mildred or Margaret not to check to see if we were home or not."

"I don't know, and right now I don't care. So let's go to bed and will talk about it tomorrow."

# Chapter 66

April 21$^{st}$ 1933
9:12 am Wednesday

I awoke to the sound of Margaret's voice telling me to get up. When I finally surfaced, she was saying the Captain wants to see me now.

Feeling a headache coming on, I took some aspirin, and got dressed. I headed for Hap's room when Margaret said.

"He's already up and downstairs waiting for you. So come eat something before you leave. The Captain can wait another fifteen minutes." Margaret said leading me to the table.

Feeling much better after three cups of coffee, Hap and I headed for the station. As we drove I looked out the window to see how much smoke the fire was still producing. To my surprise I only saw thin wisps of brown smoke.

"Well. Hap. It looks like the fire is about out. I wonder if the Fire Chief is at the station as he said he would?"

We walked into the police station and found it abuzz with speculations as to why the Fire Chief was here. Ignoring everyone's questions, I went straight to the Captain's door and opened it without knocking. As I entered I found the Captain and the Fire Chief talking over coffee and donuts. "My God Detective, you look like hell."

I started to say you're no prize either when I felt my chin. In the rush to get here I hadn't saved or showered.

"Sorry Captain, is been a long night."

"Well. I'll overlook it this time." he said picking up the phone. "Have some coffee and whatever you can find to eat and bring it to my office." He hung up the phone and looked at me. "Now tell me why Fire Chief Mitch Anderson is here?"

"As you know I have a kid named Gavin in lock-up that has set a number of fires. He's told me that the Chief has been training him on how to become an arsonist."

"Is this true, Mitch?"

"Yes and no.

I met Gavin last year at the annual fourth of July picnic in Grant Park. He asked me all sort of question about being a fireman and how he wanted to be one."

I interjected by asking Mitch, "Didn't it ever occur to you he was pumping you for information on how to set fires?"

"No, not really. You see he didn't want to be just a fireman but an investigator like me."

I was angry that a man as old and experienced as Mitch was would fall for a con job by a kid. "If that's the case,  Captain, why don't you show Mitch Gavin's confession as to how he set his fires."

"That won't be necessary, Captain. I'm, sure Detective Barronson didn't ask me down here to discuss Gavin. So Detective, what's the real reason I'm here?"

"I've been looking into your past career as a fireman. It seems you rose very quickly from a rookie to Fire Chief in quite a short year."

"So. I've worked hard to get where I am. Are you suggesting…"

"No. Chief. What I mean is you have knowledge I don't possess on fires and the people that sets them."

"Another words you want me to profile the arsonists?"

"Yes. That's part of it. I also want to know if all these fires were set by the same person or persons?"

By the time the three of us were done, I had a profile of a man who enjoyed his work. "So let me recap out arsonists. One. He is in his mid-30's who has no family or a girlfriend. Two. He probably was an only child that took out his frustrations by playing with matches. Three. He treats each fire as his family. Four. He could be selling his craft to anyone who will pay." I thanked Mitch for his time and said "Everyone gets taken in at some point in their life by an innocent face."

I left the Captain's office and went to the john to throw up. The story Mich had tried to sell me couldn't be farther from the truth. His profile he had work up for us fit Gavin to a tee. The only problem with it was Gavin hadn't set but two fires, and the last one he was in jail.

I had thought about trying to nail him today but the man had political connections.  Connections I would have to break before arresting him.

As I returned to my desk I found Nancy waiting for me there. She was talking to three detectives that were all bidding for her attention.

"Alright you three. Don't you have something to do besides harassing my niece."

"Come on Nancy, let go find Hap and well go to Kim's."

We found Hap down stairs talking to the desk sergeant about his medal. "Hap let's take a ride to Kim's."

As we walked to our car Nancy stopped. "You're kidding, right?"

"About what?" I played dumb just to watch her expressions.

"What happened to your car?"

"Nothing, Don't you like it?" I winked at Hap.

"Isn't she a beauty. I picked her out myself just today. Captain said the other car was flashy."

"Nancy looked at the two of us, "Get in the car before I change my mind and ride the bus. It's a beauty alright in 1900 maybe."

When we got to Kim's, Nancy and I went inside while Hap put water in the radiator. "Did you find out anything we missed about Mitch?"

"Not much, it seems he's been able to stay in the shadows. I did find a small byline about him and a Major McCallum." she said digging in her purse. "I wrote it down." Nancy handed the folded piece of paper to me.

Monday 1900

A new modern fire station open today in Atlanta. It was built for training new full time fireman on how to put fires out. The station was Captain Mitch Anderson's dream child that was made reality by Major McCallum's donation.

"What about this sentence? It looks as if you started to right down something. Do you remember what it was." I handed the paper back to Nancy.

Nancy read what she had written several times before she handed it back to me. "I found an article about a prisoner  that escaped from a county road gang in 1906."

"So why are you interested in him?"

"Not sure yet, it seems that was the only article written about his escape. Do you remember who he was?"

"No, before my time, but if you're still interested in him, I have a number of mugshot books?"

"Maybe Bill, let me think on that."

"Maybe you should look for him. I bet there's a reward for his capture?"

"Alright then let's start looking. I could use the money for new clothes."

We drove back to the station and started looking. Hap  brought the mug books to my desk. I knew Grace had already looked at them, but now with more information to work with I wanted to go farther back to 1905. While Nancy looked for Scruggs picture, I started looking through old wanted posters to see if there was a reward. Not finding one, I looked for Scruggs jacket in the cold case filling cabinet.

It didn't take Nancy long to find Scruggs picture in the 1904 photo books. "Here's what he looked like in 1904." Nancy said showing me his picture.

I looked in the S's and didn't find his jacket. Thinking it could be filed wrong, I looked at every folder and didn't find it. I was about to give up when I thought of one more place to look. Sometimes a folder would not be put back correctly and slid under the hanging jackets. I removed some and saw a file. Pulling out more jackets, I  freed it from whatever sticky liquid was holding it there.

As I opened the yellowing file I found it was his file.


Oscar Scrugg, 28 in 1905
Height 5" 8", Weight 145 lbs. Born 1889.
Town Atlanta. Family none. Parents unknown.
Convictions Blackmail & Arson. 4 Barns, 3 Houses, 2 Gas stations, 2 Churches, 1 Warehouse 4 Counts of Blackmail. Sentence 25 years Hard Labor County road gang. First Escaped 1908, added 5 years to sentence. Second Escape 1915, added 5 years to sentence. Third Escape 1925.


"Hap, I believe we have found our man. Look at this rap sheet."

"If I were a betting man, Captain, I'd say Oscar Scrugg would be our arsonists."

I scratched my head and lit a cigarette while thinking how to find this man. He had been on the run for 8 years now without getting caught. Which means he either left town or someone is hiding him. It then occurred to me where we could start looking. "Hap. let's head over to Ray's Pool Hall. I believe the pastor needs to start earning his percentage. Nancy see what you can dig up on Mitch Anderson's finances."

# Chapter 67

April 21ˢᵗ 1933
3:12 pm Wednesday

It had been a few hours since we had split up. My original intention was to meet up with the pastor. As luck had it our new vehicle threw a rod and left us sitting beside the road. "So what do you think of your 1928 Ford now, Hap."

"Well Captain, I suggest we take a cab to Kim's place and have some lunch before returning to the station."

"Good idea. I'll call in...ah on second thought I'll can in at Kim's seeing there isn't a radio in this car."

We took a seat and ordered something to eat. I waved to Kim as she rushed around the place taking care of her customers. We were about done when Nancy came walking in the front door. "Well I see you two are hard at work." she said taking a seat. "Tea please and a turkey sandwich. I didn't see your car outside?"

"That's because it died about a mile down the road."

"Well then I guess we all are riding around in taxis."

I noticed she had a folder in front of her. "Is that for me?" Nancy turned the folder around and slid it to me.

"This is what I have gathered on Fire Chief Mitch Anderson so far. It seems his wife and children have left him several months ago. She cleaned out the safe of, $75,000 along with all his bearer bonds as well. It seems our fire chief is more interested in political advancement than his family."

"Okay, so what else do you have for us?"

"This Bill. It seems the Chief was broke and about to declare bankruptcy two months ago. As of today he has been able to pay up or off every bill of hers and the kids."

"How did you find this out?"

"Maria. The house maid and possible new wife she hopes."

Oh the next page is his banking history until she left him."

J P MONTAGRAM SAVINGS & LOAN

| Deposit | Date | Year | Amount | Withdraw |
|---|---|---|---|---|
| June | 18th | 1904 | $3,000 | |
| December | 21st | 1908 | $5,000 | |
| August | 8th | 1912 | $9,000 | |
| May | 5th | 1920 | $12,000 | |
| October | 14th | 1923 | $25,000 | |
| April | 1st | 1929 | | $54,000.00 |

"As you can see our Fire Chief made deposits every time there was a fire. It also seems strange he would pull all his money out of the bank just before the crash."

"Have you checked to see if he borrowed or was owed the money?"

"That I can't say Bill. All I do know and the bank knows is that he shows up with a briefcase of money to deposit."

"I can't believe Mitch has lied to me about this. He must have known we would check his bank statements."

"Here's the final piece of the puzzle. The bank is part of a corporation out of New York and one of board members is John McCallum and you can guess who the others are."

"Italian I bet"

"Nancy you've done a remarkable job. Now I have another and this one could put you in danger."

"Thanks for the compliment, and don't worry about me."

"Okay. Then this is what I need to know. Who benefited from the fires besides Mitch and McCallum."

"What if I find it leads up the political ladder, say to the Mayor?"

I thought about that for a minute. "Make sure you keep your findings in a safe place. Say Kim's safe or Mildreds"

I also need to tie Mitch to whoever paid him. See if the Bank manager will give you more information?"

We left Nancy and said our goodbyes to Kim as our vacated table was scooped up by new customers. I got into the back seat with Hap as I gave the taxi driver Lee Chan's address

"Are you sure you want to talk to him? Remember last time we got together at his place he cleaned our wallets out. Heck, I still have suits and clothes I haven't even worn yet."

I had just got out of the taxi when Lee Chang met us.

"Ah! Detective, and Hap. It's nice to see you again. I have some new stock in. I'm sure you'll be interested in it."

"No, Lee, we have quite a wardrobe thanks to you. What I wanted to ask you is. Have you heard anything from the street about who the arsonist might be?"

As we entered his shop, I could see the disappointment on his face. We headed to the backroom where he had a small table, a stove heating a tea kettle.

"Sit. I make some tea."

I could tell by the way Lee was moving I wasn't going to get information unless I bargained. "Well Lee. The co-op is under way and by next month we'll need some people to help at the farm. I also wanted to let you know that I have put up a sign at the station recommending your tailor shop."

"That is too kind Detective," he said pouring us a cup of tea. "Now you ask about this arsonist. Well from what I hear it's a white man that is setting all these fires."

"Would you happen to have a name of this person, or where they might live?" I was hoping he wouldn't say Mitch Anderson and instead he said, "Oscar Scrugg."

"Are you sure about that, Lee?"

"I can't say for sure, but that's what I've heard, Detective. Do you know this man?"

"I know of him from his rap sheet. Do you know where he hangs out?"

"I believe you can find him at Ray's Pool Hall."

"Lee. I thanked you for the information and please excused our rudeness for rushing off."

"No apology necessary Detective. You Americans are always in a hurry to get things done."

We bowed to Lee and raced to the taxi. I had him call into the desk sergeant.

"This is Detective Barronson, send three police cars to Ray's Pool Hall without sirens or lights. Tell them to park two blocks away and I'll meet them there."

The taxi driver looked at us with eyes the size of saucers. "Are you two really cops?"

"Yes, is that going to be a problem?"

"Oh, no, I have always wanted to be part of a police raid. Do you think there will be a car chase?"

"I don't believe so, but when you drop us off I suggest you drive away or you might get shot."

If you had told me this I wouldn't have believed it. His eyes got even wider that they were before. "Shot! me shot! Like you did Detective Barronson. Oh my I would be the talk of the town. I might even be in the news, with my photograph."

"And the headlines would say taxi drive shot dead by stray bullet."

"Hap. Didn't I say Pastor Lyman should have had some information on the arsonist by now?"

"Yes. But it still doesn't explain all the money Mitch accumulated in his account. So maybe the three of them are working together."

"That's a possibility, but I don't see how the Pastor or Mich could profit from the fires. There has to be a third or fourth party involved."

We met the three police cars down the street from the pool hall. "I want you two men to park here and cover the backdoor exit just in case they run. You two park your car up the street and wait in case one of them gets out the front door. Hap and I with you three will enter by the front door. You two come with us and guard the entrance while we two round them up. I don't want any shooting unless it's to return fire."

We waited as the two officers slipped unseen to the back door. Hap watched the second car drive past the pool hall and park. "Alright men, let's make sure this goes without a hitch." We slowly walked up the sidewalk in single file until we reached the corner of the building.

I was about to start the rush went I saw people across the street watching us. "You. Walter, make sure those people get inside their business. We don't need one of them to be shot by mistake."

"Is everybody ready now?"

"Yes."

The two policemen went through the door first because they had on police uniforms that couldn't be mistaken.

"Police! Don't anybody move!"

I walked up to Raymond Brown while putting my gun away. "Ray is the Pastor here or at the church?"

"Detective, why the hostile visit?"

"Ray is he in or not?"

"He's not in, but I can call him."

"Okay. Tell him I need to speak to him right now."

"Detective. what about these two men?"

"Take their guns. Then Hap and you search the place from top to bottom."

"I can save you some time if you tell me what you're looking for?"

"I looking for a man by the name of Oscar Scrugg."

"Detective he's not here."

"I want my men to search the place anyway."

It took several minutes before Hap called out from the basement, "I've found a small room down here with a bed, dresser, table and chair. From the looks of his clothes he's been here a long time."

"Ray. I don't want to destroy our friendship, but I need to know is that room downstairs is where Scrugg sleeps."

"You better talk to the Pastor about that, Detective. I'm just the bartender around here remember."

I could see by his facial expression, I was putting him in a bad spot. So I dropped the subject and asked him about his coffee business instead.

"Well, Detective Barronson, why all the theatrics. I thought we had an arrangement." The Pastor said walking in the door and taking a seat. "Bring me a coffee Ray, while I find out what this is all about."

I didn't take a seat to show the Pastor I meant business. "So tell me. Pastor Lyman, when were you going to inform me you had an escaped convict arsonist living on your premises?"

I could see I had struck a chord by the look on his face.

"And what makes you think I have a fugitive living in my basement, Detective?"

"I just happen to have his jacket with me." I said showing him his complete arrest file.

"Okay. So, this Scruggs likes to burn things down. So what, every man deserves a second chance."

"Pastor. I want to speak to this man because the word around town is he's setting these fires."

"Well. I just can't give up one of my men because he escaped from that inhuman chain gang. I'll set up a time, say in one hour, at the Baptist Life Church."

"I'll agree to that. But once were done talking, I'll still arrest him even if I'm satisfied with his answers.

Now Pastor, what do you know about Fire Chief Mitch Anderson and his relationship with Oscar Scrugg."

"I have no knowledge about that Detective. As a matter of record, I was about to advise you that we have two new players in town, the Germans and the Russians."

"Okay, then your upset because there taking a cut of your pie?"

"Not my pie, Detective, your pie. The communist party have arrived and are recruiting people just as the fascist  have these past months."

"That's an FBI matter, not a local matter unless they start breaking the law. Now what about?"

"I see no reason now for you to talk to Mr. Scruggs. Detective."

"Pastor Lyman. I'm arresting you for harboring an escaped convict. Hap. Have our men shut this place down and arrest all these men as well. I'll put the pastor in a car while you put things in motion."

# Chapter 68

April 20th 1933
5:15 pm Wednesday

I placed the Pastor in the back seat handcuffed and waited for Hap to close the place down.

"Detective. I don't think you know what you're doing. Remember I have a signed document that we are working together, Remember. I gave you money in exchange for police protection."

Hap. instead of going to the station, head for J P Monogram Bank. We parked in front of the bank and before we went in I had a short talk with Hap.

We entered the Roman style bank through the double brass and glass doors. "Can I help you?" The guard asked seeing the handcuff man.

"I need to speak with the bank manager." I said showing him our badges.

"His secretary is the blond sitting at the desk straight ahead. Her names is Susan Birdie."

As we walked towards her desk I looked around and counted more guards than employees or customers combined. "Business seems a little slow. I wonder how they can afford so many guards?"

"I don't know but at least a dozen men can feed their families."

"May I help you gentleman? Susan said looking over her horn rimmed glasses.

"I need to see the bank president." I said showing her my badge.

"Just a minute officer, I'll see if he's in." she said picking up the phone. "I'm sorry Detective. Mr. Rossi must be out to lunch."

"Why don't you try the intercom, Mrs. Birdie. You see,  not answering the phone is an old trick to get rid of somebody he doesn't want to talk to."

"Detective. I can assure you.."

"Susan. I can assure you a visit to our holding cells if you refuse to use the intercom."

"Mr. Rossi. There's a two policeman her that wish to speak with you."

"Send them in Susan."

"Isn't it amazing Susan, how an intercom can solve a problem compared to a telephone."

Susan led us to a door behind her desk and opened it. We then followed her down a short hall to another door marked Bank President. Susan knocked twice and opened the door.

"Pastor Lyman. It's good to see you again. Detective Barronson, the lion tamer. I'm very pleased to meet you, and you are?"

"FBI agent, Cornelis Pepper," Hap said showing his ID.

When Hap said he was an FBI agent I thought the pastor and the bank president were going to faint.

"Well.. ah. What can I do for you gentlemen today?" he said ringing his hands as if he were washing them.

"I have it on good authority that you have been excepting deposits from Mitch Anderson for some time."

"No…no…that's not true. Pastor Lyman has. Has been making the deposits for him."

The pastor didn't say a word, but you could see the daggers flying from his eyes to the president's eyes.

"I…mean…The Pastor Lyman and Mr. Anderson are ah…friends and ah."

"Don't bother Mr. Rossi. You already have hung yourself. To deny it now isn't going to save your life from the Pastor having you killed." I watched beads of sweat appear on his brow as his eyes darted from me to the Pastor.

"I have another question Mr. Rossi. If the pastor here did all the deposits. Then how did he know to pull his money out of your bank before the crash of 29.

"Well, you see he was having wife problems, and he.. wanted to put the money where she couldn't get her hands on it."

"That sound plausible. What do you think Hap? Mitch Anderson withdraws all his savings from an account he never made a deposit in. To hide the money from his wife, so she couldn't withdraw it from an account he didn't know he had? Have I got that right, Mr. Rossi?"

"I can answer that question, Detective. You see I knew his wife well. We were business partners before she married Mr. Anderson." The Pastor said smiling at me.

"Ah, So then you and Mitch's wife were in business. And Mitch worked for the fire department."

"No! Detective. His wife worked for me before and after her marriage. I set up the account because she knew one day her husband would find out and divorce her leaving her penny less."

"I think I have all I need from you for now Mr. Rossi. I suggest you don't leave town. I may have additional questions I need you to answers."

# Chapter 69

April 20th 1933
7:25 pm Wednesday

We reached the police station and had the taxi driver drop us off at the back entrance. Hap and I escorted the Pastor into the station and to the front desk.

"Sergeant. Put this man in a holding sell for now. I got a shocked look from the sergeant. "Detective. You know he's a pastor?"

"Yes. Mike I do. That's why I didn't ask you to book him."

Once the Pastor was settled in a holding cell, I went to the radio dispatch and put out an all-points bulletin on Oscar Scruggs. "Sergeant. Send a patrol car to pick up  Fire Chief Anderson. He's probably at his office or home and bring him here."

Now I headed for the Captain's office hoping he hadn't left for the day. I knocked twice and got an answer. "Come in Detective. I've been waiting on you."

I took my usual seat before saying anything. "Captain. I've got a good lead on the arsonist. I've found an escaped man by the name of Oscar Scruggs." I said handing him the s rap sheet. I waited as the Captain read it.

"I'd say you have a good lead. How did you figure it's
him? The man's been on the run for some time now."

"I got his name from Pastor Lyman. It seems the pastor is the Boss of the Atlanta Mob, and has been hiding him at Ray's Pool Hall since his escape."

"A pastor! A church pastor?"

"Yes. If you think about it, it's a perfect cover."

I could see the Captain's wheel turning. "Captain. I have some explaining to tell you before you come up with the wrong conclusions."

I started with the co-op, and then explained about the Chinese and the Pastor's involvement. To my surprise the Captain didn't blow his

265

cork. "Detective. All I can tell you Bill is if this plan of yours doesn't work the Pastor will have you for lunch."

"Yes Sir. I know that, but I'm confident everything will work out."

"So where is this pastor now?"

"I have him in a holding cell. I'm waiting for Fire Chief Mitch Anderson to be brought in for questioning."

"The fire chief! What does he have to do with this?"

"I'll let you know shortly. Captain."

"Mich Anderson has a lot of friends in this administration. So watch your step because it's a long fall if you get my meaning."

I left the Captain's office feeling relieved I had explained my relationship with the pastor. As for the fire chief It was a horse of a different color, and right now the horse was black. As I headed downstairs something clicked.

"Hap. We need to go and bring John McCallum here as well. If I'm going to get cashiered. I might as well have everyone here that's involved." As we left I told the sergeant to put the fire chief in the same cell as the pastor.

We walked into the lobby of the Flat Iron Building and found the place empty. Entering the elevator I punched the tenth floor. When the doors opened I found two bodyguards waiting for us.

"Excuse me, gentleman, but I need to see John McCallum junior?"

"Sorry Mack. He's seeing no one this late in the day."

I brought out my badge and stuck it in front of his nose.

"I believe this gives me permission to see him," I said forcing my way past them. Hap and I went to his office door and opened it without knocking.

"Oh. It's you again. What do you want now?" his rude secretary said, blocking our way.

"Well. If it isn't Miss Personality. I see by the look  on your face the plastic surgery didn't work. Or did it?"

I walked past her and opened John's inner door "Well. Isn't this a nice surprise." I said walking in. I found  John McCallum, Mark Genovese and Henry Rossi the bank manager in the middle of a meeting.

"I'm busy, Detective. Now get out!"

"I'm glad to see the three of you together. I'll wait outside while you finish your meeting, and don't try to leave by the back door. I have more police downstairs.

I closed his door and went to the secretary's desk and picked up her phone.

"Just a minute now. This is private property."

"And this is a gun," I said opening my suit coat. So shut up and be quiet. Or you just might spend a night in jail. Sergeant. Is Mitch Anderson been brought in?"

"Yes. I have him in the holding cell with the pastor."

"Okay. Now have them driven to the Flat Iron Building along with ten policemen. When they arrived, I want two men at the side entrance and two in the lobby. The other seven can escort the Chief and Pastor to the tenth floor. I'll meet them at the elevator."

$$\text-\!\!\!-\!\!\!-\!\!\!\diamond\!\!\!-\!\!\!-\!\!\!-$$

# Chapter 69

April 20th 1933
8:25 pm Wednesday

"Now that everyone is here, I want to present my theory to all of you. I'm not going to introduce each of you because I know y'all already know each other."

"Now. Wait just a minute Bill. Does my sister know about this?" John said standing up and heading for the door.

"Sit! Down! Junior, or I'll have the officer set you down." I said pointing at his vacant chair. "Now here is my theory as I see it. Oscar Scruggs, escaped from the prison farm in 1925. I know from my years on the force he's the only prisoner to ever escaped without being caught. From reading his jacket, I discovered he never got higher in school than the sixth grade. That told me someone had to  helped him to escape and hide."

I could see by the looks of a few faces I was on the right track. "So Pastor Lyman. Will you tell everyone here why you're protecting Oscar Scruggs?"

"You're wrong about Oscar, Detective. When he came to my church I felt sorry for the man. He told me he was railroaded into a confession in order to cover up the real arsonists."

I was about to continue when Nancy entered the room. "Excuse me gentlemen." I walked out of the room so we could talk in private. "What are you doing here?"

"I think you might be interested in what I've found out about the arsonists." She said handing me a folder.

I opened it and found a birth certificate, and a marriage certificate. "Nancy, that's good work in such a short time."

I walked back into the room. "Well it seems I have some additional questions for you Pastor."

"And what would that be?"

"I have here a marriage certificate. It says you sister, Mary Lyman and Joseph Scrugg, were married in 1896 according to your own church records. She had a son Oscar who was born in 1897. That's why you have him living in the basement of Riley's Pool Hall for all these years."

"Now for you, John McCallum junior. You found yourself in debt to Mr. Genovese because of a contract your father and the Major had agreed to. It all hinged on Margaret your sister to marry Genovese son. When your father and the Major died, Margaret refused to marry him. So that left you  holding the bag for all that money the borrowed. I'm assuming you needed to stall Genovese from taking over your company in order to liquidate some of your holdings."

"Are you suggesting I burn down my own buildings! We talked about that just a day or so ago."

"Yes we did, and at the time your statement made sense. Now it doesn't."

"And why's that Detective? Did you have a vision like the ones my sister told me about?"

"No. Your insurance company did. It seems your fire insurance has paid double what the buildings are worth.

Which means you could rebuild some and still have a nice profit to pay Genovese back the money you owe.

Now we come to you, Chief Mitch Anderson."

"Bill. How am I involved in all this. I don't know these people."

"I believe that's true Mitch. But I think you do know the Pastor. Isn't that correct?"

The look on Mitch's face told me he did. "Mitch. I know your wife and kids left you without a cent. I don't know the circumstances for them to leave you. I do know the Pastor was setting you up as an escape goat if something like this happened."

"I wasn't doing any such thing. I loaned her the money when things got tight because he was the one that wanted to live well above his means. Buying that big house, donating to the politicians' elections, sending them to private schools. He thought he could be Mayor or a congressman, little did he know he was the laughing stock of the city! And if you don't believe me ask John McCallum."

I turned to Mitch and found him slumped over in his chair.

Whatever fight he had in him had been drained away by the Pastor. "Detective. I did what the pastor said, Scruggs, didn't set the fires. I did, to get back at the lot of them when I found out they were just using me."

"Hap. Put the cuffs on the fire chief now that he has confessed."

The room suddenly lit up with smiles as Hap took the fire chief away in cuffs.

"How about a drink, gentlemen?" John said lighting a cigar.

"I'm not finished yet, Pastor. You're still under arrest for harboring an escape convict. And you John are under-arrest for insurance fraud. Mr. Genovese, I suggest you get yourself a lawyer. I'm going to arrest you on blackmail. As for you Mr. Rossi I'll let the FBI handle you.

As I escorted them down the elevator. I felt Hap and I had done a good day's work. I had eliminated the Pastor's blackmailing me and the co-op. With John McCallum behind bars the fires should decrease. That left Scruggs the escaped convict who was still on the loose.

Hap and I watched as the three of them were put in the patrolmen cars and driven away.

"What about me?" Mitch said watching the red taillights fade away.

"Hap. Take off his cuffs. Mitch I don't believe you set any fires. Not as hard as you worked to put them out."

"But all the evidence you had against me. That's why I confessed."

"No. You confessed, because the Pastor was destroying your reputation. I must admit he has quite a verbal way of degrading a person. So, hop in the back seat of my new approated car and will drive you back to the station."

As we drove along I watched Mitch's face and saw the satisfaction. "I see by your face Mitch that you are happy about how things turned out."

"I sure am, except I'm still broke. But with the wife gone I can rebuild my reputation and still become a pillar in the community."

"That sounds like a good plan but what about Muller and the friends that are going to replace him." I could see the telltale signs on his face his serum was trying to take over. "Don't bother Mitch. I also have Cochran's serum in my vines as well."

"What are you talking about Bill."

"I'm talking about that other self that has all that speed and endurance that comes from the injection."

"I have no idea of what you're talking about Bill. So get off the subject or I'll."

"Okay. Forget it. I must have been mistaken."

Once we dropped Mitch off at the fire station, I got a call to report to the Captain. "Hap. I believe it's going to be a long night with the Captain. I'll have to explain why I arrested all of them."

"I'll stick around and see what can be done to find Scruggs. But before we get there, how did you figure all this out so quickly?" Hap asked.

"I had help from a young lady named Nancy Gamble. She's the best investigator bloodhound I have ever met."

"You mean she gathered all this information in two days."

"I believe she was gathering information on everyone we came into contact with since being assigned to us by the FBI."

"Damn. Then I better remember to close the blinds before taking a bath." Hap said waiting for me to step into his trap.

"Why's that?"

"If she ever saw me naked she would never find a better specimen of manhood than me." he chuckled.

"Hap. Dream on you're what sixty. That horse left the barn a long time ago. So keep plugging along and Mildred might slow down long enough for you to catch her."

Hap didn't answer me back, but I knew his pride bubble had burst.

With everyone booked I headed up to the Captains office to explain my actions. When I got there I found the Mayor already in his office.

"It's about time you got back here Detective."

"Yes Sir."

I closed his door and lit a cigarette as they started firing questions at me. "Mayor, Captain, I have explained my actions to y'all several times now. I'm sure once the District Attorney and the FBI looks things over they will be prosecuted. So for now if you don't mind I'd like to get some sleep."

By the time we got home I found Director Grayson sitting on the porch talking with Margaret. "Director, what are you doing here at this late hour?"

"We need to have a chat about the arrest you made tonight."

"Margaret, please excuse us." I sat down in her rocker and waited for him to ask questions.

"Tell me about Mitch Anderson and his connections to Muller."

"How do you know about that?"

"Let's just say a little lady told me."

"You mean Nancy. Well I was going to talk to you tomorrow, but seeing your here now. I'm not the only person that Cochran's serum has work on."

"Are you telling me Anderson is one of you too?"

"He hasn't admitted it but from what I've seen and heard he has been injected and lived. As to how powerful he is compared to what I was is any man's guess."

"I'll have him picked up right away. If he's like you will lock him up for life."

"What would you say if I said we need to leave him alone and monitor his routes. You said yourself Nancy has reported he's working with the Germans. If a war is coming then it would be better to catch all of them at once."

"I see your point and will review it with Hoover. The thing that worries me is he's stronger than you."

"I don't believe so. My serum could detect his but he couldn't detect mine. I believe he never got the Cobra venom injection like I did."

# Chapter 70

April 20th 1933
10:25 pm Wednesday

Mitch Anderson walked into his dark empty home and found Oscar Scruggs sitting in his office drinking whiskey.

"What the hell are you doing here." Mitch said looking around to see if anyone else was here.

"Don't worry, boss, I'm alone. May I try one of your Havana cigars?" he said.

"I said why are you here!"

Oscar picked up a cigar out of the humidor and lit a match. He didn't light the cigar, instead he played with the match until it touched his fingers and went out. Then he lit another, and another, before saying, "I'm here for another payment, Fire Chief Anderson. It seems the cops are getting to close, so I need to get out of town."

"I can't give you any more money because everyone with  money has been arrested except me."

"I don't care about them. I've work for you not them. So again, I'm asking nicely. I need money to get out of town or else this." Scruggs said dropping a lit match on the Persian rug."

"Alright, alright, I do have a little money in the safe, just give me a minute."

"What about Carl Muller? Isn't he still paying you?"

"No. From what I've been told he died in a plane crash."

Mitch opened the safe and picked up his 38 revolver and then put it down. "You know Oscar, I believe there's a way for you to disappear until I need you again. Here's your money!" he said throwing him a $500 pack of money.

"I'm going to need more than this, hiding out from the cop's is expensive."

"That's true so true,"  Mich said handing Oscar another $500 pack of money before shooting him.

**"Now what are we going to do with the body?"** Cochran's serum asked. "I'll set the house on fire and say a burglar got caught in the blaze. Then I can collect the insurance money and wait for Muller's replacement," the Chief said.

**"A fine solution to your problem, Heir Anderson. Now let's get to work finding a new arsonist."**

Berlin Germany

A taxi pulled up in front of a well-guarded home. Gertrude and Muller got out and were immediately met by several uniformed guards.

"We're here to see the Fuhrer."

"He's been waiting for you two since receiving your wireless."

The door opened and they entered his home and found him working in his library.

Mein Fuhrer. It's good to see you again," Major Muller said.

"I see you two made it back. Have you completed the assignment?"

"As far as setting up a network of sympathizers it's in the final stages thanks to Gertrude Becker. As far as the American Detective, his blood is worthless. I have found out he has Jewish blood in him.

"It was reported you two died in a plane crash."

"There were two passengers already on the plane when I commandeered it. One male and one female were aboard. I ordered my two agents' pilots to create a diversion so we could escape unnoticed. Once in the air they were to fly towards New York for two hours. Once they had flown the two hours they were to blow the plane up."

"Then your men died in the crash as well?"

"Yes, Mein Fuhrer," Muller said starting to sweat.

"You two are to be commended for your loyalty. For now, take a vacation in Vienna and see what you can do to set up a network there as well. I have plans to expand our Third Reich into Austria, and will need good men to enforce our laws."

Muller and Gertrude left the Fuhrer's office feeling quite pleased with themselves. "For a minute Carl, I thought we were in trouble not bringing Barronson with us. How did you find out he has Jewish blood in him?"

"I didn't. I made that story up just to satisfy him."

"Why?"

"I have another man that has lived through Cochran's injections."

"If that's so then why didn't you bring him here instead of Barronson?"

"Because unlike Barronson, this man is loyal to me not the party."

"Does Cochran know this person is alive?"

"No. He thinks the man died just like all the others. When I went to dispose of the body I found he wasn't dead. I took him to a safe hiding place and nursed him back to life."

"Does that mean he has the powers Barronson has?"

"Unfortunately for me he only got 5%. You see at that time I didn't know that the cobra venom was needed to enhance Cochran's serum to 100%."

"Well now that is interesting. Carl. With the two of us working together we could build an army for ourselves."

Gertrude said slipping her are around his.

"Yes Gertrude, it is. With my ambitions, and you at my side we could be the Fuhrer of America when we conquer it."

"Carl we need to be careful. If one person other than us talks it could go very badly for us."

They were given VIP rooms on the tenth floor that were reserved for the elite at the Berlin Grand Hotel.

"Frau Gertrude." she said knocking on the door. "It's time for me to change the sheets." she said knocking again. When no one came to the door she used her pass key to open the door and found the room empty. Three days later they found her body at the Fountain of Fairies with an 1862P penny in here hand.

# Chapter 71



September 27th 1967

"**My** that was quite an investigation your father had. I never realized the city had so many arson fires in 1933. I wonder why we never heard about them until now?

"People and the country were more worried about not having jobs than a few fires in Atlanta."

"What do you think your father meant by his last statement about the Fire Chief.

"I don't know. Maybe we'll find out when we read his next case dear. Amanda. Why don't you cleaned up while I go to the garage and pulled out the next case."

I went to the garage and pulled out the next yellow file.

"Amanda this case is called The Dixie Hwy Murders."

"I remember hearing about that. The highway was used to go from Chicago to Atlanta to Jacksonville to Miami. It brought the Northerners South for the winters just like the wagon trains heading West to Oregon and you remember what happened to many of them?"

# About the Author

I was born in Rochester New York in 1943 and married my wife in 1964 and moved to Mobile in 1968. I wanted to live some place that it didn't snow for five months. Two years later I transferred to Jacksonville.

In 1977 I moved to Douglasville from Jacksonville Florida working in the fast food industry. Finding this small town a wonderful place to live I bought my first house. Over the years I dabbled in writing but didn't have the time. As the years past and my children grew up and married it gave me some time to start writing again in the 1990s. I soon found out that trying to get published by sending in manuscripts was a waste of money and time. Shelving the idea, I kept working until I retired in 2018 due to health issues.

With all this time on my hands I once again thought about writing. Then in 2020 with Covid the lockdown I decided to return once more to getting published. In all the years of reading books I never came across detective stories or movies written about Atlanta. Researching Atlanta's history I found the 1930s was the perfect starting point for my first book.

I spent the next three months writing my first book, THE ARAGON HOTEL MURDERS. It is a story about a detective living in Atlanta who discovers two bodies in that closed hotel. At first it looked like a burglary gone wrong until he finds a gold confederate coin in the victim's hand If you enjoyed this book, you can find my other novels via Amazon, Barnes and Noble and many other fine retailers THE WISHING WELL MURDERS is book two in the series and will be released in spring. THE FIRE BUG MURDERS, hopefully in the fall. I hope you enjoy.